was born in Sydney, Australia, in 1901. The daughter of the writer and Labor politician Dowell O'Reilly, who introduced the first bill for Women's Suffrage into the New South Wales Legislative Assembly, she grew up in an intellectual and political household. She began writing early, publishing her first story at the age of nineteen.

In 1922 she married Dr Eric Dark, going to live with him in Katoomba, a town of the Blue Mountains outside Sydney. Here she combined her career as a writer with that of a doctor's wife and the mother of two sons. Her first novel, *Slow Dawning*, was published in 1932, followed by *Prelude to Christopher* (1934) and *Return to Coolami* (1936), both novels winning the Australian Literature Society's Gold Medal. Throughout the 1930s Eleanor Dark took an overtly political position in opposition to the growth of fascism abroad. In 1935 she joined the Fellowship of Australian Writers with, amongst others, Marjorie Barnard, Flora Eldershaw, Dymphna Cusack and Kylie Tennant. Eleanor Dark's political preoccupations became increasingly evident in her fiction of the 30s and 40s. *Sun Across the Sky* was published in 1937, and *Waterway* in 1938. In 1941 she published the first volume of an historical trilogy, *The Timeless Land*. Acclaimed in Britain, the United States and Australia, it has also been dramatised on Australian television. The trilogy was interrupted with the publication of *The Little Company* in 1945, but resumed with *Storm of Time* (1948) and *No Barrier* (1953).

Eleanor Dark lived for some years on a farm in Queensland, the setting of her last novel *Lantana Lane* (1959). One of Australia's most distinguished writers, she lives again in the Blue Mountains.

ELEANOR DARK

THE
LITTLE COMPANY

With a New Introduction by
DRUSILLA MODJESKA

PENGUIN BOOKS — VIRAGO PRESS

PENGUIN BOOKS
Viking Penguin Inc., 40 West 23rd Street,
New York, New York 10010, U.S.A.
Penguin Books Ltd, Harmondsworth,
Middlesex, England
Penguin Books Australia Ltd, Ringwood,
Victoria, Australia
Penguin Books Canada Limited, 2801 John Street,
Markham, Ontario, Canada L3R 1B4
Penguin Books (N.Z.) Ltd, 182–190 Wairau Road,
Auckland 10, New Zealand

First published in Australia by Collins, Sydney, 1945
This edition first published in Great Britain by
Virago Press Ltd 1985
Published in Penguin Books 1986

Printed in the United States of America by
R. R. Donnelley & Sons Company, Harrisonburg, Virginia
Set in Palatino

To
E. P. D.

"Oliver said: 'I have seen the Saracens; the valley and the mountains are covered with them, and the lowlands and all the plains: great are the hosts of that strange people; we have here a very little company.'"

—*The Song of Roland.*

INTRODUCTION

Re-reading Eleanor Dark's *The Little Company*, it strikes me as much more 'modern' than it did when I first encountered it over ten years ago. Perhaps because I am approaching the age Eleanor Dark was when she wrote her novel, and appreciate the thinking and rethinking of a woman in the middle of her life. But the novel also seems to have announced the political and aesthetic changes of the 1980s. It concerns the intellectual and political crisis of the late 1930s. The period we are living through now—of recession, nuclear threat and more failed expectations— though different in obvious ways, raises remarkably similar questions about the nature of political and cultural dissent. How can a radical write in such a world? And in view of the repeated failures of liberal democracy, the uncontrolled escalation of technological development and a threatened environment, does it matter what is written? Is there any meaning, let alone any meaningfulness in an apocalyptic world? These questions are at the heart of *The Little Company*.

The novel focuses on a family that lives variously in Sydney and Katoomba, a town in the Blue Mountains behind the city, and their contradictory and shifting responses to the Second World War. Gilbert Massey and his sister Marty are writers, their brother Nick is in the Communist Party and Marty's husband is a liberal intellectual. Through these characters and their circle of friends and through Phyllis, Gilbert's sad and conservative wife, and other family members, the narrative of their experience of wartime Sydney engages with the political and literary life of the period.

The Little Company was written during the last years of the Second World War which dominates the novel. This was the first war in which Australians faced military threat at home. Troops had, of course, fought in several imperial wars, most notably the 1914-18 War at the cost of nearly 60,000 lives and over 150,000 casualties from a population of less than five million. Although the war had an enormous impact, the actual fighting had taken place thousands of miles away; as Gilbert puts it in *The Little Company*, it was a "nightmare from which most people had awakened only to roll over with a sigh of relief, and go to sleep again. *The Little Company* is less concerned with the *fact* of war than with the *meaning* of war. Despite the war the daily realities remain mundane; because of the war, the political, ethical, personal questions are critical and pressing. The problems posed in the text are political and intellectual. There are, of course, also emotional and domestic problems which propel the narrative forward. But it is not a novel which relies on their resolution. The resolution of narrative puzzles is secondary to the revealing of the shifting state of affairs, the contradictory experiences of the characters. Intellectual and political questions are deeply entwined with the personal. When Gilbert and Elsa wake up with very different reactions to gun fire on the night Japanese submarines are found in Sydney harbour, a threat which was more symbolic than real, Gilbert "knew that no physical union, no shared emotional tumult between himself and Elsa could bring them together while they stood apart on the issues raised by those search lights and explosions. Unless you were together there, you were together nowhere." *The Little Company* focuses on the ordinary and on daily experiences and daily reactions rather than on war as a series of dramatic events. It explores the contradictions of people behaving in ordinary ways in extraordinary situations.

One way of understanding *The Little Company* is to set it against Eleanor Dark and her husband's experiences of the thirties and forties in Australia. The novel is dedicated to Eric Dark whom she married in 1922. They moved from Sydney to Katoomba where they raised their children while she wrote novels and he was in general practice as a doctor. *The Little Company*, appearing in 1945, was her seventh novel. Like Gilbert Massey, her fiction was becoming increasingly serious and she was becoming less able to regard it in any simple way as fiction. *The Little Company* was her most emphatic political statement, for which she paid during the Cold War. Eric Dark, like Gilbert Massey, was shaken by the Depression into major political rethinking. "I was a perfectly good Tory until the Depression," he said recently. "It was then that I realised we had an economic system that sterilised real intellect."[1] Eleanor Dark described him, like Gilbert, reading "from book to book till he had completed the painful process of moving from right to left".[2] For her the journey was less

1. E. P. Dark interviewed in the *Sydney Morning Herald* 5 March, 1984 p.3
2. Eleanor Dark, interview with Jean Devanny in Jean Devanny *Bird of Paradise*, Sydney, Frank Johnson 1945 pp. 253-11.

painful, having grown up in a labour voting liberal intellectual household, but for her too the Depression was a period of reconsideration and rethinking of ideas she had taken lightly since childhood. The novel traverses the Darks' experience and echoes their intellectual struggles.

Another way of reading *The Little Company* without losing sight of its personal significance for Eleanor Dark, would be to see it as "dialogic," a term used by the Soviet critic Mikhail Bakhtin.[3] He sees the novel as an expression of the many voices of social language, of all the expressions made in and through language, of the social order. For Bakhtin the individual as author answers the social world, interrogates it, responding strongly to some impulses, weakly to others, screening others out, tracking through the conflicting social voices which are based on conflicting social interests and positions. For Bakhtin the author does not speak directly but is like a ventriloquist speaking through the characters and their dialogues, as well as entering into dialogue with them. Viewed in this way one can say both that *The Little Company* is a complex of the responses of progressive intellectuals to the thirties and forties, and that it is also Eleanor Dark's own response. It is not a direct reflection of either, but a series of dialogues. One of the most argumentative of these dialogues is with the Communist Party. Neither Eleanor Dark nor her husband were members of the Party, but they were known as "fellow travellers". During the Cold War they had to leave the town because of their politics, but in the thirties and early forties, there was a social

3. See M. M. Bakhtin, *The Dialogic Imagination* (ed. Michael Holquist) Austin, University of Texas Press, 1981.

space for dissidents. The Communist Party of Australia was a focus, however contradictory, for left intellectuals whether inside or outside the Party. In *The Little Company* this dialogue is structured through Nick, Gilbert's younger brother, a Party member who is represented as dogmatic but charming. The other characters debate the Party line with him and each other and while he is shown up as often dismissive, sometimes intolerant, he is the only character with a clear position on a number of issues and in particular on fascism. He is also the only character to fight with the Australian Army. That, of course, is after the Stalin-Hitler pact, after the "phony war", when the CPA refused to recognise the war effort and were as a consequence declared illegal. For liberal intellectuals like Gilbert and Marty, the relationship with the Party was never easy. The sense of isolation for socialists in Australia was profound. A great deal of the anti-fascism that was mobilised by the war was also anti-socialist, although there was a brief period just at the end of the war which glimpsed the possibility of postwar reconstruction on progressive terms.

The Little Company evokes the wartime trauma with its title, taken from *The Song of Roland*, a medieval epic account of the last stand of two of Charlemagne's knights who were betrayed and trapped in a valley in northern Spain against the Muslim Saracens. Within the novel the quotation which prefaces the book is read by Marty after the submarine incident, referring to the sparsely populated continent holding out against its populous and imperialist northern neighbour. Japanese troops were in New Guinea and the Pacific, there were air raids in the north. The British navy had retreated after the fall of Singapore, popularly responded to as the abandonment of Australia, the model dominion. But there is another meaning which the title evokes: the little company of progressive intellectuals and radicals embattled in a complacent, timid and for the most part philistine society. *The Little Company* does not answer in any direct or conclusive way whether the CPA is able to provide an adequate base for this little company. Nick does not represent the C.P.A. Rather he offers a dialogue both with the party and the unaligned position of the other characters. He is a pivot for concepts and ideas within this dialogue. Nick's position in the novel allows the exploration of political ideas, strategies and positions.

No character in *The Little Company* is a unity. Characters become coherent only through the pattern of ideas and action into which they fit. And few are cut and dried, without contradictions, unless they belong to a different age. Old Walter Massey, the monstrous patriarch, is no more than a token, a signifier of a nineteenth century conservative father. Even Phyllis, poor hopeless Phyllis, is not without her contradictions and in her character enters into a dialogue with feminism. How is it that women can end up so pitifully? In all her novels Eleanor Dark is tough on women who conform, who accept the values of capitalism and patriarchy, who cannot lift themselves out of the domestic mire or fantasies of romance. Phyllis is Eleanor Dark's first full exploration of such a woman. In her earlier novels they are simply targets. Several years ago I argued that *The Little Company* represented a retreat from feminism under the pressure of broader political issues raised by depression and war. Neither Marxism nor liberalism was able to deal with the "woman question"; the feminism of women like Eleanor Dark had no theoretical direction. I saw Phyllis as an expression of Eleanor Dark's exasperation with women who make conventional values their own, become guardians of conservative and often misogynist ideologies. I am now not so sure. Certainly there is a shift in her feminism. In *The Little Company* gender is no longer posited as the primary social division as it was in her novels of the early thirties, but it remains a crucial division. Another way of looking at Phyllis—and at Virginia and Elsa—is as a powerful indictment of social conditions that result in such maiming of the female self. It is a dialogue about that process. We may not sympathise with Phyllis but we understand what she says.

Rather than arguing that Gilbert, as a central male figure, is further evidence of retreat, one could argue that to use a male protagonist is a different but no less feminist strategy. Although we are invited to sympathise with Gilbert as we see so much of the narrative through his point of view, there is enough from a female point of view for that sympathy to be questioned. Gilbert is a nice man, personally and politically sensitive, a writer, a type one can easily recognise. He is also something of a bore, always so troubled and serious. It is clear that he can afford this anguish as well as the long hours at his desk only because he has the massive domestic support of Phyllis; when that fails there are sister Marty and daughter Prue, supporting and believing in him. Although we cannot accept Gilbert uncritically, we should take him seriously precisely because there are sufficient subtexts to suggest that through him *The Little Company* constructs a very sophisticated dialogue indeed. Gilbert represents a way of discussing the frailty of appearances and the uncertainties of social relationships; it is a way of discussing that dialectical relationship between work and love, between conflicting human needs, between the personal and social structures of our lives. By doing this through a male character, *The Little Company* offered a way through the impasse of feminist discourse in Australia during the late 1930s and early 1940s in which gender politics either became divorced from or reduced to the politics of class and nationalism.

Nationalism was a familiar problem in left liberal fiction of the period. The defence of Australia was unquestioned and unquestionable. *The Little Company* distinguishes nationalism from patriotism. Gilbert does not crow when the submarines in the harbour are sunk: for him the horror of men trapped in steel cages beneath the water is unforgiveable. The terms of nationalism, common to the left of that period was based on what were seen as natural unities between people and nature. In this way Australia "belonged" as much to its settlers as to its original inhabitants. The critique of capitalism, technology, militarism came back, time and again, to this issue. Today we would question the terms of that relationship but in *The Little Company* they are given in a dialogue around it, rather than a value to be debated. Here is another answer to the initial question about the nature of cultural dissent. Within the terms of *The Little Company*, it is made in relation to nationalism and the defence of Australia. Gilbert Massey represents writing in defence of those unities of

people and place. Radical writing must confront and
counter the conservative narratives, the "natural" stories
of heroism and war. It is part of the struggle for other
social meanings.

The Little Company is highly self conscious of itself as
writing. It is what Roland Barthes would call a writerly
text, and poses as a central problem the nature of writing.
This of course raises problems. Characters can no longer
be seen to function as unitary and psychologically
convincing beings, but as ensembles of social relationships,
as vehicles for concepts, a site for the playing out of social
conflict. Yet at the same time Gilbert finds it impossible to
dismiss his characters as mere fictions. Writers must face
the social implications of the fictions and the characters
they write. The inner landscapes of unconscious and
memory become part of the plot and action; past becomes
part of the present, fiction part of the real. The characters'
thought and consciousness of events become more
important than the events in themselves. This may seem
contradictory in a novel about war. But The Little Company
differentiates between the war as an event, the result of
very complex forces, and the meanings of war. This is why
writing, for Eleanor Dark as much as for Gilbert Massey,
is so important: the challenging of fictions which pose as
reality with fictions which represent a different reality.

The Little Company's plot covers a short period of time and
is less important than the spirals of memory, history,
stream of consciousness, press clippings and political
argument which fill out its fairly simple lines. Although
Gilbert is a focus there is no constant viewing point. We
see the action from many perspectives and through many

eyes. Thus we are invited into dialogue with the text, questioning and requestioning. There is no unitary view. Yet *The Little Company* always deals with political issues from the perspective of dissent. This was not lost on contemporary reviewers who were clearly uncomfortable with a novel of ideas rather than a novel based on social observation and action. With the exception of those few who were radicals themselves (and usually therefore writing for small magazines) the reviewers berated Eleanor Dark more or less harshly for her "outspokenness", her "preoccupations" and her "preaching". The reviews are much more revealing of the intellectual climate in Australia during the mid to late 40s than they are of Eleanor Dark's work. It is little wonder that she found it hard to maintain the same level and intensity of writing. An irony of *The Little Company* is that while it focuses on a writer who is blocked and has been for some time because of the urgency of the political questions and the impossibility of their resolution, Eleanor Dark's own response to the crisis of war, with the exception of a brief period in 1940 when she produced only "depressing and abortive scraps", was productive. That Collins, rather than one of the small left wing presses published *The Little Company* is an indication of the constituency for a left wing novel of ideas in 1945 as well as of the reputation of Eleanor Dark as a writer which, by 1945, was considerable. Her experience of a serious writing block came later, in the fifties.

Within five years of the publication of *The Little Company* the literary and political climate had changed sufficiently to leave virtually no space for such a novel. The left was in

retreat; Patrick White had broken new literary ground
with a metaphysical alternative; while on the right writers
declared the end of ideology. The Cold War marked the
end of an era; by the late fifties radical discourse was
moving in very different directions. Eleanor Dark was one
of the several writers of her generation, productive
throughout the thirties and forties, who stopped writing
in the fifties. As Gilbert puts it in *The Little Company* "there
is a psychological strain in preserving one's own faith in
something against a mass opinion that says it isn't
important." By 1953 she had published the last two
volumes of the historical trilogy which was started before
The Little Company. Then there was nothing until *Lantana
Lane* in 1959, her last novel, very different in tone and
without the political urgency of *The Little Company*. During
those years the Darks lived on an eight acre farm in
Queensland, north of Brisbane. In *The Little Company*
Gilbert wonders whether being a novelist made him
"entitled to respect or approbation". Did the hint of
"unorthodox views make him a social outcast?" In his case
being manager of a weighty firm of booksellers which had
in his father's day specialised in Bibles, counteracted "the
vague suspicion with which writers were apt to be
regarded". But he knew his next novel would tip the
balance towards disapproval. Similarly Eleanor Dark had
counteracted the "vague suspicion" by her role as doctor's
wife. But in the fifties, with her writing becoming
increasingly outspoken, her husband was also publishing
political books and pamphlets, including *Medicine and the
Social Order* (1943), *The World Against Russia* (1948) and *The
Press Against the People* (1949). It was one thing for a writer to

be a communist sympathiser, but altogether another matter for a doctor. As early as 1940 fellow writer Marjorie Barnard wrote to another writer and mutual friend, Nettie Palmer: "Katoomba society seems to have dropped them on account of their radical views. A merciful release,"[4] She was lighthearted, but by the end of the forties, it had become serious. "There was a good deal of harassment," recalls Dr Dark, "and I lost a lot of my medical practice. I used to get letters that were addressed to me in block letters DR DARK, COMMUNIST."[5] And in another interview he recalls that "there was fairly formidable threats ... And of course a doctor is a sitting duck. I mean you have only got to be called out at two o'clock in the morning to a way out cottage. Eleanor was much more worried than I was. She insisted that whenever I got a night call from a person I didn't know she [would come too]"[6] Nothing happened but they felt they had no option but to leave. As Eric Dark put it: "At that time once you put a foot left of centre, you were dubbed a communist."[7] A very interesting account of this period in Katoomba is given in a recent autobiographical novel by Roger Milliss.[8] Roger Milliss was the son of Bruce Milliss, a store owner and communist who also lived in Katoomba. Reading Roger Milliss' account of his father during the

4. Marjorie Barnard to Nettie Palmer 18 October, 1940. Palmer Papers. National Library of Australia Ms. 1174/1/5826.

5. E. P. Dark, interviewed *SMH* 5/3/84 p.3.

6. Eric Dark, interview with Robert Darby Katoomba, November, 1980. p.45 of Transcript. Copy in National Library of Australia. Thanks to Robert Darby for showing me this interview.

7. Quoted in Leonore Baxter "Fires in the Fall". The story of a rational reformer: Dr. Eric Dark" *New Doctor* No. 32 June 1984.

8. Roger Milliss, *Serpent's Tooth*, Penguin Australia 1984.

late 1930s, always reading, his glassed in veranda-study so similar to Gilbert Massey's, the atmosphere is uncomfortably familiar. He describes the little company of mountain radicals and their work for library facilities, school canteens and cultural events and the escalating anti-communism of the late forties and fifties which forced the Darks' departure and tormented Roger Milliss in the playground. Eleanor and Eric left Katoomba in 1950 for an area where they were not known, they lived modestly harvesting macedonia nuts and citrus.

This Virago edition is the first reprinting of *The Little Company* since it first appeared in 1945. This in itself is a baleful comment on Australian publishing and cultural politics. Eleanor Dark lapsed into obscurity after the war but has returned to view since 1979 when her lovely 1938 novel *Waterway* was reprinted. In the intervening years only *The Timeless Land* (1941) remained in print. After years out of print and out of fashion, things have swung around. Now her past fits our present, her writing meets the current demand for writerly, political and intellectual fictions and the voices of women. As she wrote in *The Little Company*: "The past will coil up behind you like a spring, it will reach over your head to link up with your future where you will find it awaiting you ... [your] existence [is] an endless present moment, moving snailwise through time, carrying the past and the future on its back."

Drusilla Modjeska,
Sydney, 1985

THE LITTLE COMPANY

BOOK I

I

AUTUMN came early in the mountains; there was an edge to the air as soon as the sun disappeared, and the garden, which had bloomed bravely in gay if disordered profusion through the dry summer months, was now thrusting the pink and white of self-sown cosmos, and the sad, misty mauve of tall daisies through a tangle of neglected beds. From the Sunday paper, fallen on the grass beside Gilbert Massey's deck-chair, bold black headlines announced: A.I.F. NOT IN BENGHAZI RETREAT. He heard footsteps and voices behind him, and closed his eyes hastily. Soon it would be getting cold, and he would have to move; already the shadow of a slender gum sapling was wavering within a foot of his chair. But he did not want to talk just now, or to be invited by his wife, his aunt, and his sister to join their little expedition to the creek. He wanted to sit still and go on thinking of Mr. Matsuoka on his way home from Berlin to Tokio, to turn over in his mind the guarded but soothing prognostications of "informed opinion," and the even more soothing assurances of the Japanese Foreign Office. Yet he found that his train of thought, once interrupted, could not be resumed; and, opening his eyes warily to see the three women walking past him, he returned from international to domestic affairs, and began to wonder what Aunt Bee thought of her nephews and her niece now that—for the first time—she was having an opportunity to get acquainted with them.

But probably she didn't think at all. She was, he decided, watching her totter on her high heels down the path between Phyllis and Marty, one of those empty-headed, full-hearted old darlings who bestow affection at random in the happy assumption that everyone deserves it. Even towards the brother who had ignored her for nearly fifty years, and at whose funeral three weeks ago she had actually shed a tear or two into her scented handkerchief, she seemed to cherish no real bitterness. Gilbert had felt shamefaced then, inviting her to stay with them after the funeral, and to share, later, a week-end at their mountain cottage, because what he offered seemed such small amends for a lifetime of ostracism from her family. He felt even more shamefaced now, having watched her naïve delight at being with them—all of them, so many of them, a whole new collection of (as she phrased it) "young people," to whom she could extend her gossipy, chuckling, uncritical, indiscriminate devotion. As if, he thought, her own family were not enough! But there could never be enough for Aunt Bee. Provided already with four sons of her own, two daughters, a grandson and a granddaughter, plus an army of nephews and nieces on her husband's side, she could still take to her heart, with the excitement of a young girl, two more nephews, a nephew's wife, a niece, a niece's husband, a grand-nephew and two grand-nieces!

She accepted them all in a lump as her "young people." But he thought that perhaps last night—when Phyllis had gone off to her Christian Watchers' Circle, Pete to the pictures and the girls to a dance—had been her happiest evening. Then, while he and Marty and Nick yarned comfortably by the fire, she had knitted herself a skittish bed-jacket, and nibbled chocolates from a huge box, crying continually: "Oh, I mustn't! I'm getting too dreadfully fat!"

He had been, at first, a trifle uneasy lest their conversation should shock her. He knew, after all, nothing about her except that she was his father's sister, and seemed a pleasant old dear. He didn't want to shock her. But if she's going to know us, he had thought, she had better know us properly. As the hands of the clock went round, and she showed no greater sign of shock than an occasional affectionate cluck of disapproval, he was reassured.

"I'm too old, dearest Marty," she had said at one stage, "and—so my family tells me—much too stupid to start learning all about a new world now. Of course . . ." she wagged her golden-dyed, elaborately dressed curls at them and chuckled happily, ". . . they're all Communists, the naughty children! Or is it Socialists? What's the difference? No, Nick, don't tell me, because I shouldn't understand. But I like to see young people rebelling. It's healthy. I rebelled myself, when I was young, against your grandfather and your father." Her eyes clouded for a moment. "He was—really, darlings—not a very *kind* man, your father. Not very understanding. Just a little *narrow*, perhaps . . ." She brightened again. "Anyhow, I like rebels, and I'm used to them. You talk just like my Noel and Priscilla—though of course, being older, you're a little more restrained. A little calmer, if you know what I mean. But I can shut my eyes and listen to you and feel *quite* at home."

Gilbert sat up and bent stiffly to recover his paper. His women-folk had vanished now. He liked the little creek at the foot of the hill as much as Phyllis did, but he disliked her sentimental raptures about it, and the way she always contrived to quote, coyly: "There are fairies at the bottom of our garden!" So let her show it off alone, and be chilled by Marty's maliciously polite unresponsiveness; and then let her be cheered again by Aunt Bee's generous, garrulous appreciation—her effortless, inconsequent babbling which still, somehow, included all the right things for making everyone feel happy.

Her mild, almost apologetic criticism of their father, he thought grimly, had been a masterpiece of understatement. And idly, watching the long shadow of the tree reach out across the grass towards his chair, he wondered what common ancestor had provided the rebelliousness of Aunt Bee, the rebelliousness of himself, and Marty, and Nick, and how far back along the line of their ancestry he had lived. Or she? Rebellion, for a woman, had been a terrible matter once. Terrible, perhaps, even for Aunt Bee, wilfully getting herself "compromised" with her rich young squatter, and being, thereafter, as one dead to her father and her elder brother. But no; Aunt Bee was one of those for whom Life itself shows an unashamed favouritism. Instead of being deserted by her alleged seducer she had married him; instead of being smitten with remorse or with punishment, she had prospered. Nor were her sins visited on her children as no doubt her brother, Walter, had believed (and hoped?) they would be. Behold her at sixty-seven, the mother of a brood of handsome, intelligent children, a wealthy widow with enough zest still to rouge her cheeks, dye her hair, and sparkle flirtatiously at any man!

Beginning to feel cold, he climbed out of his chair and glanced round at the garden. It looked, he thought, more unkempt than usual at present, for his father's illness and death had put a stop to their mountain week-ends since December. Next Saturday, he resolved, I'll mow the grass and clip all that dead stuff away. From the bottom of the hill came a little shriek—Aunt Bee's—followed by laughter. She's slipped, he thought, in those ridiculous shoes; and as his eyes fell on his left hand with the tip of its little finger missing, his mind recoiled violently from that fantastic night last year, when a spade, wielded in semi-darkness, had come down a second too soon. . . .

Recoiling, jumping back to Aunt Bee and her girlish shriek, it used her as an impetus for a retreat into the past, a past where one did not go out at night carrying one end of a heavy tin trunk, and get one's finger chopped off—a past which enticed thought merely by not being the present—and yet which, when gained, betrayed one with its own painfulness.

Time had dulled that pain, though. There was only a shadow of it in this picture of himself and Marty, ten and five, standing in the front garden at *Glenwood*, and watching a lovely lady get out of a hansom cab. Some memory remained to him of loneliness, bewilderment, apprehension; he saw himself and his sister standing close together—his own expression remote, observant, non-committal, Marty's warily hostile. Of course. To Marty anyone, anything unknown was an enemy until proved otherwise. Life itself must have seemed inimical just then, for their mother was only a few days dead, leaving in her place—frightening and embarrassing mystery—a baby brother.

"Children!" cried the lovely lady swooping upon them. "Darlings!" she crooned, gathering them into an exquisitely fragrant embrace. "You don't know me, of course! I'm your Aunt Beatrice!"

Suddenly Gilbert felt inclined to laugh. He did not do so, for he was alone, and to laugh in solitude would have made him feel foolish. Yet he was amused to remember quite clearly that his ten-year-old self had promptly identified Aunt Bee with America. How, after all, could it have been otherwise? For he and Marty were, at that time, embarking upon their "education." They were being given to understand that the world was divided into the British Empire and, as Dickens expressed it, such other nations as there might happen to be. Europe, they learned, was a continent divided up into a number of countries inhabited by different kinds of foreigners. Africa and India were satisfactorily arranged for, in some unspecified way, by the British Empire. China was the country from which, at Christmas time, came entrancing stone jars in wicker baskets, containing ginger in a delectable sweet syrup. In Japan there were silkworms and cherry-blossoms. But America? America, having once belonged to the family, had wilfully and ungratefully seceded, from which circumstance it became quite inevitable that it should be associated in their minds with Aunt Bee—the more so in that both seemed to have prospered in spite of a regrettable mistake. From this fragrant and mysterious aunt they backed away, disturbed, speechless.

"Gilbert and Marty!" she exclaimed, dabbing her eyes with a fragment of lace and turning loose on the pine-scented air a bewildering breath of violets. "Gilbert, I have a little boy just a year younger than you. And another one just a year younger than Marty. And of course some bigger ones. How I hope you are going to be great friends with your cousins!"

Cousins? They had never heard of any cousins. Marty, who usually found her tongue first, asked with guarded interest:

"Where are they?"

"They're at home, darling. Awa-a-a-ay up in the country!" That awa-a-a-ay, Gilbert discovered, had been his own first conception of the largeness of his native land. "And," added Aunt Bee triumphantly, "there's a baby girl as well—just two years old! What are you looking at, Marty?"

Marty's eyes were glued to a sparkling object which glimmered among the frothy laces of her aunt's dress. Jewels. Diamonds . . .

"Are you rich?" she enquired.

But that was the end. Gilbert, middle-aged, folding his deck-chair, couldn't feel the scene any more. He remembered now, coldly and explicitly, that suddenly their father had been there, standing on the verandah, staring. Aunt Bee rose and hurried to him with an intoxicating swish of petticoats.

"Walter!" she cried. "My dear Walter, I saw it in the papers and I came straight down! You must let me help you with these dear children . . ."

A voice of icy formality:

"Will you come inside, Beatrice?"

She followed him indoors. A quarter-of-an-hour later she came out again, escorted by her brother, and she looked angry. Her cheeks were pink, her eyes bright, and she walked fast, holding her skirts high so that a foam of flounces danced round her pretty ankles and her shiny shoes. She hesitated for a moment when she saw the children still watching from the shade of the pine trees. Then she waved, called rather sadly: "Good-bye, children!" and got into the waiting cab. She shook hands coldly with her brother; old Foster trailed his whip over the back of the horse; she was gone. They had never seen her again until their father's funeral. And the next day Mrs. Miller and Phyllis had arrived . . .

"Oh, God, no," Gilbert thought, getting up and hoisting the deck-chair under his arm, "*not* a kind man!"

*　　　　*　　　　*　　　　*

To condemn his father thus, and, in the next moment, to be confronted by his son, gave him a curious shock. Pete arrived, as he did most things, suddenly and boisterously. He came round the sharp curve of the gravel drive on his bicycle, leaning out at an incredible and, as it turned out, a too ambitious angle. There was a scatter of gravel, a crash. Pete picked himself up cheerfully.

"I was broadsiding," he explained.

"Not too good for your tyres." Gilbert, still obsessed by the thought of his own father, hastily added something to remove the flavour of rebuke. "Or your hands."

Pete dabbed perfunctorily with a grubby handkerchief at his palms, where a few streaks of red and a drop of blood showed through the dirt. He grinned at his father, and the candid friendliness of his eyes was reassuring. Gilbert went on up to the house, left the chair on the verandah, and entered the drawing room by the long, french windows. Darkened by the trees outside, it was already dim. Phyllis had re-furnished the cottage two years ago, and, though he had been willing enough to see the old stuff go, he liked the new little better. He had himself, he admitted, no knack of making a room personal—no gift at all for self-expression except with a pen in his hand. He had known only two homes in all his life—the old, square stone house which his grandfather had built up the North Shore line, and this rambling, weatherboard cottage at which they had spent week-ends and the children's school holidays for the past fifteen years; in both he had been more like a lodging-house boarder than an inhabitant. Yet he was acutely aware of house-furnishing as a means of projecting personality, and he could not fail to see that this room, in its conventionality, its uncertainty, its amorphousness, its awkward efforts, always just failing, at taste and harmony, expressed Phyllis with merciless clarity. It was a room which, by the mere expenditure of money on well-made chairs and thick carpet, could offer a physical comfort; but there were, he reflected, hundreds of boarding-house "lounges" just like it. Except, perhaps for the books, and even they looked uncomfortable. Phyllis had a theory that books of a similar height should stand together, so there they were, stiffly ranked like a physical culture class at attention. Lately, too, she had read some pamphlet on the psychological effects of colour, and the room had broken out in a rash of rainbow cushions, so that the eye, wandering idly, was violently halted by the clamorous insistence of orange, vermilion, and peacock green.

The fire was laid, but not yet lit. He knelt down, struck a match, and then, without putting it to the paper, blew it out again. Phyllis had laid the fire herself this morning, he remembered, for the maid had been given the day off, and he knew from long experience that no fire laid by Phyllis ever burned. He pulled it to pieces and re-laid it, noticing that Aunt Bee had deposited her little pile of pine-cones in the hearth. She had fluttered round under the trees collecting them this morning, calling out that it would remind her so of *Glenwood* to smell them burning. Why on earth, he wondered, should she want to be reminded? But after all, if she had been able to preserve through the harsh memories of bitter enmity a happy memory of burning pine-cones—well, lucky Aunt Bee!

The flame from the paper caught the smaller twigs, felt its way up among the larger ones, licked the smaller logs, sent blue wreaths of smoke curling about the big bit of ironbark he had used as a back log. Squatting on his heels, he watched pinkish waves of firelight dart and retreat over the carpet. He decided not to turn on the light, and, rising, pulled up a chair and sat in it, feeling for his pipe and tobacco pouch.

His latest novel, *Thunder Brewing*, was now more than four years old. That thought was always in his mind, becoming, as every month passed, more of a burden to it. He would not allow himself to make the easy mistake of seeing it merely as a personal problem; of setting it aside; of saying: "How small a thing, how trivial, in the face of a crumbling civilization!" He knew very well that the immobilisation of the creative mind was one symptom of that crumbling, and that the multiplication of his own failure all over the world was no small and unimportant matter.

He had seen Marty affected, too. That disturbed him almost more than his own nightmare impotence. He knew that he was himself, as she described it, a buttoned-up person, not expansive, not prolific, not perpetually bubbling over with words. He was accustomed to finding words slowly, with infinite labour; he was accustomed, often, to not finding them at all. But to see Marty's pen halted gave him an almost superstitious chill. For her brain, quick and volatile as it was, had never been able to outpace her tirelessly scribbling fingers. She wrote as naturally and easily as she talked, and, while he recognised that her candidly topical matter, her carelessly colloquial manner might not rank as "literature" in the more austere sense of the word, he had recognised its value in a world where most people only read if they could keep on running at the same time.

Nick was impatient with them both. He wrote nothing but "factual" stuff. Give him his data, his figures, and he had an article or a letter to the paper finished in no more time than it took him to tap it out on the typewriter. He said: "What's wrong with you both? It's all there. Good God, the world was never so full of stories! You can take your pick—anything from the obscurest psychological agonising to the rankest melodrama. Nothing's too complicated or too simple to be true nowadays. And all you can do is to tear up paper!"

The rankest melodrama! Gilbert lifted his hand and studied, in the gathering dusk, its mutilated finger. Last year, the year 1940, at dead of night, carrying spades and keeping as quiet as possible, he and Gerald Avery and poor, scared little Tom Brady had gone out to bury a tin box in the orchard at *Glenwood!* "All right," he could imagine Nick saying, irritably, "there's your story!" And as for obscure psychological agonising, what else was his whole life now? But his brain still refused; it jibbed; it wandered from unproductive activity to numb inertia and back again.

Even Phyllis was getting puzzled. She, he suspected, swung between anxiety because he was not writing, and apprehension of what he might write if he did. For, like many of his friends and acquaintances, she had found herself for several years before the publication of *Thunder Brewing* in a curious dilemma. Was he, as a novelist of some repute, entitled to respect and approbation, or did the still only whispered hints of his unorthodox views make him a social outcast? As it was nearly dark now, he allowed himself the rather grim smile he felt. The tyranny of custom, of "background," he thought, had partially resolved these vague confusions. No man with a bank balance is a social outcast. No man occupying a permanent and respectable niche in the commercial world need be looked at askance. His own "background," as manager of Walter Massey and Sons, Wholesale Stationers and Booksellers, had, he realised, partly counteracted that vague suspicion with which writers were apt to be regarded.

Moreover, he reflected with some bitterness, he still lived to an extent in the odour of his father's sanctity. The firm still occupied the narrow, old-fashioned building in York Street which had housed it since its foundation as James Veetch and Co., eighteen years before Walter Massey acquired and renamed it in the last year of the nineteenth century. No one but his father, to whom the old had always been synonymous with the good, and who regarded innovation of any kind with loathing, would have continued to suffer its inconveniences. There was not even a lift. Electric light had been forced upon him by the corroding of ancient gas-pipes; and the plateglass window fronting the street was less a convenience for displaying merchandise than a shrine for the Bibles and prayer-books which furnished it. That window, Gilbert told himself wryly, was perhaps the strongest evidence of his own "respectability."

For Walter Massey had been by temperament, as his wife had been in fact, a missionary. Being in his early years a clerk (and later a substantial shareholder) in a shipping firm whose vessels plied between Sydney and the Islands had satisfied him; for the ships included Bibles and missionaries among their cargo, and that sanctified them. Being a bookseller later in life had enabled him still to deal in the Book; indeed so ardently had he specialised in Bibles, prayer-books, hymn-books, tracts and stories suitable for Sunday-school prizes, that the tottering business he had bought regained its equilibrium, and proceeded through the years in a state of dignified solvency.

A log fell from the fire, and the room shone redly for a moment while sparks rushed up the chimney. Gilbert, drawing thoughtfully at his pipe, admitted that his "background" was, through no fault of his own, deceptive. It was true that *Thunder Brewing* had caused a renewal of fluttering indecision in the minds of many readers who counted him among their acquaintance. His previous books, he suspected they would have said, had been just right. Substantial without being heavy, serious without being alarmist, thoughtful without being highbrow, their soberly critical note had been free from that insistent propaganda, that rabid agitation, that ranting bitterness which made so much fiction of the late 'thirties awkward and embarrassing. It had been possible to read them and maintain complacency at a time when the pattern of world events was beginning to look ominous even to the least discerning. The reader who, while priding himself on his intellectualism, still did not wish to be intellectually disturbed, found in them an approach and an interpretation which—though it could not be accused of escapism—was gratifyingly rooted in established values. He was left at home in a world he knew—conscious, indeed, of subterranean rumblings, but still treading a firm earth.

[17]

And then came *Thunder Brewing*. Gilbert looked back at it and at himself writing it, through a long tunnel of mental and psychological experience. It had been the expression of his first shock, and his first anger. He had been, at that time, with millions of others all over the world, going through a stage of development so painful and so alarming that even now he disliked the memory of it. The war of 1914-18, he had begun to see, was a nightmare from which most people had awakened only to roll over with a sigh of relief, and go to sleep again. Those few who had not returned to their pillows, but had, with tiresome, persistent, and ill-mannered vociferousness, disturbed the slumbers of the majority with warnings, had been unpopular people—agitators, scare-merchants, war-mongers. A few light sleepers (among whom he humbly recognised himself) had been roused by the clamour to listen, at first sluggishly, reluctantly, and then with rising anxiety, to the hullabaloo. Another bad dream called Depression had awakened a further batch with the shocking ruthlessness of a douse of cold water; but there were plenty who were still snoring—yes, even now, when the second nightmare was already twitching their limbs and distorting their mouths with grimaces of pain. And some, whose sleep had drifted into coma, would never waken. Let them die in their sleep, he thought with sudden fury—so long as they die!

The painfulness of his own awakening, which had found its way into the pages of *Thunder Brewing*, had lain less in the fear of a dark future than in the staggering realisation that the intellect of humanity in general, and of himself in particular, was totally. unequipped for facing it. One had dimly supposed oneself to be educated. But, good Heavens, this education was like a fish-net, more holes than substance, offering no resistance to the gathering gale of barbarism, no shelter from the threatening deluge of catastrophe. So he had become one of the intellectually-groping millions, feeling his way through the fog of his "conditioning," stubbing his toes against his own prejudices, bumping into time-honoured traditions, endlessly beguiled by some fancied gleam of light from a tempting by-path, only to find it a blind-alley, and return again to a road of still Stygian blackness . . .

In that mood *Thunder Brewing* had been written. There was no foothold in it for his faithful readers, for he was out of his depth himself. It had been really, he thought wearily, no more than an instinctive shout of warning and alarm. *"Look out, below!"* it yelled—and that was all. Perhaps because, striking this reverberating gong of alarm, it had chimed with a prevailing, though only half-realised mood, it had been read, it had been discussed, it had been widely advertised and reviewed—and it had sold. Thus the sanction of commercial success had again partially counteracted doubts raised by its uncompromising tone, and he had remained—provisionally at least—respectable, with a streak (so natural in writers) of eccentricity.

Yet when he tried to work again he was conscious of a drag somewhere. He had always written slowly, but steadily. Now he found himself floundering among innumerable false starts, discarding, beginning again, altering and revising until the thought he had begun with was entirely lost, and all was to do over again. He found himself continually betrayed by his own ignorance. Characters and "situations" which he would once have regarded as mere fictional material could no longer be regarded as such when they had become manifestations of a social disorder. Somewhere behind the description of a collapsing business, a society hostess, a broken marriage, a tubercular child, a swagman waltzing Matilda along the outback roads, he recognised a common truth which must be captured and expressed. His thoughts and his pen halted, arrested by his writing conscience, which told him sternly that he was giving short measure.

So he went on doggedly delving into what were nowadays known as World Affairs. He continued to question, to investigate, to read and think; he continued to discover and disbelieve, to rage and despair. He began to feel like an ant which has undertaken to remove a mountain, grain by grain. He uncovered what looked like a fact, stared at it incredulously, and threw it aside, only to find it cropping up again somewhere else. He became reluctant to the point of rebellion when he realised at last how much there was to learn. Nothing kept him at it but his growing alarm, and a certain native habit of perseverance which had made him, as a small boy, collect stamps for years with joyless patience. Even worse was the discovery of how much he had to un-learn, for he was even then approaching middle-age, and the discarding of conventions and ideas to which he had been bred was as painful as the stripping of bandages from a dried wound. His alarm, mounting with his knowledge, reshaped his impulse, detaching it from him, changing it from "I want to know" to a more impersonal and peremptory "You *must* know."

Yet, because he was a writer, with an itch in his fingers for a pen, he came back and back to his desk, dissatisfied with perpetual reading, impatient of mere absorption, obsessed by the need to produce. Only to find that he was writing on the slowing impetus of old ideas and the fading influence of old convictions; that the new forces gathering in him were, as yet, too chaotic and un-assimilated to vitalise his work. Could he say that still? No, it was something different now. He had long ago got past the stage of dragging back mentally, baulking, making nervous attempts to by-pass a problem, or scuffling efforts to avoid it altogether. He was able, now, to move about with some confidence in the socio-logical labyrinth. His forces were ranged and stabilised, his con-victions clear, his emotion strong and whole. The thing that frustrated him now was, he suspected desperately, sheer mental and emotional fatigue. His brain "faded" like a radio. Across the clarity of an idea a mist gathered. A sentence, framed to its conclusion in his mind, suddenly vanished as his memory blacked out. The simplest words eluded him. Once, alarmed by these symptoms, he had confessed them to Marty. She had shrugged in her casual way.

"I know. The same thing happens to me. Be sensible, Gilbert; it's only to be expected."

"Why?"

"Well, I know you don't like my fanciful way of putting things, but at the moment I can't think of any other way. Our brains are, so to speak, tuned-in to creativeness, and at present the mass-brain is tuned-in to destructiveness. We're suffering, Gil, my poor lamb, from 'interference.' The waves we try to give out are being jammed."

He bent forward and knocked his pipe out on the hearth, think-ing with irritated affection: "Marty!" It was true that her slap-dash, picturesque, inaccurate way of saying things often annoyed him. And yet when, knowing his distaste for untidy metaphorical statement, she looked at him slyly and said: "You see what I mean?"—he usually had to admit that he did.

* * * *

She came in with Aunt Bee and Phyllis through the French windows.

"See!" cried Aunt Bee, "he's lit the fire! How cosy it looks! Why, there he is, sitting all by himself in the dark. Gilbert, if you have burnt my pine-cones I shall be cross."

He stood up and pulled chairs forward to the fire while Phyllis switched on the light.

"I haven't touched your pine-cones, Aunt Bee," he said. "Come along and sit down here."

"Your creek," announced Aunt Bee, sinking into the chair thankfully and crossing one still shapely silk-clad knee over the other, "is quite charming, Gilbert, but *much* too far down the hill. Now, Phyllis . . ."—she settled more luxuriously into her cushion— ". . . can I help you in the kitchen? No, I'm sure I can't; I shouldn't know where anything is. I shall just sit here with Gilbert and smell the pine-cones. Ferdinand, of course. Talking of bull-fights, Gilbert, why don't you keep a cow?"

Gilbert asked mildly:

"Where?"

"Well," Aunt Bee said, reflecting, "you might buy a paddock. We always kept a cow at *Glenwood* when I was a girl. And, by the way, where are Prue and Virginia?"

"They're playing tennis at the Club." Phyllis came over to the hearth and pulled the logs about with the poker till the fire began to sulk. Her nose and hands were reddened by the cold, and the glowing embers were reflected in her glasses. She went on, clambering to her feet: "They would wear those skimpy silk frocks, and they wouldn't take anything but cardigans. I warned them it was going to be cold. And Gilbert, you must tell Pete not to ride his bicycle across the lawn. Aren't you going to sit by the fire, Marty?"

Marty, lighting a cigarette, turned from her contemplation of the bookshelves.

"I'll come and help you, Phyllis."

"There's no need." Phyllis' gift for sounding cheerful with an undertone of martyrdom was never so much in evidence as when she spoke to Marty: "Dulcie left the vegetables ready, and I'm only going to grill some chops. You sit down and smoke your cigarette."

She bustled out of the room. Marty shrugged and took the chair opposite Gilbert. At forty, her slimness had become slightly angular, and there were lines around her eyes. Gilbert, facing his own reflection in his shaving mirror, could see no outward sign of the wear and tear of the past few years, but he thought now, studying his sister's face, that they had left their mark on her.

She rested her head on the back of her chair and shut her eyes.

She was thinking of Pete, whom they had met as they returned to the house, lovingly bestowing his bicycle for the night in the little shed beside the garage. Exercise and cold air had painted his cheeks a clear crimson, his teeth and the pellucid whites of his eyes shone, his strong black eyebrows made a dark bar across his forehead. He was nearly thirteen. Philip, she thought, would have been just a month or two older if he had not been drowned in the surf at Manly when he was eight. He would have been like Pete, too. The same shaped head, the same wide-set grey eyes, the same dark brows and clear red-brown complexion. There had been moments in these last four years while she had watched the world skidding towards catastrophe, when she had told herself she was glad he was out of it, and known that she was lying. Shaken by the swift, familiar rigor which the thought of him still caused, she opened her eyes, and said, hastily, the first thing that came into her head:

"Do you want your knitting, Aunt Bee?"

"No, darling, not just now. To tell you the truth, I feel quite ashamed to be doing anything so frivolous when I see dear Phyllis so busy on her ugly khaki socks."

Marty's eyes closed again over a glimmer of amusement. Phyllis and her socks! How Aunt Bee must be wondering, with her innocent inquisitiveness, why Gilbert had ever married such a tiresome, unattractive woman! Sometimes she marvelled herself, until she remembered that strange childhood of bewilderment and repression into which Phyllis had been so suddenly introduced. Their own mother, she thought, had been so essentially a house-keeper, an attendant upon her family's material needs, that when her place was taken by Phyllis' mother, bred in an exactly similar tradition, wearing, even, exactly similar clothes, it had seemed to the children after a little while that nothing was changed. Except that there was Nick . . .

And suddenly, as if Aunt Bee had been reading her thoughts, she asked:

"Tell me, Marty, was Phyllis' mother an old friend of your mother's?" Marty opened her eyes again and threw her cigarette butt into the fire.

"She was a missionary with mother in the Islands before her marriage."

"Ah, yes. I have always," Aunt Bee said innocently, "felt sorry for the natives. Oh, my dears," she cried in protest, looking from her nephew to her niece, and finding the same smile in both pairs of eyes, "I didn't mean that!"

"Of course not."

Marty spoke soothingly, but she felt sorry for the natives, too. She had not been born and brought up in a home to which missionaries were constant visitors without learning that their profession, like every other, had its worthy and its unworthy members. She had known missionaries whose sincerity and devotion were beyond question; and she had known others who were mere posturers. But now when she thought of them she found herself remembering those island boats at whose comings and goings her father had assisted; boats bearing Bibles and merchandise, missionaries and traders, Christians and copra, God and Mammon. She knew now that her mother, worthy woman that she was, had seen nothing amiss in this unholy and unnatural association.. Nor had Phyllis' mother, Mrs. Miller, equally worthy, ever questioned it. She had done her duty according to her lights—not only towards the pagan islanders, but, later, in her dealings with three motherless children. Thus Marty dismissed her, both as a missionary and a foster-parent; but Phyllis was a different matter. Looking into the fire, she saw a big-boned, fair-haired child with round blue eyes, who had given her first lesson in hatred. Why had she hated Phyllis so? Partly, perhaps, because Phyllis had courted Walter Massey so assiduously. "I wasn't jealous," Marty thought with detachment. "I disliked Father too much to value his good opinion. I suppose I thought of Phyllis as a person with one foot in the enemy camp. A quisling." She saw her father with his hand on a fair, curly head. "Phyllis is my little sunbeam!" he said.

"You know," Aunt Bee told them suddenly, "I wrote to your father several times while you children were growing up, asking him to let me have you for holidays. It would," she added wistfully, "have been so good for you—riding, and picnicking and swimming . . ."

Marty looked at her curiously.

"What did he say?"

Aunt Bee struggled for a moment between indignation and respect for the dead. She shook her curls sadly.

"Never mind, never mind! He didn't approve of me. And yet, you know, there was nothing *in* that silly scandal. Even in those days no one would have made such a fuss except my father and

Walter. I was very young—only sixteen—and really quite pretty, and—well, I'm sure Virginia and Prue do as much as I did every time they go to a dance!"

She threw out two plump little hands, lavishly be-ringed.

"A kiss or two! And a little—what do they call it now—petting? Just a little. Anyhow, no one saw that. The real trouble was—you'll hardly believe it—that I went driving with him, in his carriage, in the moonlight—oh, it was a lovely night!—and we didn't get home till after four o'clock."

"What happened?" asked Marty.

Aunt Bee achieved an expression of mingled glee, mischief and contrition.

"I was really very rude. Father was waiting up for me. But I was feeling a little—a little *above* myself. And only a few days before I had heard someone speak of Father when they didn't know I was listening. So before I could stop myself I repeated what they'd said. I just looked straight at him and said: "Papa, you're a sanctimonious old humbug!"

She interrupted their laughter to say wisely: "Sometimes I've thought that it was really *that* . . . oh, well, it's all over long ago. But I used to wonder if you would all grow up prim and stiff and disapproving. I didn't see how you could help it. How did you help it, Gilbert?"

"I don't know that I did," Gilbert admitted. "I'm supposed to be pretty prim and stiff."

"Oh, no!" protested Aunt Bee loyally. "And not a bit disapproving."

His brows contracted in a sudden slight frown.

"That depends."

"Oh, well, of course we all disapprove of *something!* I do myself. I disapprove of . . . well . . . I'm sure there *are* some things . . ."

"Intolerance?" Marty suggested. Aunt Bee cried gratefully:

"Yes, of course—intolerance! Such a nasty thing! And I used to wonder if Mrs. Miller looked after you all properly, and if Phyllis was a nice playmate . . ."

Oh, Lord, Marty thought, a nice playmate! Poor self-righteous Phyllis, raised in sentimental godliness, working so hard at being a good, Christian child, a little sunbeam! Poor Phyllis, always yearning, craving, fishing for attention and affection; always blundering and intruding, romancing and falsifying! She reflected that in their home, as in every home where the child-adult relationship is limited to "don't" and "did you brush your teeth?" there was a subterranean emotional life which the grown-ups never suspected—except when they saw some eruption which it caused. How surprised they were then—how shocked!

"Looked after us . . ." she said vaguely. "Oh, yes, she looked after us all right. We were fed and washed and combed. Do you remember Miss Plunkett, Gilbert?"

"Yes, I remember her. A little dried-up spinster who had the audacity to run a school. Not one single qualification except gentility. She taught us what an isthmus was, and some simple arithmetic, and "The Stately Homes of England," and—what else? To recite the rivers of New South Wales from north to south. And once she hit me with a ruler, Marty, and you kicked her shins."

"How splendid!" cried Aunt Bee sincerely.

"And she tried hard to make snobs of us," Marty said.

"But she couldn't," added Aunt Bee fondly.

"No credit to us," Marty objected. "I suppose it was about the time when the air was beginning to be less charged with snobbery. And there were the Dodds. They lived in that little hovel that used to be grandfather's groom's cottage before he sold that bit of land—you remember, Aunt Bee?" She laughed. "We weren't supposed to play with them—I could never understand why. Now I realise that though there was never any Mr. Dodd there was somehow always a baby. The eldest was Sally. She was my bosom friend."

In the idle silence that fell they could hear Pete clattering about on the verandah. Marty was thinking of the paddocks and the bush about *Glenwood*, the leafy shelter of the orchard, the blackberry-smothered fences, the slopes of bracken, shoulder high. Plenty of cover for small, hunted animals, and that's what we were, Sally and I, alert for the voices of grown-ups, still and silent in hiding as footsteps went by, swift and invisible in flight . . .

And Phyllis, always following and prying. Always trying to get herself included in the games, admitted to mysteries and whispered secrets. And then, rejected, running off to her mother with tales, covering her betrayal from herself by pretending that she had a duty towards Marty—naughty, disobedient little Marty who mixed with undesirable companions!

She rose suddenly and stretched across the mantelpiece for another cigarette.

Aunt Bee protested:

"Darling Marty, you smoke too much."

"I know."

"So do I," said Aunt Bee placidly, accepting one from the box. Marty sat down again, curious, interested because she found that even now she still cherished a sense of injury against Phyllis for having provoked all through those childhood and adolescent years, her worst, her most unlovely qualities. Phyllis had never been a match for her. Her own naturally sharp tongue had developed a razor-edge for wounding. Her quick wits, her instinct for seeing into motives and hidden impulses had found no better outlet in those days than scheming for Phyllis' humiliation and discomfiture. That sewing-class! Phyllis incorrigibly clumsy-fingered, slaving over her botched sampler; and herself, bright-eyed with malice, manœuvring for a seat just opposite, contriving that her own sampler, neat and smooth, with every stitch correctly placed, should be consistently visible to Phyllis' resentful and sometimes tearful eyes!

Now that she was grown-up she could see the pathos of a human being who wanted so badly to be loved and admired—and never was; who wanted to excel, and always failed; who worshipped efficiency, deftness, brilliance, wit and learning, and who remained bungling, clumsy, dull, slow of speech, and hopelessly muddle-headed. Over the arm of the chair not three feet away from her hung the mud-coloured socks which had abashed Aunt Bee; even from here Marty could see that the heel was in a mess. There's no excuse for me now, she told herself sternly. I understand now that she must have her compensations. If she can be nothing else, she can be a martyr—can one grudge her that?

She got up abruptly.

"I'll go and see if I can give Phyllis a hand."

She threw her half-finished cigarette into the fire, and went out into the chilly passage.

II

PETE, beaming, came in from the frosty air to the kitchen, and sniffed the odours of cooking with frank enjoyment. Phyllis, loading the traymobile, looked at him and felt herself stabbed, as she so often was, by his resemblance to his father. Incapable of analysing her own emotions with any detachment, she knew only in a vague, aggrieved way that the undeniable good looks of her children left her not altogether pleased. She had been pleased enough until Pete arrived; for Virginia and Prue both had fair hair and blue eyes, so she had always assumed that they were like her. No one had ever contradicted her—except Pete. He contradicted her every time she set eyes on him, for there was no denying he was the image of his father, and also the image of his sisters. Looking from her children to her husband she could not fail to see that she had contributed nothing to their appearance except the colour of the girls' hair and eyes. Thus, when people complimented her, as they often did, on her good-looking family, she felt it like a prick—an implied criticism of herself. Indeed, there had been occasions when a tactless hint of surprise had crept into the congratulations. "Why, but they're *lovely* children!"

"It wasn't, she always hastened to tell herself, that Gilbert was so handsome. He wasn't. It was just that somehow the children seemed to have taken his features and improved on them. Pete, poking among the dishes on the table, asked:

"Can I scrape this, Mum? What is it? Teacake?"

"Oh, yes, you can scrape it. Put it on the sink when you've done with it. Did you get that kindling wood in when I told you?" Pete stopped with a spoonful of golden dough half-way to his mouth.

"Gee, Mum, I forgot!"

Phyllis, lifting the saucepan lid from the potatoes, felt a rush of steam scald her wrist as he spoke. She rationalised as instinctively as she breathed, and the exasperated anger of momentary pain transferred itself to Pete without a second's hesitation. She said sharply:

"Put that basin down! No, if you can't remember to do a little thing like that when I ask you . . ."

"But, Mum, you *said* . . ."

"Put it down at once! And go and wash your hands."

Pete glowered. He said with heavy sarcasm:

"*You* never forget anything, do you? Oh, no!"

"Don't be impertinent!" Phyllis snatched the basin, dumped it in the sink, and turned the tap on it. Pete, his brilliant colour more brilliant than ever with mounting resentment, stormed:

"The other day I asked you to mend my football jersey, and you said you would, and when I asked for it you said you'd forgotten!"

The potatoes boiled over. Phyllis, grabbing a dish-cloth, rushed for the stove. Pete jeered maddeningly. She said, shrilly:

"Go away out of the kitchen this minute! How dare you speak to me like that? What if I did forget your jersey? I'm going from morning till night, and you have nothing to do but play! Go and wash your hands immediately, or I'll get your father to deal with you!"

Pete went, muttering. Phyllis restored order on the stove, transferred used dishes from the table to the sink, and then, quite suddenly, sat down on a chair and slumped, her hands heavy in her lap. Her mind busied itself instantly to justify and account for the tears she felt rising to her eyes. Four other women in the house, and I have to get the meal alone. Aunt Bee's a selfish old woman—one expects no help from her. But Marty—she'll offer once, and when you politely protest she'll sit down at her ease with her everlasting cigarettes. Prue and Virginia should have been home long ago. It's quite dark, they can't have been playing this last hour. Gossiping instead of coming home to help their mother . . .

For a moment her thoughts checked upon the image of Virginia. Wasn't she almost *too* pretty? Wasn't she too pleasure-loving, and didn't she think too much about her clothes and her appearance? Phyllis reflected upon these failings more often and more earnestly than she would have done had it not been for the fact that she was jealous of her elder daughter. Remembering her own sober and restricted youth, she looked askance at Virginia's "good time," substituting an anxious maternal disapproval for the envy she would not admit. All this lipstick and powder and nail-varnish. . . . When I was a girl such things weren't used so much. We relied on our own complexions. And I was *married* at twenty-two. Well, perhaps after all it's natural for a young girl to be a little frivolous. More natural than to be interested in politics, and go to lectures and meetings more than to dances, and read queer books, and that ridiculous modern poetry, and reports on housing and malnutrition, and even venereal disease. . . . No, I don't think I need to worry so much about Virginia, even if she does flirt and drink cocktails more than I like; she's normal—but I just don't know what to *make* of Prue! It isn't natural for her to think about such things . . . venereal disease . . . ! A child of twenty-one! Grandfather was quite right to oppose the idea of her bookshop. It wasn't as if she *had* to earn her own living. He said it would give her wrong ideas, and see how right he was. He said she'd be safer and happier helping me at home. But of course her father always gives way to her. . . . She was always his favourite because she's so mad about books. . . .

Instantly, with the accidental conjunction in her thoughts of "Gilbert" and "books," her mind bolted like a horse at the prick of a spur. When thought became difficult, disturbing, confusing, she always tried to drown it in physical activity, and to restore confidence in herself by the performance of domestic tasks. She jumped up now and busied herself feverishly. It did not matter in the least, to-night, what time they had their meal; her glance at the clock was merely to set her right with herself, to account for the sudden bustle in some way which saved her from recognising it as a symptom of panic.

"I never understood Gilbert—never!" She pushed the traymobile into the dining-room and began laying the table. How many of us? Five in the family, Marty, Nick, Aunt Bee, that's eight. Knives, forks, table napkins, salt and pepper, even when we were children there was always that—secretiveness in him. Those flowers looked faded. Prue should have done them this morning; and it wasn't as if I didn't try . . .

She stood with her finger to her mouth looking critically at the table. Under cover of this attitude her thoughts were of the old man, just buried, who had called her his little sunbeam. What if he was a bit—old-fashioned? He was a good man, the life he had tried to make was steady and solid and respectable, and he had appreciated her. Always, right up to the end, he had depended on her. Why, if it hadn't been for her insistence that they must look after him, Gilbert mightn't have agreed to live on at *Glenwood* after they were married. There wasn't one of the three of them who wouldn't have left him in the lurch without a second thought.

As it was all the weight of it had fallen on her. During the last few years when he was so old and forsaken, and so angrily bewildered by the changing world, it had been herself who tried to shield him, reassure him, agree with him, make him feel that there were still some people who remembered old standards and old ways. His own children wouldn't bother. So she had gone every night to sit by him while he read his chapter from the Bible, and she had bent her head and murmured "Amen" to his prayer. She had brought him the paper every morning, and read the leaders to him when he was too tired to read for himself; and she had listened to his comments, and shaken her head with him over the wickedness of a world forsaking God, over women who smoked and wore trousers, over Sunday sport, over modern art, over strikes, over James Joyce, and contraceptives, and Bolshevism, and cocktails. And, if he *was* old-fashioned, wasn't he right? Hadn't things been better in the old days?

Gilbert said "No." The steadiness and conviction of his "no" was the root of her confusion, for she had not lived with him for most of her life without learning unwillingly to respect his opinions. Yet when he tried to explain, to justify his "no," she was not convinced. She had memories of a time when everything had its place, and stayed there. He said that was an illusion. He said that even then there had been turmoil, and the stirrings of that unrest which burst out at last in 1914 as war—but she hadn't known, because in those days it was still covered up from people of their sort. Thinking back, she had remembered mornings at the breakfast table when Uncle Walter had thundered about politics, and shaken his finger at her mother, saying that, mark his words, these Trade Unions and Labour Governments would bring disaster on the country. Well, perhaps he had been right there, too? Couldn't you trust a man like Uncle Walter, upright, and God-fearing and scrupulous, to know what was best? But once, answering this with a grim face, Gilbert had said a dreadful thing:

"Could you? With the Dodds' starving on his doorstep?"

"*Starving?*" She looked at him in horrified resentment. "Gilbert, don't be ridiculous! They weren't starving!"

He said relentlessly:

"How do you know? Did you go and see?"

She answered trembling:

"You know we weren't allowed to go there!"

"Marty went." He spoke coldly. "She went once—for the first time, though she and Sally had been friends for years—when she was about sixteen. They were eating bread and jam and tea without milk. All of them, down to the three-year-old. Sally said that was what they usually ate."

Phyllis had said sharply:

"Well, why *was* there a three-year-old? There wasn't ever any Mr. Dodd that I knew of!"

That had silenced him—but Gilbert's silences were sometimes more disconcerting than his words. Yet the fact that she felt disconcerted was, in itself, another infuriating bewilderment. Were you to condone immorality? Was that what Gilbert meant?

Coming out of her trance, she hurriedly straightened a knife, moved a salt cellar, and bustled out to the kitchen again, trundling the traymobile in front of her.

No, I never understood him. Even when we were about four-teen and he first began writing. He wouldn't show me his things, or talk about it, though he and Marty had their heads together all the time. Of course she put him against me. Well, I beat her in the end! For a few years how nice he was! Just for a few years! When we were first engaged—just a pair of children— eighteen and nineteen! His lovely letters when he was away at the war, and my trousseau . . .

Her mind jumped from the trousseau. It was necessary to her own conception of herself that she should not admit failure in any of those accomplishments which she thought proper to womankind, so the knowledge of her own ineptitude at sewing and cooking was hustled from her mind whenever it threatened to intrude. It was proper for a girl to make her own trousseau, and it was proper for her to dream over the task. She had done both, but, unwisely, she had once allowed her desire to score over Marty to tempt her into speech about it. Sewing away on the verandah at *Glenwood*, she had met Marty's unsympathetic gaze, and said, with gentle triumph that hopes and plans of her future with dear Gilbert were being woven into these white ruffles; and Marty, looking at the large, ungainly stitches, had said sourly: "Look out they don't fall through."

Jealous. Poor Marty, she had always adored Gilbert. The chops are done, but the potatoes need a few minutes more. There are the girls coming in. Is Nick back yet? Well, I'm not going to wait for him. He and Marty between them are simply ruining

Gilbert. Now that his father's dead—well, what? Won't it make him have more—more steadiness, more sense of responsibility? After all, he is the head of the firm now. Of course he has been, actually, for years, but there was always the feeling that it didn't really belong to him. Oh, those potatoes will have to do! Good Heavens, the teacake! Well—yes—it's burnt. That's Pete's fault, he got me so upset. . . .

Prue, her racquet still under her arm, stood in the doorway, frowning slightly. Phyllis asked:

"Are you ready for tea, dear? Where's Virginia?"

"She's staying the night at the Johnson's, Mother. She said to tell you she'll be back by ten to-morrow."

"Oh, well!" Phyllis turned the potatoes into their dish, and set the dish on the traymobile. Marty wandered in from the passage. "She knows we're leaving on the eleven-fifteen, doesn't she?"

"Yes, she knows."

Marty said:

"Shall I carry that in for you, Phyllis?"

"Don't bother, Marty. Just go and tell the others we're ready. Oh, and Marty, see if Pete has washed his hands. Prue, you dish up the other things."

"All right, Mother."

Left alone in the kitchen, Prue began to frown again.

*   *   *   *

The meal was almost over before Nick came in. But for Aunt Bee, conversation might have languished. Phyllis' depressingly determined brightness met with little response; Prue, having repeated to her father that Virginia was staying the night with the Johnson's, had nothing further to say; Pete was sulking, on his dignity. As for Gilbert, he never spoke for the sake of politeness, of convention, of tiding over an awkward moment. He was unaware of awkward moments. A silent company, he presumed, was a company which did not desire conversation, and was quite within its rights. So it was left, and could safely be left to Aunt Bee, who chattered with happy garrulity, mostly about the past.

That was natural enough just now, Marty reflected. Their father's death had turned all their thoughts backward during the last few weeks; and on that she had looked up to see Nick in the doorway, and to admit that the past never held his attention for more than an impatient moment. He looked, as usual, angry. She had never been able to make up her mind how much of this characteristic expression of his was a reflection of his uncompromising attitude to life, and how much was due to the structure of his face. The high cheekbones which they all had were so emphasised in Nick as to give his cheeks a hollow gauntness. His mouth, being larger than her own and Gilbert's, looked thinner; his chin was definitely more square. His thick black eyebrows, almost meeting over the bridge of his nose, were halted by the two deep, frowning furrows between his eyes. How much, Marty often wondered, could you rely on faces as a guide to character? Nick looked both ascetic and at least potentially fanatic. The quality of their father's belief had descended upon him; and, though he placed Marx and Lenin where Walter Massey had placed the Bible, Marty found his attitude towards his own faith curiously reminiscent of the old man's remorseless and immovable conviction. Nick was a modern evangelist, sternly scientific, substituting for the Scriptural thunder with which his father had rebuked the unbeliever, a deluge of statistical data. He was tireless, self-denying, austere in his personal habits, a stripper-away of what he regarded as inessentials, a condemner of complacency, a voice crying indefatigably in the wilderness of political inertia. He would not, his sister knew, have been willing to see himself as a spiritual descendant of John the Baptist. Yet listening to him speak from a platform, hearing him exhort the incurious to ask, hearing him urge the heedless to wake up, for the New Order was just round the corner, she heard also the echo of a voice saying Repent ye, for the kingdom of Heaven is at hand.

Of the three of them, he, who most resembled their father, was the most bitter and ruthless in his condemnation of their father's creed. She felt the same narrowness in him, the same dangerous flavour of bigotry, the same threat of intolerance; yet she applauded Nick for daring to be a rebel, which their father had never been; for daring to apply his theory to life, which their father had never done; for daring to present his faith as something that might, and must be practised as well as professed. He made her angry very often, and sometimes he made her afraid, but she respected him.

To-night, however, that air of having a mind full of grim and dammed-back furies was not so much in evidence. He had been out walking all day with his latest girl, Brenda, who seemed to show encouraging signs of responding to political education, and something of the enjoyment and stimulus of open-air and exercise had made him look younger rather than, as was usually the case, older than his years. He said:

"I'm late, Phyl. We got tangled up with a creek-bed—couldn't get out of it for over an hour. And then I saw Brenda back to her friend's place, and got talking to her friend's husband. God, what confusion, what ignorance! He's one of those who think socialism wouldn't let you own your own toothbrush. Have you got anything cold to drink, Phyllis?"

Phyllis, who in her attitude to him still clung to the rôle of nurse and devoted (though now disapproving) slave, which she had adopted during his infancy, answered fretfully:

"Can't you *ever* stop talking politics? No, there's nothing cold but water. Sit down and I'll bring your dinner in; I've kept it hot for you."

Gilbert asked:

"Where did you go?"

The question which might have been, from anyone else, a mere conversational politeness was, from Gilbert, a serious request for information. For he had recently decided that he needed more exercise, and that he could find it both pleasantly and cheaply in week-end bush-walking. Nick poured himself a glass of water and drank thirstily.

"Right up on top of Solitary, and back across the valley."

Phyllis, returning, placed a plate before him, and complained:

"You should never have gone. Your cold's worse—I can see it is. I wish you'd take some of that mixture that I give Pete and the girls."

"Don't you, Nick!" Pete advised with his mouth full. Aunt Bee said firmly:

"Hot lemon drink, with a little something in it, and aspirin. But above all, bed. Because one looks such a fright with a cold."

"Thanks." Nick, who had discovered that his aunt appreciated a little horseplay, gave her a playful dig in the ribs, so that she squealed happily. "As a matter of fact," he added, "my cold's better. What's the news, Gil?"

"Looks bad in North Africa," Gilbert said gloomily. "Japan's still sitting on the fence, and Matsuoka's on his way to Moscow." Nick snorted.

"He won't get anything out of that. Don't wait for me if you've all finished." He looked at the empty chair beside Prue, and enquired:

"Where's Virginia?"

Phyllis said:

"She's staying the night with the Johnsons."

Nick flashed an alert glance at Prue, who met it with an expression instinctively defensive. He felt a cynical amusement at thus sharing with his niece an unspoken secret, and at the knowledge that she was looking at him, wondering: Now how does *he* know that isn't true? Phyllis rose cumbersomely, pushing down on the table with her hands.

"We won't wait for you, Nick. Aunt Bee, you go and sit by the fire again. I'll be in as soon as I've seen to the washing-up." She added heavily: "And everything."

Prue pushed her chair back and began gathering plates together.

"I'll clear away and wash up, Mother. You go and talk to Aunt Bee."

"Oh, all right." Phyllis looked grudgingly at the table, as if afraid that without her supervision even so simple a task could not be properly accomplished. "Don't forget the milk-jug, and leave a note saying we won't want any more till next week-end."

Marty said:

"I'll put the kettle on while you clear, Prue." She vanished with a pile of plates into the kitchen. Phyllis, following her husband and Aunt Bee to the door, said sharply to Pete: "You'd better bring in some more wood for the fire. And mind the walls when you're carrying it through the hall. And lock the woodshed door after you." Nick, left alone with Prue, grinned at her, and asked:

"What's the lovely Virginia up to now?"

"Up to?" Prue countered, avoiding his eyes.

"She's not at the Johnson's."

"How do you know?"

"Because I saw them all outside their gate on the way home. They were just leaving for town."

"Leaving?" Prue said blankly. "Oh, damn! Have you got a cigarette, Nick?"

He threw a packet across the table to her.

"Where is she, then?"

Prue gave her shoulders an angry shrug.

"How should I know? She told me she was going to the Johnson's. Of course," she added coldly, after a slight pause, "I didn't altogether believe her."

"One doesn't," Nick agreed equably. He remembered that five years ago, when Virginia was just leaving school, Marty had said to him:

"Poor Phyllis' sinlessness is going to be visited on that child. She's going to work off all her mother's complexes before she's finished. You watch."

It had been, he thought, worth watching. Virginia, he held, was a useless little bit of pink and blue and golden decoration. As such, believing passionately that the young must cultivate a militant enlightenment, he despised and detested her, but he had to admit that she brought to her paltry purposes an astonishing strategy and technique. Aided and abetted by her mother and her grandfather, she had dodged training in any trade or profession. "Why," Phyllis had demanded, "shouldn't one of them be just a home-girl?" "Home-girl, my eye!" Nick thought cynically. "When is she home?"

Prue wheeled the traymobile, laden with crockery, out to the kitchen. Nick finished his meal alone, and then joined the rest of the family in the drawing-room, dismissing Virginia from his mind.

*   *   *   *

Lying in bed on the verandah, watching the frosty glitter of the stars through a tracery of branches, Marty cursed Aunt Bee and her reminiscent mood. She had been rather startled by her own reluctance to remember, but she found now that the thick black curtain she had hung between her adult life and her childhood, having once been drawn aside a little by Aunt Bee's artless chatter, tempted her to draw it still further. And, while she lay awake thinking of what had been for so long forgotten, stars had moved from the black line of the verandah roof across the sky to the tree-tops.

Thought—its forms and techniques so various! Memory, too. Aunt Bee remembered like a child turning the pages of a picture book. Gilbert—how? Probably in a sober, methodical way, as an array of facts, as one remembered things to write them down in an examination paper. For herself memory was either sharp and detailed and poignant—or non-existent. She knew, from hearing other people speak of events in which she had participated, and of people she had met, that there were blind spots in her memory, but when she did remember it was a departure from the

body, an excursion into a fourth dimension. She could not remember and not feel, taste, smell, hear—*be* in the past. To-
night, resist as she would, anchor her mind as she would by
watching the stars, by thinking how pure and cold was this mountain air, by grabbing at the eiderdown as it slid towards the floor,
her thoughts escaped continually, annihilating time, leaving her
middle-aged body tenantless, to inhabit the wraith of a child-body,
and make it flesh and blood again.

A restless flesh and blood, informed with rebellion, coming to
terms with life only in one secret, mystical way. How Nick and
Gilbert would laugh at that "mystical!" How Richard, her husband, would laugh! How Phyllis would jeer! Marty—mystical!
Yet in a childhood which had been more full of resentments and
confusions than most childhoods, she had had her one jealously-
guarded, intimate source of tranquillity. The years belonged to
her. Curious faith, curious abiding comfort! How had she discovered it—when had it begun?

That was lost—so it must have been very, very early. Probably
from some words of her mother's, while she played with blocks on
the floor. "Marty and the Twentieth Century were born together,
you know. Practically to the minute!" It had made the century
seem peculiarly her own; she had resolved quite early in life to
live until December 31st, 2000, so that she could die with it too.

Thus, an accident of birth had invited her to see her life in a
slick, chronological pattern; the century had grown with her in
the slow, slow tempo of their mutual childhood. Its days were
long, though its moments flew, things happened in dream-like
isolation, events momentarily disturbed an endless flow of weeks
and months, and only now she realised that a life which had then
seemed so solidly inevitable, was unstable, fluid, breaking down
into chaos. At the time, she and the Century had seemed to
share, up to the year 1914, an age of innocence, of unsophistication, of downright naïvete. The violence of the next four war-
years had inevitably identified itself with the storms and stresses
of her own ignorant and rebellious adolescence. She had emerged
into young womanhood, discovering life and love, with the century
still sympathetically matching her mood in the rosy, pleasure-
mad years of the early twenties. The years were hers, she had
believed; they kept step with her. Now, in the cold consciousness
of maturity, she saw herself as keeping step, willy-nilly, with them,
learning throughout the uneasy thirties worry and disillusionment

and apprehension, being dragged with them, nervously, nearer and nearer to the climax, borne down with them into catastrophe.

Now she could look back on those early years and see that she had conceived them, in the boundless egotism of childhood, as taking their colour from her. No one had ever suggested to her that she was living in history; no one had ever analysed or dissected those years for her, or even in her hearing, so that she might look at them, and at herself inhabiting them, with comprehension. She had been forced, long after she grew up, to learn laboriously from books, the significance of events in which she had participated; and she reflected now, turning restlessly on her pillow, that the intelligence of children was grossly underestimated. How blandly fatuous, she thought, is our assumption that this topical question, or that current problem, is "beyond" them! As well say that the air they breathe is "beyond" them—and leave them asphyxiated! Are they ghosts, disembodied wraiths blowing through their world like smoke? Why do we hold this black screen of ignorance before their eyes? Is it fear of being shown up? Fear that the searching, logical child-mind which has not yet learned to be afraid will uncover the indolence, the shirking, the confusion and hypocrisy of adult thinking? Is it jealousy of a new generation, stepping forward to take control?

Something ugly, anyhow, she told herself grimly, or there wouldn't be such a drapery of sentimental fondness spread. Let the little darlings be care-free while they can! They will have to face the wicked world soon enough! Old heads on young shoulders! Keep them carefree, keep them merry, and above all, for Heaven's sake keep them ignorant while we wreck the machinery of their lives! She sat up, snatching irritably at the eiderdown and thinking bitterly: "There aren't enough millstones on the earth, the ocean isn't deep enough to receive us all . . ."

She dropped back on the pillow with a shiver. Oh, well, I was ignorant. Gilbert and I, we were both quite stupendously ignorant. We floundered. But at least we rebelled. What were we taught of the fundamental relationship between man and man? There were "nice" people—and others! We weren't exactly told —not in so many words—that the others were nasty; that was left to the logic of implication. But bad as it was, it might have been worse. It would have been worse thirty years earlier, just as it's a little better now, thirty years later.

Her anger quietened at the thought, and she lay on her back

looking at the sky, trying to estimate and analyse the social atmosphere, the *zeitgeist* of her childhood. Still pretty rigid, but beginning to give in places. Still complacent and self-righteous, but
pricked here and there by doubt. Social conventions, which still
flourished lustily in the long-established society which had bred
them, necessarily suffered change and dilution in a community still
in the throes of shaping itself to a new environment, still experi-
mental, still urgently developing its own character. Yes, she
thought, rigid as they might remain, and uncompromisingly as they
might be cherished in the minds of such people as her father,
they were already being discarded by the general public. It was
an unconscious by-product of impatience—not a policy; life was
too busy here; too mixed up; there was too much interdependence;
there simply wasn't time, except among a small, ridiculous, wealthy
section, for the little ceremonies and conventions of class-distinc-
tion. Shedding them was like shedding a coat and collar before
embarking on strenuous physical work. She felt a rare prick of
pity for her father, who could no more shut out this intrusive
social evolution than he could shut out the air, but who had
continued to the end of his long life in a stubborn opposition,
still denouncing and protesting long after the battle had passed
over his head.

Yet he had succeeded—believing that he was protecting them—
in condemning his children to a life over which there hung a
perpetual mist of confusion. He had given them, in place of
guidance, a series of tabus and prohibitions; in place of enlightenment a series of condemnations. The clearest and most dominant
conception they had was of guilt; and from this conception flowed,
inevitably, the pitiable, lonely secrecy of bewildered childhood.
So that when they began to write, she and Gilbert, they had at
first hidden their new impulse jealously even from each other,
vaguely alarmed by anything so demanding, insistent, and mysterious, sure only that, being something sprung from themselves,
and lacking parental sanction, it must be carefully hidden, and
surreptitiously indulged.

If it had not been for the accident that the Laughlins came
suddenly to live in the little cottage at the foot of the hill, what
would have become of that writing impulse? Had it been strong
enough to survive and develop quite alone, or would it have died
when the driving power of adolesence failed? She remembered
her own interest (never revealed, never expressed) when she found

that another little girl a year or two older than herself had come to live so near them; she remembered, too, and saw it now as significant, that she had not been at all surprised, angered, or even disappointed when it became clear that the Laughlins were not "nice" people, and that the little girl was, therefore, not a suitable playmate for her. Her reaction had been, quite simply, that it would be necessary to play with her by stealth, as she played with Sally Dodd. She neither knew, nor was interested to know, the reason for her father's disapproval; but she was more than interested—she was staggered—when she discovered that Janet Laughlin not only "wrote things" too, but actually showed them to her father! ,

Inside the hall the clock struck three. Marty heard it, but only vaguely. For her memory was departing again, and there remained with her body only enough consciousness to count three, and then fade. She was still in bed, but not here; it was not night, but morning—the morning of her twelfth birthday. She was sitting up, barely awake, but already filled with the familiar, pleasing sense of sharing her birthday with a year which was one of a hundred years, part of the Twentieth Century, whose vast potentialities, stretching away mysteriously into the future, lent significance to her own small life.

Phyllis still slept in the opposite bed with her mouth slightly open. She would, when she woke, make New Year resolutions of extreme virtue, but Marty's, though having the added potency of being birthday resolutions as well, would be less concerned with virtue than with getting her own way. Already she was scheming to escape unobtrusively after breakfast before Aunt Ada could summon her to dust the drawing-room. It was a lovely morning, but alas, a Wednesday. On Wednesdays throughout the holidays the three elder children were required to learn a passage from the Bible and recite it to Walter Massey at the end of breakfast. Marty glowered at her Bible, lying on the edge of the washstand near her bed, reached out for it unwillingly, opened it at the marker, yawned and began to read. *"Children, obey your parents in the Lord; for this is right. Honour thy father and mother, which is the first commandment with promise, that it may be well with thee, and thou mayest live long on the earth . . ."* Marty gabbled it over to herself, bored, secure in her own faith that she would see her century out, commandment or no commandment. *"And ye, fathers, provoke not your children to wrath . . ."* The meaning of those words penetrated, halted her, set her musing pleasantly. It would be nice saying that to Father; it lit the dreary task up with a purpose. She memorised the rest sketchily, discarded the Bible, and turned eagerly to matters of more importance. She felt beneath her pillow for a crumpled bit of paper which she unfolded and smoothed out carefully on her knee. There should have been a pencil too, but there wasn't, so she hung out of bed in her calico nightdress with its long sleeves and its pin tucks and its lace-edged collar, and peered about on the floor for it. Her brown hair swept the linoleum, her cheeks already pink from sleep, grew crimson, but she saw the pencil, stretched, craned, grabbed, and sat up again, triumphant.

She was having trouble with this poem. She looked sadly at two angrily scribled-out lines.

> *"The bush beyond the creek is lit*
> *As if with sunshine by the wattle,*
> *And fragrant is . . ."*

But after all there were no rhymes for wattle except bottle and throttle, and how *could* you . . . ? She swept her hair back from her face impatiently and chewed the end of her pencil. She was vaguely resentful of this tyranny of rhyme, but did not know quite how to escape from it. And yet when rhymes did fall into place with a lovely inevitability there was something very satisfying about them. She studied the only complete verse she had achieved with considerable doubt:

> *"The rose, they say, is queen of flowers,*
> *The loveliest 'mongst them all,*
> *I would not for the rarest give*
> *One golden wattle-ball."*

She put her head on one side, studying it. " 'Mongst," she decided, was wrong. You oughtn't to have to chop bits off words, and anyhow it was an ugly, silly-looking word. No, it wasn't right at all. And yet she was loath to condemn something which, she dimly felt, did express not only her thought, but herself. She was able to recognise her own independence when it leaked out from the tip of her pencil and confronted her on paper; it gave her a moment of awed pleasure, as if she had worked a miracle by accident. She grabbed the Bible to serve as a table and wrote:

> *"O lovely golden flower, shine*
> *In shadowed places 'neath the trees . . ."*

'Neath! 'Mongst! She looked at it despairingly. Words wouldn't behave for her like they did for Janet, taking their places smoothly and sedately, making a sequence of sounds good to roll upon the tongue. But the thought of Janet suddenly reminded her of something so painful that she stopped thinking about her poem altogether, and stared unhappily out of the window. The Laughlin family had been, for her, in the past year or so, a new, exciting and delightful experience. Mrs. Laughlin, with her amused smile, her casual friendliness, her pretty fair hair, her habit of sitting down at the piano and strumming delectable tunes, was so unlike Marty's mental picture of what mothers were that she had found it easy to romanticise her. There was something about the Laughlin household which stimulated her—an emotional undercurrent, of which she had seen only the happier manifestations—until last night. Mr. Laughlin, coming home in the evening, would kiss his wife—not with a routine peck such as Marty dimly remembered having seen her own father bestow on her own mother, but vigorously, with enjoyment and ardour, lifting her off her feet, squeezing her till she laughed and pretended to protest, and winking at Marty as he did so. She had felt an expansive and benevolent delight as she watched, but at the back of her mind there had always been an uneasy wonder because Janet did not seem to share that delight. Janet could be merry with her father, or with her mother, but with them both together she became watchful and remote.

And last night Marty had learned, with bewilderment and pain, that love and hate can be disastrously mixed. The emotional aridity of her own home had made her peculiarly susceptible to the warm demonstrativeness which she had found in the Laughlins, and so, hearing them quarrel last night when she had gone down to wait for Janet, and had sprawled on the grass under an open window, had almost stopped her breath with shock. For it was terrible quarrelling, cruel, hurtful, tormented. Nothing they said gave her any clue to what it was all about, but she had felt their desperate love and hatred of each other as if they were physically belabouring her. She had rushed home, not waiting for Janet, feeling a horrified pity for her friend who, surely, could not know of this peril of instability which hung over her home.

This morning she was not so sure. It seemed almost as if things had fitted together in her mind while she slept, and now she remembered Janet's face wearing that strange, observant look of critical detachment; she could hear the queer, dry note in her voice which suggested that she wasn't going to take anything at its face value; she remembered that Janet had always made her feel that she was childish in her own overt rebellions; and she realised that Janet had not only a knowledge, but an inner strength, a refuge, which she lacked. In her conscious thoughts it boiled down to a discovery that "Janet knew," and that Janet had her own way of meeting the situation.

Suddenly it occurred to her that Janet and Gilbert were rather alike. When things went wrong they withdrew inside themselves, as you might go into a room and shut the door. She was overcome by an alarming and unfamiliar sense of humility, which formed itself into the incoherent thought that she herself was "too noisy" and "too rude," and she must somehow get to be quiet like Jan and Gilbert, and manage life in a more dignified way.

Subdued and chastened, she bent over her paper again. Slowly, cautiously, as if daring the words to present her with further problems, she wrote:

"Under the trees in shadowed places . . ."

She felt more hopeful over that. "Places" ought to be an easy rhyme. Faces, races, graces, braces . . . She giggled. Phyllis woke up. Preparing, even as she rubbed her eyes, a magnanimous forgiveness with which to meet Marty's ungracious reception of "Many Happy Returns of the Day," she was thoroughly taken aback by a muttered "Thank you," and a grimace which, however forced, was meant to be a smile.

Phyllis, now nearly sixteen, was at that intermediate stage when childish prettiness has vanished, and adult prettiness not yet arrived. The emotionalism of adolescence, being connected with sex, was something which, in her mother's view, could only be ignored. Obscurely conscious of its floods and tides, Phyllis let them escape through the only outlet she knew—religion. She had become very devout. She had also become very fat, and her once

[43]

petal-clear complexion was afflicted with spots. The hatred which Marty had invited was now lavished on her, but being Phyllis' hatred it had to work under another name. The name she had found for it was Duty It was her duty, she told herself, to exercise a good influence over wilful little Marty; and so, in devious and innocent-seeming ways, she contrived to let her mother and Uncle Walter know when Marty was with Janet or Sally. When Marty played hookey from Sunday-school it was somehow always discovered. Phyllis also had a duty to little Nick, and adroitly she sowed and fostered a legend that Marty didn't take very good care of him, so Marty was not often allowed to take him out. Marty often forgot to wash his ears, and see that his teeth were brushed, so Marty was not often allowed to preside at his bathing.

Now, staggered by unexpected politeness, her brain set about swift adjustments whereby she might see it in some light which would be a spotlight on herself. This, she told herself, was surely the first sign of that grace which she had prayed might descend on Marty. She jumped out of bed and floundered across the room.

"Marty darling!" she whispered from an enveloping embrace. "Let's be friends, Marty! Let's be *great* friends!"

To Marty's hard and still skinny child-body Phyllis seemed unpleasantly and rather obscenely plump. She didn't like feeling overwhelmed by this large soft flesh, so she drove her elbow hard into Phyllis' stomach and snapped:

"Get out! Leave me alone!"

Phyllis smiled at her with sorrowful, forgiving tenderness.

"It's New Year's Day, Marty. Let's make a resolution to be friends this year!"

Marty glared at her. New Year's Day was *her* day. She wasn't going to share it with any fat Phyllis. Her impulse of self-criticism, with its unconscious and spontaneous resolution, had borne its one small, meagre fruit, and was now dead. She said viciously:

"I don't want to be friends with you. You're silly and you're mean." She paused for inspiration, and found it. "And you're fat, and you've got pimples."

Phyllis burst into tears. Marty got up and began to dress.

*   *   *   *

Somewhere just before Phyllis' advance, Phyllis' embrace, memory had slid towards dreaming, and become infected with the obscure horror of nightmare. Marty came wide awake with a start, feeling cold and realising with exasperation that the eider-down was on the floor again. She got out of bed, re-arranged it so that it hung well down between the bed and the wall, and pushed the bed hard up against the weatherboards. She was shivering as she climbed back between the sheets, and she had never felt less sleepy.

Ours wasn't a home, she thought, where the giving of birthday presents could be made into a ceremony; we were all too self-conscious, and too mistrustful of ourselves and each other. She remembered five presents awkwardly thrust upon her before break-fast; Father, brushing her cheeks with his beard, too close to see her grimace—but surely conscious of her pull away from his encircling arm—saying deeply: "God bless you, my daughter!" and leaving her with a new prayer-book in her hand., Mrs. Miller, busy in the kitchen, giving her a hurried kiss and a work-basket, wicker, with padded pink satin lining. Phyllis with a tissue paper parcel inscribed "To dearest Marty, with love from Phyllis," and containing two sky-blue hair ribbons. . . .

Marty smiled, hearing the clock strike the half-hour, probing with cold amusement into the emotion which had caused Phyllis' blue eyes to overflow as she offered her present. That she should be bestowing a gift while her eyes were still red with tears which the recipient had provoked, was an act of nobility which affected her so much that they overflowed again. Yet, the hair ribbons were blue. Blue was not Marty's colour, but it became Phyllis very well. Oh, bitter, wounding, merciless little girl standing against the wall in the long passage, looking into those lachrymose blue eyes with hatred and contempt, saying sweetly: "You keep them in *your* drawer, so you'll be able to find them easily!" Phyllis blundering away down the hall with flaming cheeks and incoherent sobs . . .

And Gilbert . . .

Marty's smile lost its bitterness. To this day Gilbert knew only one birthday present—handkerchiefs. Handkerchiefs, and a tight, hasty, but honest smile. And seven-year-old Nick, presenting a needlebook to match the work-basket, adding a hearty hug and a sticky kiss. . . . I wasn't the only member of the family, she thought, who found an outlet for damned-back emotions in Nick.

Breakfast . . .

Somehow the memory of breakfast was of a cheerful meal. It could only have been because of the sun coming through the big windows, lying in blocks and streaks across the starched white tablecloth, revealing the steam going up from the blue-bordered plates of oatmeal as an intriguing vapour in which you could actually see each separate particle of moisture. It glittered on the silver toast-rack and the silver jam dish with marmalade in it, and made Mrs. Miller's perfunctory arrangement of flowers in the centre of the table fairly blaze.

At breakfast father read the paper, and conversation was limited to "Pass the butter, please," and "Eat up your porridge, Nick," and "Marty, don't gobble so." The children all hoped that the news would hold Mr. Massey's attention, for occasionally, when it did not, he would put the paper aside and ask them awkward questions, which was his way of taking a paternal interest in their childish affairs. They were careful, therefore, to be quiet, lest they should distract him from his reading. While he held the newspaper in his left hand, and spooned porridge methodically into his mouth with the other, they were all tensely aware of him; even Mrs. Miller ate absent-mindedly, watching so as not to miss the exact moment for pouring his cup of coffee. This came when he lifted the second last spoonful of porridge to his lips. By the time he put his plate aside his cup was full; passed by Mrs. Miller to Gilbert and by Gilbert to Marty, it arrived in its appointed spot two seconds before his right hand began to feel for it.

The newspaper, so the children gathered, gave him (as, indeed, did most things) ample reason for disapproval. The rumblings and mutterings which came from behind it were welcome sounds to them—evidence that his attention was still blessedly fixed on "this fellow Holman," and "this mountebank, Hughes." That, they knew vaguely, was "politics," but it had no personal import-ance for any of them—not even Mrs. Miller—beyond the fact that it kept Mr. Massey temporarily unaware of his family. He found it necessary, now and then, to have an audience for some comment his reading provoked, and then he addressed himself to Mrs. Miller, who said: "Really?" or "Yes, indeed!" or "How disgraceful!" without having the faintest idea what he was talking about. Thus, in a dim way, as one knows of things one has seen or heard in dreams, Marty was aware that "this fellow Holman" was bent upon squandering the public moneys by building double-track country railways where single-track ones had always been

good enough before. But her own suburban train bore her punc-
tually to and from school every day, and beyond that railways
were obviously no concern of hers. Explosions from behind an
angrily crackling paper conveyed to her and to Gilbert that there
were mysterious and sinister organisations known as Trade Unions.
Denunciations whose tone could not fail to remind them of Mr.
Mackness' more eloquent moments in the pulpit, revealed that there
also existed a hobgoblin personification of evil, a kind of first
cousin to Beelzebub, called Eyedoubleyoudoubleyou.

Children and animals, Marty thought sadly, learn to listen for
danger-sounds or danger-silences with some sort of extension of
their senses. To us politics were a lightning-conductor; politics
kept us safe at the breakfast table. And yet, on that first day of
1913 an alarming thing had happened. Suddenly, without warning, politics lost their remoteness. Father uttered an explosive
exclamation, lowered the paper, glared across the table at Mrs.
Miller, and said with fierce contempt:

"Our neighbour appears to have political ambitions."

Mrs. Miller gaped at him.

"Neighbour . . . ?"

"Laughlin. Wants to contest a seat in the State elections!"
He became conscious that his daughter and his elder son were
gazing at him with startled attention. He said with tremendous
emphasis: "If men of that stamp are to govern the country, we
shall have anarchy! Mark my words—anarchy!"

Gilbert recovered first. His face regained its usual closed im-
passivity, and he helped himself to butter. Marty wriggled in
her chair, remembering miserably the scene she had overheard
last night, rebelling violently against the creeping suspicion that
Father might—*might* have been right about the Laughlins. What
did it mean—"contesting a seat?" Was it a very bad thing to
do? Should a country be governed by people who quarrelled with
their wives? And what did "anarchy" mean? Mrs. Miller said,
with an anxious attempt to soothe:

"Perhaps he won't get in."

"I trust not." Mr. Massey's face was still quite red with anger.
"I most sincerely trust not. These Labour Governments will ruin
the country. A set of agitators and windbags!"

Nick giggled so suddenly that he spat out a little shower of
porridge. Mrs. Miller asked hastily: "Another cup of coffee,
Walter?" But she was too late.

"You may leave the table, Nick, as you seem unable to behave properly."

Nick climbed down from his chair, his face suffused, his eyes watering somewhere between laughter and tears. Marty, watching his small retreating figure, suddenly dropped her spoon noisily, pushed her chair back, and prepared to follow.

"Marty, how dare you leave the table in that unmannerly fashion? Sit down immediately and finish your breakfast!"

She said stormily:

"I won't! And I like Mr. Laughlin, and I hope he does govern the country!"

Outside the door she found Nick. They fled, hand in hand, to the orchard where they cried for a few minutes and then began to eat half-green plums.

"You got out of saying your Scripture," Nick pointed out consolingly. But Marty frowned.

"I wanted to say it," she complained. "*This* time."

Suddenly she giggled and proclaimed: "*And ye, fathers, provoke not your children to wrath!*" Nick beamed. They began to chant it together, stamping with their feet in a corroboree rhythm to emphasise these delectable words which held the full flavour of their protest, and which could yet be spoken without fear of rebuke, for they came out of the Bible. Nick stopped, clutched her arm, and urged: "Sh-h! There he is on the verandah!" Yes, there he was, Bible in hand, looking round for her. He called: "Marty! Marty, I am ready to hear your Scripture." She was suddenly deliriously and defiantly conscious of her invulnerability. After all, it was her birthday and the birthday of the year. Time was friendly, time was her own, time was on her side—and now the Bible was on her side too. She called out quite loudly: "*And ye, fathers, provoke not your children to wrath . . .*" Nick choked with gleeful apprehension. "He'll be *wild!*" Sharp and ominous came the voice from the verandah: "Marty! Come immediately when I call you!" She answered dutifully: "Yes, Father: I was just saying my Scripture over to learn it." She winked recklessly at Nick. "See? He can't say anything! He can't hurt me!" She sniffed with magnificent contempt. "*Nothing* can hurt me!"

Nick believed her, and she almost believed herself.

*   *   *   *

Well, they both knew better now. Or perhaps she was wrong about Nick. Can you be hurt if you have no doubts? There was something, she felt, almost inhuman in Nick's didactic certainty. Being so sure of himself, so certain of the unassailability of his formulæ, gave him a kind of rigid strength; but she suspected that in a shifting world-scene, where conditions altered overnight, where tremendous events and dynamic emotions acted and reacted continuously upon each other, it meant a certain weakness too. His brain was furnished less with thoughts than with blueprints. He would produce one for any problem at a moment's notice; his attitude was: "There it is; take it or leave it."

So could anything hurt him? Things did anger and disgust him —and what did that mean, after all, but that he was being hurt all the time? Without even, perhaps, the consolation which she and Gilbert could find in a creative interpretation. Nick saw men and women as they are drawn in those diagrams which present a human outline as representing ten thousand of population. She and Gilbert could at least fill it in, colour it. endow it with speech, fears, hopes, the capacity of joy and suffering . . .

At last she was really sleepy. Inside the clock struck four, and outside the gate clicked, and footsteps came softly down the path. Marty's eyelids struggled up again; a slender, white-clad figure flickered across the verandah and vanished through the french windows of the drawing-room. "Virginia," Marty thought. rolling over and clutching the bedclothes round her shoulders. Dimly the words "home with the milk" strove to formulate themselves in her mind, and drifted instead into a rambling dream about a milkman hiding in the orchard at *Glenwood*, while Walter Massey, ten feet high, and dark with judgment, stood on the verandah holding a blue jug.

III

GILBERT, Nick and Prue, being business people, left for the city next morning before the arrival of the newspaper. It was barely light when they breakfasted; they carried the luggage out to the car under an overcast sky in a raw cold which stung their cheeks and fingers. Driving down the winding mountain road, they saw the even grey of the clouds break up, and watery gleams of sun-light coax the sullen tree-tops to a momentary brilliance. Lakes of white mist still lay in some of the valley beds, and drifts of it hung above them. No other cars were abroad yet; they had the road to themselves for the first hour, and Gilbert, who enjoyed driving, swung round its curves, playing with himself the game of keeping his right-hand wheels on the white line.

"I didn't know it rained last night," Prue said.

"Early this morning," her father replied. "Not much. About half-past four."

After a small silence Prue asked:

"Didn't you sleep well?"

Had he, she wondered, heard Virginia come in? Dressing in the semi-darkness, she had glanced now and then at the dim shape of her sister, wondering what sort of explanation she would have ready for her mother's insistent enquiries. Well, it was her own silly business. If Dad had heard, he had said nothing. It was difficult to know from Dad's silences what he knew, or what he thought. Now, as he merely answered: "Not very," she acknowledged that she was left exactly where she began, and, with a sudden feeling of irritation against Virginia, and uncertain sympathy for a father whom she vaguely felt was not as happy as he should be, she patted his knee, and then, embarrassed by her own demonstrativeness, opened her bag and began to powder her nose.

Gilbert, his eyes on the road, asked:

"Warm enough, Prue? There's a rug in the back."

He had been thinking of Virginia ever since four o'clock, but by degrees she had merged into the whole problem of his marriage, and then his marriage had merged into the still larger problems which involved the war and all humanity. He pulled hard on the wheel as they swung on to a bridge across the railway, built for the leisurely days of horse and carriage, and never adapted to the needs of motor traffic, thinking: "Enough to keep you awake!" His whole instinct since he had become a father had been to leave his children alone—a reaction, he supposed, almost morbid in its intensity—from the intolerable restrictions and repressions of his own childhood. Yet the effect had been, he realised now, that they had been less left alone than left to the confused care and the constantly changing theories of their mother. What should he— what could he have done? For he knew himself to be awkward and inept in his emotional dealings with other people. The light-hearted, skylarking friendliness which some parents, he observed, were able to achieve with their children, would seem in him forced and unnatural to the point of indecency. He remained himself because he could do nothing else; having no gift for gregariousness, he preserved his own imposed and conditioned attitude of slightly formal detachment, and though he believed that his children felt an affection for him, something of the chill of his own repression inevitably tinged their approach to him. If there was reassurance in Prue's hand on his knee, her quick retreat from that involuntary gesture seemed to him a measure of his failure. She said brightly: "No, I'm quite warm."

He thought heavily that he should never have consented to stay on at *Glenwood* after his marriage The influence and the atmosphere of his father's bigotry survived there. Not that any of them—except Phyllis—had pandered to it. Indeed, the one thing in his boyhood upon which he could look back with some satisfaction was the sureness, the unrelenting determination with which he had grown away from his father's authority, grown beyond his tyranny, and maintained a stubborn resistance to his narrow standards and conceptions.

And in nothing—fortunately—had he resisted with such energy as in the matter of Scott Laughlin. He had often marvelled since at the unerring instinct which had led him—and Marty—through the fog of confusion in which their father's prejudice had shrouded this man. And he found himself remembering a certain Friday afternoon in the summer of 1911, when he was fifteen, and had stayed behind after school to watch a cricket match with his friend, George Cole.

*   *   *   *

It was George's idea. He was aspiring to the Seconds, and Gilbert, though no cricketer himself, regarded a polite display of

interest in his friend's favourite sport merely as one of the normal
decencies of conduct. He had not been bored, for he was at that
stage of adolescence when the discovery of the pleasures of the
mind is sometimes made, and becomes a kind of gentle intoxication.
He could enjoy it quite as well sitting on a wooden bench outside
the railings of the oval as anywhere else; and indeed, the mellow
warmth of the afternoon, the shadows of the Moreton Bay figs
lengthening across the grass, and the placid cooing of doves in
their branches had provided a scene and an atmosphere peculiarly
friendly to his mood. He was still using the thought of others
rather than manufacturing his own: emotions which were formless
in him shaped themselves into patterns within the rhythms of
newly-discovered poetry, and he was content to see them thus,
dressed in the words of other men, and yet poignantly his own.

In those early years of the century when the aim of the educational system to standardise was still an instinct rather than a
policy, the school uniform—that outward and visible sign of an
inward and spiritual mass-production—had been adopted by only
a few schools, of which Gilbert's was not one. As the boys
alighted from the train at their home platform the only similarity
between them lay in their hats and hatbands, and the leather bags,
heavy with homework, which they carried.

"See you to-morrow!" said George, waving farewell from the
top of the steps. Gilbert's way lay to the east of the railway
through the tiny township, and he walked briskly, whistling because an outward nonchalance seemed to counteract the inner
uneasiness which he resented. For he had promised to go to a
tennis party next day. He did not know why he disliked social
occasions, but unlike Marty, whose simple philosophy was to get
out of doing things she disliked by fair means or foul, an instinctive
self-respect prevented him from avoiding them. So far no one
had been discerning enough to suspect that his rather expressionless face and his rather flat voice were symptoms of a control too
rigid for his years.

He passed the few small shops, unseeing until he came to the
last one, before whose window he paused. This was the general
store, the biggest store, which sold mostly groceries, but also pots,
pans, brooms, bran, corn, crockery, oilcloth, carpenter's tools and
stationery. It was at the window where the stationery was displayed that the schoolboy halted, his obscure creative urge to
express himself stimulated by the sight of exercise books—shiny

black covers enclosing virgin pages. He went in soberly and bought one—a large one, for there was so much he had to say—and as soberly came out again into the fading sunlight and walked on, carrying it under his arm. The mere act of buying it was an assuagement of unrest; he felt more peaceful, as if the payment of a whole week's pocket money for paper upon which singing words could be written, even if they never were, gave him a kind of affinity with Keats and Browning.

He stopped once again for a moment at the doorway of the blacksmith's looking into a semi-darkness lit by the red glow of the forge, at the patient horses and the bent, leather-aproned figure of the smith, and then went on, leaving the paved street for a red earth road, rising gently to vanish over the top of a hill from which he could see the pine trees of his home.

At the gate was a sulky which he recognised, and his pace slackened. His habit or technique of accepting life as it came had not yet allowed him to dislike anyone with conscious violence, but he preferred, if possible, not to meet his father's most intimate friend, the Rev. Maurice Mackness. Some half-conscious repudiation of hypocrisy lay, perhaps, behind this unwillingness. He knew that his father thought of him as a "good steady boy," in whom his own strong religious tendencies and his own dogmatic beliefs were faithfully reproduced. Gilbert was just beginning to feel sure that he was wrong. He went to church every Sunday morning, wearing his best clothes, walking with Phyllis and Marty, who crackled crisply in starched muslin, followed by his father and Mrs. Miller, and Nick in a sailor suit with blue anchors on the collar. Every evening in the dining-room he knelt for prayers. His father's endorsements and tabus still dwelt passively in his mind. Yet lately his discovery of books, and more particularly of poetry, had made him aware of some spiritual satisfaction which his father's creed had failed to provide, and conscious that he had another life besides the one which had been shaped for him in his home. His knowledge that it was one which would be regarded without parental comprehension, and even with misgivings, put him faintly on the defensive, and the clergyman became a symbol in his mind for a faith which he had found insufficient. He shrank from a greeting whose hearty approbation, he felt, would have been considerably modified if Mr. Mackness had been able to see beyond his guarded eyes.

By dawdling, by pausing to tie a shoelace, he was able to delay his arrival at the gate, and the sulky clattered towards him while he was still fifty yards short of it. He raised his hat decorously in response to the clergyman's flourished whip and heartily shouted, "Well, Gilbert, my lad!" and went on to join his father who, having sped the parting guest, now awaited him, holding the gate ajar.

Walter Massey, though only fifty-one, already looked elderly. He looked, indeed, more like a clergyman than Mr. Mackness did, and the main effect of his greying beard was to make one suspect a hidden clerical collar. He had put on flesh, and moved with a ponderous deliberation; he brushed his hair carefully across a bald patch on the top of his head, and wore gold-rimmed pince-nez on a black cord.

Walking up the path, observing the cap lying on a cane chair by the front door, Gilbert was, naturally, quite unaware of a turning point in his life. His mind did baulk for an instant before the incongruousness of such an object there, in his home, where the hats which his father and his father's friends hung on the hall-stand were well-brushed black bowlers. He heard Mrs. Miller, who had come to the door to meet them, utter an annoyed exclamation as she picked it up.

"Walter, look! Mr. Laughlin has left his cap!"

Gilbert felt a little shock of astonished excitement. His father said "H'm," taking it from Mrs. Miller's hand and turning it over with obvious distaste, as if he had never seen such a thing before, and did not want to see it now. Gilbert, hesitating in the doorway, stopped to stroke the cat which had come to rub against his legs, and was unaware that he was using it as an excuse not to go indoors at once.

Mr. Laughlin had been here? It was typical of his relationship with his father that he asked no question about a subject which so stirred his curiosity, but waited passively to see if anything would be said to explain it. Not from actual words, but from adult silences, adult glances, from the implacable objection to Janet as a playmate for Marty, and from the reserved tone of an occasional "Good morning" required by mere neighbourly courtesy, he had absorbed the knowledge that his father disapproved of Mr. Laughlin; but it never occurred to him to ask the reason.

Somewhere, sometime, the word "atheist" had been uttered. Gilbert did not know when, or where, or by whom, but only that it hung in the air like thunder whenever the Laughlins were seen or mentioned. Certainly they never went to church. Gilbert himself had seen Mr. Laughlin walking home with bottles of beer under his arm, not even wrapped, and a connection between atheism and alcohol seemed to him natural if not inevitable. He was not censorious about it, but neither was he yet quite ready to discard the effects of fifteen years of conditioning, and though his instinct was to accept the bottles of beer without prejudice, as bottles of beer, that conditioning could not fail to suggest to him that they *might* be evidence too.

Moreover, Mr. Laughlin was a journalist, and this (said the atmosphere of the Massey household) was a profession only on the outside edge of respectability. For journalists, apparently, lived a life which was, not very explicitly, described as "Bohemian." To Gilbert's enquiring and bewildered eye Mr. Laughlin's life seemed blamelessly domestic, but the whole question might have remained merely abstract if he had not discovered that Mr. Laughlin was also a poet. This made it a personal problem for him, as Janet made it personal for Marty. In those days when he was first succumbing to the lure of words, he could not fail to be intrigued by a neighbour whose poetry was actually published—or slightly uneasy because it was published mainly in the *Bulletin*, that rampageous pink-covered weekly which his father would not allow into the house, and which, therefore, Gilbert was compelled to buy with his own pocket money, and leave in the train after he had cut out Mr. Laughlin's poems. All the same, so strong was his conditioning that he could not get rid of a suspicion that the natural sequence of ungodliness and intemperance might be extended to include the writing of poetry; but here he rebelled. If it did, then drink and atheism must be accepted, for poetry could not be outlawed. On that point he was already quite clear.

Mrs. Miller was saying with a faint note of apprehension:

"He might come back for it."

His father frowned, turned a speculative eye on his son.

"Gilbert, my boy . . ."

"Yes, Father?"

"You might just run down to Mr. Laughlin with this. Tell him he left it on our verandah."

Mrs. Miller patted his shoulder.

"Don't be long, dear. Tea will be ready soon."

"All right, Aunt Ada."

He put his bag and his book down, took the cap, and ran out into the road again. He hurried along to the corner and turned down the hill. Though the afterglow of sunset still touched the tops of the pine trees it was already dusk in the hollow, and across the road in a paddock abandoned to blackberries a swarm of Dodd children ran and shrieked in the last frenzy of evening playtime. Three small figures—Marty and her two forbidden friends—ducked under the fence and ran across the road; Gilbert could see them standing with their heads close together for a moment or two before one turned down the hill and the other two climbed through the Massey's fence and disappeared, shadow-like, into the orchard. Gilbert's mood began to be damped by shyness and his pace slackened. He found himself envying the Dodd children, envying his sister and Janet Laughlin, realising with a slight shock that he had left behind for ever that happy age when only playtime is real. He understood suddenly that, having grown beyond it, he had, as yet, no substitute; this street, harbouring an adult world inside, and a child world out of doors, had no place in it for him.

Not to be a child any longer, and not yet to be grown up. . . . He had a painful feeling that in losing the child world he had been robbed; he did not know how or when he had passed out of it, but he did know that the adult world which would not yet receive him was a world lacking the unity and the simplicity of the one he had lost. There was, he perceived, only one child-world, and if you were a child you belonged to it. But how many adult worlds were there? How did you know which one to enter? Could you choose? Feeling, now, nothing but nervousness, he left the road, crossed the footpath to the Laughlin's half-open gate.

The front door, too, stood ajar upon an unlighted passage, and music, coming from an inner room, ceased abruptly as he pressed the bell. A door opened inside letting out a bar of yellow gas-light, and Mrs. Laughlin stood before him, saying enquiringly:

"Yes?"

He explained awkwardly:

"Father said to bring . . . er . . . Mr. Laughlin's left his cap——"

She asked vaguely:

"Cap? Oh! Where did he leave it?"

"At our place. This afternoon."

Forlornly conscious of his exit from the child-world, he felt an anxious eagerness to be admitted to hers. For she seemed young-looking in the dusk, and the light behind her made a halo round her hair. These impressions, stumbling over each other in his mind, were only his instinctive contribution to a friendly relationship, but she quenched them with another question:

"And who are you?"

Even as he retreated into his no-man's land he knew that her intention had not been unkind. She was not trying to snub him; she really had no idea who he was. This, he saw, was only a result of those divisions in the adult world of which he had just become aware. As if he had known her all his life, he understood that she was not only unconscious of neighbourly disapproval, but oblivious of the neighbours themselves. Her eyes, in the months since they had come to live in the street, had probably recorded them as they would record a fence, a telegraph pole, a rut in the road—no more. She would know of the elderly widower living at the top of the hill, and of his little girl who sometimes played with Janet; but long, long ago she must have seen that they inhabited one world and she another.

He accepted it all, back in his accustomed solitude. His voice was normally toneless again as he replied:

"I'm Gilbert Massey. We live up there—in *Glenwood*."

"Oh, yes!" She gave a little laugh as if she found the thought of the Masseys amusing. "Of course!" The inside door opened again and Mr. Laughlin came out.

"What is it, Denny?"

"Your cap."

"Eh?"

Gilbert explained once more with wooden patience, and turned to go, but Mr. Laughlin was heartily hospitable.

"Thanks very much; very good of you. Come in, won't you?"

"I don't think . . ."

"Oh, come in for a minute or two, anyhow! What's your name, now . . . ?"

"Gilbert."

"Of course, Gilbert." He pushed open the door of the lighted room, still talking cheerfully.

"Come along, now, and meet Jerrold Kay. Here he is. Jerrold, this is a young neighbour of ours, Gilbert Massey. Sit on the sofa, Gilbert. Have some beer? No? Well, listen to some music, then. D'you like the 'Waldstein'? Go ahead, Denny."

Gilbert sat on a sofa with a faded chintz cover. Music began again. The room, which had seemed to him, in his shyness, a ball of spinning light, spun more slowly, and after a confusion of sight and sound he began to see normally, and to listen. Janet slipped into the room from the hall, glanced at him with that wary, secret half-smile with which children acknowledge each other in adult company, and sat in a leather chair with her long, black-stockinged legs hanging over its arm. Gilbert still felt slightly breathless from too sudden an introduction to unfamiliarity, but with the music for the present ensuring him against the perils of conversation, he gradually recovered his calm, and began to observe.

His first impression was of untidiness. No room in his own home ever looked like this one. Three large bookcases had over-flowed on to the mantelpiece, and even on to the linoleum-covered floor. Gilbert stared at them with hungry curiosity for a few minutes, and then noticed that the linoleum was not polished as it would have been even in the *Glenwood* kitchen, and that the green cloth over the table at the far end of the room had a large hole burned in it. It was littered with books, newspapers, magazines, music, a bundle of sewing, three beer bottles, two glasses, a plate with a few sandwiches on it, and a typewriter.

He looked longest at the pictures, and, looking at them, found himself seeing in his mind's eye the five which adorned the draw-ing-room walls of his own home. He had never thought about them before, but he thought about them now, and there appeared on his brow the faint frown which usually developed when pre-occupation made him forget himself and his surroundings for a moment or two. He was absorbing his first impression that pic-tures could be intimately related to life; that something in him nodded recognition of the queer, brown gum-trees on the opposite wall, the watercolours of streets and houses so familiar that he might have walked along them and knocked at their front doors, of the rocky bush-covered headland sloping down to blue water. But if he felt recognition of these, his mind shied away nervously from a group of small drawings in pen and ink which looked like originals. They were nude figures—some of them only bits of bodies, shoulders, arms, backs, headless torsos. He did not like to look at them too hard, and transferred his attention to a number of black and white cartoons fastened with drawing pins to a green baize-covered board. And suddenly his mind rang a bell of association between them and the name by which Mr. Laughlin had introduced his other visitor. His eyes widened, jumped sharply to the man lying back in a cane chair, holding his half-empty glass of beer on its arm.

Often on his way to school Gilbert had paused by the bookstall on the wharf to look at the placards displaying Jerrold Kay's weekly cartoon. By such standards as he had they were crude, vulgar, violently provocative in their satirical assaults upon people and customs which he vaguely felt to be sacrosanct because they were established. Their political message was lost upon him, for he knew nothing of politics, but he liked to look at them as a later generation was to look at comic strips—for the symbolism and fantasy in them, for their rough, sardonic humour, and their strong, brutal caricature of life.

This, then, was Jerrold Kay. Gilbert felt safe in studying him, for he looked half asleep, and Mr. Laughlin was rummaging among the music on the table, with his back to the room. Kay sprawled in his chair, a lean, untidy figure with bony hands and a bony face. Black hair, already receding from his temples, made his forehead look even higher than it was. The surprised expression of inky, Mephistophilean eyebrows was contradicted by half-shut eyes, suggesting indolence. His sallow cheeks were almost starvation-hollow, but a large mouth with a full underlip had nothing of the ascetic in its permanent half-smile. He wore baggy flannel trousers, a white shirt open at the neck, and not very clean black boots. With a sharp twinge of uneasiness Gilbert's mind dashed for the sanctuary of his home standards, as in childhood he might have fled from the alarmingly unfamiliar to his mother's skirts. Perhaps his father was right to disapprove? Everything about these people was—queer. Their room, their house, their manners, their pictures, their visitor . . .

He found himself looking at Janet.

Their daughter . . . ?

Her eyebrows lay like bars over her blue eyes, staring absently at the opposite wall. She seemed to be listening to the music, but not as if she enjoyed it. Gilbert, once alarmed into a mood as near to censoriousness as his detached and judicial temperament would allow, reflected that Marty would never have been allowed to sit like that in the drawing-room, her legs sprawling over the arm of the chair so carelessly that there was actually a glimpse of bare skin and white frill . . .

The music ceased. It was not finished, it just stopped. Mrs. Laughlin got up suddenly from the stool, flung round to face the room, and said angrily:

"Oh, damn! I'm out of practice."

Jerrold Kay, holding his glass up and studying the amber-coloured beer against the light, said casually:

"You aren't the musician you used to be."

Gilbert, who believed that the only possible sequel to a drawing-room piano performance was a polite murmur of admiration and gratitude, stared in an indignant astonishment which became embarrassed dismay as she turned furiously upon her guest.

"How should I?" she asked bitterly. "What chance do I get to practise?"

She gave a look round the room then which Gilbert never forgot. It was the look of one to whom, in a moment of stress, walls become symbols of a spiritual captivity, and must be scanned for the hope, however slight, of escape. Gilbert, shocked, saw that her eyes, angry as they were, had tears in them. The next moment she had gone, the door slammed behind her, and there was no sound left but the hissing of the gas-jet.

Jerrold Kay had not moved; he still seemed interested in his beer. Laughlin, who had turned sharply with some sheet music in his hand, stood looking at the door, frowning slightly. Janet remained motionless, her eyes lowered, her fingers fiddling with a pleat in her serge skirt. Gilbert stood up hastily:

"I must be going, Mr. Laughlin."

Mr. Laughlin did not seem to hear him. Kay, moving only his bright black eyes to look at the gawky schoolboy so oddly introduced into the scene, asked blandly:

"Well, what did you think? Pretty ragged, wasn't it?"

Gilbert said stiffly:

"I thought it was very nice. Mr. Laughlin, I'll have to go. It's getting . . ."

Janet swung her legs over the chair arm and stood up.

"Come on."

He muttered an awkward good-night to the two men and followed her thankfully through the dim hall and out on to the verandah. Behind them they heard Mr. Laughlin's rapid footsteps in the hall, the sound of knocking on a closed door, his voice saying urgently:

"Denny! Denny, I want to talk to you! Let me in, darling . . ."

Gilbert was struggling in a kind of panic with the gate, which would not shut. Janet called angrily:

"Leave it open—it never shuts. Good-bye."

He left it, and hurried up the hill towards the lights of his own home at a pace which suggested flight.

*   *   *   *

He heard Prue say:

". . . how soon do you think?"

"Eh?" He glanced hastily at his speedometer, relieved to see that while his thoughts were absent his hands and feet had still controlled the car at a steady forty. They were down the mountains now; the sun was shining palely, and the road went ahead in a straight grey streak to vanish over a hilltop half a mile away. He said:

"What, Prue? I didn't hear you."

She repeated:

"I keep on having enquiries for those books. You know; I gave you a list. Do you know yet when you can let me have some?"

"No. Soon, I hope." He frowned. "There was a consignment on one of the ships for me, so Matthews says, and it was taken off to give priority to something else. God knows when I'll get them now."

He noticed then that worry and annoyance had expressed themselves in a pressure of his foot; the speedometer said forty-seven. He slowed, still frowning, and said over his shoulder to Nick:

"There's a box ready for Prue at the office. You'd better collect it when we get there, and drive it down for her."

He glanced sideways at his daughter. Interwoven with his uneasiness about the fate of all books in a world destruction-mad, was a strand of personal worry for Prue, working hard and devotedly at her tiny shop and circulating library, doing (so he liked to imagine in a proud, parental way) something which, on its own modest scale, was useful and constructive. Small as it was, he knew that already it had made a place for itself; students found their way there; people who, like himself a few years ago, were embarking painfully on a course of self-education, haunted its shelves. More than once he had had to beat down his father's

[61]

hostile objection to the books he imported for her, books which, in the days when the old man had exercised despotic control over his own business, would never have appeared on the invoices of Walter Massey and Sons. Absurd, the grandfather had stormed when she left school, to let a girl of eighteen set up in business on her own! Even if her father were there to back her. Ridiculous, he had said a year later, to keep on throwing good money after bad in this way. Of course the shop wasn't paying! How could it? What did Prue know of business matters? Why couldn't she stay at home like Virginia, and help her mother? Wicked, he had raged later still, for a young girl even to know of the existence, let alone sell and circulate, such books as these which (on the occasional excursions to the office in which he had persisted to the end) he found listed among the firm's papers.

Gilbert had had to fight him over this as he had fought him over so many things all his life. He admitted, not without a grim regret, that he had been hard on the old man. You had to be hard with someone who would use any advantage, even his own age and dependence, to impose his ideas on a granddaughter struggling to form her own. Prue had got her shop and her library, and, he swore, she should keep them so long as he could go on supplying her with books. How long would that be? He had no illusions. He looked into the future and saw paper becoming scarcer, man-power becoming scarcer, the effort of honest writers, honest publishers, honest lovers of good literature, clashing with the effort of self-seeking tradesmen, concerned only with the selling of printed dope to a bemused and escapist public. He saw also, needing to look no further than himself and Marty, a drying up of honest writing at its source. He saw the creative mind staggering under the repeated hammer-blows of destructiveness, getting groggy, getting exhausted, drawing on its own reserves till they were gone, and then finding in its environment not enough communal creative spirit to renew them. . . .

Well, the reserves weren't gone yet. He took his hat off and threw it on the back seat, feeling gratefully the rush of cool, grass-scented air on his forehead. Actually, of course, he told himself rebukingly, they wouldn't ever dry up altogether; to believe any-thing else was intolerable. There were always new springs of energy in the young; it was his own generation, having seen two wars, which was getting tired. And even in himself there were—

there *were*, he insisted—some reserves still. He had never been better equipped to write than he was now. And as if that state-ment had been made (as it might well have been) by Nick, he found himself arguing against it as he might have argued with his brother.

Better equipped—yes, intellectually. But that's only part of the equipment. Knowledge—even wisdom—stored in the brain is not enough. The brain has to be fresh, Nick, it has to be alert, it has to be confident. What brain can carry the load of present-day human suffering and not go more slowly, more stumblingly, more uncertainly? Well, yes, maybe some brains can do it, but they ain't the brains that create. For if you're to describe and record humanity you must first feel it; a rapture of meeting, an agony of parting, a loneliness of flight between blacked-out earth and inky heaven, a bleakness of isolation for unpopular belief, a bayonet thrust in the stomach. We have to take the impact of these things on our minds as a pugilist takes blows on the chin. We have to describe and record—that's our job—but by Heavens we have to crash and drown and kill and grieve and yell out in pain a thousand times to do it . . .

He thought wearily: Oh, well—that's how it is. So our brains stumble after a time. Then we go off and do things with our hands because we must do something. And the flood of books thins out to a trickle. Because, after all, where are the youngsters who should be taking over? Doing things with their hands too. Flying planes, firing tommy-guns, making munitions, driving lorries, cooking meals, typing lunatic Army documents in triplicate.

He said to Prue:

"It's getting worse all the time. And it won't be solved by printing here. We," he added bitterly, sounding his horn as a milk-cart came out from a side street, "will have only enough paper soon for the really important things like official forms and questionnaires, and advertisements, and movie posters, and cheap magazines."

"Paper shortage," Nick said in his detached way from the back seat, "will be only a cover-up for censorship. Everything the re-actionaries don't want printed won't be printed, and paper-shortage will be a grand alibi. There'll still be files a yard high in the Public Service, and twenty-seven Army memoranda to account for a broken tuppenny egg-cup."

[63]

Prue broke the depressed silence with an attempt at cheerfulness: "I think it's going to be fine after all."

Gilbert thought furiously:

"Damnation! Why should her youth be made hideous like this?"

Wasn't it, he asked himself, to ensure that her generation should grow up in peace that his own had been martyred twenty-five years ago? And knowing her armed, as he had not been, with at least some enlightenment, some understanding of the forces which were tearing her world to shreds, he still found it painful—a kind of sacrilege—that she should have to carry such a burden of unlovely knowledge. He turned his head, answering her remark with: "Seems like it" to cover his momentary stare at her face. He thought her better-looking than Virginia, whose greater vivacity and more vivid colouring usually attracted more admiration, but sometimes the sadness of her mouth in repose had stabbed him, as it did now, with a resentful pain. Most young faces, he thought restlessly, convey that curious suggestion of fragility—defencelessness. Probably, because quite apart from good looks, they have a smooth perfection of surface and contour that looks—well—precarious. Easily damaged. His eyes, on the road again, held an image of Prue's white forehead, her bright hair springing up from it in a wave that curled forward like a breaker in an artful golden roll, her fine dark brows, her upward curving lashes. Behind that forehead—what? Knowledge of duplicity, hypocrisy, swinish greed, inhuman brutality, endless stupidity, insatiable lusts for power. Burdened as his own youth had been, it had carried no such load as that. Nothing but his own personal problems had exercised his youthful mind; and then the words, "Bear ye one another's burdens," flicked up into his consciousness by association, made him acknowledge that perhaps, after all, Prue was more fortunate than he had been.

For he had known nothing—nothing! He had been, at fifteen, at eighteen, even at twenty-one, in the mud of Flanders, sublimely ignorant, not only of international issues, but even of the domestic national policies of his own country. He knew that there were State Parliamets and a Federal Parliament. He knew that there were two "Parties," Labour and Liberal, and that sometimes one was in power and sometimes the other. Either way, it seemed to him, life went on just the same. He had been taught that his country was a "democracy," and saw no reason to doubt it. Democracy meant voting when you were twenty-one, and everyone indubitably did do this. Had he not heard Mrs. Miller being coached by his father about where she must make her crosses on the ballot paper?

He was not interested in politics; he was interested, at that time, in poetry. So efficiently had his mental conditioning been achieved —so neatly had his mind been divided into watertight compartments—that he could segregate sections of human effort, aspiration and achievement from each other and remain quite unconscious of absurdity. He knew that Shelley was a rebel; he had remembered to record that fact in his senior exam. Yet without so much as the shadow of a suspicion that politics and poetry might be inextricably entangled, he had been able to recite by heart:

> "*Men of England, wherefore plough*
> *For the lords who lay ye low,*
> *Wherefore weave with toil and care*
> *The rich robes your tyrants wear?*"

Not once until that morning when his father, snorting angrily, had poured scorn on Mr. Laughlin's intention to contest a seat in the State elections, had his mind fastened even for a moment on politics. And then, with a flash of startled enlightenment while he reached for the butter-dish, he had understood that the real reason for Walter Massey's implacable hatred of his neighbour was not the hint of atheism, not the beer, not the journalism, not even the poetry—it was politics! Mr. Laughlin was "a Labour man"!

And still, he thought painfully, that meant less than nothing to me. It "went" with the other things. It was dimly unrespectable. That was all I knew!

Entering the outer suburbs the traffic grew thicker. He called his mind to attention, and concentrated on the road.

*　　　　*　　　　*　　　　*

Reaching the office, pulling the car into the kerb, Gilbert looked at his watch, and said:

"A quarter to nine. A bit over the two hours. Nick, if you come in with me we can get those books for Prue, and you can drive her and them down to the shop."

Nick climbed out of the car and stamped his cold feet on the pavement, looking gloomily across the road at the small, narrow, dingy building opposite.

"If it weren't," he remarked, "that Japan will be running amok in the Pacific before long, I'd feel like putting a stick of gelignite under that monstrosity. No doubt a bomb will do it for us some day."

Gilbert, running the keys around on his ring till he came to the office latchkey, said:

"I did think of moving. But now . . ."

He would not admit—not with Prue there—that his thoughts had been close to Nick's. He had no more faith in his Government's policy of appeasing the enemy to their near north than he had had three years ago in that other appeasement which led to Munich. Only a few weeks back, reading of Paternoster Row gutted by incendiary bombs, of millions of books going up in smoke, he had known that it could happen here. That the fury now loosed against China might well—now that supplies no longer sped to her along the Burma Road—triumph, and turn south for further spoils. He knew all that; he had said it, and said it, and said it, watching uneasy faces become closed and hostile, feeling distrust of himself spread like a fog, feeling the herd's suspicion of anyone whose opinion dared to diverge from the dictated mass-opinion of Press and official pronouncement. Yet he had felt, too, with a shadow of hope, that his own certainties were already beginning to stir as doubts in many minds. Angrily resisted doubts. Doubts finding no answer but the immemorial parrot-slogan of colonial dependency: "After all, there's the British Navy!" Look them in the eye and say gently that, unfortunately, the British Navy was fully occupied elsewhere, and the suspicion flared into open resentment. "It's true what they say! This fellow's anti-British! He must be a communist!" He had found a sour, rueful amusement in that. To be looked at askance by the conservatives for being a communist, and to be simultaneously regarded more in sorrow than in anger by the communists for not being one, placed a man, he thought wryly, in a very select sort of isolation. Still, the doubts swelled, the undercurrent of uneasiness ran more strongly, and gave him hope. These, he insisted to himself, were not docile people. This was not, thank God, a country living on its past, but still struggling away from it. It had begun badly;

it grew up the hard way. Physically, mentally and spiritually handicapped, it had sweated and blundered its way out of the dark era when human flesh and blood, having suffered the deterioration of poverty, having endured nightmare voyages in the hell-ships of the day, had still by some miracle lived to tread a new earth, and kept enough vitality to reproduce itself. Human minds, warped, hardened, illiterate, and full of hatred, had still clung to the idea of survival and perpetuation. Human spirits, damned almost to impotence by the tradition of their own worthlessness, had still kept alive, instinctively, a spark of faith in the possibility of regeneration.

Walking across the road with Nick, leaving Prue sitting in the car, he was trying to persuade himself that his fellow-countrymen were not yet—not completely—demoralised by the terror of thought. They had had dope poured into their ears like the people of other nations; clothed in "glamour," it had flickered hypnotically before their dazzled eyes. But they had—oh, merciful dispensation!—a brief, brief history. They were not yet too helplessly in the grip of a legend, or bemused into imagining that they could ride triumphantly into the future on the back of the past. Their ancestors were only their grandfathers, or at most their great-grandfathers, and such national memories as they had led them not very far from the life of their own knowledge and comprehension. It was so short a time ago that the mere necessity for survival had been a challenge that they met with every breath they drew, and they were now conscious of that time less as a tradition than as part of their own experience. Nor was this short history an alluring one, gay with the pomp and ceremony of courts, picturesque with elaborate ritual, colourful with pageantry, romantic with legendary incident. It was more like the sober, practical review of achievement which a man might make, with aching muscles, and a hard day's work behind him. It was a history of obstinate striving, of hardship, ugliness, loneliness, success and failure, effort and more effort . . .

Walking through the dim passage with Nick behind him, down the steps, across the asphalt yard to the adjoining warehouse, his brain went on arguing anxiously. We had to fight in those days, so we fought. We fought the country, we fought the heat and the cold, the drought and the bushfires, the bad soil, the floods, the solitude. But above all we fought the conception of ourselves that had been imposed on us, the tradition of servitude. Is it conceivable that we should go back on that?

"Is this it?" Nick was pointing to a crate. Gilbert said: "Yes, that's it," and stooped for his end. But carrying it back across the yard, up the steps, and along the passage, he was still thinking of this last incredible eighteen months, when the people of whom he could not bring himself to despair, had watched their films, their plays, their books and their radio-talks censored, and preserved (except for a few intransigeants) an open-mouthed, docile equanimity. He remembered how they had submitted, apparently without alarm, to legislation which, at a stroke, threatened to deprive them of rights they had been battling to win since Magna Charta; how they had contemplated, with every appearance of bovine incomprehension, attacks upon their freedom of speech and assembly, the framing of regulations which could condemn them to secret trial and summary detention, which could expose their homes to search, their books to confiscation, and leave them totally at the mercy of any "officer" who might choose to suspect them of being "about to commit" an offence. Did they care about democracy? Did they even know what it meant—or was it just the signal for a cheer—the stimulus for a conditioned reflex . . . ?

Prue had a morning paper. When the books were safely bestowed, and Nick in the driver's seat, she held it out to her father. GERMANY INVADES YUGOSLAVIA AND GREECE said the black headlines. He watched them drive away, and went back slowly across the street to the office.

*   *   *   *

It had been a private house in the days when the city was little more than a township—one of a long row, of which it was the only survivor. Its passage was dark and narrow, its stairs even narrower, and lit only by a small window on the landing. Gilbert had two flights to climb now that he had, since his father's death, moved the managerial office to the top floor, and he admitted as he climbed that it was not reasonable, and certainly bad business to expect his customers to climb them, too. Old Polkington, the chief accountant, who had been with the firm for more than thirty years, had been openly shocked; but Gilbert, in the grip of a defiant mood, had not found it necessary to tell him—or anyone else—that the big downstairs room where Walter Massey had presided for forty years kept too strong a flavour of the old man's

personality for his liking. He had said, blandly, that he preferred
the view from the top storey. There were some small advantages, he reflected, as he attacked the second flight, in being a
writer. It was understood that such people were slightly mad.
The upheaval of long-established custom, the laborious removal of
office furniture up the stairs for the sake of a glimpse of very
distant tree-tops, and a meagre flicker of blue water could be—
and was—attributed to literary eccentricity.

More demonstrations of eccentricity, he thought grimly, were in
store for Polkington. If I have to be a bookseller, so his thought
ran, I'll damn well sell the sort of books I want to sell! And he
brushed aside as unimportant the warning of a business-sense,
which the routine of years had developed in him, that a long-
established clientele, a reputation, a "goodwill" are things not to
be lightly cast away.

He reached the top of the stairs briskly, noting with approval
that he was not puffing, for if he had one vanity it was his physical
condition, and his tailor never failed to please him by remarking
that his waist measurement had not changed in the last fifteen
years. He sorted out the key of his office, unlocked the door, and
went in. Crossing the room to the window, he lifted the heavy
sash and looked across the narrow laneway through a gap between
the taller buildings, which dwarfed his own two storeys, to his
"view." He admitted that his employees were to be excused for
their polite astonishment; it was really not much of a view. But
at least it was something to look at—a bit of sky when he lifted
his head from his work.

Turning to the desk he saw the big, battered tin deed-box standing against the wall. Into it he had bundled, a fortnight ago, the
formidable stack of letters and papers he had found tied in neat
bundles in the capacious bottom drawer of his father's desk. A
cursory glance had shown them to be mostly personal letters—the
accumulation of God only knew how many years—and he had put
them aside, feeling curiously reluctant to examine them, to find,
perhaps, new light shed on the character of a man whom he had
known only as a domestic tyrant. "Some day," he thought restlessly, "I suppose I'll have to go through them. . . ."

Miss Butters, resplendent in a new frock, her blonde hair elaborately dressed, her lips brighter than any geranium, her fingernails so long that Gilbert often wondered how she typed, and so

vividly lacquered that he sometimes blinked as she laid papers before him, appeared smiling at the door. It had both amused and infuriated him that his father, upon first setting eyes on her three years ago, had looked at his son with a sharp, unmistakable suspicion. Miss Butters, however, in spite of looking (as Nick put it) like the answer to a sugar-daddy's prayer, was a pleasant, efficient, and simple-minded young woman. She said brightly:

"Good morning, Mr. Massey. You're in early to-day."

He hadn't Nick's gift for small-talk. There seemed to be nothing to say to this but "Yes," so he said it, and sat down unwillingly at his desk. Miss Butters, disappearing into her tiny adjoining room (Gilbert suspected that once, long ago, some downtrodden under-housemaid had occupied it) began the busy, subdued clatter of her daily routine. Resting his arms on his blotter, staring blindly at his inkwell, he thought: "So now it's Greece .."

IV

FOR nearly a month it was Greece. Day after day, travelling to town in his morning train, Gilbert read the unfolding story of disaster. A.I.F. MOVE TO BATTLE STATIONS. YUGOSLAVS RETIRE IN SOUTH. GERMAN TROOPS BREAK THROUGH TO SALONIKA. ALLIED LINES MOVE BACK. YUGOSLAV RESISTANCE ENDING. 2000 AUSTRALIANS HOLD NAZIS. GERMAN TROOPS ENTER ATHENS. THROUGH HELL WITH ANZACS. GREEK FORCES ON LEFT CAPITULATE. ORDERLY WITHDRAWAL CONTINUES. 45,000 TROOPS EVACUATED.

The curtain came down on Greece. "That's that," said Nick, briskly, folding his newspaper. For every man, Gilbert thought. his own approach to horror, and his own defence against it. He knew his brother too well to believe that the eye of his imagination could not pierce that curtain, or that he failed to realise the tragedy of fear, persecution and starvation which would be played out, though no audience watched. But the approach Nick had chosen was the scientific detachment of the doctor; the world was a "case," its agony a "disease." Good enough. All kinds of thought, functioning in all kinds of different ways, would be needed for its regeneration. It was Nick's good fortune, perhaps, that his profession did not demand of him that suffering should be personified, that imagination should not stop at a mass-concept, but go down with every insignificant individual into his own individual hell. For himself he could not feel brisk about Greece.

Nick, writing it off, turned to campaigning for the coming State elections. Gilbert saw little of him during the first ten days of May, but heard a good deal in querulous complaint from Phyllis.

"If you want," she said, heatedly, to Gilbert, "to get mixed up with these ranting, mischief-making people yourself, you might at least not encourage Nick. It isn't fair to the girls, either. Virginia says Mrs. Heath asked her the other day if it was her uncle who was speaking in the Domain on Sunday. In the Domain! A soap-box orator!"

"A soap-box orator." Gilbert repeated the words slowly.

[71]

"Well, for that matter so were Christ, and Socrates, and Huss, and Wat Tyler, and hundreds more. He isn't in bad company. Many of the best things have been said from soap-boxes."

Phyllis looked at him suspiciously. "It's quite different," she insisted. "It isn't the same now."

"It never was," Gilbert quoted shortly. "Anyhow, Phyl, can't you remember that Nick's grown up? I couldn't discourage him if I wanted to."

"You don't want to!" she retorted. "You're every bit as bad yourself. After all, Nick is much younger than you. You have some responsibility."

Gilbert said, in exasperation:

"He's thirty-five. For Heaven's sake stop trying to treat him as if he were three."

She flared out:

"All right! But I will not have you—or Nick—putting your mad ideas into Prue's head. Virginia's sensible enough, but Prue's getting impossible. She was at a meeting the other night where there was quite a disturbance. People started throwing things. I told her she was *not* to go to any more."

Gilbert's sight blurred with sudden anger, but he said quietly enough:

"Look here, Phyllis, I won't have you interfering with Prue. She won't take any notice of your prohibitions anyhow, and she's perfectly right. But leave her alone."

She said in a shaking voice:

"You actually encourage her to disobey me?"

"I encourage her to do what she thinks is right."

"You mean what *you* think is right!" She stared at him for a moment, the inevitable tears gathering behind her glasses. "You make me almost believe what people say about you. I used to try and comfort your father, and say it was just silly gossip. But when you talk like this, I" . . . she twisted her apron nervously . . . "nobody would say such things unless he were a—a communist!"

"Oh, don't be silly!" Gilbert said wearily. "You haven't the faintest idea what a communist is."

*   *   *   *

Nick came in, jubilant, late on the evening of election day.

"It's going all right," he said. "A regular swing-over. It looks as if we win fourteen seats. I've brought some beer to celebrate.

Get us some glasses, Prue." He glanced at Phyllis, bending in silent disapproval over her knitting, and winked at his niece. "The millenium," he said, "is just around the corner. No work, and free beer for everyone—eh, Phyllis? Put 'em here, Prue, and stand by to mop up the froth. Here you are, Gilbert. Come on, Phyl, won't you drink damnation to all capitalists . . . ?" He dropped into a chair and put his glass on the floor beside him. "Heck, I'm tired!"

Phyllis rose, put her knitting down, and left the room. She told herself that she would not stay and listen to such nonsense. The resentment which had been rising in her for years as she found her husband and his brother and sister more and more engrossed in political, sociological and economic questions, had to be accounted for. To admit that it was actually resentment against conversations in which she could take no part would have been to admit ignorance or failure in herself. That would have been intolerable; so they talked nonsense.

Only when Marty's husband, Richard, joined the group could she bear to listen, for she cherished a tremendous respect for Richard. She liked his tall, lean, distinguished figure, his almost white hair, his kindly blue eyes, his attitude of scrupulous deference to herself, and, above all, she liked his background.

Somewhere in it there was an Earl. This was a source of the deepest satisfaction to her; it was, indeed, the only reason why she continued to be even moderately pleasant to Marty. She had never been able to discover just what relation the Earl was to Richard, so she referred to him as "my brother-in-law's cousin," which wasn't, of course, quite accurate, but you couldn't very well say "my sister-in-law's husband's cousin."

The fact that the cousin of an Earl could join amiably in Gilbert's and Marty's and Nick's interminable discussions, the fact that he could smile, the fact that he could give their unnerving, preposterous, extravagant ideas a courteous attention, seemed to her proof not only of an astounding magnanimity, but also of the immeasurable superiority of his own character and ideas. To these she could listen, mentally applauding, saying to herself: "That's exactly what I think!" and "Isn't that just what I said to Gilbert?"

She had, in fact, neither thought nor said any such things. But when Richard spoke she really felt that she had done so. She

could *recognise* what he said. He put into words her own confused, amorphous impressions of what men should be, of how they
should behave, of a world governed by high ideals, of human
beings living at peace with one another, of those noble qualities
whose names she loved to roll on her tongue—tolerance, faith,
justice, wisdom, unselfishness . . .

And then Gilbert—or Marty—or Nick would say:
"How?"

And at once the conversation became sordid again. At once
her ears were assailed by ugly, tiresome words—unemployment,
slums, exploitation, markets, undernourishment, venereal disease,
war. At once the talk bristled with incomprehensible phrases—
effective demand, means of production, tariff walls, bank credit,
capital goods . . .

Richard was so broad-minded. He would concede this, and
admit that, and allow the other. He never became annoyed when
they spoke tactlessly—even bitterly—against things which were
part of the Earl's background, and, therefore, of course, his own.
He kept on smiling, nodding, listening, putting up his own arguments so clearly and wisely and politely that she blushed for Nick
when he knocked them spinning with a caustic phrase. And when
he went away with Marty, her arm linked in his, he wrung Gilbert's hand and Nick's just as if they hadn't been insulting him
and all he stood for the whole evening . . .

"Nonsense!" Gilbert would say when she protested in the
privacy of their room. "These things aren't personal questions.
Richard knows we aren't insulting him. I have a great respect
for Richard."

And so he should have, she thought indignantly, going into her
bedroom and switching on the light. As for Marty, Richard's
loyalty to her was moving—it was heroic! She wasn't worth it.
She chalked it up as another black mark against Marty that, whereas these detestable politics seemed to be widening the gulf between
herself and Gilbert, they had no apparent effect on the marriage of
Gilbert's sister. No *apparent* effect, she insisted. For, of course,
it was nothing but Richard's tolerance, his kindness, his perfect
breeding, his strict regard for the sacredness of the marriage tie,
which kept things outwardly serene. What he must suffer in
secret! She had even heard Marty speak before him in her un-

pleasant sarcastic way of "the old school-tie," when everyone knew that Richard had been to Harrow!

The week's laundry was lying on the bed waiting to be sorted. Phyllis began separating handkerchiefs into four piles; the girls must sort their own—she never knew which were Prue's and which Virginia's. Her thoughts came back to a problem which had been worrying her more and more over the last four years. Gilbert wasn't writing.

For years after their marriage she had not taken his literary activities at all seriously, though she had tried to fulfil what she regarded as a wifely duty by feigning a polite and admiring interest. It had been just free-lance stuff in those days—short stories and articles. And occasional poems—though these had ceased quite soon, and she had been glad on the whole, because she had felt embarrassing emotional depths in them which made her husband seem unfamiliar.

She hadn't been able to feel really impressed by these snippets. They didn't make much money, and they took up a lot of Gilbert's time which, she thought, should have been spent with her and with his children. But when, astonishingly, he had written a novel when he was just thirty, she had felt quite proud. There was something solid about a book with covers. There was something to show for the hermit hours, for the midnight oil, for the preoccupation, for the evading of social calls, and chopping wood, and putting a new washer on the tap. She had not been able to come any nearer to him through this writing than through the other; in fact, she remembered now that reading his first book, even, she had caught herself looking at him with surprised curiosity, as though he were a stranger. "My instinct," she told herself solemnly, laying five shirts in a pile, "was quite right."

The next book had been much the same. She read it with the surface of her mind, and didn't really enjoy it. But she could, and did, point to it. She could, and did, say: "My husband's second book." As the years passed she could say, with mounting complacency: "My husband's third book, "My husband's fourth—fifth —sixth book." She hadn't much wanted, somehow, to draw attention to his seventh . . .

She had strong views as to what was right and proper. Culture was right and proper. She wanted it in her home just as she wanted wall-to-wall carpets and a lounge suite. When she spoke

of the arts her voice took on the same reverential hush as it did
when she spoke of religion, and she went to concerts and art
exhibitions in the same mood of vacant piety as she went to
church. A writer-husband, she had felt, gave her a kind of
vicarious standing in what she thought of as "the literary world,"
and she learned to enjoy it during the years when his seven novels
came out at fairly regular intervals.

They had been increasingly uneasy years, all the same. She
was resentfully conscious, for one thing, that time was treating
her husband more kindly than it was treating her. By 1935 she
had already begun to look bulky and to move slowly; the bright
colouring, which had been her chief claim to prettiness, had faded
from her cheeks and eyes; her hair was greying; she wore glasses,
and she had an upper plate. Gilbert, on the other hand, though
his body had acquired the solid outline of maturity, and though he
was rather grey at the temples, and though he wore glasses for
reading, had kept his waist-line, his hair and his own teeth. She
thought: "Men! It's a pity they don't have to have children, and
look after them!"

For she was beginning to realise that, with the failure of her
physical hold on him, he was breaking loose from her altogether.
She couldn't interest him any more. She couldn't hold his attention with household gossip, with accounts of tea-parties, or even
with talk of the children, for they were not children any longer,
but young individuals whose surprising ideas, activities, and interests seemed only to provoke new arguments between herself and
their father. The bad years of the depression had changed her
vague discontent to definite alarm and resentment. She became
aware that what she had persuaded herself was her husband's
normal, understandable anxiety about his own business affairs was
something much more—an anxiety about the world in general, a
nagging dissatisfaction, a mounting anger, a sombre obsession.

Thunder Brewing was finished in the autumn of 1937, and during
the months before its publication she noticed that he had nothing
to say about a new book. Instead of writing, he began to read
more than ever—to read endlessly, to read with an almost passionate concentration. Af if, she thought in bewilderment, he
were studying for an exam.!

She prided herself upon her wifely tact, and during his absences
at the office she tried spasmodically to read what he was reading.

"A wife," she often said, with that profound air which she reserved for her cliches and slogans, "must share her husband's interests." She struggled through the first dozen pages of a score of books; their closely printed pages, peppered with statistics, with the polysyllabic words and obscure phrases of economic jargon, failed utterly to hold an attention which wandered helplessly to the pleasanter intricacies of a knitting pattern, the contents of the larder, or the material for Virginia's new frock. There was an obscure hurtfulness in this; the realisation that her husband's brain could cope with something from which her own persistently retreated, made it necessary for her to assert herself. That was not easy with so detached a person as Gilbert. Where was he? What was he at? What was he thinking? Watching him grow away from her, finding that she could not keep up with him, she was only able to save herself by deciding that he was not worth keeping up with anyhow. He was going quite the wrong way.

If his way was wrong, then hers must be right. In her growing unhappiness, she too began, after her own fashion, a search. Her wanderings from one creed to another were more like a maze of aimless tracks than a road. But though they had no constant direction, though they crossed and re-crossed each other, faded out into nothing, led her round in circles, she trod them without slackening, goaded by the one unvarying impulse of self-justification. She had tried philosophy, but her mind, wandering from Kant as wilfully as it had ever wandered from Gilbert's books, sent her off on the track of Pelmanism. That, in turn, crossed the path of Coué, and deflected her again. Coué had seemed, at last, but a stepping stone to Freud, from whom, vaguely scared and repelled, she fled to the higher realm of Theosophy. This had involved her in Vegetarianism for a time, but she was a big, energetic woman, and fond of food, so she had scrambled back at last to more spiritual regions with the help of the Christian Watchers' Circle.

And there, she told herself, and anyone else who would listen, she had found Peace. Peace, Peace, Peace. It had, like all her abstract ideas, a capital letter; she saw it, indeed, as a word, a written word which she might have invoked with the same fretful urgency with which she might have called a dog. And so strong were her powers of self-deception—so immeasurably stronger than anything else in her whole make-up—that she was able to believe that the pleasant, complacent sense of righteousness in which she found consolation was really the touch on her brow of some celestial visitant bestowing Peace.

This, then, was the problem over which she knit her brows as she looked at Virginia's frivolous and extremely scanty scanties, disapproving of them because she herself, at twenty-two, had worn fuji bloomers with elastic at the knee. She pursued her "way" which was right, and Gilbert pursued his, which was wrong. She had a kind of stupid, unimaginative gallantry; she would go on butting her head against a brick wall till she died of it. There-fore, it still seemed possible that through her Gilbert might even now be wooed from his mistaken ideas, and she was beginning to toy with the thought that possibly her father-in-law's death might point the way.

Her own intense respect for property made it seem incredible to her that possession of it should not have a steadying, stabilising effect. Gilbert, had she confessed the thought to him, would have assured her grimly that in ninety-nine cases out of a hundred she was perfectly right. Now that he was actually head of the firm, she thought, now that the whole responsibility of the business rested on his shoulders, surely he would be in a more—a more *reasonable* frame of mind? Surely this was her chance to turn him from the queer ideas he seemed to have developed, and the still queerer acquaintances he made? If she could only persuade him to let this house—a thing that the old man had always refused even to discuss—and live permanently in the mountains, would he not by degrees break loose from the discontented, eccentric people he mixed with—get interested in gardening—take up golf . . . ? At the back of her mind, also, was the thought that this might separate him to some extent from his brother and sister; for though she accused him of having a bad influence on Nick, she also accused both Nick and Marty of having a bad influence on him.

Gathering up a pile of her daughters' clothes, she hurried along the passage to their room. Virginia was at the mirror, trying a new way of doing her hair. Phyllis said eagerly:

"Here are your things and Prue's, darling. Tell me, Virginia, how would you like to *live* up the mountains?"

"Live?" said Virginia. "How could we? Come and hold this bit of hair for me, Mummy."

Phyllis persisted.

"I think it would be fun. Dad could drive down every day— lots of people do. And you have plenty of friends up there, haven't you?"

"Oh, yes." Virginia studied her lovely reflection with passionate and searching attention. It mightn't, she thought, be bad for a while. After all, George was up there every week-end, and she never saw him in town anyhow, because of his wife. And there weren't so many dances now, since the war . . .

Phyllis said:

"I think that style's too old for you, dear. Why not just let it fall naturally?"

Virginia's blue eyes met her mother's in the mirror. A calm stare, a calm silence, and no pause in the busy movement of her fingers. Phyllis said defeatedly: "Oh, well . . . !" and went back to her own room.

*   *   *   *

Richard's sciatica had been bad again. Marty walked down the path from the front gate, through the hall, up the stairs, holding one newspaper under her arm and the other open beneath her startled eyes. Richard had been in pain all yesterday; she had been busy renewing his hot-water bottles, bringing him aspirin, and sitting by the window while he dozed, working on the script of her next month's broadcast. They hadn't had the wire-less on all day, so the news which the headlines proclaimed set her mind racing with shock.

DRAMATIC ESCAPE OF HITLER'S DEPUTY. PROFOUND EFFECT ON NAZI PARTY.

On the landing she paused. Even to herself, she thought, who had learned to distrust headlines, there was a temptation to suc-cumb to the authoritative appearance of the printed word, to accept it at its face value—particularly when it cried so enticing an encouragement to one's hopes. But already the temptation was fading. Already, reluctantly, her mind was responding to the heavy, unhappy knowledge that in a disordered world you must, it you want truth, hunt for it, build it laboriously from a thousand tiny assembled scraps of data—and, having built it, still not accept it fully, but set it aside for the confirmation or denial of time. She went on slowly, still reading: *It is authoritatively stated in London that the flight was an escape, and that Hess brought no peace overtures or messages. He left in defiance of the authorities.*

She crossed the hall into Richard's room, laid the open paper across his knees, and stood watching him as he put on his glasses and bent over it.

"Good God!" he said, reading avidly. She was thinking: "No. It doesn't make sense. Not escape. Not Hess . . ." Richard looked up, a curious glow of excitement which she found unbearably poignant on his face. She knew what Richard, the Londoner, had suffered during these last terrible months of the air blitz on England. There had been an almost stupefied pain in his eyes when, only two days ago, he had read to her: *From dusk till dawn waves of bombers streamed across London . . . there was not one moment of relief from mass bombers in the first five hours of the raid. Casualties were heavy. . . . Famous streets became channels of fire. After midnight the city burned so fiercely that the flames leapt across streets and set fire to buildings on the opposite side . . ."* She thought now: What straw of hope would not a man's mind catch at, drowning in such grief for his homeland and his countrymen? He said with suppressed excitement:

"This could mean anything, Marty! It could be the beginning of the end! It could mean the collapse of the Nazi Party! It could . . ."

He stopped, looking at her face, and asked with a return to his normal quietness: "What do you think?"

She turned away and went over to the window. She had met Richard on the boat returning from England when she was twenty-three and he forty. In those early years of the peace which she had not yet recognised as phoney, there had seemed to be no belief, no viewpoint, no interest which they could not share with the happiest whole-heartedness. They had talked of books, of music, of gardens, of a world come safely through agonies which had made it safe for democracy, they had seen a future which seemed to offer no reason for doubts. She had been, even then, observant, and not unaware of problems; but she had been content to see salvation in human goodness without examining those influences which so often turned human goodness bad. And only in the last ten, tormented years had she realised, finding her own maturity, that the man she had married had been mature when she met him. Nothing but the mutual forbearance of their love for each other had made it possible that their steadily diverging beliefs should bring only sadness—not enmity. No, she admitted, there had been something more, contributed not by her impatient self, but by Richard. There was much to be said for manners, for a courtesy so ingrained that it never failed, even when she herself became bitter, vehement and sarcastic. And it was not—not by any means—that Richard was mentally ossified. He wasn't what one called, nowadays, a reactionary. He wasn't a Blimp. No one so kindly, tolerant, humorous and sincere could be a Blimp. He was (if one must, like Nick, pin a label) a Liberal, and she de-fended his Liberalism emphatically and with conviction against that friendly but uncompromising radical, her younger brother.

"You're a hopeless dogmatist, Nick," she told him. "You and your kind need people like Richard—Heavens, how you need them! You have what he lacks—I grant you that—but he has what you lack, and you won't admit that you lack anything. You know all the answers. You have your plans and blueprints. But you're dealing with a world of semi-to-uneducated people, and Richard can influence such people, while you do nothing but alarm and antagonise them. I've seen him do it. I've seen him do more in one evening to shake the complacency of wealthy morons than you could do in your whole lifetime. He doesn't take them as far as you want them to go, because he doesn't go as far as that himself; but he does shift them. They do listen to him. Why can't you admit that all people who want the right things are allies—even if they disagree about the detail of methods?"

Nick couldn't admit it. With exasperated amusement she thought how alike they were really—Nick and Richard—in their inflexible loyalty to their own ideas. So that she herself became a kind of liaison-officer, seeing the valuable qualities of each —struggling to make an alliance where they would have nothing but a watchful, friendly truce.

She said slowly:

"I haven't read it all yet, Richard."

She sat down on the window seat and opened the other paper.

HITLER ABOLISHES FUGITIVE'S POST. NAZI SPLIT SEEN AS REASON FOR SENSATIONAL FLIGHT.

She looked out the window into the garden, and felt a denial of those headlines rise strongly in her mind—a half-contemptuous denial with something of irritation in it, as if she had been asked to believe that the moon was made of green cheese. She thought:

It's a habit of mind, this Nazism—like liberalism, like radicalism—
and you don't discard it overnight. And it has no frontiers. She
smoothed the paper out on her knees and read: "*An authoritative
British statement, issued after the examination of Hess, states
that he escaped to Scotland in defiance of Nazi authority. He brought
no messages or peace overtures with him.*" She looked up to find
Richard watching her.

"Well?" he said.

She shrugged.

" 'The lady doth protest too much, methinks.' "

"You think he came to offer terms?"

She answered unhappily:

"That's my guess."

"What terms?"

She could find no words. She thought despairingly that among
the many poisons which war injected into human minds, the
shrinking, supersensitiveness of national pride was not the least
dangerous. So careful, so terribly careful you must be not to hurt
people in this raw, vulnerable spot! Yet unless Richard knew, by
now, how profound was her own love for his countrymen, what
had their marriage meant? Unless he understood without even a
shadow of doubt that the measure of her love for them was her
hatred of the policies which had led them into that martyrdom of
which he had read to her two days ago, what was left to them
from their long years together? She looked at him with a misery
which faded as she saw in his eyes that he did know; yet even
then she spoke with reluctance.

"I think he came to say: We'll lay off you if you lay off us while
we attack Russia."

He took his glasses off and began to polish them absently on a
corner of the sheet. She thought anxiously that he looked suddenly
old; not even the pain of his illness had made his face as gaunt
and wretched as it was now. He said slowly:

"I can—hardly believe that. If he did such a thing he must
have had—some reason to believe that he could succeed."

When she made no reply, he asked:

"Do you expect him to succeed?"

She knew her own face was as wretched as his. She said desperately: "How should I know? Is the Red Bogey dead? How
effective have the years of propaganda been?" She stood up and

began to walk restlessly about the room. She stopped and asked him with sudden fury: "How long will people put up with having their minds belted about like shuttlecocks?"

He said in a tired voice:

"Cheer up, Marty. I can't think you're right about this. But even if you were—no, it couldn't be done."

"Don't you think," she asked, not looking at him, "that there are people in England who would be willing to see it done?"

He acknowledged impatiently:

"Yes, yes. A few. Of course. But Germany doesn't want war with Russia. She never has wanted a war on two fronts . . ."

"No," Marty agreed dryly. "Hence Hess, to settle the Western Front."

He made a sharp, goaded gesture of protest. She said quickly:

"But I believe you're right, Richard. It won't happen. But it's—well, it's ugly that it should even have been attempted . . ."

"If it has been attempted." He was poring over the newspaper again. She went to sit on the bed beside him. The heavy black print challenged her mind's obstinate resistance, and the very feel of that resistance reassured her. It said: Up to a point we can be fooled; just so far, and no farther. She noticed that her husband's hair was thinning on the top, and touched it with her hand in a quick caress.

"You shouldn't be sitting up so long," she told him briskly. "Lie down and rest for a while before the doctor comes."

He lay back obediently and shut his eyes. Watching his tired, ageing face, she asked:

"Could you sleep?"

"Perhaps."

She drew the curtains and left him, but he did not sleep.

*　　　*　　　*　　　*

A few days later Gilbert said to Miss Butters as she prepared for her midday Saturday departure:

"Will you see if Mr. Nick's still here, Miss Butters, as you go down? Tell him I'd like to see him for a moment."

Nick, appearing in the doorway ten minutes later, found his brother bending over the black tin box which stood open on the floor by his chair. He said gloomily:

"I suppose we must go through these sooner or later. I thought I'd stay back for an hour or so this afternoon. How about you?"

He added, seeing Nick's grimace: "After all they're as much your concern as mine."

"Oh, all right." Nick pulled a chair up to the desk and lit a cigarette. "Pitch me over a bundle."

"Most of them look like private letters. It beats me why he kept them here instead of at home. Here you are. Or why he kept them at all, for that matter."

Nick asked:

"Don't we get any lunch to-day?"

"You go now, if you like," Gilbert said. "I'd rather get on with this, and have a bite later on."

He took, at random, a bundle of papers from the box, and untied the pink tape that bound them. Unfolding the first, looking at his father's familiar, pointed writing, realising that they were love-letters, he felt in rapid succession an impulse to throw them all away unread, and that faint pricking of the novelist's incorrigible inquisitiveness, which finds material in any human document. He read: *"What you tell me of your work fills me with uneasiness for your health: and yet I console myself with the thought that you are doing the Lord's business, and that He will watch over you. The darkness of error in which those unhappy people have been living for so long is being lightened by your labours. I try to remember this, and not to be impatient for the end of the year, when we shall be united. I am having the house painted, and have bought some new pictures and furniture— quite handsome, I think—which I hope will please you. That God will protect and strengthen you is the nightly prayer of your devoted*
"Walter."

On the other side of the desk Nick made a small, explosive sound, between amusement and disgust. Crumpling a few sheets of paper in his hand, and pitching them with violence into the waste-paper basket, he passed a page across to his brother and said: "Read that bit."

Gilbert took it. The pointed writing said: *"I have received a letter from Beatrice which has greatly distressed me. She shows no feeling of regret for that indiscretion (to call it by no harder name) which, I am sure, hastened our father's death. She tells me of the birth of a son, whom she has called John, and speaks of visiting us when we are married. You will readily understand how it grieves me to say such a thing of my own sister, but I cannot feel that you would welcome her to your house, nor should I wish you to do so. I have therefore written to* her to say that *I fear we have chosen different paths, but that we will always remember her in prayer. Indeed, I have done so most earnestly, ever since she left home . . .*"

"And you say he wasn't altogether a hypocrite!" said Nick. "Here, give me something else. I can't read this stuff."

Gilbert threw another packet across the desk without replying. For himself, he found that such letters put flesh and blood on the skeleton which was all he had ever known of his parents' life; they built a little more reality, a little more detail, on to his understanding of the curious, confused, groping, infinitely various methods by which human beings governed their spiritual life. And although this particular letter showed the narrow-minded pettiness of a censorious and unforgiving man, had not the other showed—or at least suggested—one to whom more kindly and even more generous emotions were not unknown? Wasn't there, behind the stilted phraseology, a real devotion? Wasn't there some eager tenderness in the hope that the new furniture would "please her"? Wasn't there, even, a hint of human ardour in his impatience for the time when they would be "united"?

Nick cried delightedly:

"This is marvellous! Who . . ."—he turned a page and spelt out a name laboriously—". . . was Alfred B. Hetherington?"

"Never heard of him," said Gilbert.

"Well, he knew all about you. Listen to this. Date, 1915 Written from some place in England. . . . *"I am still living in this home for retired clergy. Spring is commencing, flowers appearing, and birds beginning to sing. But, alas, this terrible conflict is still going on, now perhaps at its height, or nearly so. I am glad to be able to make contact with some of our men whom I meet on my walks, by giving them a special edition of St. John's Gospel. I note in your last letter that your eldest son was then fifteen, so he will now (if he has been spared to you) be eighteen, and will perhaps be coming to this side of the world to play his part in the struggle . . .*"

Nick, looking more puzzled than Gilbert had ever seen him, put the letter down and shook his head. "Well," he said in a baffled voice, "what do you know?" Still frowning his bewilderment, he picked up another letter in the same old-fashioned writing, and began to study it as he might have studied the obscure heiroglyphics of some unknown, primitive tribe. Gilbert felt faintly amused. Ten years, he thought, can make quite a difference. That

world, which seems incredible enough to me now, is quite incredible
to Nick. Marty and I grew up in it defenceless, but by the time
he came along we were big enough to act as buffers between it
and him. To Nick, he realised, still with that faint amusement,
the thought of an elderly clergyman waylaying troops in country
lanes and handing out Gospels to them was fantastic. But why?
He found that it gave to himself a curious feeling of triumph. For
it made him realise afresh that the moment man has a belief to
communicate he turns to the printed word. He saw that frail old
parson handing out Holy Writ, he saw Hitler handing out *Mein
Kampf*, he saw Lenin handing out Marx and Engels, he saw the
Left Book Club handing out red books, and the Right Book Club
handing out blue books, he saw the Henry George Society and
the Douglas Credit Society, and the Christian Scientists and
Jehova's Witnesses handing out pamphlets. And he saw, with an
uncontrollable twitch of his lips, Nick himself, striding round the
Domain in his raincoat handing out "literature":—

He picked up a pen absently, dipped it in the ink, and looked at
its tip, shining with a drop of black fluid; his memory searched for
the bold words of Tom Collins: *". . . the whole armoury of the
Father of Lies can furnish no shield to turn aside the point of the tireless and terrible PEN . . ."* Unfortunately, though, the Father of
Lies could wield a persuasive pen himself. The power, then, was
not in the pen alone, but in the contact it was able to establish
between the minds of writer and reader; the words it inscribed
were dead till they lit a spark behind the eyes that read them. He
reached for another bundle and began to unfold the brittle, yellow-
ing sheets; Nick was reading aloud again, but almost to himself,
as if he needed to hear the words spoken before his brain would
really believe in them: *"Well, my dear Walter, I think the Lord's
coming is not far off. I have been reading in my Bible of Enoch who
walked with God. May it be so with you and yours! This is an age
when many have forsaken the old moorings, alas! But the old paths
are best and safest. . . ."*
He looked up, no longer puzzled, but merely amused now that
the last sentences had given him that label without with no human
being was comprehensible to him. Obviously, poor old buffer, a
reactionary. And a bit mixed in his metaphors. He gathered the
rest of the bundle together and dropped it in the waste-paper
basket. "I needn't go through all these," he said; "it'll just be

more in the same vein. Give me another lot."

They read for a while in silence. The basket filled and over-flowed; they threw the crumpled sheets round it on the floor. Gilbert said once:

"Here are our birth certificates—better put these aside." And again: "I don't suppose you want a photo of yourself in Lord Fauntleroy curls?" Over a sheaf of tattered pages he paused for a few moments. Most of them bore his mother's writing: "Gilbert's first map, June, 1903." "Drawn by Gilbert, 1905." And, above a brief "Marty, May, 1905," sprawled a characteristi-cally Marty-ish protest in straggling capitals—"I DOAN LIKE SKOLE." Had his father, cherishing this revolutionary document for thirty-six years, actually felt an indulgent sympathy for its rebelliousness? Or had he merely been proud that his daughter, at four, could achieve it? He dropped them among the litter on the floor without showing them to Nick, and unfolded another sheet of paper. The signature at the foot of a page of bold, black writing caught his eye, and he read with sudden, sharp interest:

"Dear Mr. Massey,

"I can hardly believe that, having had your attention drawn to the condition of the houses of which you are the owner, and understanding how injurious those conditions are to the health of at least one family inhabiting them, you propose to take no action in the matter. When I called on you yesterday afternoon I felt sure that you would accept my information in the spirit in which I gave it, and rectify a situation of which I could only suppose you ignorant. The note I received from you this evening suggests that you found my 'intrusion' into the matter an impertinence; I can only say that it was intended as no such thing, and add that I am at a loss to understand how you reconcile the re-ligious principles, which I am told you profess, with responsibility for dwellings which are (and, apparently, are to remain) unfit for human habitation.

"Yours faithfully,
"Scott Laughlin."

Past and present rushed together in Gilbert's mind so that their impact was like a blow on his consciousness, from which it re-covered slowly to find the black writing still accusing him. He looked at the date. Dec. 8th, 1911. So that was it! He had had to wait nearly thirty years to discover why Scott Laughlin had called on his father that summer afternoon, and left his cap lying on the verandah chair—but he knew now. And with that knowledge came the once-familiar, writhing effort of his mind to escape from a painful problem, to evade or postpone a decision almost impossibly difficult. For those houses were still there, and now they belonged to him. Not to Nick, or Marty. For some reason best known to himself, the old man, while dividing the rest of his worldly goods equally between his three children, had left this property to Gilbert alone.

From across the desk, but sounding so remote that it might have been from across the world, he heard Nick say:

"Crikey, Gil, look at this!" And then, after a pause, more sharply: "Gil! Wake up!"

He stretched his hand out mechanically to take the paper his brother was pushing across the desk to him. A few minutes were enough to show him the sequel to that afternoon call. A couple of solicitor's letters advising Mr. Massey that he had no case for libel against the author of the article in question, for his name was not mentioned, nor could his identity be regarded as established by anything it contained. And, attached by a pin, the article in question. He read it through.

Suddenly he swung around on his chair so violently that when he rose he left it spinning. He snatched up his hat, saying shortly to Nick: "I'm going. Leave this. We'll finish it some other time . . ."

He went down the stairs, along the passage, out into the street, hardly knowing what he was doing. Nick, left alone, picked up Laughlin's letter and read it thoughtfully. Poor old Gil, he thought, got himself too emotionally worked up over these things. Can you live on a muck-heap and not get befouled? Of course not. The fool wastes his energy scraping filth from his clothes; the sensible man starts cleaning up the muck-heap. He lit another cigarette and went on reading.

V

MARTY'S restless, energetic, but untidy mind saw things in flashes, in pictures, in metaphor; she was content to do so, recognising these lightning-sketches of her brain as a short-cut technique of thinking not without its value in a temperament which she admitted to be volatile, and impatient of discipline. They were a means whereby some one aspect or facet of a problem was lit to brilliance while she had a good look at it, but automatically blacked-out when its validity failed, as the validity of a metaphor usually does somewhere. Such pictures, she knew, were useful to her, for they were her brain's only illumination; she merely laughed unabashed, when she caught herself making a metaphor to explain her use of metaphor—showing her herself feeling her way through a dark room, striking matches as she went, seeing a chair, the corner of a table, a shelf of books leap from obscurity for a moment, and then going forward more confidently in the darkness for having seen so vividly even a fragment of the whole.

Yet, like Gilbert, she found now that the thinking which must supplement her flashes, and through which alone she could build them into a coherent idea and project them on the outer world, had failed her. The flashes themselves played as continuously as summer-lightning; falling back inevitably on metaphor, she told herself that she was receiving better than ever before, but something had gone badly wrong with her transmission.

Lunching with Gilbert one day in June, telling him glumly that she had just torn up her eleventh false start, she became cranky at his well-meant effort to console her by suggesting that she had not yet found the perfect starting-point. She snapped:

"Good Heavens, Gil, you know there's no such thing. That's just one of the little vanities—the little poses of writers trying to make much of the "technique" of their art. Any point's the perfect starting-point if you treat it properly."

He knew her danger-signs by now. She was not in a good conversational mood, so he left her to her silence and set his own mind methodically to work on what she had said. He himself knew to his sorrow the long torment of unfruitful hours, of scribbled pages scored through with rejecting lines, of a room gone suddenly blank and lonely with the departure of the creative impulse. He suspected that the very simplicity of writing might be its terror. Alone with your sheet of paper, he thought, you know that there are no rules. Nothing but your thoughts—and words. Ranks, armies, a whole world of words, but not helping you, not ordered or catalogued, not to be used (except, indeed, by politicians) in groups or sets, but single, elusive, uncompromising, each perfect for its purpose. From this mass you must somehow extract your thought, not building it so much as finding it, whole and inevitable, so that what you feel as it flows from your pen is not accomplishment, but recognition. Perhaps, as Marty seemed to suggest, all this talk of 'technique' was just a frightened denial of so baffling a simplicity? Perhaps it was nothing but a pathetic gesture of self-importance? A buttress of self-respect in a world of technicians? Perhaps the poor writer, lest he be bereft of the glory which a chemist or a mechanic wears as an undisputed right, must invent his patter and his jargon, make his rules and formulæ, classify his plots and climaxes, jabber of characterisation, timing, contrast, style, understatement, tension and what have you. . . .

If so, then Marty must be right. There is no 'beginning' and no 'end.' To recognise that was, perhaps, to achieve a proper humility—to recognise that 'your' art was not yours at all, but merely a minute contribution, possibly inept, possibly abortive, to a continuous human record. No matter where you begin, someone else has brought the story to that point; no matter where you end, someone takes over from you and carries it on. All you can do is to record a fragment of human experience—anywhere, any time, for every moment gathers in the past and propels the future. No moment is more significant than any other moment, for all hold germ and growth, maturity and decay. No 'deciding on' character, either, for a human being is not a house to be planned, but an incalculable organism to be twisted and shaped by emotions and events. Nor can you marshall events to some orderly pattern, for the human beings you create will disorder them, deflect them, rend them. So you are no clever puppeteer pulling strings, but merely a fragment of human mind, groping in the chaos of 'your' art as you grope in the chaos of the life it mirrors. You see the shadow of a place—what place is it? How can you know until you give it existence by writing it down? How can you write it down until you know? Was this, he wondered, the whole burden of the writer's art—to hold himself poised, receptive, while words and emotions flowed together in him and fused? And when among thousands of ghost-ideas, clamorous for the substance of words, none achieve this fusion, the writer lives and moves and has his being in a very special, subtle kind of Hell. He thought: "It's rather like that agony of impotence in nightmares—trying to run, trying to climb, trying to hold . . ."

"I suppose you're right about beginnings," he said. "After all, if you want to tell the story of one human being very exhaustively where *do* you begin? If you take his birth as a starting point you're begging the question of his conception."

She shook off her despondency.

"Even his conception," she said, "doesn't account for the time when he was, as they say, no more than a twinkle in his father's eye. Are you to go back and back till you find yourself up against a twinkle in the eye of a great-great-grandfather? It hardly seems decent."

She yawned, waving the subject away impatiently.

"What's the time, Gil?"

He looked at his watch.

"Nearly two. What time is your broadcast?"

"Three o'clock." She met his eyes and asked: "What are you grinning it?"

"Was I grinning?" But he knew that he was, for he had been thinking that it was like Marty to fall back on a microphone. He felt inclined to suspect sometimes that with her colloquial style, and her lively preoccupation with topical events, it was her proper medium. It had entertained him to observe how adroitly (recognising that blind spot of officialdom which fails to realise that there is no such thing as an uncontroversial subject) she had contrived to say at least a good deal of what she wanted to say despite the blanket of censorship. Knowing that any subject must finally reveal itself as part of the whole social pattern, she chose titles of such astounding innocence that even her father would never have suspected them of covering unsettling ideas, and introduced here and there small, sharp comments, like pins, to prick the lethargic minds of armchair listeners.

She asked suddenly:

"What about the Burt Street property, Gil?"

He answered without looking at her:

"I don't know. I'd like to sell it. I'd like to be rid of it." He added, after a moment's silence: "Of course, that's only an escape—a personal escape."

She enquired, looking at him with sympathy.

"Have you been down there?"

His brows came together sharply and his face tightened. "Yes," he said, and added violently: "A row of pig-styes!"

She said slowly:

"If you did sell them—what then? They'd only go to some landlord who probably hasn't your scruples. I should think the only thing you can do is to put them in order and lower the rent."

"I'll do that, of course, if I keep them. But nothing on earth will ever make them a proper environment for children." He looked at her hard. "And they helped to pay for your expensive and practically worthless schooling. And mine. And Nick's." He held a match for his sister's cigarette, and lit his own. "I've been hunting up the history of them. I've got it pretty well pieced together from old letters that Father kept, and the legal papers. It appears that our great-grandfather, Henry, got the land as a grant in 1820." He laughed shortly. "Believe it or not—for farming!"

"Good God!" said Marty, interested. "How did he make out?"

"I gather that he died a disgruntled man. There's a letter he wrote to a brother in England—somehow it came back into Father's possession. He talks of "a society abandoned to every kind of wickedness," but his greatest grievance seems to have been that the land—as one would expect—was hopeless for farming. He left it to his son, William, and William built the houses on it."

Gilbert stared out the window beside him, recalling his tour of inspection. He had stood in the narrow street trying to imagine it in those middle years of the last century, before, spreading out over the shores and promontories of the harbour, the city had at last engulfed it. Well, however barren it had been for crops, it had sprouted a luxuriant growth of houses. Built faithfully after the prevailing English model, they stood in grim and hideous terraces, wall to wall, with a pocket handkerchief of back-yard, and ten feet of clipped buffalo grass to separate a respectable spiky iron fence from a respectable front door with coloured glass, and a white china doorknob.

Thus, in the evening of his days, Grandfather William had found himself a substantial property-owner. Godliness had saved him from succumbing to the lure of an ostentation he could well have afforded, and he had retired, instead, to what was then "the country"—the heights of the North Shore—where he built his large, inconvenient stone house, square and solid as a gaol, named it *Glenwood*, married the daughter of a clergyman, and begot eight children, of whom Walter, the eldest, and Beatrice, the youngest, were the only survivors.

Just before Marty was born Walter had forsaken his shipping office, and bought the failing business of James Veech and Co. He had designed, with patriarchal pride, a handsome letterhead, renaming the firm "Walter Massey and Sons," but prudently awaited the new baby's birth before having it printed. When Marty arrived he sadly erased the final "s," which was, however, triumphantly restored five years later with the surprising advent of Nick. But nearly half of his income still derived from that property upon which his grandfather had so unsuccessfully grown crops, and his father had so successfully built houses. They were old houses now. The years, though they had passed in sober and godly monotony over the Massey household at *Glenwood*, had been years of exuberant, planless, greedy development in the young city. Well-to-do people built their homes farther and farther afield, no longer tempted by terraces in the heart of what was rapidly becoming a district of factories and warehouses. They grew dingier and shabbier—they lacked amenities which modern-minded people demanded, their slate roofs leaked, their paint peeled and blistered, dust filmed over them, their floorboards rotted, their back yards filled with the accumulated rubbish of innumerable tenancies, and rats took possession. Nevertheless they were still inhabited, and rents continued to be paid into the account of Walter Massey, who had never seen them since he was a little boy, and who never thought of them save as investments—a legitimate and respectable source of income. His children never knew of their existence until they were grown up. In childhood they understood vaguely that their father had "private means," which came from "property," and they were given to understand that this was a state of affairs to which a certain amount of prestige attached . . .

Marty jabbed the stub of her cigarette in the ash tray and began to pull on her gloves.

"I must go, Gil. It's after two, and I have to do some house-hold shopping before three. Are you going to the mountains this week-end?"

"No, I don't think so. Phyllis is helping at some bazaar on Saturday."

"There's a meeting of the Writers' Guild on Friday night—are you going?"

He said, picking up the bill, and feeling in his pocket for change: "Oh, I don't know. I might."

They pushed their chairs back and went across together to the cashier's desk. Outside on the sunny pavement they parted, but he watched her for a moment as she walked off briskly down the street, reflecting that she probably wore that rakish little red hat because it was not black, and she was supposed to be in mourning.

$$*\qquad*\qquad*\qquad*$$

Sitting waiting for her cue to begin, Marty studied the green baize-covered desk before her, thinking how like a lectern it was, and idly toying with the pleasing thought that in a fit of absent-mindedness she might hear the announcer say: "Mrs. Ransom," and, with bent head and folded hands, begin: "Dearly beloved brethren, the Scripture moveth us in sundry places . . ." In a way, she thought, it would hardly be surprising. After all, the rituals of church attendance had been graven on her mind through all her childhood. The memory which was forced, now, to struggle if it wanted to retain the detail of more recent reading, could still produce the Creed, the Absolution and Remission of sins, the Venite, the Te Deum, and sundry Collects with smooth mechanical word-perfection—like a slot-machine producing chew-ing-gum. That echo of prayer, and a chance encounter not fifteen minutes ago, flowed together in a stream which floated her thoughts back to childhood.

In the street just outside she had run into Gerald Avery with a thin, dark-haired girl. She had felt a faint shock when he in-troduced her as Elsa Kay, and during their few minutes' conver-sation she had been forced to analyse her dim reaction of hostility and dismiss it as senseless. Those moments of self-examination had taken her back to 1914, to find it, in her until then unconscious mind, less a year when civilisation collapsed than a year when the bottom fell out of Janet Laughlin's world. She had never known, and could now only guess at the causes of the domestic tragedy

which both she and Gilbert had glimpsed in the Laughlin household. Somehow she had an impression that Scott Laughlin's
failure at the polls in the 1913 election had brought things to a
climax. At all events, it was on her own thirteenth birthday that
Janet, dry-eyed, unemotional, curiously remote, had said to her
almost casually: "Mother's gone away with Mr. Kay."

Marty remembered now that her confusion, her distress, had
amounted almost to a panic. She had been just awakening to the
knowledge of sex as being something more than a tiresome accident
which imposed extra restrictions upon her without, so far as she
could see, offering any compensating advantages. All her life she
had known that while Gilbert might hang upside down from a
tree branch, such behaviour was, for her, indecorous and forbidden. Boys might be noisy, but girls must be quiet. Boys were
not required to set tables, or make beds, but girls must be at all
times dutifully willing for such tasks. When Gilbert tore his
trousers, Mrs. Miller mended them, but a rent in Marty's petticoat
was a matter for her own needle and thread. Gilbert travelled
alone in the train, but Marty must have a companion. Gilbert
and Nick, when they grew up, would become important people,
partners in Father's "business," but she would have to stay at
home still making beds and setting tables. Gilbert and Nick were
the "Sons" on Father's letter-paper; why wasn't it "Walter Massey,
Sons and Daughter"?

All these vague grievances had been, during the last year,
brought forward into her consciousness and reinforced by another.
She was waking up to something, but waking in the dark, and
even the terror of her appeal to Mrs. Miller one dreadful morning
met with nothing but hasty ministrations and evasive answers. No,
she wasn't ill. Of course, she wasn't going to die—don't be silly,
Marty! This was something that just happened. Why? Well—
it's just Nature . . .

Guessing at depths, tides, potentialities in herself, governed by
an obscure power which she did not begin to comprehend, she
was frightened, and hated the cause of her fear. Small wonder,
she reflected now, that when it manifested itself as something that
had hurt and harmed Janet, she should see its whole hatefulness
personified in Denny Laughlin and Jerrold Kay.

How she had hated them! She hated them because they took
her friend from her—at first spiritually, when Janet seemed with-

drawn into a world from which Marty felt herself debarred by shameful, childish ignorance—and then physically, when the furniture went away from the cottage in vans, and Janet, still with her smitten, aloof air, came slipping through the orchard for a good-bye tryst. She hated them because they brought about the end of those precious hours which she and Gilbert and Janet had spent having their writings criticised by a real writer. She hated them because now her father—not in so many words, but with looks, snorts, and oblique references—was able to say: "I told you so!" And somehow, quite without conscious thought on her part, that hatred had transferred itself into a diluted form to the daughter of whose birth she had heard Mrs. Miller speak later to a friend—saying, in a hushed voice, significantly: "Seven months!"

So this was the daughter. How old would she be now? Twenty-six—twenty-seven? A queer-looking girl, badly dressed, rather subdued, or was it that most people seemed subdued when they were set against Gerald Avery's irrepressible liveliness? That one novel of hers, written in the dead-and-alive little Queensland town where she and her mother had lived since Jerrold Kay's death, had been not without merit—and not at all subdued . . .

She heard the announcer say:

"We are now to hear a talk by Mrs. Martha Ransom on 'The Art of Reading.' Mrs. Ransom."

*   *   *   *

Going home in the train she read the evening paper, and, having read it, dropped it on the seat beside her and stared out the window. The obliteration of the old Milson's Point wharf and railway station, to make room for the sweeping concrete curve of the bridge, was one of those facts which still occasionally gave her a slight shock; a scene which continued to live so vividly in the memory remained a real scene, reducing its visible and tangible substitute to the level of an illusion. Going to town had meant for her, in her childhood, crossing the harbour in the ferry, embarking and disembarking at a wharf where an old man with a white beard sat year in and year out, playing on a concertina.

That high, windy sound, plaintive and sweet, was the sound of homecoming, for though Marty disliked the atmosphere of her home she liked its environment, and escape from the city, whose allure had never held her long, meant return to this wharf, meant climbing the ramp with the sound of music diminishing behind her, meant lagging a moment by the window of the fruit and sweet shop, meant sniffing the steam-and-cinders smell of the railway station, and finding the train waiting. It still seemed impossible, in unguarded moments, that all this should be gone, dissolved in the air as though it had been no more substantial than smoke, and that there should no longer be, just around the corner, that steeply sloping street where the trams waited. Swept away, vanished in the dust of demolition, they endured obstinately in her memory as things still existing in all their substance of bricks, mortar and asphalt pavement, hot even through shoes on summer days, and ringing to the hurried tramp of crowds.

Now the electric train, tearing across the bridge, rattled up the gently climbing hills where long ago the steam train had puffed and laboured. One got home from town much faster. Did that matter? In her mood of dejection, she asked herself what all these technical advances were but a stream-lined super-mechanism for making mistakes more quickly, being stupid on a larger scale, doing evil more efficiently, and telling lies to a greater number of people at a given time.

Now they were past the lower suburbs where brick bungalows, square, like boxes, stood ranked in endless rows, facing pavements on to which the formal trees, pruned to the shape of dish-mops, spilled dark discs of shade. Now they were coming into that pleasanter realm where the gum-tree, at last belatedly discovered, had been spared—and even planted; its steely leaves flickered among greener and darker foliage like polished coins. Here houses had been built singly by those who were to inhabit them, instead of in batches by contractors seeing them as investment. They stood quiet in gardens, their walls a cool cream instead of a hot red, surrounded by gay flower-beds, and tempting, shadow-striped grass. Marty looked at them sourly. A lifetime lived "up the line" had made her familiar with the average life lived in those pretty homes. An existence innocent enough, in that it did no harm, or did it unwittingly—but guilty in that it did no good. Pleasant people, kindly people, tending their gardens, caring conscientiously for their children, going soberly to and fro between home and office, playing golf on Sundays, giving each other tea-parties, bridge-parties—organising bazaars for charity—undoubtedly pleasant people. Going to concerts, subscribing to lending libraries, visiting art shows. People honestly, yes, quite honestly—

looking for culture and feeling about for enlargement of their minds. Marty had sat at their bridge tables, sipped tea in their drawing-rooms, bought gay aprons and embroidered kettle-holders at their bazaar stalls. She knew them. She knew they believed that the books they brought home from their libraries, the symphonies to which they listened, the pictures they stared at, would, without effort to themselves, make them all that they desired to be. I suppose, she thought dejectedly, that when they eat a meal they forget how much hard work their stomachs have to put in before it's any use to them. Let us "do," they said; "let us "go," let us "make," let us "look," "listen," "read." But let us "think"? Oh, no; oh, dear me, no! For who knows where thinking, once begun, will end? May it not sweep you out of your pleasant life into one hard and unfamiliar? May it not set the firm ground beneath your feet rocking? May it not suggest, and finally prove (as it had proved to herself and her brothers) that you have won your own serenity at the cost of someone else's? Can pleasant people, kindly people, be expected to endure such thoughts?

The train stopped at her own station. She gathered her parcels together and stepped out on to the platform, admitting wryly that it was no wonder her neighbours seemed to find her increasingly "difficult," increasingly prickly. "No one," she thought, "could accuse me of being a pleasant person."

VI

IT was not ten o'clock when Gilbert came down in the lift with Paul French and Elsa Kay and a round little man, with a foreign accent, whose name he did not know. He felt to-night as he usually felt on the rare occasions when he attended these meetings of the Writers' Guild—slightly depressed, slightly exasperated, and more than slightly critical of himself and his unhappy inability to mix. Some time during the evening, someone had mentioned Joseph Conrad, and his feeling of isolation had found expression in a remembered passage which ran through his head during the rest of the proceedings: "Woe to the man who has not learned while young to laugh, to hope, and to put his trust in life." He had never learned that, and a world in chaos was hardly a good classroom for learning it now. There had been talk of a memorial plaque to be set up to the memory of a dead poet, and he had found himself thinking irritably: "Good God, aren't there his poems? What other memorial does he need?" There had been a proposal to hold regular weekly meetings at which members could discuss "matters of literary interest." With supper at one shilling. There had been an announcement of a short story competition with a prize of ten pounds. There had been satisfaction expressed at the number of new members enrolled. It had taken nearly two hours, and the room was cold.

It was not until he was about to leave that he had become involved with a small group also edging towards the door, and someone had introduced him to Elsa Kay. He looked at her with interest. A nervy sort of person, he decided; restless, one of those people whose quietness does not succeed in concealing tension. She reminded him of a stray cat, thin and wary, with a sort of watchful hunger in her dark eyes. He wondered if she would, like a cat, grow sleek and contented in a safe domestic atmosphere, and decided that she might. He had read her first novel a few years ago when it came out; he remembered that he had found it amusing in a sharp, pungent way, but that he had felt it in the sour flavour of a grudge. He had decided that it came from a mind obsessed by some sort of frustration. He asked as they walked from the lift to the street door:

"Are you working on anything new, Miss Kay?"

She answered briefly without looking at him:

"Only in my head."

Paul French struck in:

"Is anybody getting anything down on paper? Except frantic articles about Democracy and the New Order, God help us!" A sharp glance from Elsa at his fair, schoolboyish face intercepted a faintly startled glance from Gilbert in the same direction. There was a moment's pause, and then she smiled rather maliciously.

"You too, Mr. Massey?"

He felt that he looked sheepish, and was annoyed. She added, pulling on her gloves: "Paul's at it, and Max Brown's at it, and Evelyn Hilliard's at it—and so are you, it appears?"

"Gerald Avery," said French, "is writing a play. It's about himself:

Gilbert asked curiously:

"About himself?"

"Yes—it's a comedy. He's calling it 'Subversive Mr. Avery.' It appears that all the other tenants in his flats complained to the landlord because his friends went to see him carrying copies of the illegal *Tribune* and books with red covers. And he says he got some marvellous material when the police raided him last year. So he's writing this play, and he's going to send all the other tenants complimentary tickets for the opening night."

Elsa said with a laugh:

"I'll buy one myself."

The round little man announced gravely:

"And I, too."

Gilbert said nothing. He had been visiting Gerald on that night last year when the Law invaded his flat, and though he admitted that Gerald had contrived to make it good comedy at the time, and would, no doubt, make it even better on paper, it still remained tragedy to him. The police had found nothing, and they could hardly have been expected to connect his own still bandaged hand with that fact. Some streak of obstinate pride had prevented him from burying his own books along with Gerald's and little Tom Brady's. By keeping them where they belonged on his shelves he had seemed to himself to be defying the mediævalism of political persecution; but he had been bound to admit that it was less likely to descend on himself than on poor

Tom, scratching a living with pick and shovel—or even on Gerald, scratching one hardly less precarious with a journalistic pen.

It had been, he remembered, about eleven o'clock when his host, rising to answer a ring at the door-bell, had found two policemen—a sergeant and a young constable—standing bulkily on his threshold. Gerald had, of course, immediately spread his veil of comedy over the whole ugly business. No sooner had they made it known, with irreproachable civility, that they had come to search his flat for subversive literature, than he had swung gaily into his rôle: hospitality and willing co-operation were his line.

"Ah!" he had cried. "The Gestapo! Come in, come in!" He flung the door open with such abandon that it cracked on its hinges. "Here they are," he had continued, ushering them assiduously across the room to his shelves. "You'll forgive me if I can't be very helpful—our ideas of subversiveness are probably so different. . ." For a long moment there had been an awkward pause while he stood with his head on one side observing his visitors baffled contemplation of some thousand books. They were both, Gilbert had realised, watching from his armchair, embarrassed; he noted it as a healthy sign that they did not take kindly to this unsavoury job. A slow tide of colour which had dyed the younger man's cheeks from the utterance of the word "Gestapo," had now reached his ears. They were all Gilbert could see of him, but they were large and protruding, and they flamed like a sunset.

"Politics?" Gerald enquired tentatively. "Sociology, perhaps? Economics? I'm afraid there isn't much. Mind you," he added, "there are some pretty hot passages in the Bible. Things like 'the love of money is the root of all evil,' and that bit about it being easier for a camel to go through the eye of a needle than for a capitalist to enter into the kingdom of God."

The sergeant looked at him with an expressionless, boiled eye, and said heavily:

"Rich man, wasn't it?"

"Well," Gerald conceded handsomely, "you may be right. But after all, what's the difference?"

The sergeant recited stolidly:

"We have instructions to search for books advocating doctrines prejudicial to the efficient conduct of the war."

Gerald achieved the expression of a draper regretting his inability to supply the required suspenders.

"You know," he said apologetically, "I simply haven't any of those. My own feeling is all for more efficiency in that direction. But," he added encouragingly, "you just look around, and you may find some to suit you. You'll excuse me, won't you, if I finish my beer? May I pour you a glass?"

The sergeant declined. The young policeman stared unhappily at a row of Thackeray in gilt bindings. The sergeant, bending bulkily to read titles, moved slowly along the shelves. He passed by an abridged edition of *Mein Kampf*, and hesitated long over a highly orthodox volume on economics. He brooded for a moment or two over *The Wealth of Nations*, pulled it at last, silently, from the shelf, and handed it to his offsider. Encouraged by this first kill, he reached too hastily for another book and passed it over, murmuring with an oblique glance of triumph at Gerald:

"Political Works of Shelley . . ."

"Poetical," corrected Gerald gently.

The sergeant snatched it back, examined its cover, opened it mistrustfully, read a line or two of "The Revolt of Islam," with deep suspicion, and replaced it on the shelf with a faint sigh. Gerald returned to his armchair, winked at Gilbert, and lit a cigarette. The young policeman, embarrassed by his own inactivity, reached tentatively towards a solid-looking volume which bore on its spine the title *Dialectics*. Gerald glanced at Gilbert and closed his eyes; for a moment the fate of one book they had overlooked hung in the balance. But the sergeant, moving crabwise towards his subordinate, brushed the hovering paw away reprovingly. "Not that," he admonished, and added explanatorily: "Food". The young policeman blushed redder than ever. Gerald choked, recovered, and called cheerfully:

"Having any luck?"

The sergeant turned ponderously, produced a notebook and thumbed its pages; this, he had found, was a bit of business which often overawed people who showed signs of getting fresh. But when he looked up at last to observe results, the young man was holding a match for his friend's cigarette, and seemed quite unaware of him.

"We have information," he said, "that you are a member of an organisation known as the 'Left Book Club.' "

[102]

Gerald said protestingly:

"Look here, excuse my mentioning it, but I'm a writer, and I hate redundancy. Suppose I were to say that I understood you were a member of an organisation known as the Police Force? You see what I mean?"

The sergeant inquired with monumental patience:

"Are you a member of the Left Book Club?"

Gerald beamed at him.

"There, you see? That's the perfect sentence. No ambiguity, economy of words. Yes, I am. Or, even better—yes."

The sergeant wrote in his notebook, and proceeded woodenly:

"Where do you keep the books you procure from the organisa— from the Left Book Club?"

Gerald tapped his forehead and smiled disarmingly.

"Here."

The sergeant digested this in silence for two whole minutes. Then he asked:

"Where do you keep the books themselves?"

"Aha!" said Gerald playfully.

The sergeant, too, Gilbert noticed, was becoming slightly red, but he maintained an admirable calm. He said coldly:

"We shall have to search the rest of the flat." Gerald waved hospitably at the opposite door.

"Go right ahead, my dear chap. There's only one bedroom and the bathroom. I eat downstairs."

He and Gilbert had finished their beer and smoked two more cigarettes before the Law emerged from the inner rooms, empty-handed.

"Nothing?" Gerald asked sympathetically. "Well, how about a glass of beer now to wash the kapok out of your mouths? I really must get a new mattress before you call again. Well, I'm sorry you won't help us finish the bottle." He conducted them to the door. The sergeant said correctly:

"Sorry to have troubled you, Mr. Avery."

"Not a bit!" Gerald reassured him sincerely. "Look in again, and smoke a pipe with me some evening."

Returning to the chair, he said reflectively:

"Decent fellows, you know." He splashed an inch or two of beer into their glasses. "Come on, Gilbert, cheer up! Here's to Democracy!" And suddenly he was doubled up with laughter.

*   *   *   *

Gilbert, remembering it, admitted to himself that there were gaps in his sense of humour. He hadn't found it funny. He had been conscious all the time of this democracy as a fraying rope, snapping strand by strand as they all hung on it over a precipice. And, curiously enough, his main concern had been for the policemen themselves. Decent fellows, Gerald had said. But what happened to the decency of fellows whose minds had never been trained to liberal, analytical thinking, whose education had denied them access to culture, but who had been for years sub' jected to a discipline which left them with no standard of be' haviour save to "obey orders"? In the moment when those orders violated their sense of decency, what was there to save them if they could not save themselves? And how many were there among them who, from long dealings with the dispossessed dregs of society, had acquired a mentality which only awaited the sanc' tion of authority to express itself in terms of the truncheon and the jackboot? He had been very conscious, that night, watching the tragi'comedy from his armchair, that here, as in other lands, such authority could rise. He knew also that such raids had not always been so "decently" conducted. . . .

They came out into the Neon'lit glare of the Friday night shop' ping crowds in King Street, and paused for farewells. Paul French, grabbing at a passing newsboy, called over his shoulder:

"Good night, Elsa. Good night, Massey. Are you coming, Werner?"

The little man with the foreign accent shook hands cere' moniously.

"I have enjoyed your books, Mr. Massey. Already before I left Austria I have read one, and I am eager that you should write again."

To Gilbert's relief—for he was inept at answering compliments —he was given no time to reply. A formal little bow was dis' tributed between himself and Elsa, light flashed on the crown of a bald head, and they were left alone. He asked politely:

"Which way do you go, Miss Kay?"

"I'm at Kirribilli just at present."

Resignedly he asked:

"Can I give you a lift, then? I live up the line, and my car's parked in Clarence Street."

"Thank you," she said sedately.

They crossed George Street, and set off along the comparatively uncrowded footpaths. Marty had told him of her encounter with this young woman, and glancing down at her as they walked he remembered his sister's description—"a predatory waif." It was not without its aptness, he thought. A small-boned creature, thin, and rather pale. But, on the edge of feeling sorry for her, you were baulked by a feeling that she was not defenceless, and became curious about her instead. A writer who did believe in "perfect moments" for beginning a story, he reflected, might well embark on hers with that scene which he himself had witnessed so many years ago. It remained in his memory, he found, like a tableau on a brightly lit stage—Denny Laughlin looking desperately round the room, Jerrold Kay staring fixedly at his beer, Denny's husband lifting startled eyes from his sheets of music, and himself, a panic-stricken adolescent, thinking only how to escape from a room still ringing with the echoes of Beethoven, and burdened with the mystery of adult emotions. He had recognised it, even at fourteen, as a pregnant moment—and here at his side walked its offspring. His curiosity became suddenly acute, and he yielded to an impulse.

"How about a cup of coffee? Those meetings make me thirsty."

"That would be very nice."

A prim little piece, he thought, and felt puzzled because he did not really believe she was prim. Already half regretting his invitation, he said:

"There's a place just across the road a little further up."

She said:

"I met your sister the other day."

"Yes, she told me."

"You have a brother, too, haven't you?" It was not a question, but a statement. "Is he a writer, too?"

"He writes articles and pamphlets and things of that kind."

They crossed the street and went down a flight of steps between under-nourished dwarfed cypresses in blue tubs into a basement room full of tables, and dim with yellow lights through a blue haze of cigarette smoke. At the far end of it, on a low dais, sitting slackly in their chairs, moving their hands automatically over their instruments, and staring blankly in front of them, two men and a girl were making mechanical, hypnotic music on a violin, a piano and a 'cello.

Elsa made for an unoccupied table at the far end of the room. Over its blue cloth and its vase of half-opened iceland poppies he stole a few glances at her face. It was by no means beautiful; he did not even think it pretty, but he studied it with interest because it was at once so like and so unlike the face of her father, whom he had seen only once, but whom he still remembered with surprising clarity. Her mouth, like Jerrold Kay's, was well-shaped, with a full underlip, but unlike his it looked tight, and had a restless twitch. Her eyes, bright and opaque, reminded Gilbert vividly of a stare which had once disconcerted him, of a voice saying blandly: "Well, what did you think? Pretty ragged, wasn't it?" Her cheeks were hollow, her heavy eyebrows black and arched— and yet, in spite of these definite, and even arresting features, her face remained unremarkable, without accent, without animation. He felt himself staring, looked awkwardly away, and then, helplessly, back again. Perhaps it was this very emptiness which was intriguing. His mind struggled for a word or a phrase to describe that emptiness. Impassive? Not with that tense, nervous mouth. Detached? Not with those restless, unrevealing eyes. Negative? Yes, he was getting warmer, but that wasn't all. *Stubbornly* negative, he thought suddenly. It was not emptiness, but concealment. You saw nothing because she was hiding—whatever there was. With this thought he became more curious than ever; it roused the novelist in him like a challenge. He looked from her face to her clothes, searching for a clue. Didn't all women have a technique of dressing which expressed them? In Phyllis a desire for frills and ribbons fought a losing battle against her belief that dowdiness was a sign of virtue. Marty sometimes enlivened a gift for austere elegance with spirited audacities and sometimes betrayed it, in sheer absent-mindedness, with surprising blunders. Virginia knew that her own beauty could dominate any extravagance of style or colouring, and used flamboyance merely as an extension of her self-confidence. Prue enjoyed pretty clothes like a child, and like a child became unconscious of them ten minutes after she had put them on. What the devil did this girl's clothes suggest? They hovered oddly between the drab and the picturesque. Her thick coat was a muddy brown, and badly cut, but it had a very broad patent leather belt of bright scarlet, and she wore a red and green scarf with a certain insouciance. She had pretty, slender legs, sheathed in good silk stockings, but her shoes were old, and had not been polished that day. Her black, thick hair stood out round her head in a rather untidy bush, but her small hands were carefully manicured, their nails vivid with scarlet lacquer. She wore a diamond engagement ring. She looked up at him from the handbag in which she had been rummaging, and he asked hastily:

"What will you have?"

She replied in her composed, reticent way:

"Coffee, please, and sandwiches. I didn't have any dinner, and I'm hungry."

It was, surprisingly, on the tip of his tongue to say: "I know you are." She had given him the adjective he had been searching for. She *looked* hungry. She had what he supposed spiritualists might call an "aura," and it was not a comfortable one. He produced cigarettes, and asked, holding a light for her:

"Do you often go to these meetings?"

"Mostly."

"Do you think," he went on, feeling for words, "that they—help, in any way?"

She looked at him, and again he recognised Jerrold Kay's noncommittal, observant eyes.

"Help," she repeated. "How? And who?"

"Help anyone. To write. To have what they write published. I suppose actually what I mean is do they serve in any way whatever to encourage or advance the production of literature?"

He spoke the last sentence rather sharply, conscious of a return of his irritated mood. She said:

"Oh, yes, I think so. I think people need that kind of thing to give them—what shall I say?—faith in the importance of what they're trying to do."

He stared at her.

"Are you serious?"

"Yes—why not?" Finding him still frowning at her, she went on:

"There isn't much else, is there? I mean in the way of extraneous support. Even in peace-time the writer is apt to be regarded by the bulk of the population—if he's regarded at all—as a sort of entertainer. A passer of idle moments. So that in wartime, when there aren't officially supposed to be any idle moments, he becomes almost an object of contempt. What's called an "ineffective." So perhaps getting together with a lot of other writers is a comfort to him."

He was still puzzled.

"Does it have that effect on you?"

She shrugged.

"To some extent, I suppose."

He looked so obviously bewildered that she asked dryly.

"You don't agree?"

He said uncertainly:

"I never felt—myself—any need for that kind of support."

She blew a cloud of smoke up towards the light, and asked with an inflection which made him feel that she did not believe him:

"Why do you go, then?"

He frowned.

"I don't as a rule. But I always have an uneasy feeling that there *may* be something in it—even if one doesn't feel the need oneself—some germ of a—a movement, a unifying and strengthening process that one doesn't want to—well, to stand aloof from. I've expressed it badly. Here's our coffee."

She drew the cups towards her.

"Sugar? Well, perhaps there is that, don't you think? In my own case, of course, there's another motive as well. I just like a little human company now and then."

"Oh!" He felt rather nonplussed. "Do you live alone, then?"

She answered that she did, and volunteered no further information. He took a sandwich from the plate and tried another conversational opening.

"I used to know your mother years ago, when I was a schoolboy."

"I know," she said calmly. "She used to speak of you and your family. She was very interested in your writing. I think *Thunder Brewing* was the last book she read." And suddenly she added, looking straight at him: "I've been curious about you for the last few years."

"Oh?" Now that he met her eyes he realised that her habit of speaking without looking at the person she was addressing made her occasional direct stares disconcerting.

"How many books have you published altogether?"

He did a rapid mental calculation.

"Seven novels, and a book of short stories, and a collection of verse, which tactful people don't mention nowadays. Why?"

"I was wondering if I had read everything. I haven't read the short stories or the verse. Was *Excursion Trip* your first?"

"Yes."

"How long ago did you write that?"

He reflected.

"Well, it must have been fourteen years ago. It was published just before Pete—my son—was born, and he's thirteen."

"What do you think of it now?"

"Now?" He laughed. "I haven't looked at it for at least ten years, but my impression is that it must be pretty awful. What do you think?"

"I thought it was pretty awful myself."

He felt slightly nettled, not by her dislike of the book, but by the casual, offhand decision with which she announced it. He said with an attempt at lightness:

"Show me the writer who has no skeleton in his cupboard. But did you say you had read *all* my novels?"

"Yes."

He asked point-blank: "Why?" and felt that she curled up and shrank like a snail when it is touched. She countered sulkily:

"Why not?"

He had an impression that she was unfairly trying to escape from a subject which she had herself introduced, and it made him obstinate.

"I asked you why. I don't believe it was because you liked them." He felt surprisingly sure on this point, and her evasive glance told him he was right. "What interested you then? Enough to make you seek out seven novels by one writer?"

She replied, speaking so slowly and carefully that he knew she was inventing:

"I was interested in your developing point of view . . ."

"Wait a bit," he interrupted ruthlessly. "Did you read them in order?"

"Yes, I read the first four all in a bunch."

"How old were you then?"

"Oh, I suppose about seventeen."

He looked at her grimly. He had an intelligent daughter of his own; he measured her against Prue in his mind, and was able to tell himself without hesitation that at seventeen she had not read four successive novels for the sake of a critical estimate of their writer's developing point of view, but he only said: "Well—go on."

She was glib and hostile.

"There was an impression of someone getting older and wiser that can be taken for granted. But I felt that it was being a—painful process. That was what made me curious. You see I had formed an impression of you as a successful person—a secure, contented, well-fed, well-housed person, socially respectable and respected."

He contemplated this portrait of himself for a moment in a startled silence. Of course, there was malice in it; she had been deliberately spiteful, paying him out for having bullied her, for having cut off a retreat which, for some reason, she wanted. It was a true enough answer she had given, perhaps, but she had made it untrue by transposing it in time; she had not formed that impression while she read, but after she had read—quite recently. And he had asked why she read at all. Well, evidently she was not going to tell him, and he pushed the puzzle to the back of his mind and considered her estimate of him, in which, despite malice, he still felt enough truth to be uncomfortable. Successful? His books had all been published, and had sold reasonably well. Secure? If she meant financially secure that must be passed as correct; always enough money—not riches, but comfort. Contented . . . ?

That, of course, was the point of departure into that painfulness which the girl had recognised. Contentment had forsaken him long ago. Of course, that was painful, and, of course, if you wrote, that painfulness showed through. He said rather sharply:

"You don't expect the writing of a man of forty to be—as care-free as when he was thirty. Especially when the intervening years have been anything but conducive to contentment."

"Yes, yes, I know." She spoke impatiently. "I only wondered why—and how—it had come to touch you so sharply. I mean, your kind of life is usually the last to be touched. Mother used to tell me about you and your family—all shut up—and isolated in a kind of world-proof life . . ."

He interrupted quite angrily:

"Nonsense! No life is world-proof now."

"But yours *was*," she insisted. "How did you get out of it? Did you fall, or were you pushed?"

Still incomprehensibly irritated with her, he decided that he was not going to withold his tribute to Scott Laughlin because of any personal embarrassment that name might cause her. In the next moment he recognised that thought as one inspired by some rem-nant of his own conventional upbringing. Why should she be embarrassed, after all?

"The person who did most to get me out of it," he said, "was your mother's first husband, Scott Laughlin."

She looked up quickly: her eyes met his for a moment, and slid away.

"Really? Did he? Tell me about it."

Tell her about it? How on earth, he wondered, could he make this girl understand the atmosphere in which he had grown up? How could she realise the almost feverish excitement he had felt, at fifteen, in finding a companion with whom writing could be discussed as a sane and normal occupation? Could he describe how his first agonised shyness in showing his poems had dwindled and vanished before Laughlin's matter-of-fact criticism? Could she conceive an environment which had never allowed one to forget guilt? In which, if one were not actually guilty of anything at the moment, the chances were that one would be shortly? Could she understand how inevitable it was that in such circumstances any new, strange impulse in oneself became suspect; that, when he had found himself driven to covering pages of his exercise books with strange combinations and arrangements of words which he would never have used in his daily life, the feeling that he was doing something very abnormal and (even worse) very silly, had filled him with tormenting confusion and anxiety?

Not only to himself, but to Marty, secrecy had become a habit. They had concealed and concealed, even from each other. So that it had been left to Scott Laughlin to disclose to him that his sister also inhabited, in secret, his own secret world.

"This isn't bad," he had said, frowning over one of Gilbert's laboriously hand-written stories. "It's queer how utterly different your style is from your sister's."

"My—my sister's . . . ?"

Blank amazement. Did Marty "write things," too? Even the

heady discovery that he had a "style" was overwhelmed by this astounding revelation.

He knew now, of course, that Laughlin's casual, seemingly accidental remark had been his way of throwing open a door too long closed. He was saying: "Get together, you floundering, lonely young idiots!"

"Yes," he had continued in his detached, judicial tone, "Marty's line is quite different. I don't think she'll ever do more than some competent rhyming, but she'll probably develop a lively prose style some day. Of course," he had added gravely, "she's younger than you, so it's natural that your writing should have more—maturity."

Looking down at his coffee cup now, thirty years later, Gilbert remembered that word "maturity" and smiled. He had been still afraid of his writing—still tentative and apologetic. The word "maturity" had been adroitly used. He had not realised with what tact and skill Laughlin had built up his confidence in himself until, in adulthood, he had come across a remnant or two of the writing of his adolescent period, and found its crudity and its pathetic awkwardness almost unbelievable. Nor, he suspected, had Laughlin failed to realise that Gilbert as a writer and Gilbert as a human being were one and indivisible. The word "maturity" had affected not only his relation to his writing, but his relation to his father. He had awakened with a throb of triumph to the knowledge that he was now beyond coercion, and his father knew it.

He said at last to the girl watching him across the table:

"He just took us seriously. I don't know why I say 'just'; it was a superhuman feat of patience and understanding. He took our crude rubbish and really criticised it. His daughter, Janet— your half-sister, of course—and Marty and I took to having regular weekly sessions with him. Under the rose, as it were, because our father didn't approve of him. Actually it was under a certain large gum-tree by the road, half-a-mile or so from his house, where we all 'happened' to meet every Thursday afternoon."

She said briskly:

"I never knew him, of course, except from hearing mother speak of him. She made a bad mistake, you know, in leaving him for my father. She admitted it afterwards. She felt bad, too, about Janet." She looked at him again in her sudden way, and he was momentarily startled by something like a flash of avidity in her eyes. "Tell me about Janet," she said.

Slightly confused by the discovery that when he did, for a second, see beyond the surface of those eyes, he learned no more of her but was, rather, increasingly bewildered, he searched back among his memories, and began uncertainly:

"I rather think she wrote better than any of us. Technically, anyhow." He smiled. "Sometimes Marty and I were jealous of her."

Her eyes were as unrevealing again as black jet, and her mouth looked almost puckered in its close control. Gilbert found that, now he had uncovered them, his memories of those roadside classes were vivid, and unexpectedly poignant. There had been moments of intoxicating pride when one's own "thing" was acclaimed as good; moments of cataclysmic despair when Laughlin said: "Oh, God, no, Gilbert, this won't do at all!" Moments of unhappy resentment when Marty's "thing" was better than his, or Janet's obviously best of all. And yet everything had added up to a new impetus for living, a new motive, a new purpose. . . .

"He used to manage us very cleverly," he told Elsa, "by analys-ing our several qualities. He insisted that I had something Marty lacked, and Marty expressed something Janet missed, and Janet used her words in a more workmanlike way than we did—and so on. He drummed self-respect into us."

He saw Laughlin sitting on a fallen log with his elbows on his knees, his toes turned in, his pipe in his mouth, and sheaves of paper in his hands. Gilbert's writing, he proclaimed, had "body"; it had substance and solidity, but he was too conventional, as yet, in his approach. Marty was vehement and explosive; the violence with which she felt her ideas led her into over-emphasis, and even into vituperation. "Being angry, Marty," he said, "is all right, but being abusive is silly." Gilbert must loosen up a bit, but Marty must learn literary self-control. Janet put words together as if she were building houses of cards—delicately, gingerly, so that one read her sentences with a feeling of astonishment that they did just support each other in some kind of frail, precarious sense. "Matter first, my girl," he used to say to her, tapping her paper sternly with the stem of his pipe, "and manner afterwards."

He heard Elsa saying:

"I don't think Janet would ever have done anything much, even

[113]

if she had lived. That smooth, polished style of hers—too remote, surely, to express modern trends and problems. Almost academic."

He looked at her in surprise, not at her words, but at the strength of the impression they made on him. And yet, strong as it was, it was elusive. There was something behind what she said—something acid and purposefully destructive; there was some resentment, perhaps, some unacknowledged hurt . . . ?

He said slowly:

"I always admired her writing very much—especially what she did in the last few years before she died. It was—deliberate, I suppose, in style. Measured and carefully constructed. Nothing slipshod about it. But there was nothing slipshod about Janet herself, I should think, though I never saw her after she was about fifteen. She had a sort of integrity and balance."

His own words gave him his first moment of illumination, and he thought, looking at her: "Which you haven't got, young woman!"

She made her characteristic shrugging movement.

"A matter of opinion, I suppose. You know I think Scott Laughlin had something to do with my being a writer, too. My own father died, you know, only a few years after I was born. I grew up on mother's stories about her first husband and her first home, and she had a lot of cuttings of things he wrote . . . what are you looking so black about?"

"I was thinking," Gilbert said painfully, "that all the thanks he got from me was that I allowed myself to be told he was a traitor. He went to gaol, you know, during the last war."

"I know. Mother used to tell me about that."

"He'd gone over to the West after—after your mother left him, and he took on the editorship of a little Labour paper. I don't know what charge they got him on—something comparable to our own modern 'conduct prejudicial to the efficient prosecution of the war,' I suppose. I was in France when I heard of it. And I was still as innocent of politics as a new-born babe. I was shocked—and disillusioned." He made an angry gesture. "Disillusioned! Well——" He poured himself another cup of coffee. "I've lost a lot of illusions since then, but at least . . ."

He broke off abruptly and changed the subject.

"That's all ancient history. But it answers your question, doesn't it?"

"Only partly." She looked at him curiously. "I still wonder why there's been nothing since *Thunder Brewing*. In that you seemed to be getting ready for something. I thought it read as if it were going to be the beginning of a flood. As if you had discovered a gold-mine to exploit. And then—nothing!"

He moved restlessly. It had been as obvious as that, had it? For he could not bring himself to believe that this was a young woman of any peculiar perceptiveness. What he had imagined to be his own private problem was matter for anyone's recognition and curiosity. She asked insistently:

"Are you *doing* anything? There does seem to be a sort of creative paralysis abroad. It's true what Paul was saying—we aren't getting things *done*."

He asked, looking curiously at her:

"Are you stuck, too?"

Again her self-possession seemed to crack, and again she took refuge in sulkiness.

"Oh, yes, I'm stuck."

Trying to probe her, to find any depths at all, he asked:

"Do you think it really matters if we're all stuck?"

She replied dryly:

"It matters to me all right. I don't like living on my meagre salary."

"That wasn't what I meant." He wondered why she was pretending to misunderstand him, and what instinct made her flinch from the exposure of anything but the surface of her mind. She lit another cigarette and admitted:

"I know it wasn't. I don't know if it matters or not. What do you think?"

He answered heavily:

"Of course it matters. It's a job—even if it isn't recognised as one. We're allowing ourselves to be—deflected."

She said suddenly and despairingly:

"I can't do anything—not anything at all!"

He was startled. Counting the stubs in the ash-tray, he realised that she had smoked three cigarettes to his one, and that there was a faint but definite and continuous tremor in the hand that lifted her coffee cup. He remembered his own thoughts as he drove down from the mountains a couple of months ago; his own reassurance to himself that the young ones, at least, would remain

[115]

active. He had a momentary guilty memory, too, of his own desk at home. How bare and barren and tidy its lying top! And in its drawers the piled chaos of four years' unproductive effort—the notes, the half-recorded ideas, the slender sheaves of a dozen abortive beginnings. Mute evidence of defeat, of what she had called 'creative paralysis.' How many desks, like that, he wondered, all over the tormented world?

For the first time he felt sorry for her, and said kindly:

"Well, you're young. There's plenty of time. The war . . ."

"The war!" She made an impatient movement. "The war's only a bit of life, it's only a mass of material. Writers ought to be able to fall on it and use it!"

He objected irritably:

"You talk as if writers weren't human beings, units of a community. The war falls on them as it does on everything else. I know. I've been guilty of scraps, too. What was it French called them . . . ? Frantic articles about Democracy and the New Order. Scraps are no good in themselves, but if they're there, clamouring, you have to get them out of your system before you can do anything that has direction and coherence . . ."

Suddenly he saw that she was not really interested. This problem —all problems, perhaps—were not general to her, but personal, and he was tired of trying to guess at the machinery of a personality which did not greatly appeal to him. He became moodily silent, and she asked at last:

"What happened to your gold-mine, anyhow?"

"Gold-mine?"

"The one I thought you seemed to have discovered."

"You can't work a gold-mine without some sort of technical knowledge." He felt, and sounded, depressed. "I was deplorably uneducated. Your generation was born into strife and insecurity, so though your formal education hasn't been much more help to you than ours was to us, you've had the advantage of growing up —with the jungle mentality, let us say. Alert, and suspicious, and always conscious of danger. You couldn't understand how naïve we were, how smug, how colossally ignorant. How much accumulated mental rubbish we had to get rid of before we could learn to think . . ." He paused, looking back at himself with wonder, and admitted: "I used to think of slums, for instance, as one problem, and juvenile delinquency as another, and ignorance as a third, and war as a fourth, and so on. When I did at last realise that I had a jig-saw puzzle on my hands—well, I had to stop writing and start learning instead . . ."

"So you've been piecing things together . . . ?"

He wondered with some annoyance why he had talked so much. She was not, he reflected, a sympathetic sort of person at all; her dark, concealing eyes held, indeed, some sort of hostility which included him even if he did not directly inspire it, and he was glad when she looked at her watch and said briskly:

"Well, thanks for the coffee. Shall we go now? I have to be up early in the morning."

They crossed the room together. She watched him as he paid the bill, just as she had watched him at the meeting while he sat with his hands in his pockets and his pipe in his mouth, looking bored. She had felt a faint antagonism then because she had construed his boredom as superciliousness, and she found it curiously pleasant to find that he was not quite as invulnerable as he looked.

VII

As he opened the front door with his latchkey, he was met by a
stench of burning sugar. Phyllis called from the kitchen:

"Is that you, Gilbert?"

"Yes." He went along the passage and stood in the doorway,
looking through a pungent-smelling smoke at his wife, distractedly
skimming a scummy froth from the top of a huge preserving-pan
of jam. She wore an apron over a frock whose colour rather
distressingly matched the mauvish-pink flush of her hot cheeks,
and bedroom slippers on her feet. The sink was littered with
sticky saucepans, spoons and saucers; a row of glass jars containing
an opaque yellow-brown substance stood on the window-sill, and
another row, empty, on sheets of newspaper on the table. Phyllis
greeted him over her shoulder, pushing back wisps of hair with
her forearm, her eyes harassed behind steam-dimmed spectacles.

"It won't set properly," she complained. "I've been at it all
the afternoon, and again ever since dinner. The recipe must be
all wrong—I put *exactly* the amount of water it said. That's the
first batch over there, and I don't believe this is going to be any
better."

He looked at the mess with an irritation amounting to rage. He
had been telling her for the past ten years that she need not make
jam. She need not make cakes. She need not make clothes. All
these things, he urged, they could afford to buy. He had so far
refrained from telling her that indeed the ready-made product
would be far cheaper than her continual and costly failures, but he
felt the words hovering on his tongue to-night. He shut his lips
over them and asked:

"Where's Dulcie? Why don't you get her to help you?"

"Friday," she said tartly, "is her day out; you ought to know
that by now."

Well, perhaps he ought. He forced himself to realise that all
this jam-making was part of her idea of model wifehood. He
could admit quite sincerely that whatever her efforts towards
making a success of their marriage had lacked in imagination they
had been heroic in their stubborn persistence. She asked coldly:

"I suppose you had dinner in town?"

"Yes—with Nick. I told you I was going to a Writers' Guild meeting. Where are the children?"

"Pete's in bed, of course. Long ago. The girls went to the pictures." There was a silence while she skimmed, and then she said in a different voice—the voice of one trying to be amiable: "Did you have a good meeting?"

He made an effort to respond.

"Oh, not bad. Not very many there. I met Elsa Kay—you remember?"

She looked up from the stove with quick interest.

"Kay? You mean the daughter of that woman who used to live down at the bottom of the road when we were children? The one who ran away with the artist?"

"Yes—Jerrold Kay. We had Elsa Kay's book in the house— you read it, didn't you?"

"Yes." She sounded defensive again now, as she had learned to do when she spoke to her husband of books. "I didn't like it. I thought it was hard and sarcastic."

"Oh, well . . ." Gilbert did not want to argue about that. "She seems a nice enough sort of girl. She had a cup of coffee with me afterwards:

Phyllis skimmed for a few moments, and then asked:

"What's she like?"

Her husband's brows contracted. He had spent an hour trying to find out, and now while he searched for an answer his mind was blank. He said vaguely:

"She seemed—intelligent."

"I mean to look at."

"Oh!" He felt inclined to quote Marty, but he knew that "predatory waif" would convey nothing to Phyllis. "I hardly know. Dark, and thin . . ." Suddenly he remembered her clearly —black eyes and hair, white face, scarlet lips and fingernails— scarf flaunting the gay colours of a mountain parrot. The word "vivid" shot into his mind, but he decided not to say it. He thought of her diamond ring, and mentioned that instead. "She was wearing an engagement ring."

"Who's she engaged to?" Phyllis asked.

"I don't know—I didn't ask her. Are you ready to wash those things yet?"

"No." Suddenly she was snappish again. As if he could look inside her head and see her brain working, he knew that she was resenting his offer of eleventh-hour assistance. She had been working while everyone else amused themselves, and she was not going to be deprived of the dregs of her martyrdom. He turned abruptly, went up the hall to the drawing-room and switched on the light, furious with her because she had provided him with an excuse for evading so detestable a task, and furious with himself for grabbing it so promptly.

He sat down in the armchair by the fireplace and put a few sticks on the dying fire. He got out his glasses, lit his pipe, and picked up the morning paper at which he had, so far, only glanced. He had seen a *Sun*, so the news would be stale by now, but he wanted something to read—anything—an anchor for his drifting thoughts.

TURKS SIGN PACT WITH NAZIS. FATE OF ALLIANCE WITH BRITAIN. GERMAN PRESSURE ON RUSSIA. . . .

The sudden shrilling of the telephone bell made him realise after a few moments that he had been reading with only half his attention. This curious splitting of thought was another recent symptom which disturbed him. He found that while one part of his mind noted the significance of what he read, weighed the possibility of a German drive on the Middle East, contemplated between hope and acute dread, a Nazi clash with Russia, another part was steadily and disconcertingly looking inward at himself, Gilbert Massey, a writer not writing.

He heard Phyllis go to the 'phone, and noticed that her voice, even when it was being agreeable as now, had acquired a high pitch, a permanent note of querulousness.

"Yes," she was saying, "I'll be there. No, I haven't finished that pair yet. Oh, I've been making jam all the afternoon and I'm so tired I can hardly stand. No, not yet. Well, I got the fruit so cheaply, you see—a case. . . . What time does the meeting start? Oh, that's dreadfully early! No, I can't possibly get there before half-past. All right, I won't forget. Good-bye."

She padded away again down the hall. Gilbert sat still, the paper across his knees, and his absent stare became suddenly fixed.

Good God, those pictures! Now that Father's dead we must get rid of them. He had, for a moment, a sense of hopeless, exhausted

bewilderment because everything seemed suddenly inextricably entangled and related, and it was too much for his mind to cope
with. A writer not writing. That joined up with Elsa Kay and
their conversation that evening; and Elsa Kay joined up with that
bright tableau in the Laughlin's house so many years ago; and
that tableau, because it had been the beginning not only of Elsa,
but of himself as a writer, had an accusation in it for the writer
who was not now writing, but sitting looking at the pictures he had
thought about that night, and read about in a letter only a week
or two ago. In this inter-relation of things, events, personalities,
in this action and reaction upon himself of past and present, he
found confirmation of Marty's theory that so far as the story of
any one human life was concerned you might as well make your
first plunge anywhere. The past will coil up behind you like a
spring, it will reach over your head to link up with the future
where you will find it awaiting you. The writer's trick of presenting a life as the steady onward march of a personality, leaving the
past behind, advancing on the future, must be, then, nothing but
a lazy device to make his own task easier—a recoil of his mind
from the technical intricacy of recording a man's existence as an
endless present moment, moving snailwise through time, carrying
the past and the future on its back.

He had lived, he thought angrily, with these damned pictures
all his life! He stared up at the one over the mantelpiece which,
although not the largest, held pride of place because, portraying
the incident of the loaves and fishes, it included a figure of the
Saviour. He looked from it with a kind of disbelief to the one on
the opposite wall; a young woman in flowing white was
having her hand kissed — had been having her hand
kissed for at least forty - five years — by a side - whiskered
gentleman in a garden where doves clustered at the foot of a
sundial, and a peacock walked on a distant lawn in the shadow of
crenellated walls. He had not looked at it for years, he had not
thought of it since that night when, at fifteen, he had studied very
different pictures on the Laughlin's walls. This monstrosity, he
thought, must have been, along with the new furniture, one of the
"handsome" purchases which his father had made as a fond gesture
to his missionary bride. He did not turn his head to look at the
one behind him, but he could see it all the same. It had no title;
it was merely a basketful of puppies. The largest, on the wall

opposite the fireplace, depicting village lads and lasses dancing round a maypole, was called "The Gaiety of Youth."

Remembering how far from gay his own youth had been, he felt suddenly bitter towards a parent who could enshrine this synthetic frolicking on walls within which his own children's exuberance was so unmercifully subdued. He studied the last picture with cold detachment. It was a large framed photograph of s.s. *Larapaita* which had carried his mother on her missionary voyagings. "I suppose," he thought, "I was a fool to go on living here. 'Soft' as Marty says. She was quicker to grasp the—the inevitability of Father than I was. She saw that he was at once the product and the perpetuator of an attitude." He remembered that in one of her books she had brought that point out by holding up to simultaneous ridicule a character of whom their father was undoubtedly the prototype, and the newspaper which he read. He got up and went across to the bookshelf; wasn't it in that caustically amusing thing she had called *I'll Tell You What?* He carried the book back to his chair, hunted up the passage, and read:

"*The old man walked slowly down the path to where the 'Daily Messenger' lay, an enticing white cylinder on the gravel path. Stooping is an action which only the young can accomplish with real grace, yet Mr. Blenkinson, though he bent ponderously, managed to retain even from the back view, which his daughter commanded, a certain stateliness.*

"*Watching him, she was teased by the thought that a natural affinity existed between him and the paper which he was already unfolding as he walked back to the verandah. That he seated himself with deliberation, opened his spectacle-case without hurry, shook out a clean handkerchief, polished his glasses, and gave some care to the precision with which he re-folded the pages before he began to read, seemed but an inevitable tribute from one established dignity to another.*

"*For this was not the kind of paper that he who runs stops dead to read. No sensational headlines lured one into a greedy gobbling of news instead of a sober, leisurely (and indeed sometimes somnolent) perusal. Between it and the Mr. Blenkinsons of the community there existed, therefore, a long, acknowledged, and well-tried regard. It was a paper which could be trusted never to shock their moral, nor disturb their political prejudices; and in return they could be relied upon to read its leading articles faithfully. 'The Daily Messenger,' they said devoutly, 'is my Bible.'*

"And indeed its leaders were worth reading. They brought to a high degree of perfection the art of saying nothing with great dignity and conviction. The vulgarity of vehemence found no place in them; they relied instead upon a subtle flattery of their readers by inviting them to austere reflection. 'Mature consideration' was a favourite phrase, varied by 'a careful weighing of the pros and cons.' That useful cliché about confusing liberty with license had not yet become a joke; it had many years of life still before it, in which to abash the simple-minded by suggesting that their timid groping after a broader culture and a truer democracy was merely an undisciplined grabbing for indulgences.

"Any unwise outburst from some irresponsible person against established custom was gravely rebuked. Any suggestion that all was not for the best in the best of all possible worlds was swiftly damned with the word 'agitation.' Any anxious advocacy of reform was treated with benign indulgence, which never failed to include a nostalgic sigh for unattainable Utopias. Anything, in short, which threatened to disturb the public complacency was promptly, decently and efficiently buried beneath mountains of well-chosen words, interspersed with Latin tags to titillate the erudite and awe the unlettered . . ."

Gilbert shut the book with a sigh. He could see his father, dignified and patriarchal, spectacles on nose, reinforcing and being reinforced by the no less dignified press advocacy of the status quo. Thus community thought could be made to flow in a vicious circle, from the Blenkinsonian mind to the columns of the Blenkinsonian newspaper and back again. The strength of that barren inter-change was the strength of death. It had made a sepulchre of this house. His own marriage had never generated the spiritual vitality to combat it, and yet he had lived on here, taking, in this one matter, the line of least resistance. It had seemed a small enough concession to make to his wife and his father in return for ruthlessness in other directions. But now he regretted it, thinking of his children, and feeling a hunger in himself for some sort of completeness, some fitting congruity between the life of his mind and the environment of his body. "You drift into things," he thought wearily. "You don't rouse yourself to break away completely. You try to compromise, to split the good life into sections, to win in one section by submitting in another. . . ."

He reflected that writers should, perhaps, make it their especial business to stir people's resentment over the mutilation of their little share of time. Look here, you silly saps, life is endless, but your share of it is only threescore years and ten. If you stand in a queue for two hours and then get a bad seat for the show you're fighting-mad. But you wait a million years to get born, you let all the fun be grabbed out of your little span—and do you raise hell about that? Not you! A little comfort, a little febrile gaiety, a little dope—and your turn is over, my lads! You vanish in a nailed box through the door marked "exit," and the million years to come write you off as a dead loss. . . .

Some sort of awareness like that was behind my rebellion and Marty's. It was our turn, and we wanted to function. We couldn't because our minds had been tied up. Life had been reduced by the merciless repetition of dogmatic statements to a rigid pattern which we felt must be false because we couldn't move, stretch, breathe in it. Yet we were too ignorant to know where it was false; it *looked* all right, but we couldn't find any meaning in it. . . .

And when the first World War burst on us it had the same maddening air of lunatic simplicity. Someone had murdered an Archduke. Why? Well, it was in the Balkans, where one expects such things to happen. Germany was invading Belgium. What had that got to do with the Archduke? That doesn't matter; the point is that a great big bully of a nation is invading a gallant little neighbour, and no man of British blood can stand by and see that happen. Now can he?

Of course not—but . . . ?

Why is Germany invading Belgium?

Because Germany is a great big bully.

The dangerous, fearless logic of the young mind getting to work must be countered. Germany is a *country*—how can a country be a bully? Are the German people bullies? *All* of them? Beethoven, Goethe, Heine, the old Fräulein at Marty's school, the kindly young man who held Nick on his shoulder once to see a procession . . . ? Is it the rulers? Is it the Kaiser? Is it . . . ?

But questions must be stopped, thought must be drowned, emotion must be degraded into emotionalism, men must be pushed back towards their primitive origin—or how can they ever fight a war? Phrases must be marshalled quickly to arouse anger and hatred. Blood and Iron! Deutschland uber alles! But *we* say:

'Rule Brit . . . !' Be quiet! A scrap of paper! Might is right! Gott strafe England!

There's no chance for the adolescent mind. Its emotions are wide open like a flower inviting fertilization—how can it fail to reach out ardently towards a new, exciting atmosphere, born over' night? There comes a quickening in the leisurely tempo of life, a faint, new throb like drums, swelling to an intoxicating crescendo. Suddenly we knew the Belgian national anthem, and the Belgian flag. Suddenly, indeed, we knew all sorts of flags—Serbian, Rus' sian, Japanese, Italian—the sky was bright with their fluttering, and every colour in their flaunting kaleidoscope thrust down into our silly, undefended hearts with a stab of exultation. They dazzled our physical eyes, and phrases were the flags we flew in our minds to their bemusement and confusion. The Lion's whelps. The lads in khaki, the boys in blue. The last man and the last shilling. A World fit for heroes to live in. The War to end War . . .

Well, they overreached themselves there, the purveyors of slogans! A catastrophic phrase! A phrase which now, remem' bered with bitterness, drove millions into cynicism. A phrase which, once used and betrayed, could never be used again except with the irony of disillusionment; whose promise, though it were one for which the whole world cried out, could never again be believed with the same wholehearted faith . . .

And there, he thought, was the weak spot. A democracy with' out faith is just a machine without power. Nothing can make it function except faith in itself, in the ordinary man and woman. For once you say in your heart that they are no good—incorrigibly apathetic, sentimental, superstitious, ignorant and undisciplined— what is left to you but force? Force—and a Führer! Hadn't he heard in a thousand scrappy conversations that ominous note of despair and capitulation? Hadn't he seen the vast majority of his country's seven million inhabitants moving through life in the bewitchment of a familiar routine, stepping from to-day's problems to to-morrow's, declining to meet those of next week half-way? They knew there was fighting going on in China—but, cripes, when wasn't there fighting going on in China? They knew that Mussolini was dropping bombs on Abyssinian natives—but when haven't natives got it in the neck? They disapproved in theory; this Musso, they thought vaguely, was beginning to throw his

weight around too much. Look how it put ideas into other
people's heads—Hitler, for instance; but if they were on the dole
they were too busy trying to keep alive to bother, and if they were
in a wage job they were too busy trying to keep it, and if they were
in executive positions they were too busy trying to show a profit,
and if they had independent means they were too busy gardening
and playing golf. So, really, no one had time to think about it
except a few cranky, tiresome people who seemed to have nothing
to do but stand on soap-boxes in the Domain and lay down the
law about things they couldn't possibly understand.

There was still an army of unemployed, though. Many of them
were on the road, but you didn't notice them much because the
police kept them moving. Draw your dole in this town this week,
but by next week you must be many miles away—or no dole.
Unemployed people get talking when they settle down together,
and that's bad; they get thinking, even, and that's worse. So they
knock at your back door and ask for an hour's work, or a bite of
food, or a couple of bob, and then they drift away. . . . Well,
times are hard . . .

In the papers you might see that there's to be a call-up; if you
happened to go down to the wharves to meet an incoming ship
you might see a drab-looking, patient crowd of men waiting around
the gates. In Hyde Park or in the Gardens or down the sunny
slopes of the Domain there they were again, sitting on the grass
with their hands locked around their knees, or lying asleep with
a newspaper over their faces . . .

Something wrong somewhere. But a man has his own life
to look after, and it's no picnic. All the same when there's something wrong somebody has to be blamed, so you say angrily to
your mate on the job, or your friend at the Club, or your visitor
in the drawing-room:

"Politicians! We ought to string them up to lamp-posts all
down the street!"

And your friends say, shrugging:

"Well, we elected them!"

What's that but a slap in the eye for Democracy? So you did
elect them. You put a mark on a ballot paper because you knew
you'd be fined two quid if you didn't. And your cross helped to
elect John Snooks—but what the hell did you know about John
Snooks? Something wrong somewhere!

Nothing but a malaise as yet—like the first faint pangs of indigestion that you ignore, hoping it will pass away. But a new pang is delivered to your door every morning with the paper. This Hitler—what's he up to? We settled Germany once—have we got to do it all over again? What about the Peace Treaty? Was it too hard, as some say, or too damned gentlemanly, as others say? Can you flatten out a whole nation and keep it flattened—and even if you can, should you?

All the same, you can't have nations just walking in and grabbing other nations. Look at Austria. Look at Abyssinia. Maybe they were just a bunch of savages, but all the same . . .

What was the League of Nations for? I read that Covenant of theirs once—it sounded all right. If one member nation was attacked, all the others had to go to its help. Abyssinia was a member, and so were we. The works slipped somewhere. Why?

Mind you, Germany and Italy are pretty strong, and we aren't armed properly; we have to go carefully. But, Hell, they grow stronger with every country they grab—we have to draw the line somewhere or we'll be next ourselves . . .

What's this in Spain, now? This bloke Franco—what does he think he's doing? Crushing Bolshevism? Well, the Spanish Government was elected, wasn't it? Cripes, no, I'm not a Red—but if the Spanish people want a Red Government what do I care? Well, if it's a civil war I suppose this non-intervention is all right. But they say Germany and Italy are all out helping Franco—where does that put us? Do we want Spain to go Fascist, too? No concern of ours? Jesus Christ, when all Europe's Fascist we'll have to start and be concerned all right!

Well, now, my dear chap, let's take a look at this Fascism. Calmly and without prejudice. A man I know was in Germany last year, and he said it was impressive what Hitler had done. Perfect roads, all the country looking like a garden, marvellous service in the hotels. Concentration camps? For God's sake, old man, you don't want to believe all this sensational stuff they dish out. Floggings and torturings—those things went out with the Middle Ages! Do you know what it is? Those people have a *leader*. They know what they have to do, and they do it. We could do with some discipline and organisation like that ourselves. Look at these confounded Trade Unions running the country—look at the strikes we have—look at these ranting Reds without an "h" to bless themselves with, standing up in the Domain day after day preaching Communism! I tell you we could use a Hitler here!

What was all that, Gilbert thought, but the decay of faith, the power of democracy running down? This was the thing he hated and feared—this drifting of the human mind, anchorless, swinging helplessly to and fro to the pull of unscrupulous propaganda. This, finally, was the issue which split the world in two, split nations, split parties, split friendships and families—do you believe in human beings, or don't you?

*   *   *   *

It was, Gilbert acknowledged, coming back reluctantly to his personal life, the issue which had finally finished his own marriage. Suddenly he was sorry for Phyllis—and for himself. Not for the querulous, muddling woman in the kitchen, not for the middle-aged harassed man in the armchair, but for two young people whom he could see across a gulf of years, becoming aware of each other, stealing glances, feeling an exciting difference pervade their familiar brother-and-sister relationship. He was sorry for a slight, reserved boy who had just passed his Senior exam. with a distinction which astonished himself, and set his father boasting complacently; a boy intellectually and emotionally hungry, and snatching food where he could find it—for his brain in books, and for his emotions in the artificially overcharged atmosphere of the times. The War had meant only that for him—a subject for romantic reverie, a peg upon which to hang shy, private dreams of valor and sacrifice, life and death. And he was sorry for the anxious, inept girl, blossoming into her brief, pink-and-white, milkmaid prettiness, suffering her own confusions, hiding even from herself her own bewildering desires, abandoning herself to the spurious emotionalism of the period, doing war-work in a state of romantic exaltation, dreaming, no doubt, of a young soldier-lover for whom she would wait in patient constancy.

And there he was. Himself at nineteen, coming home for the first time, shy and gawky, in uniform; queerly disturbed by his own abrupt transformation from a schoolboy to a man upon whose shoulders rested at least some of the fate of civilisation. Seeing Phyllis' blue eyes stare, shine, and overflow; realising that being a man involved many things, including the awareness that she had just put her hair up, and that she was prettier than he had ever noticed before.

[128]

The family had rearranged itself. His father and Mrs. Miller were the old people, Marty and Nick were the children. Between stood himself and Phyllis, flung at each other by their new adult-hood, finding companionship and refuge from their uncertainties in each other's eyes. During the uneasy year in camp he had come home on leave charged with all the impressions and emotions of a new, rough, male life, to find Phyllis always there, eagerly sym-pathetic, flatteringly attentive, pretty, slow-speaking, patient to-ward's Marty's unrelenting animosity, sewing on buttons for him, knitting him socks which could be treasured if not worn, and looking up at him with blue, adoring eyes. He was still shy and awkward, and she was the only girl he knew intimately; penned in her narrow circle, inhibited by her own and her mother's pru-deries, she knew no other boys. Spinning in an atmosphere of synthetic emotionalism like bits of thistledown in a gale, bemused by the patriotic legend, stupefied by martial music, intoxicated by the miracle of their own participation in stupendous events, they had mistaken the loneliness which drove them together for an abiding compatability, and the awakening clamour of their senses for love.

Out there under the blossoming apple-trees on his last leave, looking from the starlit sky to Phyllis, mysteriously ghost-like in her white frock, thinking of death, thinking of never coming home, there had been no chance for him—for either of them.

"Phyllis . . . !"

"Oh, Gilbert!"

It had been as easy as that. Once her head was against his shoulder and his arm round her, the thing was done. They were engaged; nothing else was conceivable. And a fortnight later he was on his way to France.

*   *   *   *

Yes, he was sorry for Phyllis now, in a remote, regretful way, as for something long finished and past rectifying. She had had a joyless sort of life. She had been taught to be afraid of joy, so she had sought, instead, the dreary satisfaction of conscious rec-titude. She had always felt, and she still felt (out there in the kitchen among her sticky saucepans) that so long as she was, like Martha, burdened with many cares, she was being unassailably virtuous; and so she piled up her cares, believing that thereby she was piling up virtuousness. And yet, in a blundering, laborious way, she had tried to respond to the slow widening of her horizon. She had realised that many things which had been alien to their common upbringing were becoming not only permissible but desirable, and she had struggled to be what she pathetically called "broad-minded." She had even made the supreme gesture of being "broad-minded" about religion—but it was only a gesture. It had done nothing but knock away a spiritual prop which she needed, and she had clutched instantly, in panic, for another to replace it; the procession of her various "faiths" over the last ten years had made even the children smile.

And now the world had begun to invade her home. Poor Phyllis! Her anger, her resentment, her fear! She didn't want the world inside her home; its proper place was in the newspapers. Let it stay there; let Gilbert leave it alone, too, and attend to his business!

The clock on the mantelpiece struck eleven. Time for the news. But Gilbert did not move. Too much trouble to get up and walk across the room and switch on the wireless. He had no stomach, just now, for the rounded, platitudinous phrases, the stereotyped propaganda, the tedious quotation of unilluminating "statements." "Mr. Churchill explained . . ." "Mr. Hughes went on to say . . ." "Mr. Menzies made it clear . . ." He had no reserves of patience at the moment to endure all that for the few meagre grains of news among the chaff of verbiage. What a world! No wonder poor Phyllis persisted in her obstinate, instinctive, foredoomed efforts to keep it at arms' length!

Does she know, even now, that it has her beaten? Hasn't she, even now, some last, desperate hope that she can still ignore it, and persuade me to ignore it, too? Doesn't she understand yet, after all these years, that I have to follow such intelligence as I have where it leads me? Actually I believe she is less confused now that the war has begun. She has a set of reactions for war— a precedent for correct "war-behaviour." But the few years before were outside her experience—they terrified her. Something that wasn't war, and yet was something that even she couldn't call peace. Yet so long as it lasted—that phoney peace, rotten and tottering as it was—how fiercely and irrationally she clung to the idea that to talk of war, even to think of it, somehow brought war closer. Primitive, that. The genie, the evil-spirit, the debbil-debbil who is invoked by the sound of his name. Just don't think about it, don't even glance at it over your shoulder, don't move and hardly breathe, and it may go away—recede—vanish . . .

No use saying to her, back in 1934, that the war had already begun. "Oh—China!" That was not our business. Then, "Oh, Abyssinia . . . well . . . !" Then Spain. "But, Gilbert, that's a civil war." Oh, shades of half-digested history books, the red rose of Lancaster and the white rose of York, Prince Rupert of the Rhine, and take away that bauble! Then Czechoslovakia—and Munich. "But he's trying to keep the peace, Gilbert! He's *trying!* I think it's magnificent of him!" And at last the snapping of patience, the torture of nervous stress, of anxiety, of exasperation and despair. "Oh, don't talk rubbish, Phyl! Can't you see? There *is* no peace to keep!"

She couldn't see. "*We* weren't at war," she said angrily. "Not yet." She looked at him with hatred—not, he knew, a personal hatred of himself, but woman's hatred of man's mysterious, mischievous, destructive activities. He opened Marty's book again, remembering wryly that she, too, had had barbed words to say upon what she described as "the man-question." She, too, had launched an indictment not easily to be refuted.

"Why all this pother, anyhow, about a 'woman-question'? Women are simple creatures, with simple and rational desires. But what of the desperately urgent man-question? What of this world almost entirely and almost uninterruptedly governed by man, and now in such a state of chaos that woman's creative instinct—a steady light in all previous storms—is blown and shaken like a candle in the wind?

"Was there ever a man-creature who, from his first jam-stealing onward, did not rationalise his misdeeds? And now, perturbed by the dimming of the one fudamental source of light (whose failure would have passed unobserved by him had he not provided himself with complicated figures which he is pleased to call Statistics of the Birth Rate) he searches wildly for something to blame—anything to blame—so long as it is not his own criminal muddling. Women, he cries accusingly, are selfish and pleasure-loving. They prefer parties to parturition—fie upon them! And women, who have poured themselves out with misguided, sacrificial recklessness through the long centuries of his silly blundering, to keep that light alive—women who have stunted their brains, lost their alertness, narrowed their vision, and all but renounced their very humanity to make good his senseless orgies of self-destruction, are now

*dumb, lacking knowledge, lacking direction, knowing only (and with-
out statistics) that the flame they have tended is going out, and the
principle of life, whose devotees they are, has been too often, and too
brutally violated . . ."*

He moved impatiently in his chair. Well, that was Marty, with
all her slapdash vehemence. But it was also Phyllis. Not in
headlong torrents of words, but only in that look of hatred. The
same thought, the same deep bitterness, the same deadly accusation
from two such different women. But Marty could at least see that
in the fury which had possessed him over the last ten years to
learn, to probe, pry, analyse and criticise, to come to grips with
the man-made forces now almost uncontrollable by man, he was
making an effort which was for her and all womankind. Phyllis
couldn't see that. It was "politics," it was "economics," it was
banking and credit and industry and wages; it was trade unions
and living conditions; it was imperialism and socialism and capitalism. It was just more of that dangerous, wilful man-stuff, wrap-
ping up simple things in all the complications men delight in.
There was no *need* for such complications. People only had to be
sensible and good. "I don't *believe* there'll be another war!" she
had cried. ""Everyone remembers the last one too clearly. They
just couldn't be so silly!"

And that's Phyllis. Instead of being educated like a human
being she has been domesticated like a cat. Her whole life was
planned to that end, and she's no more to blame for the result
than a goose destined to provide *paté de foie gras* is to blame for
its enlarged liver. Should *I* blame her? Heaven forbid! Didn't
I take my hand in that training? Didn't I, for years, accept it as
natural that she would have no thoughts beyond caring for my
physical comfort, and looking after the children? All the same I
did try to wake her up when I began to wake myself. I did try
to drag her along when I set out on this ghastly road of trying
to cram a lifetime's education into a few years. She didn't want
to come; perhaps she couldn't come. . . . Anyhow, I left her
behind . . .

He almost jumped, hearing her speak suddenly from behind him.
"Gilbert, I want to talk to you."

She came into the room and sat down heavily on the opposite
chair.

"I've been wondering if—now that Uncle Walter's dead—we couldn't live up the mountains. Permanently, I mean."

He stared at her, and unconsciously echoed Virginia:

"Live there? How could we? I have to get into town every day, and so has Prue."

She picked up her knitting; it was one of her favourite boasts that her fingers were never idle. She said persuasively:

"Quite a lot of people go up and down every day. It isn't really far, and you say you always enjoy driving. Pete was going to boarding-school anyhow at the end of this term, so it wouldn't make any difference to him. And it really would be much cheaper living, you know."

It was characteristic of her that she could weave her secret thoughts behind a screen of candid works without suspecting that he might do the same. Secure, because her eyes were on the stitches she was counting, he looked at her thoughtfully.

"Would you like it much better yourself?"

"Oh, yes!" Her tone was ardent. "You know how I've always loved the mountains. And the children, too. Of course, Pete would only be there for holidays, and an occasional week-end, but the girls would love it. Personally, I'd like Prue to give up her shop; I don't think it's good for her, and she's been looking quite peaky lately—but you wouldn't notice that. I believe it would do you good, too, Gilbert, because . . ."

She went on elaborating her case without touching on its real motive, but he was not listening any longer. He was thinking: "Good God, it's a solution!" A little shocked at his own relief and his own dawning excitement, he forced himself to recognise the crude fact that he wanted to be rid of the tiresome company of this tiresome woman. His life with her had developed in him, by now, a fear of mental dishonesty which had become almost an obsession. Her own habitual self-deceptions so horrified him that he was kept painfully on the lookout for a similar failing in himself. Gradually, as his own habit of thought had clarified and matured, he had watched her mental and spiritual flounderings with increasing repugnance; it had seemed alarming and almost incredible that any creature endowed with the mechanism of thought should so misuse it, should be capable of so much mental dishonesty, should be so utterly astray in her own brain, so certain of her own strength and rectitude, and yet so pitiably eager to grasp any ready-made faith to supply her with the spiritual support she would not admit she needed.

Not that he could not understand her craving for support. Understand—yes. Even sympathise. But endorse—never! He had to hate this thing from which he had himself escaped by the skin of his teeth—this dependence on symbols and slogans and the faiths of other people. He had to hate it in her as he had hated and overcome it in himself. So he admitted bleakly that the less he saw of her the better he would be pleased; and if they lived in the mountains it would be easy to absent himself pretty frequently without being obviously neglectful or overtly brutal. There was Nick's flat where he could stay overnight, and Marty would always put him up . . .

He said slowly:

"We'd have to let this place."

Actually, he was thinking, it was a providential suggestion. It was true that living would be cheaper in the mountains; he knew, without regrets, that his business was likely to suffer—at least tem-porarily—from the drastic changes he contemplated, and that his plan of action for the Burt Street property would make it more a financial liability than an asset. Driving up and down from the city would hit up the garage-bill a bit, of course, but against that he could set the rent of *Glenwood* . . .

"I daresay," he said, "we could try it for a year or so, if you like."

She looked up, beaming through her spectacles. It had really been absurdly easy. She said happily:

"I'm sure it would be a good move, Gilbert. I've thought for a long time that you needed a change, and you'll have such lovely air and surroundings to come home to every night. And I believe you'd write better there, too." She became earnest. "I've been planning. We can fix up that glassed-in corner of the verandah as a lovely study for you. I was sitting there last time we were up and I thought that anyone would just *have* to be inspired by that view. I'm sure the city atmosphere must be rather stifling to the artist. Of course, you have to be there through the week, but I'm sure it will *renew* you to escape to the mountains every week-end. You'll be able to look at the view while you're writing . . ."

Suddenly he felt almost murderous. During these last unproductive years he had many times been flinchingly conscious that she looked on with disapproval at what she obviously considered his wilful and self-indulgent idleness. To her a stack of paper, a pencil and a writer equalled a book. When the book was not forthcoming, she added "inspiration" in the shape of a view, and thought: "Now there's *no* excuse!" He could not bear to have her blundering in on that particular sore spot, and he found himself saying disagreeably:

"I usually look at my paper when I'm writing."

It was, he thought furiously, the sort of cheap snub she invited. He felt ashamed of himself, and angrier than ever with her for provoking him into ill-natured sarcasm. She gave him a hurt, long-suffering glance, and bent her head again over her knitting. He picked up Marty's book and opened it at random—a hint to her as clear as he could make it that the subject was closed, and the conversation over.

VIII

SIGNING his name on the last of the cheques and letters which Miss
Butters had laid before him, Gilbert said:

"Tell one of the boys to go out and get me a *Sun*, will you?"

She blotted his signature and gathered the papers together.

"Mr. Nick just went for one, Mr. Massey."

"Oh, all right. That's the lot, I think, Miss Butters; don't
forget to register this."

He yawned, took off his glasses, and looked at his watch. It
was ten to five; he was finished for the day, and he could not
remember a day when it had been harder to concentrate. They
had all spent the week-end up the mountains, making arrangements
for painting and minor alterations to the cottage, but the news
which had come over the radio at midday yesterday had driven
every other thought from Gilbert's mind. He had left Phyllis
gaping confusedly, at a loss for the correct reaction, and gone out
into the cloudy midwinter day alone. He had walked for miles.
He had a dim recollection now of the stony path he had followed
over a high, windy tableland, of the huge valleys far below him,
blue-grey, deepening to a cold purple towards late afternoon; of
an eagle swooping, soaring, floating above him; of a creek where
he had stopped for an icy, moss-tasting drink; but all the time he
had been struggling with a new hope and a new horror. So much
effort now to be deflected from construction and turned to the
insane destructiveness of war—so much achievement now to be
endangered—so many people who had tasted stability and discovered a motive power for existence, and who must now go back
into that lunacy of danger and suffering out of which they had
struggled in twenty-five momentous years . . .

Miss Butters, he realised, was lingering; he glanced up to find
her looking at him with a curious expression of anxious eagerness.
She said hurriedly:

"I just wanted to ask—I mean—do you think Russia has any
chance against Hitler, Mr. Massey?"

"Good Lord!" he thought. "Already!"

He had always got on well with his employees. He had brought with him to his managerial desk a certain understanding tolerance which made him personally popular. But he would have needed to be more lacking in sensitiveness than he was not to have noticed, during the last couple of years, the faint reserve, the awkwardness, the uncertain stiffness which had invaded a once cordial relationship.

He admitted that they had all been tactful—even forbearing! They had loyally tried not to see the dubious pamphlets, newspapers, magazines and books which lay about among the papers on his desk. They were conventional people, conditioned to obey the law, and conditioned also never to question it, but it was their sense of propriety, more than anything else, which was outraged by the idea of having an employer who was, if not actually Red at least definitely Pink. They accepted what they were told, and what they had been told for many years now was that there was a bogey called Communism, which dwelt in a terrible country under the sway of a ruthless dictator, its people starving, barefooted, ignorant, denied their religion, hounded and oppressed by a sinister secret police. The bogey, they had been endlessly assured, was on the march; even here, in their own country—the pattern of democratic freedom—it was being slyly introduced by means of subversive books. Gilbert had borne them no grudge for their uneasy sidelong glances, at the time; what were they to think, after all, when they saw these very books lying on their employer's desk?

He looked hard at Miss Butters, and she returned his look with a shade of embarrassment, blushing slightly. The young, he thought, are full of curiosities, thank God. All this time when they disapproved consciously, perhaps, unconsciously, they wondered? Throughout this long day, ploughing through his work, he had felt one question nagging at his mind: "What is going to be the effect of this?" It amused him that here, within a few hours, was one effect, trivial in itself, but perhaps full of portent as a symptom? He had noticed that his staff avoided discussing the war with him, and Nick had reported the same experience. Now he was being asked, point-blank, as one having knowledge of forbidden mysteries, for his opinion!

But he was suddenly annoyed. It had been a difficult time for people who had committed the unforgivable sin of trying to investigate. He could support that kind of unpleasantness himself with equanimity, for he had always been, by nature, solitary, but he was angry now on behalf of other people, less detached, who had suffered in being treated like lepers, ostracised, suspected, even cut dead in the street. He reached across the desk for that morning's *Herald*, folded it open at the leader, and tapped it sharply with his pen. He said shortly to Miss Butters:

"Read that. Just there."

She bent over it. "*It would be foolish to entertain great hope that the Red Army will be able for long to resist the Germans.*" She looked up at him unhappily. Still irritated with her, he said:

"Well, there's one opinion; now I'll give you mine. Russia's very strong. If Britain and America pull with her Hitler hasn't got an earthly chance. Take your pick." He rose and went across to where his overcoat hung behind the door, got a packet of cigarettes out of its pocket, and added more brusquely than he had ever spoken to her before:

"See that all those letters go off to-night, Miss Butters."

*　　　*　　　*　　　*

"My dear," giggled Aunt Bee, bustling into Marty's dining-room, "if you hear a loud pop at dinner time it will be my waistband. I can't think why I'm getting so fat." She bent to the sideboard mirror and arranged her curls. "It's charming of you and Richard to have me, darling, and I love my room with its glimpse of the water. Is it just a family dinner to-night?"

"Not quite." Marty gave the table a last look and took her aunt's arm. "Stop admiring yourself, and we'll go and sit down till the others arrive. I think I'm tired. There'll be our three selves, and Gilbert and Phyllis, and a young man called Gerald Avery, and a girl called Elsa Kay. I asked Nick to come, but he couldn't."

"What does he do, this Mr. Avery?"

"He's a journalist for his bread and butter, and he writes short stories and radio plays, and acts in them sometimes."

"And the girl?"

"I really don't know much about her. I knew her step-sister when we were children—before she was born. She published a novel a year or two ago, and she earns her living at some sort of secretarial job now. Aunt Bee, your hair looks perfect; if you fiddle with it any more you'll spoil it."

She dragged her aunt away from the mirror, across the hall to the drawing-room, where Richard was standing on the hearth-rug with his back to the fire, reading the evening paper. Aunt Bee sank on to one end of the sofa, and sat up again abruptly, crying: "Marty, I *must* remember to sit straight, or goodness knows what will happen." She accepted a glass of sherry from Richard, a cigarette from Marty, and said comfortably: "Now tell me *all* the news!"

Marty, sitting on the arm of a chair, racked her brain for family gossip, and offered: "Gil has let *Glenwood*—you know that, I suppose?"

"Oh, yes, Prue told me in a letter. And they're going to live up the mountains. It seems very—very *odd*, Marty, and unnecessary—poor Gilbert driving all that distance every day." She sipped and smiled flatteringly at Richard. "What *good* sherry! Not that I can tell, really. The children all say I only know the difference between champagne and lemonade by the colour. Of course, that's an exaggeration. But I know this must be good if Richard chose it. Anyhow, Marty, whose idea was it?"

"Idea . . . ?"

"About letting *Glenwood?*"

Marty shrugged.

"I don't know. Gil seems quite satisfied. And if he needs to be in town he can always stay here or at Nick's flat."

"Ah," said Aunt Bee. She considered; she brightened. "That's perfectly true, Marty, and I hope he often will, because sometimes I think Phyllis . . . Well . . . Darling, that wine-colour suits you perfectly, but you should have a lipstick to match; that one's much too vermilion-y."

Marty said impenitently: "It's the only one I have. There's the bell. Will you go, Richard—I expect it's Gilbert." She looked at her aunt with speculative amusement. "You'll get on well with Gerald; soul-mates, you'll be. I don't know about Elsa; somehow I think she mightn't measure up to your standard in lipsticks either. More enthusiasm than discretion."

Aunt Bee said indignantly:

"I *don't* judge people by their lipsticks! Though I do find people who don't wear *any* a little—unsympathetic. Ah, Gilbert, my dear boy! No, you'll have to bend right down, because . . . well, just because." She peered round him at the door. "Where's Phyllis?"

Gilbert sat beside her on the sofa and took a glass of sherry from Richard.

"She sent her apologies, Marty. She's been helping at the canteen all day, and she had a headache. When did you arrive, Aunt Bee?"

"This afternoon. And I had a most comfortable journey down in the train, and there was such a *nice* woman sharing the sleeper with me, and we talked about our children and grandchildren, and really the time passed so quickly that I could hardly believe we'd arrived." She patted her nephew's knee. "Are you feeling happier about the war now, Gilbert?"

"Well—in a way, I suppose."

"You looked so *worried* before. When Russia came in I thought to myself: 'What a *comfort* this will be to dear Gilbert!'"

Flicking her ash delicately into a tray, she was happily oblivious of a flabbergasted, three-cornered glance. Gilbert blinked and replied meekly:

"That was very good of you."

Marty said:

"I can hear Gerald and Elsa coming up the path. No, Richard, I'll let them in; you give Aunt Bee some more sherry—I want her to sparkle to-night."

"Aunt Bee," Richard answered gallantly, "needs no sherry to make her sparkle." The glance he exchanged with his wife as she went to the door made fun of his gift for blarney, his adroitness in playing up to whatever an audience or a situation demanded of him. Aunt Bee, Marty foresaw, would spend an entrancing week flirting with him, and join the legion of people who already spoke of him as "Marty's *charming* husband."

Elsa, she observed, ushering her two newly-arrived guests through the hall and into the drawing-room, was certainly not reticent with her lipstick. She looked more waif-like than ever in a long-skirted black front which emphasised her thinness almost to emaciation. Her scarlet lips and fingernails brought to the surface of Marty's mind the words "red in tooth and claw," and the thought, linking on to her half-formed impression of semi-starvation, made her feel a faint spasm of distaste.

Performing introductions, she reflected that it was perhaps just as well that Phyllis had a headache. She had one herself, and she knew that the conversation would demand less of her if it were not being stalled every now and then by her sister-in-law's inept comments. Gilbert was asking Gerald Avery about his play.

"My dear chap," Gerald said, "it's ruined. My chief character has been sabotaged. My title's a washout. How can I call it *Subversive Mr. Avery* now that I'm not subversive any longer? I've been double-crossed."

"Don't worry," Gilbert remarked dryly, "you're still subversive."

"I give you my word," Gilbert protested, "that I was bowed to this morning by the lady in the flat opposite. And my editor came to me, cap in hand, for an article on collective farming. I tell you it's unnerving. An artist sweats blood to build up a conception of his character, and then the world takes his conception and wrings its neck."

"I know," Aunt Bee said sympathetically. "There was a paper the children used to bring home and leave lying about when people they didn't like called—so that they would go away quickly, you know—and it worked so well. And the other day when they got it out for Mrs. Merivale-Hooper she *borrowed* it. Do we go in now, Marty dear?"

She had been right, Marty thought, when the soup was finished, in guessing that Gerald and Aunt Bee would hit it off well, and she relaxed, letting her thoughts wander to the fantastic time through which they had just passed. Citizen though she was of a sport-worshipping nation, she had always found the antics of the human mind more entertaining than the antics of the human body; but not all her forty years had afforded her such a spectacle as these six short weeks. Had ever an ally been so grudgingly welcomed? Yet the ugliness of petty prejudice and mean-spirited distrust had been shot with its own sharp, sour humour. It had been almost awe-inspiring to watch how minds, floundering among false values, wriggling, dodging, evading, doubling back on their tracks, became enmeshed at last, inevitably, in obvious contradictions, and cornered by the logic of events. Can you refuse any longer to fly the flag of an ally? Oh, tormenting sight—that we should live to see the hammer and sickle flaunt against our pure blue sky! National anthem . . . ? God forbid—is our very air to be polluted? Anyhow, we have no records. But time and history press forward together, so powerfully that there's nothing to do but put a good face on it, retreating step by step—for lo! there is the flag, there is the anthem, there is the announcer saying: "M.

Stalin, the Russian dic—er—Premier . . .," there is the Lord Mayor drinking vodka with a Russian captain, there are the people besieging the bookshops for information about The Bogey, there are subversive pictures breaking out of custody to show fine buildings, healthy children, buxom women and purposeful men. Oh, yes, it had been funny in its way . . .

She roused herself to say to Elsa:

"How has the comedy of the right-about-face to the Left struck you, Miss Kay?"

Elsa looked at the table, frowning slightly.

"I don't think I have a very strong sense of humour," she said dryly. "Everything that strikes me as funny seems tragic the next moment." Marty noticed that Gilbert, sitting between Elsa and herself, gave the girl a quick look.

"Of course," Gerald said, "it's a literary device as old as history to mix comedy and tragedy so as to heighten the effect of both. But you have to live through a time like this to see the principle in action."

That's true, Marty thought. Is it funny, or is it terrible to see minds halted in mid-stride, baulking, jittering, shuffling, looking round wildly for some convention to take the place of the one that has been so rudely snatched from them? Millions of human minds, huddling like sheep waiting to be told which way to go. Looking with an anxious, ovine gaze for the Parliamentary sheepdogs to manœuvre them into a suitable, safe pen. And finding their erstwhile shepherds no longer brisk, purposefully snapping at their heels—but avoiding their eyes, every bit as bewildered as their docile flock! *Lacking a definite official lead from Whitehall, the Federal Ministry is temporarily confused in defining its attitude to Russia's entry into the war."* The truth is, my fleecy friends, they don't *know* which pen you're to go into now!

"It's becoming quite confusing," Gerald was complaining to Aunt Bee. "Before all this happened the people who took an intelligent interest in the U.S.S.R. were quite a select little fraternity, but nowadays all sorts of people go round talking about Russia at the top of their voices." He sighed. "You know, Gilbert, I could find it in my heart to resent these upstarts who are beginning to gate-crash our subversive seclusion."

Gilbert could smile at foolery, but he could answer it only with seriousness. "It wasn't a particularly enjoyable seclusion," he said thoughtfully. "We were avoided, and whispered about. Some of us lost our jobs, and some of us got run in, and lots of us had books confiscated by the police. Ill-informed dim-witted people who never put two ideas together for themselves in their lives had the colossal impudence to accuse us of being traitors. And," he added, after a pause, "I wouldn't be too sure that it's going to be very different now. Less overt, perhaps."

' Well," said Gerald, amiably charitable. "Heaven forgive them for their prejudice!"

"Not at all!" snapped Marty. "Heaven smite them for their ignorance! They know nothing now in the way of essentials that they couldn't have known for the past six or seven years at least."

"True, true." Gerald nodded judicially. "They just hadn't grasped the elementary fact that the first duty of a democrat is to read banned books."

Elsa looked at him with a faintly malicious smile.

"You make me wonder, Gerald, if snobbery isn't the one failing we'll never cure ourselves of. Must you re-act like an aristocrat to the nouveau-riche?"

Gerald chuckled.

"Why not?" he enquired unrepentantly. "Don't you think we've earned the little luxury of saying 'I told you so'?"

She made an impatient movement with her shoulders. It suggested to Gilbert, watching her, that she was trying to wriggle away, as she had done on the first night he met her, from a subject which had become unwelcome to her, or in which she had lost interest. Or that she wanted to shake off the responsibility of defending a position she had taken up. Was it lack of conviction, lack of confidence, cynicism—or just inertia? She said indifferently: "Oh—perhaps." But Marty objected.

"No, we haven't, Gerald. No matter how small or how understandable a snobbery is, it still breeds antagonisms. It's still the germ of a new set of 'class distinctions.' Nick—my younger brother, Miss Kay—is always so busy with the War of the Rich Class against the Poor Class, that he forgets there are a thousand other forms that class antagonism *could* take."

"For instance . . . ?" Gerald asked.

"Oh, the manual class versus the intellectual class, or the technical class versus the artistic class, or the active class versus the contemplative class, or the gregarious class versus the solitary class . . ."

Richard interrupted:

"But why 'versus'? There may be an intolerance, or as Miss Kay calls it, a snobbishness between those classes—but not the bitterness and hatred that spring up between the haves and the have-nots."

Marty insisted:

"Why not—in time? Supposing we do adjust the economic structure so that there are no longer haves and have-nots. During the long period while we're getting ourselves educated to tolerance and the idea of co-operation, what's to prevent those minor snobberies from becoming hatreds? A crack can become a chasm. The superiority of one group over another only has to be accepted —to become a legend—and the group that's regarded as inferior will begin to feel resentment." Her head was aching badly now, and preoccupation with the world's future was overwhelmed by preoccupation with a sharp pain behind her temples. She passed on the effort of conversation. "Or won't it?"

Gilbert said in his deliberate way:

"I don't see why it should. So long as he has a job, a home, enough to eat, and a reasonable freedom, I think the average human being is tolerant enough. He can keep his minor rivalries good-tempered. It's when he's cold and hungry and worried that he turns nasty—and how right he is!"

"There's machine-snobbery," Richard suggested. "Particularly air-machine-snobbery. I can foresee trouble there. Swooping about in the air is still new enough to cast a glamour. Can't you imagine the emergence of a class of bird-men, quite superior to ordinary earth-bound mortals?"

Marty could not resist that; she nodded emphatically, and flinched.

"I can indeed. And there's the physical symbolism, too. People are still so primitive about symbols. Here are these people *above* them; they look *up* . . ."

"Pilots' uniforms," proclaimed Aunt Bee, "are so exciting, aren't they? A sort of adventurous polar-exploration look, they have. If I were young I'm sure I should fall madly in love with an airman."

"You see?" Richard twinkled amusedly at his wife's aunt. "Aunt Bee has succumbed already!"

Marty's eyes were suddenly arrested by the sight of the water in Elsa's glass. It was slopping about crazily as the girl drank; her hand was shaking so much that a drop ran down her chin. She replaced the glass on the table with a faint click, and lifted her napkin to her mouth. Marty, in that paralysed moment of surprise, saw that she was struggling against tears.

Gerald was saying:

". . . as soon as Japan starts throwing her weight about . . ."

No one else seemed to have noticed. Aunt Bee cried anxiously:

"Oh, dear, Mr. Avery, are we going to have trouble with Japan?"

"And how!" replied Gerald cheerfully.

Marty saw with relief that whatever emotion it was that had so abruptly shaken her, Elsa seemed to have subdued it, and she blessed Aunt Bee, whose voice, rather wistful now, was prattling on:

"You know, Gilbert, we went to Japan for a trip once, my husband and I. Such a lovely *clean* place, Richard, and the gardens so perfect, though somehow not very comfortable gardens, I thought, I mean to lounge about in and for children to romp in, but I may be wrong, of course, or perhaps it was just because my own children always had such miles and *miles* of country to ride about in, and it seemed a little bit—well, restricted; and very polite people they seemed, and I always did think *The Mikado* quite the most charming of the Gilbert and Sullivan operas, and then there's *Madame Butterfly*, too, and their wonderful flower paintings, I mean you can hardly *imagine* that they would . . ."

For a moment, as her voice trailed off into silence, her gallant, synthetic, youthfulness became a very apparent mask, and Marty found herself looking at an old, tired and bewildered woman. This party, she thought, only just refraining from clutching her aching head, is getting difficult, and she said briskly:

"Talking of gardens, ours will simply cease to exist if we don't get some rain soon."

Oh, Lord, she though, crude, very crude! But Richard. . . . She caught his eye and relaxed thankfully, knowing that she could depend on him to pick up this inept changing of the subject, and invest it with conversational ease. Elsa was looking quite composed again; Richard was skilfully developing the weather-theme into a general discussion of droughts—a subject upon which Aunt Bee, as a country woman, could speak with authority, and so have her confidence happily restored. Marty sighed and left her dinner party to take care of itself for a few moments while plates were removed, and sweets arrived. She came on duty again to hear Gilbert saying to Elsa.

"I'm sorry my brother Nick couldn't come to-night. He wanted to meet you. He was very keen on your book."

Elsa answered politely:

"I'd like to meet him very much."

A stab of pain across her forehead made Marty ask herself with almost vicious uncharitableness: "Now, what does that prunes-and-prisms manner cover up?" She said:

"Be accurate, Gilbert. Nick was keen on the 'ideology'—detestable word!—of Miss Kay's book. He'd have been just as keen on a pamphlet expressing the same ideas."

Elsa gave her a small, oblique smile.

"He's that sort, is he? There are people who'll read propaganda into anything."

Gilbert turned his head and looked hard at her.

"Do you believe in the theory that art should be divorced from propaganda?"

"Not entirely divorced, I suppose," she answered. "But when the propaganda content is too high the art seems to suffer."

"I don't think so. It may be true that the better the art the less one is conscious of the propaganda—but it's there in all the best art, and always has been."

"The word itself," Richard pointed out, "has the same derivation as the word 'propagate,' which means an act of generation. Doesn't that suggest that it's peculiarly a function of the creative mind?"

"Maybe so," Elsa said shortly, "but at present, anyhow, it seems to be the happy hunting ground of the dogmatic mind."

"All the more reason, surely," Gerald argued, "why the artist should get busy and claim his own again. Instead of which he often comes over all fastidious, and says he wants no part of the nasty, vulgar thing. Why, Gilbert? Sour grapes? Or dropping his bundle because it has got too heavy?"

Gilbert said moodily:

"Something like that, I suppose."

"If I have to be preached at," Aunt Bee said with a hint of defiance, "I like to be preached at in a nice, interesting story."

Gerald cried delightedly through their laughter:

"And you're perfectly right! You know, Gilbert, the reactions of people like Mrs. Butler are greatly to be trusted. It's a strong, sound instinct that prefers its propaganda humanised. People don't want to see their social trials as abstract problems, and themselves as units in a row of statistics. They want to be made to feel what things mean in terms of individual human experience. Nick should sit at Mrs. Butler's feet and learn the elements of psychology."

"Oh, dear!" murmured Aunt Bee, awed and flattered, "should he?"

Richard protested:

"You're all a bit hard on Nick. He's a very useful sort of person."

Marty said cantankerously·

"I don't deny his usefulness; but I don't like the way his mind functions. It's like a gramophone record. A very good one. Everything he ·has to say is good, and the way he says it is good. But there's just the one record; turn him on with a word, and he'll play the whole thing through for you."

"Well," Gilbert said mildly, "don't we all?"

"Friend Adolf, for instance,·' Gerald suggested. "Jews, communists, international finance, blood and soil, herrenvolk and lebensraum. Repeat as before."

"Oh!" cried Aunt Bee, scandalised. "How can you compare dear Nick with Hitler? I won't have it."

"Quite right, Aunt Bee." Richard spoke seriously. "There's a similarity of technique, because they're both fanatics. But they're pulling in opposite directions. And we do all play our own tunes, Marty—even those of us who aren't fanatics."

"I know," she admitted. "I suppose what I really object to is Nick's pose of omniscience. He hasn't earned it. He has a brain that's absolutely unproductive. It's just a cold-stirage room for other people's ideas . . ."

"Marty," Gerald explained to Elsa, "has a passion for metaphor. Don't mind her jumping from gramophones to cold-storage rooms —it's just her way."

"Be quiet, Gerald," said Marty, unabashed. "What I mean is that when Nick talks I get no impression that his mind is working on what he says. He's just reproducing. Whereas when Richard talks, for instance—though I frequently don't agree with what he says—I do feel that his words are coming out of a living mind and not a machine. Nick keeps his borrowed ideas in refrigeration, all stacked and fresh, and hands them out to anyone who will accept them."

"And very useful too," Gilbert said stoutly.

Marty scowled at him.

"Useful, useful! I concede his usefulness. I applaud it. But when he calls himself a 'Marxist thinker' I begin to bristle. Look here, Miss Kay, wouldn't you agree that one's thinking should be —to some extent at least—original thinking?"

"Original?" Elsa looked sceptical. "That's asking a lot. Haven't most of the good things on fundamental subjects been thought long ago?"

"Of course they have, but there's always a new set of circumstances that they have to be related to. And I don't mean original in an absolute sense, anyhow—only original for oneself. I mean that it's necessary to break one's own intellectual trails. Never mind if you have an idea and then discover that Solomon had it when he was a boy—it's still your own. But Nick never had an original idea in his life. He's a born follower—like King Wenceslas' page, trotting along in the footsteps of his master . ."

"Every prophet has his disciples," Gilbert said.

Marty sighed.

"I suppose so." She added truculently: "But all the same, I dislike a conversation that's really a series of recitations from *das Kapital* and the *Communist Manifesto*."

Richard looked amused.

"I grant you," he said, "that your disciple is the world's worst conversationalist. But, after all, his job is conversion, not conversation."

"Suppose," Marty insisted, "that he achieves his conversion, and gets his reform—what then? All he can do is to go on playing the same old record . ."

"God!" murmured Gerald, "she's back on gramophones!"

". . . and the world goes past him, and conditions change, and the needs and capacities of people are different, and hey presto, he's a reactionary, obstructing the ideas of the new generation."

"I pray," Gerald said devoutly, "that I may live to see Nick a crusted old Tory telling his son that all these new-fangled ideas will never take the place of good, solid, well-tried, old-fashioned Marxism."

"But," Elsa objected, "the Marxist teaching does insist on change and flexibility, doesn't it?"

"I wasn't talking of the theory," Marty said. "I was talking of human minds and how they work."

"They'll work differently when they've been differently educated," said Gilbert. His sister looked at him.

"Let's hope so. But, presumably, the physiological changes in human brain-cells will continue. They'll still deteriorate with age. Perhaps that could be coped with by compulsory retirement from administrative jobs at—say—fifty-five?"

Aunt Bee cried enthusiastically:

"Dear Marty, that's a wonderful idea! I've always thought that young people should manage the world."

"You know, Marty," Richard said to his wife, "Aunt Bee refutes your theories. Here she is at—well, at a good deal more than anyone would think to look at her—all agog for innovations. What we really need is Nick's encyclopædia knowledge and his singleness of purpose grafted on to Aunt Bee's charmingly large-hearted nature, and all our troubles would be solved."

Marty laughed as they rose.

"Perhaps it sounds as if I don't like my brother, Nick," she said lightly. "I do, but I often wish I had smacked him more when I had the chance."

Back in the drawing-room, Gerald, declining coffee, sat down at the piano and began to strum, keeping up a stream of badinage with Aunt Bee, who held herself very straight in her chair while she ogled him, for she had dined well, and her waistband felt tighter than ever. Elsa, wandering to the window, took her coffee cup from Gilbert, and said:

"The city looks lovely from here. All cities should be seen from a height and a distance—and at night."

"You don't like cities—otherwise?"

"Not to live in."

He realised that he had never considered his own feeling for his native city, so he considered it now, stirring the sugar in his cup, characteristically oblivious of any need for continuing a con-versation which seemed to have lapsed quite comfortably. He had lived, he decided, not so much in this city as with it; it had seemed less an environment than a loose outer skin. He liked its easy informality the more, perhaps, because he was himself by nature stiffish. Bullock-teams, not surveyors, had determined its first streets, and the bright, intrusive fingers of the harbour had always shaped its plan. It and its inhabitants had built their characters together in a happy-go-lucky harmony. Its vitality and theirs were of the same kind—a vitality not necessarily expressed in movement or in "progress"; a vitality of existence rather than of performance, falling, sometimes, under the hot sunlight, into an idle trance which had something of sluggishness, but nothing of debility. Yet the people, too, he reflected, were capable of that cold violence which possessed the city when a bleak wind roared through the funnels of its narrow streets, and the harbour whipped itself to a fury of white-crested waves.

He admitted with regret that it was a city rescued from man by the sea. Buildings crowded over its low hillsides to the water's edge. The unscrupulous greed of "development" had indeed been curbed here and there by a sad flash of that intermittent homage which man pays to beauty; a few bays and promontories had been left to the bush. But it was through no plan or virtue of its inhabitants that the city remained an adjunct of the harbour, and not the harbour of the city. Only at night, from surrounding hill-sides such as this, when it looked like a sky of stars below, could they claim to have added to beauty—and then by accident. Beyond the protection of its blue water, defenceless, the city became any city. Coming into it by train you left the bush behind, and then the paddocks, and then the stray vacant allotments; and with the multiplication of the railway tracks it closed about you in a whirl of black smuts and hot, tarry smells. The terrible backyards of the slums streaked past, and the human individual became lost in the city-concept of mass humanity which he had created, living and dying within crumbling walls, behind dingy curtains in labyrinthine lanes . . .

And in rat-infested Burt Street terraces . . .

He said abruptly:

"Come up to the top of the steps at the back of the house, Miss Kay. The view's really good from there at night."

She put her coffee cup down and went with him through the verandah door, across the gravel path, across Marty's lawn, now languishing in the drought, and up the steps cut out of the rock wall to the back gate. From there, looking over the roof-top, they could see most of the city and a great deal of the harbour, but when Gilbert spoke it was not of the view.

"I've been thinking of that 'creative paralysis' you mentioned. Perhaps 'productive paralysis' would be a better term?"

"Doesn't it come to the same thing?" she asked flatly.

"If it continued, of course, it would. But why should we assume it's going to continue just because we're going through a barren patch ourselves? What's the matter?"

She had moved sharply, and drawn a quick breath. She thought that it was like this slow, serious, middle-aged man to utter so clumsily a phrase that flicked her like a whip. The incessant torment of her own 'barren patch' had almost betrayed her into making a fool of herself at dinner when they began talking about airmen; she had felt an almost murderous exasperation with them all—these well-provided-for people with their comfortable relation-ships, their strongly established private lives, their easy theorising. And yet she had wanted to meet this family—wanted it almost morbidly because they were part of a life which, though only a story on her mother's lips, had been more real to her than her own. And having met them she did not want to let them go; it was as if by entwining them with her own life she could borrow some of their psychological stability. Now that Bill. . . .

She said hurriedly:

"My cigarette burnt my finger. What were you saying?"

"I wondered if this feeling of paralysis were a result of our having been—as writers, you know—kept at arm's length by the community. We haven't ever been made to feel that there's a population demanding our products, just as it demands food or clothing. So that when life falls into chaos as it is now, there is no established bond between the public and its writers . . ."

She knew that her face had fallen into sullen lines, and her eyes into the strained stare which she sometimes surprised in the mirror when she was alone; but in the darkness it didn't matter. She said: "There should be, by now," and then, realising that her tone had matched the invisible expression, she added quickly, forcing more interest into her voice: "It's not as if our writers have lived in ivory towers. What more could they do?"

He said quite heatedly:

"No more. No writer can do more than write. But when what they write has to go out into the market place and compete on equal terms with a new pair of stockings, or an evening at the cinema—well, what can you expect of a public that left school at fourteen, and whose literary taste stops short at the comic strips?"

She said unsympathetically:

"You sound like your sister. But does that explain why we sit chewing our pencils by the hour like third form children with an essay to do?"

"I think it does. Writers live on their times; they have no material except the life around them. And they live *with* their times in a sort of holy wedlock, for better or worse, till death do them part. So when that life doesn't accept them fully, or recognise them as contributors, it throws the whole burden on them instead of taking half itself. Writers are only human beings; they get tired like anyone else, they get depressed . . ."

"And then they start bellyaching about creative paralysis."

"I suppose so. But there *is* a psychological strain in preserving one's own faith in something against a mass opinion that says it isn't important."

She was not interested in the abstract problems of collective writers. Her own private misery was so demanding that she shied away impatiently from anything which endeavoured to distract her attention from it. She said coldly:

"My cigarette's gone out. Have you a match?"

Holding one for her, he saw its light wink back at him from the diamond on her finger, and asked abruptly:

"You're engaged to be married?"

She stared down at the city lights in a silence which lasted for so long that he began to think, feeling irritated, that she had resented his question. He was just about to propose to return to the house when she said slowly:

"No. No, not now. My fiance is—was—in the Air Force. He went to England quite early in the war. He was one of those who—didn't come back from Dunkirk . . ."

He saw her drop her cigarette-butt and stamp out its glowing end. She said in a dull, expressionless voice:

"It's rather cold, isn't it? Shall we go inside again?"

He followed her silently down the steps.

IX

In the mountains, nights were long and dark and piercingly cold; days were rent and maddened by bitter westerly winds. In the early morning taps were frozen, the ground stood up on tiny stilts of ice, and pavements rang like iron underfoot. Down in the gullies where the sun came late or never, plants and undergrowth were no longer green, but powdery white—brittle and unearthly like frost flowers. Under the towering tree-ferns, among the mossy rocks and decaying logs, the lyrebird, embodiment of a perpetual green twilight, stressed the silence with his midwinter song of mating. The smell was of loamy soil, rich with the rotting leaves of centuries.

Up on the tableland above those wide gullies and narrow gorges the sun shone through an air so icily pure that every breath of it was to the lungs like the shock of cold water to the body; there was a shiver in the thinnest tracery of shade. Shopkeepers strayed to their doorways to loiter for a moment in the sunshine, rubbing their numbed fingers. Postmen and tradesmen were more leisurely on their rounds, housewives dallied when they came out to shake their mats, and holiday makers, stretched in deck-chairs on boarding-house verandahs, basked rapturously, newspapers and knitting forgotten on their knees. Afternoons died quickly under lengthening shadows, and sudden sunsets, as gorgeous as mountain parrots, flamed out across the purple valleys. When they faded only a cold, bluish haze was left, and smoke began to rise from every chimney to meet and mix with it. People retreated indoors to huddle over fires, leaving the streets deserted, the town beleaguered by darkness.

Gilbert, in the town but not of it, found himself observing with the mild interest of the casual onlooker its reactions to its environment. Phyllis, by now firmly entrenched as a permanent resident, provided him with the keynote. As a whole, he discovered, the town took small notice of the valleys. They were its livelihood, its reason for existence, but they dwarfed it, and some half-conscious resentment, perhaps, at being dwarfed, tempted the town-folk to assert themselves by creating an atmosphere of complacent

suburbanism. They made indeed a grudging gesture of ack-
nowledgement to scenic immensities by constructing sedate and
easily accessible vantage points from which visitors could gape,
and turn away. Smooth paths skirted the cliffs for the tourist,
broad roads invited his car, signposts directed him, refreshment
rooms beguiled him, rubbish bins invited, but did not always
receive the litter of his picnics. And yet the valleys were omnipresent; no one ever quite forgot them. Looking innocent enough
from above, their tree-tops endless and unbroken, like moss, soft-
ened by the blue haze, dipping and darkening to some hidden
creek, rising again in a sunlit talus to the foot of some perpendicular
cliff, they offered a perpetual challenge. Looking-glass country;
country in which the surest way of not reaching a given spot was
to walk straight towards it. Country that tempted you forward
with a vista of gentle undulations, and then stopped you dead with
an unexpected cliff. Country that camouflaged its contours with
dense undergrowth, enveloped you suddenly in an impenetrable
veil of white mist, left you floundering, disorientated; country
which quietly swallowed the inexperienced hiker and held him
prisoner. . . .

During the week-ends, Gilbert escaped to it. He found a certain
stimulation in the austerities of the weather, and the pleasure of
novelty in winter loveliness. It was a beauty, he felt, to awe
rather than to gladden the heart; there was nothing in it of the
sensuous enjoyment of summer beauty—of grass, and flowers, and
hot, strong-scented earth. But it fitted his mood. He could walk
himself to physical exhaustion, he could pit himself against the
stubborn wildness of the country, he could explore, and climb,
and trudge, finding comfort and reassurance from the threat of
middle-age in the hardy response of his body.

His escape was not from his thoughts, harassing as they were
during those winter and spring months of 1941; he took his
thoughts with him to a place where he could examine them free
from the intrusions of his personal life. The end of August
brought a political crisis in his own country, and he watched its
development with a kind of uneasy hope, measuring the extent
of his earlier anxiety by the breath of relief he drew when the
first Federal Labour Government for nine years was precariously
established early in October. Life nowadays, he thought, found
its peaks in pathetically fervent gratitude for small mercies. People

had forgotten how to expect good things; they could only offer wondering thanks when they were not as bad as they might have been.

He knew that his absences on such expeditions were at once the cause and the result of his wife's increasing bitterness. He went to escape from her complaints, and she complained because he went. And yet he knew also that during the week she was well content without him, fussing with the house and the garden, giving and attending tea-parties, making a life for herself which was serene because she could build it to her own pattern, without his intrusion. She did not really want him, but she wanted the conventions of married life to be observed. She was, he found, essentially a small-town dweller, and he realised now how the more impersonal life of a city must have chilled and bewildered her. She liked small communities, small problems, small issues, small scandals and small talk. In the little mountain town she found herself transplanted to a soil in which she could thrive. Here she discovered a compact and cosy circle of respectable matrons with whom she could endlessly exchange calls, recipes, knitting patterns and gossip; here her penchant for organising found an unfailing outlet in church bazaars, local charities, functions in aid of war funds, and sewing bees. As the wife of a novelist, she assumed, too, the responsibility for nourishing culture in her home town, and founded a "literary circle" at whose meetings literature played second fiddle to afternoon tea. She was so busy and so happy for the first few months that she ceased to worry about Gilbert, assuming that the carrying out of her Machiavellian plan was the same thing as its success.

And indeed, except for his selfish, solitary excursions into the bush on Sundays, it seemed to be working out quite well. Ignoring his unenthusiastic response to her offers to accompany him, she insisted, once, on going. She packed an elaborate lunch, and chattered with determined cheerfulness as they walked. And walked. Cheerfulness faded as they toiled up the fourth long, stony hill. She protested querulously:

"How much further are you going? There was a perfect picnic spot back there."

He looked at his watch.

"We haven't been walking two hours yet. Do you want to stop here?"

She looked round discontentedly.

"There's no water."

"There may be some in the next creek. But it wasn't much more than a trickle last time I passed it."

"How far is it?"

"About two miles."

"Two miles! I can't possibly walk that far, Gilbert!"

"Well, we'll stop here if you like."

"But what about tea?"

He said irritably:

"I can't conjure water out of the thin air. If we stop here we can't have tea—that's all."

She contemplated a tealess lunch with horror.

"I suppose we'll have to go on."

There was no water in the creek. She sat down and took her shoes off, almost in tears.

"I can't *imagine* why you want to come all this way! There's always water down by the falls, and a good path, and seats and tables, and fireplaces for the billy and everything . . ."

It didn't seem worth while, in this unattractive spot, to spread the little cloth she had brought. There was grass on the banks of the creek, but it was tall and wiry and parched by the drought. There were no trees—only thickets of low-growing callistemon, and when she sat near them to get some shade she was disturbed by movements and rustlings that made her think of snakes.

Gilbert wandered away down the dry creek-bed. It was a pity, he thought, that Phyllis could not have seen it as he remembered it before, when the creek was running—though her main interest in water seemed to be as a means of making tea. He shrugged, looking down at the dry sand under his feet, and the hard-caked mud of the banks, picturing it transformed by the flash and gurgle of the little creek tumbling merrily from one limpid pool to the next until it reached the lip of the falls, and leapt over in a flutter of diamond drops and a gauzy veil of wind-blown spray. He moved cautiously nearer to the edge of the cliff until he could lean over and look at the soft, sage-green tree-tops far below. He craned, trying to see what became of the creek down there, but his view was partially interrupted by a ledge jutting out from the cliff-face not ten feet below him. He saw a clump of unfamiliar blue wildflowers growing on it, and was studying the rock, toying with the idea of climbing down to look more closely, when Phyllis called him.

"Gilbert! Gil-bert! Aren't we ever going to have any lunch?"

He turned away from the cliff. Getting down might have been easy enough, but getting back would be difficult. He made his way up the creek-bed again to find Phyllis nearly in tears.

"This place is swarming with ants, Gilbert! I had to put every-thing away again in your pack, and even then they keep crawling in. And the flies are nearly driving me mad! Of all the silly places to come to!"

She sat on a bare flat rock with her back to the view, and sulked. Gilbert ate a couple of sandwiches standing. Most of the picnic had to be carried home again. She arrived limping painfully on a blistered heel, and went straight to bed. After that Gilbert went walking alone.

*   *   *   *

It was not until the winter was over, the maples in the garden in young green leaf, the lilac in bloom, and one old apple tree reminding her, as it always did, of the blossomy scene of their betrothal, that Phyllis began to fret again because the inspiration she had so carefully provided for her husband's muse still failed to inspire. She could not quite clarify her own wishes on the subject. For a time after *Thunder Brewing*, she had hoped that he would write no more, that he would rest upon the laurels he had already won, and give their friends no further cause for doubtful glances. But she had discovered—with some indignation—that the world was curiously forgetful. She had realised that a writer whose name was not continually blazoned on the bookstalls is soon for-gotten, and it irked her to discover that more and more of her new acquaintances had never even heard of Gilbert Massey. As Pre-sident of the Literary Circle, she wanted to be able to say again: "My husband's new book," and she felt that in making this im-possible he was letting her down badly. She began to question, to hint, to exhort.

"How is the new book going, Gilbert?"

"I haven't started yet."

"But, Gil, you were writing yesterday—and last week-end."

"Nothing of importance—just notes."

She was puzzled. He never made notes. She knew that, at least, from hearing him talk to other writers. Nevertheless, "notes" sounded professional. Perhaps, she thought, he was working out a new technique. That was a good phrase, and she used it with effect at the next meeting of the Circle. But when she enquired again he still said he had not really started on anything new. She became importunate.

"But, Gilbert, why don't you? I'll see that Pete doesn't turn the wireless on while you're working. After all, you've had a *good* rest from it—four years! There's really *nothing* to disturb you here!"

He stared at her, looking into her mind with amazement and despair. Nothing to disturb you! Turn off the wireless, and the voice of humanity is silenced, shut the door and the world is outside! Then, in a dreamy void, in a vacuum, in an exquisite nothingness—you can write! With what? Why, with a pencil, on a sheet of paper! Looking up when your words fail to a blue view, and drawing from that some nebulous inspiration for creating a safe world, a gentle world, a rosy-golden-tinted world unrelated to the savage one so happily excluded! That was how she saw it. Could he tell her that he carried the world in his mind, that no matter how profound the silence she provided for him it was still clamorous, that those clamours, that "disturbance" were the ingredients of his craft, that he could not shut them out, and would not if he could?

He said wearily:

"I'll get going on something soon."

But when her enquiries began to grow querulous, he took refuge in a stony, forbidding silence which daunted her until she persuaded herself that it was her duty to remain undaunted, and began again. He countered that by beginning to stay in town overnight one and sometimes two nights a week, until she understood at last that she had not removed him from the influences which she dreaded, but had merely removed herself so that she could no longer efficiently police his actions. Watching her, he had seen her growing more and more into the life of the township, building herself a place in it, becoming, as he grimly phrased it, the big frog in the little puddle; and when he saw the realisation of her mistake dawning on her he threw down a challenge.

"If you don't like my being away at night occasionally, perhaps we had better sell this place and go back to town."

She cried hastily:

"No, no—no, there's no need for that! But . . ."

sounded professional. Perhaps, she thought, he was working out a new technique. That was a good phrase, and she used it with effect at the next meeting of the Circle. But when she enquired again he still said he had not really started on anything new. She became importunate.

"But, Gilbert, why don't you? I'll see that Pete doesn't turn the wireless on while you're working. After all, you've had a good rest from it—four years! There's really *nothing* to disturb you here!"

He stared at her, looking into her mind with amazement and despair. Nothing to disturb you! Turn off the wireless, and the voice of humanity is silenced, shut the door and the world is outside! Then, in a dreamy void, in a vacuum, in an exquisite nothingness—you can write! With what? Why, with a pencil, on a sheet of paper! Looking up when your words fail to a blue view, and drawing from that some nebulous inspiration for creating a safe world, a gentle world, a rosy-golden-tinted world unrelated to the savage one so happily excluded! That was how she saw it. Could he tell her that he carried the world in his mind, that no matter how profound the silence she provided for him it was still clamorous, that those clamours, that "disturbance" were the ingredients of his craft, that he could not shut them out, and would not if he could?

He said wearily:

"I'll get going on something soon."

But when her enquiries began to grow querulous, he took refuge in a stony, forbidding silence which daunted her until she persuaded herself that it was her duty to remain undaunted, and began again. He countered that by beginning to stay in town overnight one and sometimes two nights a week, until she understood at last that she had not removed him from the influences which she dreaded, but had merely removed herself so that she could no longer efficiently police his actions. Watching her, he had seen her growing more and more into the life of the township, building herself a place in it, becoming, as he grimly phrased it, the big frog in the little puddle; and when he saw the realisation of her mistake dawning on her he threw down a challenge.

"If you don't like my being away at night occasionally, perhaps you had better sell this place and go back to town."

She cried hastily:

"No, no—no, there's no need for that! But . . ."

had forgotten how to expect good things; they could only offer wondering thanks when they were not as bad as they might have been.

He knew that his absences on such expeditions were at once the cause and the result of his wife's increasing bitterness. He went to escape from her complaints, and she complained because he went. And yet he knew also that during the week she was well content without him, fussing with the house and the garden, giving and attending tea-parties, making a life for herself which was serene because she could build it to her own pattern, without his intrusion. She did not really want him, but she wanted the conventions of married life to be observed. She was, he found, essentially a small-town dweller, and he realised now how the more impersonal life of a city must have chilled and bewildered her. She liked small communities, small problems, small issues, small scandals and small talk. In the little mountain town she found herself transplanted to a soil in which she could thrive. Here she discovered a compact and cosy circle of respectable matrons with whom she could endlessly exchange calls, recipes, knitting patterns and gossip; here her penchant for organising found an unfailing outlet in church bazaars, local charities, functions in aid of war funds, and sewing bees. As the wife of a novelist, she assumed, too, the responsibility for nourishing culture in her home town, and founded a "literary circle" at whose meetings literature played second fiddle to afternoon tea. She was so busy and so happy for the first few months that she ceased to worry about Gilbert, assuming that the carrying out of her Machiavellian plan was the same thing as its success.

And indeed, except for his selfish, solitary excursions into the bush on Sundays, it seemed to be working out quite well. Ignoring his unenthusiastic response to her offers to accompany him, she insisted, once, on going. She packed an elaborate lunch, and chattered with determined cheerfulness as they walked. And walked. Cheerfulness faded as they toiled up the fourth long, stony hill. She protested querulously:

"How much further are you going? There was a perfect picnic spot back there."

He looked at his watch.

"We haven't been walking two hours yet. Do you want to stop here?"

She looked round discontentedly.

"There's no water."

"There may be some in the next creek. But it wasn't much more than a trickle last time I passed it."

"How far is it?"

"About two miles."

"Two miles! I can't possibly walk that far, Gilbert!"

"Well, we'll stop here if you like."

"But what about tea?"

He said irritably:

"I can't conjure water out of the thin air. If we stop here we can't have tea—that's all."

She contemplated a tealess lunch with horror.

"I suppose we'll have to go on."

There was no water in the creek. She sat down and took her shoes off, almost in tears.

"I can't *imagine* why you want to come all this way! There's always water down by the falls, and a good path, and seats and tables, and fireplaces for the billy and everything . . ."

It didn't seem worth while, in this unattractive spot, to spread the little cloth she had brought. There was grass on the banks of the creek, but it was tall and wiry and parched by the drought. There were no trees—only thickets of low-growing callistemon, and when she sat near them to get some shade she was disturbed by movements and rustlings that made her think of snakes.

Gilbert wandered away down the dry creek-bed. It was a pity, he thought, that Phyllis could not have seen it as he remembered it before, when the creek was running—though her main interest in water seemed to be as a means of making tea. He shrugged, looking down at the dry sand under his feet, and the hard-caked mud of the banks, picturing it transformed by the flash and gurgle of the little creek tumbling merrily from one limpid pool to the next until it reached the lip of the falls, and leapt over in a flutter of diamond drops and a gauzy veil of wind-blown spray. He moved cautiously nearer to the edge of the cliff until he could lean over and look at the soft, sage-green tree-tops far below. He craned, trying to see what became of the creek down there, but his view was partially interrupted by a ledge jutting out from the cliff-face not ten feet below him. He saw a clump of unfamiliar blue wildflowers growing on it, and was studying the rock, toying

with the idea of climbing down to look more closely, when F called him.

"Gilbert! Gil-bert! Aren't we ever going to have any lunc

He turned away from the cliff. Getting down might hav easy enough, but getting back would be difficult. He ma way up the creek-bed again to find Phyllis nearly in tears.

"This place is swarming with ants, Gilbert! I had to pu thing away again in your pack, and even then they keep in. And the flies are nearly driving me mad! Of all places to come to!"

She sat on a bare flat rock with her back to the view, an Gilbert ate a couple of sandwiches standing. Most of th had to be carried home again. She arrived limping painf blistered heel, and went straight to bed. After that Gil walking alone.

*   *   *   *

It was not until the winter was over, the maples in t in young green leaf, the lilac in bloom, and one old reminding her, as it always did, of the blossomy scen betrothal, that Phyllis began to fret again because she had so carefully provided for her husband's muse st inspire. She could not quite clarify her own wishes on For a time after *Thunder Brewing*, she had hoped tha write no more, that he would rest upon the laurels he won, and give their friends no further cause for doub But she had discovered—with some indignation—tha was curiously forgetful. She had realised that a w name was not continually blazoned on the bookstalls gotten, and it irked her to discover that more and mor acquaintances had never even heard of Gilbert Mass sident of the Literary Circle, she wanted to be able "My husband's new book," and she felt that in ma possible he was letting her down badly. She begar to hint, to exhort.

"How is the new book going, Gilbert?"

"I haven't started yet."

"But, Gil, you were writing yesterday—and last we

"Nothing of importance—just notes."

She was puzzled. He never made notes. She least, from hearing him talk to other writers. Never

"All right. If you want to stay here we will. But when I have business in town at night, or a meeting, or the weather's bad, I'm not going to do that drive twice a day just for the sake of sleeping here. I can always stay at Nick's flat."

Beaten, puzzled, she said resentfully:

"Oh, very well." An idea came into her head which had never entered it before; but because she was angry she welcomed it. She added with a sour little laugh: "So long as that's where you *do* stay!"

* * * *

After his first astonished anger he tried to brush the remark aside, but found it returning to goad him into an uneasy self-examination. He realised that he was forty-five, and that he had been soberly faithful for more than twenty years to a woman he had never loved, and now heartily disliked. He discovered, more-over, that he had lately become a more active member of the Writers' Guild than ever before, and bullied himself into admitting that the reason for this sudden enthusiasm was that Elsa Kay was usually to be found at its meetings.

He was profoundly startled by these discoveries. He would have said, if questioned, that he did not greatly like the girl, and it would have been the truth. Why, then, in Heaven's name, was he seeking her out? Standing with her that night at the top of Marty's steps, he had been moved to an intense compassion for her—and that, surely, was natural. There was enough in what she had told him, wasn't there, to account for compassion? And yet, was there not also another more personal impulse behind it? Feeling some obscure psychological confusion and distress in her, was he not identifying her with the confusions and distresses of his own youth—being sorry not so much for her as, vicariously, for himself? The threads which stretched between them were too cobweb-frail to be called bonds. They were threads of association, perhaps—her association (so nebulous as to fade before thought, and reassert itself only in moments of unguarded emotion) with what he called the Scott Laughlin period of his own life; her association with himself in the pangs of "creative paralysis"; and in their common knowledge of loneliness. "I like a little human company, now and then," she had said. Something in his own nature, solitary not from choice, but from the never-to-be-escaped inhibitions of his childhood, had responded to that.

And she was often stimulating. As one of a younger genera·
tion with which he had had few personal contacts, she stirred his
interest. He compared her dry scepticism with the groping,
amorphous idealism of himself at the same age, and probed, not
without anxiety, for some depth of conviction in her which he had
not yet discovered. Was he regarding her, instinctively, as
material as a point of view and a set of reactions hitherto un·
familiar to him, but which, as a novelist, he must understand? Or
were all these conjectures merely defences which he was setting
up against the incredible possibility that he was falling in love
with her? At his age? Nevertheless, he was forced to recognise
what (but for Phyllis' barbed remark) might have remained
obscure to him for many months yet—that she was often in his
thoughts, that his eyes looked for her at any gathering, that some·
thing in him quickened if she were there, and died if she were not.

He told himself dispassionately that he was at that dangerous
period of life, and in those dangerous matrimonial circumstances
which tempt middle·aged men to make fools of themselves with
girls young enough to be their daughters. Elsa, of course, was
not quite young enough for that, but still . . .

All through November he kept away from the Writers' Guild.
He accepted an invitation from Gerald, and made a last·moment
excuse when he found that Elsa was to be one of the party.
Through those uneasy months of Spring and early Summer, while
one part of his mind watched the shaping of events—the political
crisis in his own country, the beginning of the siege of Leningrad,
the attempted assassination of Pierre Laval, the assault on Moscow
—another part worried at this personal conundrum which threat·
ened, unless he were very circumspect, to complicate further an
already complicated life. This young woman, he told himself
brutally, could mean nothing to him; to her, he realised, remem·
bering his own youthful impressions, he must seem old. He
struggled to detach his mind from her by fastening it on some·
thing else, and set himself doggedly to the reorganisation of his
business, and the renovation of his terraces.

Yet he found no real refuge in these activities. They were jobs
performed almost automatically, guided by the surface of a mind
which was incessantly restive, impatient to be about its own work.
So, one Sunday afternoon, early in December, he went off in a

mood bordering on desperation to the glassed-in corner of the verandah which was his study, and shut the door.

He had always thought that there were just two good moments in the writing of a book—the moment before beginning, when an idea demands expression, and a stack of virgin paper beckons, and the moment of ending when, with the last word written, there comes an intoxicating sensation of release. Like most writers he had an affection for his tools of trade—an affection which, as manager of a wholesale stationers, he was peculiarly able to indulge. Three reams of paper, their wrappings still unbroken, lay in the right-hand drawer of his desk. He could afford to be extravagant with typewriter-ribbons and carbons. He had an abundance of pens, pencils, india-rubbers, paper clips. He had pots of gum, elastic bands, patent box-files and folders with spring clips. He had red, green, and the best blue-black ink, envelopes of every conceivable shape and size, and a gadget for punching holes in stacks of paper. All these, neatly arranged on his bare and spacious desk, or stowed away in those drawers which were not stuffed with his scraps and failures, awakened that anticipatory eagerness of the craftsman to handle his tools, with which he was pleasantly familiar. Nevertheless, he knew from experience that in the throes of production this barren tidiness would give place to chaos, and it was the chaos he wanted really—the scattered papers, the mess of cigarette-ash and india-rubber fragments, the overflowing wastepaper basket, the screw of discarded carbon, the pages mad with interpolations and erasures, and the productive impulse throbbing at full power like a noiseless dynamo.

So he sat down and waited for the dynamo to switch itself on. He lit a cigarette and stared out through the panes of glass at the glimpse of blue valley framed in trees, not drawing inspiration from it, but reflecting idly that, though he had become a mountain-dweller for ulterior motives, he was beginning to enjoy it; had it not been for the pile of paper before him, a white and silent challenge, he could have relapsed into a mood of beatific receptiveness, observing how dramatically the cobalt of the distant valleys contrasted with the fresh green of the maples in the garden.

Forcing his eyes from them, he stared down at his paper and began to doodle. He drew a black square very carefully, and surrounded it with an intricate pattern of right-angled lines spreading out and out across the top of the sheet. It formed a maze through which his pencil-tip absently wove its way, and all the time he was thinking: "How do you begin? Damn it, the others began themselves!"

His cigarette was finished. He lit another and stared out the window again. He thought angrily:

"This isn't getting any work done."

If you can't write, he thought, how about writing about not being able to write? He scored a black line under his doodling and began with obstinate laboriousness:

There may be certain educational value in being unemployed—for a time. To imagine the frustration, the lowered "morale," the general sense of personal deterioration which inevitably goes with unemployment is not the same thing as experiencing it. The writer who cannot write—who cannot, despite long hours at his desk, achieve anything in which he can feel that independent life which is his signal that what he is doing will (in the mountain-climber's phrase) "go," is unemployed; and the moral blight of unemployment descends on him. Perhaps there is nothing left for him then but to get words down on paper somehow—any old sequence of words—or perish as a writer. Perhaps he must forget whatever writing aims he may have had in better times, forget that he wanted to write in a certain way about certain things, and go back to the elementary function of his job— recording. Perhaps into a mass of such recording some fragment of interpretation will find its way at last, and set him off on his own track again. So it becomes a matter of recording fast and continuously —and to hell with literary effect. It is a matter of driving through that invisible, intangible obstruction in oneself, of putting one's head down like a labouring ox, and going ahead. And if one's brain, dulled and blunted and half-anaesthetised by its necessary, self-preserving defence against too frequent and too brutal assaults, has ceased to be a fine precision tool for the marshalling of words into beguiling patterns, and the building of shapely phrases, perhaps it can remain a more humble but no less prideful implement—something which, like a hammer or a spade, needs no trained skill for use, but can claim the sober value of utility. . . .

Full stop. He thought: "Oh, damn!" and tore the page in small pieces. He got up and went to the window from which he could look down the hill towards the creek; and among the broom, and the grass-trees, and the low-growing black wattle, and the mountain-devil bushes, he saw Virginia being kissed by a young man.

He returned hastily to his chair. Astonished by his own discomposure he asked himself if he were going to be like his grandfather, and disapprove of his daughter for an innocent kiss. All girls got kissed, and girls as pretty as Virginia no doubt got kissed with particular enthusiasm. Was it not altogether more right and natural that she, at twenty-two, should be kissed than that he, her father, at forty-five, should imagine himself kissing Elsa? All the same, he told himself stubbornly, there were kisses and kisses. This one which he had inadvertently seen had been a very intense, passionate, experienced kiss; and he found himself remembering a morning earlier in the year when Virginia had unexpectedly come home at four o'clock . . .

So had poor Aunt Bee, some fifty years ago . . .

He had asked Phyllis about that morning.

"Why didn't Virginia stay with the Johnsons after all?"

"They had to go down to Sydney at the last moment, so she and Betty Bradley drove down with them half-way and came back by train. They had to wait over two hours on the station. I told her it was a silly thing to do—but you know what girls are nowadays." She had seemed quite unconcerned.

He stood up again and began to pace restlessly about the room, keeping away from the window. He was suddenly afraid—horribly afraid—that the shock which he had felt when he saw that kiss had its origin not in paternal anxiety, but in paternal resentment because his daughter was young and ripe for kisses, while he himself was—or should be—long past them. This demonstration of sex-passion in Virginia underlined for him unmercifully the knowledge that his own time for it was passing him by without fulfilment. Was he angry with Virginia, furious with her young man merely because they goaded him with a glimpse of something he had never known? Was he in danger of that sour, middle-aged puritanism which resents in the young its own missed and now never to be experienced ardours?

No. He was really worried—for Virginia. Standing still, glaring into himself with almost inimical ruthlessness, he was able to say honestly that if it had been Prue in the young man's arms he would have felt differently. He wouldn't ever feel afraid for Prue—even if she did, as the old-fashioned saying went, throw her cap over the mill. She would be armoured in her own personal integrity against the results of any escapade; she would bring something with her out of any experience to enrich her life. But Virginia? There was something irresponsible and undisciplined about Virginia. She would follow her sensations and her appetites into any kind of mess, taking all the time, giving nothing, and so building nothing from her mistakes . . .

He felt suddenly helpless and humiliated. Remembering his own violated solitudes in childhood, he had tried so hard not to intrude into his children's lives that now there was no common ground on which he could meet them. This, surely, was a job for a mother? Almost as if she were there in the room with him he could see Marty cocking a quizzical eye at him and asking: "Why?" Children, she always maintained, were a joint responsibility of both parents. Together, male and female, they could represent for a child a complete, sane embodiment of adult humanity; singly they split his world in half. That was her theory. Well, if it were a true one, Heaven help his children, for he and Phyllis had never been "together" in that sense. What could Phyllis, with her irritating, scolding manner, her shrinking pruderies, and her alternating fits of hectoring and sentimental appeal, do for this hungry, unstable, and far too beautiful daughter? What could he do, reserved, awkward in emotional contacts, and now inhibited by a long habit of detachment? Well—could he not at least have a look at this young man?

He went out quickly along the verandah, down the steps, round the gravel path, across the lawn. He found himself coughing loudly as he went because it was unbearable to him that he should seem to be spying on Virginia. She, seated gracefully on a rock, smiled sweetly at him as he approached, but he was unconscious of her in the shock of discovering that her young man was not young at all. He was, Gilbert judged, not more than three or four years younger than himself—a well-dressed, middle-aged man with a red face and rather protruberant brown eyes. Virginia said kindly:

"Hullo, Dad. This is George English. My father, George."

"How do you do?" said George.

"How do you do?" said Gilbert.

They shook hands.

"Charming place you have here," George remarked. He studied

Virginia's father curiously, having read two of his books, heard rumours of his pink politics, and decided that, being a writer, he must be slightly mad.

"We like it." Gilbert heard himself sounding as abrupt as he felt, and left it at that because he was no good at dissimulation, Virginia said composedly:

"I've been showing George the creek. But he prefers fairways."

"Oh?" said Gilbert.

George cleared his throat.

"Are you a golfer, Mr. Massey?"

"No," said Gilbert.

Virginia, he observed with fury, was looking amused. She said lightly:

"George is teaching me. He says I'm doing pretty well." She added demurely: "Except on the eighth hole—somehow I never seem to get a good score there." Gilbert saw a glance flash between them, and a slight deepening of the colour in the man's already florid cheeks.

He said shortly:

"I'm going down to the creek."

As he picked his way down the stony path he heard them exchange some remarks in an undertone, and then Virginia laughed. Standing on the rocks, looking down at the trickle of water sliding over the stones, he thought: "It'll be quite dry soon, if we don't have rain . . ."

      *   *   *   *

In the morning, driving down to town with Prue beside him, he asked:

"Do you know this friend of Virginia's—George English?"

She answered briefly: "Yes—just."

He drove for a mile or so before he spoke again.

"I'm worried about Virginia. It doesn't seem fair—and it's not what I would want to do—to push those worries to you, but— well . . ."—he hesitated again—". . . there are things I don't feel I can profitably discuss with your mother."

She replied awkwardly:

"I know, Dad, but I don't think it's any use *worrying* about Virginia. If she's man-mad that's the way she is."

"But hang it all," he burst out, "I must worry about her, mustn't I? I'm her father."

"Just what are you worrying about?"

"I don't like the look of this chap English."

He tried to add that the chap was nearly twenty years older than his daughter, and found that he could not say it. Prue said it for him.

"Of course he's much too old for her."

To his annoyed astonishment he heard himself objecting quite hotly:

"That in itself needn't matter. Look at your Aunt Marty; she and Richard have made a perfectly successful marriage . . ."

"Marriage?" He saw from the corner of his eye that she turned and looked at him for a moment. "There isn't any question of marriage between George and Virginia, Dad. He's married already. He has two children round about Pete's age."

He managed not to show the shock he felt. There had been something almost pitying in her voice. Poor old innocent Dad, said her tone. She tried to reassure him.

"I don't think it means anything more than—all the others, you know. Virginia has always had men trailing after her ever since she left school. She's really absurdly *young*, Dad—I mean un-developed, and irresponsible, like a kid. She only cares about having a good time, and George is well off, and he has a car, and he takes her to expensive places where she can show off her clothes and be admired. That's all it means to her."

"Is it?" he asked, remembering that kiss.

She did not answer, and they drove for a few miles in silence. He wanted to say: "What about his wife and children?" and found that he could not say that either. Again she seemed to read his thought.

"I gather he doesn't get on with his wife. Hasn't for years. She's—sort of fat and middle-aged, and perfectly happy so long as she can play bridge all day. I suppose you can't blame him for being mad about Virginia."

He asked slowly:

"You wouldn't blame a married man with children for having a love affair with a girl twenty years younger than himself?"

She said impatiently:

"Oh, Dad, we don't know that it is a love-affair. Why shouldn't it be just a flirtation like half a dozen others she's had?"

He made no reply to that, admitting to himself that he was out of touch with the modern techniques of flirtation. Prue said almost apologetically:

"Anyhow, what can you *do* about it? I mean Virginia's of age, and you haven't any hold over her except money, and you wouldn't cut her off with a shilling—at least I can't see you doing it—and if you did she'd only get herself into a worse mess than ever."

He said heavily:

"No hold over her, eh? We must have been shockingly bad parents, Prue."

She replied with detachment:

"Mother's not a good parent because she's not a good human being. I mean her intentions are good, but she's all muddled and sentimental. I'm quite fond of mother, but I feel as if she's the child and I'm the adult. And if she really knew the extent and variety of Virginia's flirtations she'd only scold and exclaim, and make a fuss, and say that modern girls are no good, and Virginia would go straight ahead her own way without taking the slightest notice."

He asked with an effort:

"How about yourself? Have I no hold over you, either, except money?"

"Would you want to have a hold over me?"

He said with violence:

"No!" And then added: "Not a hold, Prue, but at least a say if I saw you getting yourself into a mess."

She said lightly:

"Do you think I'm likely to get myself in a mess?"

"No—no, I don't really. But if you did?"

She laughed and patted his knee.

"I'd give you a fair hearing, Dad."

He felt reassured, and smiled at her.

"You're an impertinent brat. See if you can't talk some sense into Virginia, Prue."

She said with a sigh:

"Sense doesn't seem to take with Virginia. But I'll try. And get called a prude and a sourpuss for my pains. Oh, Lord, Dad, just look at those burnt-up paddocks!"

They were going down the long, curving slope of the foothills, and below them the plains spread out, parched and brown except for the green ribbon of trees which marked the winding river.

"When the drought breaks," she said, "let's stay at the hotel up there and sit on the verandah and watch them turn green."

He glanced up at the cloudless sky and grunted discouragement.

*   *   *   *

That day Nick burst into his office.

"Well, it's happened at last, Gil. The Japanese are running amok. They've bombed Pearl Harbour . . ."

While he listened Gilbert noticed with a novelist's detached curiosity that the effect of this news was to send a flood of energy through his body—as if it wanted to leap out of the chair and start doing things straight away; as if the sudden awareness of crisis with its merciless challenge were stimulating (as, indeed, it probably was) automatic physiological reactions. That passed, and there remained nothing but the intolerable burden of intellectual realisation. He laid his pen down, took off his spectacles, rubbed his eyes, reached mechanically for a cigarette. He told himself, putting it carefully into words: "The Pacific isn't pacific any more."

BOOK II

I

Not for some years now had Marty, waking on her birthday, been able to feel that friendly affinity with the New Year which had consoled her childhood. She had learned to think of years as ominous, hiding heaven knew what disasters, and none had ever seemed more laden with menace than this 1942, which greeted her with a blaze of heat through her bedroom window, reminding her that one could not even enjoy sunlight any longer.

This, she thought, was to be a year when normality itself would seem abnormal; when to see trains running, people shopping, housewives hanging out their washing on Mondays, would seem curiously unreal against the more urgent business of shatter-proofing windows, fixing blackout paper, despositing buckets of sand about the house, digging air-raid trenches, learning A.R.P. and first-aid.

This was to be a new kind of life, calling for profound psychological readjustments; and she remarked to Richard a few weeks later how easily this adjustment was being made. It seemed strangely simple, she said, to revert to the conception of life as a perilous thing—precarious, insecure. Could one measure the thinness of the civilised veneer by observing how readily one ceased to think of human society as walled about by law and order, invisible defences through which no outer barbarism could break? She added:

"I'm homesick for the future. A thousand years hence—two thousand . . . ? For the time when we learn that only the invisible defences are sound."

"We're fifty years nearer to it," her husband said, "than Edward Carpenter was when he wrote that man loses his inner and central control, and declines on an outer law that must always be false."

"Nearer to it? Are you sure?"

He drew her hand through his arm and patted it.

"Oh, yes, we're nearer."

She moved restlessly.

"I believe that, too, really. But one wants to be able to enjoy living in the present. One doesn't want to be perpetually battling against the temptations of escapism. Because I suppose being homesick for the future is really as escapist as being homesick for the past.

"No, it isn't," he comforted her, "looking back is escaping, but looking ahead is a contribution."

"You can't live ahead," she objected.

"No, you can't do that. You have to live," he paraphrased, "in that stage of human evolution into which it has pleased God to call you. But, unless there had been a few people always able to think ahead of their stage, where should we be now?"

She wondered: "Where are we now?" but did not say it. She was thinking again how easily the civilised veneer stripped away from the ancient jungle-law—thinking that what is emotionally easy to accept is still likely to be accepted, no matter how frantically it may be intellectually denied. Once you thought of living life; now you thought of defending it against death. Evidently it was even harder than one had imagined to put on the habit of civilised thought—far easier than one had imagined to cast it off.

A little more was shed with every morning's headlines. Those territories which optimists had for so long continued to call, in the teeth of geographical fact, the Far East—those islands which they had preferred to describe as bulwarks rather than as embarrassingly placed stepping-stones were already in the front line of battle. Hongkong had been engulfed, Thailand had capitulated, resistance in the Phillipines was nearing desperation point, and the word Singapore was fast losing its mystical reassurance.

No, it was not surprising that under the recurring assault of the headlines an atavistic memory should stir. SINGAPORE'S FATE A MATTER OF HOURS. JAPANESE LAND ON SINGA-PORE ISLAND. PALEMBANG IS OCCUPIED BY JAPAN-ESE FORCES. These were daily blows that hammered the loose-knit exploratory mind of the civilised human being into a cohesive mass, hard, solid and resistant. The sensitive feelers which it had put out in wonder to investigate and interpret its great world were now withdrawn; its world became its own threatened existence; its purpose narrowed to survival. TWO BIG AIR RAIDS ON DARWIN. AIR RAIDS ON BROOME AND WYNDHAM. This was their own earth trembling beneath their feet. THREE WEEKS' LIFE FOR JAVA. And then?

People were studying maps. They were measuring distances. They were saying: How many 'planes have we? How many tanks? How many of our fighting men are overseas? They were thinking of the vast, unprotected northern coastline of their continent, reckoning the range of bombers, worrying about rubber and petrol, wondering where their little Navy was. They were looking inside themselves, too, estimating their own qualities, finding no reason to doubt themselves until the voice of the Department of Information bade them to do so. Marty, listening, ground her teeth with rage; Gilbert, outwardly expressionless, seethed inwardly; Richard looked as though he were smelling drains; Nick was coldly attentive, cynically unsurprised. Hate propaganda of the crudest sort insulted their humanity; fear propaganda insulted their courage; querulous scolding, impertinent jibes, and sickly sentimentality stabbed viciously at their nerves, Marty said one night, silencing the voice with a savage flick of her finger.

"If our 'morale' stands up to this, it's indestructible."

Nick shrugged.

"We're partially immunised—that's our salvation. This stuff is just advertising, done by people with advertising minds, and we're hardened to it in other forms. So we can ignore it. If we expected to get anything from it—any guidance, or strength, or statement of purpose—it would kill us psychologically."

"The point is," Gilbert said, "that the method has no relation whatever to the subject. The subject is, actually, spiritual, and the method is commercial, as Nick says. People may not put it into words, or even think it very clearly, but they know you can't sell morale as if it were a breakfast-food. So when they hear someone trying they just don't listen."

"Let's hope they don't," Richard said dryly.

"But," Marty protested, still furious, "apart from its stupidity, and its vulgarity—what right have these ignorant dunderheads to assume that we need lectures on morale?"

"What else can they assume?" Nick asked. "They're commercially-minded people. They know nothing about the abstract qualities of the human mind—they only know about commodities.

In the past when they wanted people to become permanent-wave conscious, or safety-razor conscious, or refrigerator-conscious all they had to do was to put across a line of sales-talk on perms and razors and refrigerators. Now they think we should be made morale-conscious in the same way; they'd only gape if you told them that morale's like digestion—the less you think about it the better it is. Can you expect them to believe that the public already has something they haven't sold it? Why, Marty, it would undermine the only faith the poor saps have."

Nick was in uniform now. He had taken, since the war began, the view that sooner or later his own country would be threatened, and that he would not voluntarily risk on the other side of the world a life which would be needed nearer home. He had pointed out that he took this stand from no narrowly nationalistic view. The war, he recognised, and continually emphasised, was global. There was a task—and not a light one—to be performed as part of that global war, in the Pacific. He saw no sense in denuding a large, sparsely populated continent of its fighting men, nor in taxing already overtaxed shipping by transporting abroad troops which would later have to be transported back again. He pointed out that the cry from Europe had always been shortage of equipment, not shortage of manpower. Some of his liveliest arguments with Richard during the earlier stages of the war had been upon this point.

"We don't know," Richard had insisted, "that Japan *will* attack us."

To which Nick replied:

"Why shouldn't she? The British Navy tied up on the other side of the world, the United States with one eye on Europe and the other on Isolationism, Russia watching her German border, China crying out for enough supplies to defend herself—what the hell's to stop her attacking us and the Dutch East Indies when she gets good and ready? We know what her political set-up is. Haven't you ever read the Tanaka Memorial?"

Now invasion streamed south like a dark glacier. March began with the assault on Java; a booklet called *If Invaders Come* found its way into once tranquil homes, and was read by sober-faced citizens. Life quickened and thrummed to the lightest touch, like a violin string tightening. In the second week Batavia fell, Rangoon fell, the first Japanese landings in New Guinea, and the first bombing of Port Moresby brought the enemy a stride nearer. The third week began badly with news of the loss of the cruisers *Perth* and *Yarra*, and Darwin had its fourth air-raid. Marty, teased by a half-remembered quotation, went and looked it up. *"Oliver said: 'I have seen the Saracens; the valley and the mountains are covered with them, and the lowlands and all the plains: great are the hosts of that strange people; we have here a very little company.' "*

*   *   *   *

Gilbert and Prue had taken over Nick's flat. Suddenly Gilbert found his own personal problems reduced to an almost disconcerting simplicity; without any action on his part events had imposed their pattern on his life, and the fact that it was the pattern he would have chosen was irrelevant—a mere accident. Now, with petrol becoming as precious as champagne (or, he reflected, as water, in this merciless drought), driving over a hundred miles a day became out of the question. Even Phyllis could find no justification for it. Equally absurd, as he pointed out to her, would be a deliberate removal from the mountains back to a city from which many people were already evacuating their children.

"Prue and I," he told her, "have to be in town. But when we have the cottage here already there's no sense in your leaving it. Pete will have to give up boarding school for a time, and go to the local school."

"But, Gilbert," she protested, "I don't want us to be apart just now. I want to be with you."

Physical cowardice, he acknowledged, was not one of Phyllis's faults. He patted her shoulder, feeling hypocritical.

"I'll have to be out with the V.D.C. most week-ends," he said, "but I'll get up as often as I can. And Prue can come up, even if I don't. There really isn't likely to be any trouble so far south, but you must see that we can't deliberately expose Pete to even a possibility of danger so long as we have an alternative ready-made for us."

"I don't see," she insisted, "that we're any safer here than we'd be in town. What's sixty miles to a 'plane?"

"Bombs," he said grimly, "are much too precious to be wasted on a little place like this. Besides . . ."

But suddenly she was weeping wildly.

"It isn't that!" she wailed. "You *want* to get away from me! I've seen it coming for years! You don't care about me any more because I'm getting old, and because you're afraid of the Truth I want to show you . . ."

Bewildered, he stammered:

"Truth . . . ? What do you mean?"

Then, to his horror, she began to rave. A mad, rambling incoherent diatribe against his wickedness and the wickedness of the world, and the falseness of his ideas, and the stubbornness of his mind which had forsaken old simple teachings and the faith to which they had been bred. All this killing, all this evil, she raged, had been loosed on the world by such minds as his because they were "materialistic," because they looked all the time for salvation through human effort, and not through the Grace of God. And just because she had lost her figure through bearing his children, and because she thought more of being a good wife than of painting her lips and doing her hair and wearing smart clothes, he was tired of her. And he had been given a great gift, and instead of using it to make people better and happier he had used it to make them discontented. That last book of his had been a wicked book, full of anger and unsettling ideas. But if he had only joined the Christian Watchers' Circle with her, as she had begged him to do, he would have learned that nothing matters except keeping your thoughts pure and serene. So God was taking his gift away from him—didn't he even understand that? Oh, yes, she knew he hadn't been able to write, and she knew why. He wasn't worthy of his gift, so it was being taken away from him. And she had had to bring up the children quite alone—almost as if they hadn't a father, so little interest he took in them. Except to encourage them in all their silliness. Couldn't he see how Prue was becoming infected with all his own ideas, and losing her womanliness and having her purity tarnished by mixing with bad people, and thinking materialistic thoughts, and would Virginia have become so frivolous, and would she have used so much lipstick if he had helped her as a father should, and set up high ideals for her . . . ?

He sat on the edge of the bed where she had flung herself staring at her in dismay. She seemed quite frantic. Her voice rose and rose till it was almost a scream, her hands waved and clutched and beat on the counterpane, her face was distorted, and blotched with tears. Several times in the last few years she had had semi-hysterical fits, but never one so violent as this. Forty-five, he thought, looking at her with an aversion which pity could not altogether overcome. A bad time, anyhow, and now made worse than ever by the anxiety which hung over them all. Was this a frenzy of dying sex, directed against himself because he had never satisfied it, rationalised by her mind into any kind of accusation which would serve as a cloak for its real nature?

Whatever it was, he thought, with a grateful sense of detachment, events had the situation in hand now. Events, perhaps, had always had it in hand, slowly separating him from her emotionally during their long years together, and now making the break definite and complete with a physical separation. He realised that events were doing this to people all over the world. They were breaking down human society as if by some vast chemical action, so that individuals of one kind were separated from those of another kind; so that disregarding all minor ties, all minor expediencies, they found themselves ranged irrevocably in opposite camps, committed irrevocably to different paths . . .

The thing was done now. Returning to the city, he had set about making—but not so much making as acquiesing in—a new life. The flat was small, but there was room in it for himself and Prue, with an extra stretcher which did duty for Nick or Virginia when either of them turned up for a night or two on leave. Virginia, having carefully considered the uniforms of the various women's services, had decided to become a W.A.A.F. Prue, after hesitating for a few weeks, finally said: "I think I'll keep on with the shop and the library, Dad. Books *are* important, aren't they?" Gilbert was issued with his V.D.C. uniform, and congratulated himself, during arduous week-end exercises, on the bush-walking that had kept him fit. He went with Prue to first-aid classes at night; together in the flat they swathed each other in bandages and slings, joking about it to subdue the heavy knowledge that they might some day have to use their skill in earnest. The life of which they were a part, and its environment, underwent a curious, slow, implacable change. The city, once so light-hearted and happy-go-lucky, began to look dingy and unkempt. Under the now intolerable sunlight the parks languished, the trees wilted, the grass went straw-coloured and crackled underfoot. Housewives shatter-proofed their windows and wrestled with rolls of blackout paper. Dumps of sand appeared in the streets; buckets were filled from them and borne off to stand incongruously in peaceful suburban hallways. Shop windows vanished behind boards, notices

appeared saying AIR RAID SHELTER, piles of sandbags blocked
entrances. Motor traffic dwindled as the owners of private cars
jacked them up in garages. Those that remained in the streets
bore white-painted mudguards and running boards, and their headlights were masked. From the top of Marty's back steps, where
he had looked down on the city with Elsa last winter, Gilbert
looked down on it again now, thinking it a symptom of lost innocence that what was once a bird's-eye-view had become a bomber's-
eye-view. In that happier "once" a characteristic zest had tempted
the city to bedizen itself with electricity; the harbour was its
mirror, making each light two lights, and it hugged the foreshores,
in love with its own reflection. From the outer suburbs it might
have been a giant fun-fair; from farther still an orange glow in
the sky; from the mountains a luminous mist. Now, robbed of its
glitter, no longer ablaze with the old carnival gaiety, no longer
wearing the lights of its streets like ribbons, the lights of its houses
like spangles, the lights of its ferries like emeralds and rubies, the
lights of its bridge like a tiara, it was a city waiting for the sirens
to wail, and its harbour reflected nothing but the stars.

By daylight it gasped and sweltered. All over public buildings
and private homes a rash of small red-lettered notices warned
DON'T WASTE WATER. Taps were sealed, hot baths tabu;
well-loved and tended gardens died slowly, dust was added to heat,
and flies to dust. People began to see their country as a map, to
picture the bush, dry as tinder, ringing its small, isolated villages,
its country towns, creeping up to the very threshold of its cities.
They imagined a few incendiary bombs dropped into it; they remembered, and wryly repeated old lines of Henry Lawson's:

> "*And is it our fate to wake too late to the truth that we have been
> blind,*
> "*With a foreign foe at our harbour gate, and a blazing drought
> behind?*"

They shrugged and answered his question with more of his own
words:

> "*The warning pen shall write in vain, the warning voice grow
> hoarse . . .*"

Here they were, the drought and the foreign foe, and for the
moment the drought seemed the more insupportable. "Being

without water," Marty sighed, trying to wash up with one small kettleful, "*is* lowering to the morale." A people to whom sun was a necessity like air or food—a people whose bodies had learned to welcome and absorb it, now began in that drought-stricken summer to feel their very flesh drying up, to feel a physical craving for rain, as though the pores of their skin could soak it up like a sponge. Even the gum-trees, evolved to endure heat, went brown, and stood rustling on hillsides which looked as though they had been swept by fire. In the gullies, where Gilbert's V.D.C. activities took him sometimes in the week-ends, the creeks were bone dry, and the once emerald green moss fell to powder beneath a touch. Standing in the bed of one such creek, feeling even through his boots the heat of the rounded, water-worn stones, noticing the curious, dead silence, the patient enduring stillness of the bush, he thought how triumphantly, despite its grim moods, it had captured and held the imaginations and the love of its step-children. Yes, despite drought, despite their own small numbers, despite insufficient resources, they would fight like demons to hold this parched, half-desert continent. They would retreat, if the final necessity drove them to it, into the aloof, inhospitable bush— and they would die at last of thirst and hunger, but still die content because they were there. He tried to imagine it owned, occupied —even loved—by Japanese, and found it quite impossible. Yet he knew with his mind that it was the land which shaped men, and not men who shaped the land. He remembered—with his mind— how the first English settlers had hated it. He asked himself— with his mind—whether after a few generations Japanese might not also become quite different from their countrymen "at home," learning it, loving it, perhaps treating it better than it had been treated by its first invaders. Yet thinking such things and feeling them were, he acknowledged, entirely different. His mind could tell him that the aborigines were the real Australians, just as the Red Indians were the real Americans; his conviction still said: No. The country is here inside my body, and its air is the breath out of my lungs.

*　　　*　　　*　　　*

Suspense, he observed with interest, acted upon different people in different ways, but he saw little of that depression, that "de-featism" which official propaganda did its best—or worst—to keep in the public mind. Mostly it was irritation. Now, he reflected, seeing the cranky bewilderment of people who had turned their eyes resolutely from unpleasant possibilities, one had one's bleak reward for having looked into an ugly future. Seen for so long as a possibility, it had few new terrors as a fact. He had a moment of amused compassion for a little old lady who had lived faithfully all her days by the strength of reassuring phrases, and who confessed to him with a tremor in her voice that it was dreadful—really *dreadful*—but she was getting quite anti-British! He, at whom she had once looked in shocked condemnation because he reviled English Toryism, now found himself in the comical position of acting advocate to her for the British Navy; of pointing out that it could not be in two places at once. But she had left his office still tremulous and bewildered—frightened not of Japs, but of a world in which her conventions had let her down; of an incomprehensible world in which it had become necessary for a British Dominion to look for help not to the Union Jack, but to the Stars and Stripes.

For by the middle of March, officialdom had informed them of what everyone had known for weeks—that American troops were landing in the country. General Macarthur had arrived, too—and it was raining. Recovering from a bout of 'flu which had overtaken him during a week-end in the mountains, Gilbert had lain in bed on that Tuesday afternoon when the General's arrival was announced, and heard the blessed drumming of rain on the roof. It was a mere prelude. By the end of the month it was falling in torrents; the parched plains lay feet deep beneath flood waters; the menace of war was extraordinarily alleviated by the jubilant tidings "Hot baths again. Water may now be used for domestic purposes at any hour."

* * * *

It was Marty's turn to be ill. Listening with only half her attention to the low, seductive strains of the wireless by her bedside, she thought drowsily that it would not be difficult in these exacting times to become a *malade imaginaire*. She had not seen a newspaper for three days; her body, aching and feverish had made her a super-isolationist—the war and the world must get along without her. But she was better now; the aches and pains had left her, and she felt only a not unpleasant lassitude. Already, though she was still obstinately ignoring the world at large, household cares were beginning to stir her mind to restlessness; she wondered how Richard had been feeding himself in their now servantless household, and whether the laundry had come back, and if he had managed to get a new lot of coal delivered for the boiler. She knew that Gilbert and Prue had called to see her, for she could hear their voices downstairs, talking to Richard, but she was too tired to ring the bell on the table by the bedside and let them know she was awake. They would come up in due course; and in the meantime she let her thoughts drift idly about them. Dear Gilbert, whom it was almost, but not quite possible, to call poor dear Gilbert! That he had for so long endured marriage to that tiresome woman—whom it was possible in one's more tolerant moments to call poor Phyllis, but never dear Phyllis—was only another demonstration of that self-contained, stubborn patience which all their life had alternately awed and infuriated her.

How it had exasperated her, during those first years of their intellectual explorations! He had taken it all so hard—and so slowly! It had sometimes seemed to her that his laborious sifting of evidence, and verifying of figures, and accumulation of data were almost wilful stalling. Where he, thorough and painstaking, insisted on fact and detail to build a principle, she had regarded fact and detail merely as useful confirmation of some principle she had already accepted. At a time when some of his acquaintances were calling him a dangerous radical, she had said, in a fever of impatience, that he was a dyed-in-the-wool conservative. And then turned on Nick in a fury for saying the same thing.

His technique, she acknowledged now, had been sound. From that time—when was it?—somewhere in the early 'thirties?—when they had stiffened to painful alertness (as a miner might, who, entombed underground, hears the first warning crack overhead) he had moved step by step, testing each as he went, and never beguiled into haste by Utopian allurements. In the alarming darkness of sheer ignorance she had sometimes felt panicky and despairing. But Gilbert had gone on hunting methodically about the apparently solid prison walls of custom, conditioning, prejudice and propaganda, finding cracks here and there, probing and testing till he knew where the weaknesses were. They were old hands now; they knew the nature of the prison, and they were accustomed, though not resigned, to the knowledge of captivity. It was a formidable dungeon—but not impregnable; in that faith Gilbert was more steadfast than herself. . . .

The music had ceased, and a voice, deep and fruity, was saying: *"The British people have fought many wars, but in every one we can trace the same motive—the motive which inspires all Britishers—the love of freedom and justice. This is not a policy, nor even something which needs to be taught; it is inherent in the race, it is natural to our blood and our native soil . . ."*

Marty sighed. The Herrenvolk! Need he paraphrase Hitler quite so blatantly? She wanted to switch him off, but her hand, heavy on the counterpane, refused to move.

"Let us pause . . ." said the voice, and paused. *"Let us pause before we cast away the precious heritage which has been built for us, to snatch at some fantasy of internationalism which will prove but a will-o'-the-wisp, and turn to dust and ashes in our hands . . ."*

Marty, lover of metaphor, winced, and began to struggle up on her elbow with determination. Shaky, but implacable, she reached out for the dial. Someone said: *". . . and why should we suppo . . ."* Someone else said: *". . . ladies' fleecy-lined . . ."* A girl crooned moaningly: *". . . you held my ha-a-a- . . ."* A woman said firmly: *"No, Mrs. G., if you suspect your hus . . ."*

"Oh, God!" murmured Marty, turning desperately. She saw Prue peering round the doorway, and begged, subsiding on her pillows:

"Come in and turn this thing off for me."

Prue silenced it and sat on the foot of the bed.

"Are you better, Aunt Marty?"

"Yes—I'm really all right now—only weak and lazy."

"Do you mind if I smoke?"

"Not a bit."

"Will you . . . ?"

"Heavens, no! I'll have to be really well before I start poisoning myself again. Aren't you going up to the mountains this week-end?"

"No," said Prue, cupping her hands round a lighted match. "We're having some people at the flat to-night." Her voice was just too casual, and Marty had a quick ear. She said "Oh?" and waited, but Prue was silent, her head tilted back, her blue eyes watching the smoke from her cigarette, her thoughts busy with a new preoccupation of her own, out of which, rather painfully, she was building a new conception of her father.

Since they had shared Nick's flat she had felt that she was learning to know him better than ever before. And just as she was feeling that, she had found reason to wonder if she knew him at all. She liked living with him alone, away from her mother's complaining restlessness and incessant martyrdoms; away from Virginia and her tiresome flirtations. She liked most of his friends who came to the flat in the evenings to talk, she liked the informal suppers they had, and the hour after the guests had gone, when they washed up plates and glasses in the tiny kitchen, and discussed the evening's discussion. But one night, a week or two ago, she had seen him looking at Elsa Kay, and the shock which had run through her was only half astonishment, though she was curiously unwilling to analyse the other half. And a few days later she had, by accident, seen them going into a restaurant together at lunch-time, and to-night Elsa was coming to the flat again. . . .

She asked suddenly:

"How old is Dad, Aunt Marty? Forty-five?"

"Let me see—yes, that's right, nearly forty-six. He's five years older than I am."

"He must have married very young."

"He did."

Prue slid off the bed and prowled about the room. As a child, she remembered, she had always liked exploring Aunt Marty's house; her possessions managed to be businesslike as well as pleasing to the eye. Mother, Prue thought with a sigh, divided her possessions into two classes—those that were "pretty" and useless and those that were useful and ugly. Forty-five, she thought, isn't old—not *really* old. And how was she, feeling as she did just now—as she had felt ever since that morning when a voice had said to her: "Pardon me, do you have any books on wild-flowers?"—to think of Dad and the way he looked at Elsa with anything but sympathy?

Her ear had pricked up in the first syllable the rounded, trans-Pacific "r," and she had marvelled as she scrambled to her feet from the case of books she was unpacking that this accent, so familiar on the screen, should sound so exotic and improbable in one's daily life. Next, confronting a tall young man with a pair of observant dark eyes, she had been unhappily conscious of incongruity between military uniform and a request for wildflowers.

But when she had led him across the shop and found a book for him, she had seen that, as he looked at her over its open pages, there was no suggestion in his tentatively friendly smile that he

shared her thought. She had been forlornly pleased by this discovery—obscurely encouraged to find that bloodthirstiness was not
necessarily put on, nor an interest in innocent things discarded,
because one stood clothed in the trappings and accoutrements of
war. The smile seemed to demand speech of her, so she asked
lamely:

"Are you interested in wildflowers?"

"I don't know much about them," he admitted, "but my mother's
crazy about flowers. She has a garden full of them back home,
and she likes to get new kinds and grow them. So I thought
maybe I'd send her a book about the Australian ones."

He returned to a study of the coloured plates, and she looked
at him with some curiosity, for though the Yanks were a familiar
feature of the streets by now, and though Virginia had already
collected a couple to add to her retinue, this was the first she herself had spoken to. He was just foreign enough to be intriguing,
and she was so intent on her scrutiny that she had felt a little
flustered when he looked up from *Leptospermum persiciflorum* and
smiled at her again—but still tentatively.

Now, standing by her aunt's window, looking out at the sunlit
garden without seeing it, she was angry—with Virginia. A convention—an inhibition—had stood between her and a free response to that tentative smile. Was it a kind of cowardice, she
had wondered, or a kind of miserliness, to withhold oneself from
strangers? Now she knew that it was because the Virginias of
the world took the open-hearted techniques of friendship and made
them tawdry that she herself was impelled to guardedness and
reticence.

That smile had worried her; there was a sort of question in it.
She had felt responsible—and annoyed with herself for the feeling. Absurd! But after all, why not? Wasn't he a stranger in
a strange land—her land? The old, hard-dying tradition of hospitality which had sprung up in a country of vast distances where
homes were few and scattered, and wayfarers must be welcomed
and entertained, still nagged at her in a large city. And again,
why not? Could anything be lonelier, more unfriendly, than a
large city? But a soldier, she had objected to herself, impatiently,
is not alone; he's part of an army, he has his community ready-
made, everything is arranged for him—food, shelter, amusement . . .

Nevertheless, there *was* a question in his smile, and she had
smiled back, though not without reserve.

"Do you like that one? I think it's the best, really. It's thirteen-and-sixpence. There's another one here . . ."

He rejected it with a wave of his hand.

"This one's swell. I'd like to have you send it for me. I'll give you the address."

Leading the way to the desk, she had reflected that even after years of movie-going it still sounded strange to hear that word accented on its first syllable. He picked up one of a pile of cardboard book-marks which bore the legend: "PRUDENCE MASSEY'S BOOKSHOP AND CIRCULATING LIBRARY," and pointed to her name.

"Is this you?"

Constant association with Virginia, to whose more vivid and arresting beauty she was accustomed to seeing male glances turn, had made her less confident of her own attractiveness than she might have been; but she could not fail to read admiration when it confronted her so frankly. She had bent hurriedly over the desk to hide a blush.

"Yes, that's me."

She picked up a pencil and began to scribble to his dictation. Mrs. George B. Grover. She wondered if his name were George too—George B. Grover, Junior—and, thinking of George English, found herself hoping, ridiculously, that it was not. Then, annoyed with herself for feeling any personal interest at all in a mere casual customer, she wrote down "Boston," looked up, and asked sternly:

"How do you spell Massachusetts?"

"You don't," he assured her gravely. "Not any more than 'Mass.'"

There was no doubt about it; he was inviting her to smile and be friendly. But she couldn't be friendly yet because the word 'Boston' had made her think of Sacco and Vanzetti, and she was feeling depressed because of the way the world and its problems lay always in wait, hidden behind innocent words, sights, incidents, thrusting themselves into moments when one would have liked to forget them for a little while. Looking slightly discouraged, he asked:

"How much did you say the book was?"

"Thirteen-and-six."

He stared hard at a fistful of notes and silver, frowned, and dumped the lot on the desk before her.

"Here," he said, "you take it. I guess it'll be a while before I get round to understanding this money of yours."

"You haven't been here long?"

"We only got in last week."

Feeling motherly and protective, she had picked up a note and proceeded to instruct him.

"This is a ten-shilling note, and this is a two-shilling piece, and this is a shilling, and this is sixpence. Thirteen-and-six. See?"

He grinned at her, pocketing the change.

"I guess so."

Suddenly they had both realised that the transaction was at an end. She said quickly:

"I'll send the book off for you at once."

But he was looking round the shop again.

"There's another one . . . I just can't recall the name of it . . ."

"If you could tell me the author . . . ?"

He shook his head. With the knowledge that he was only seeking an excuse to prolong the interview, she became very demure.

"Well, perhaps you'll remember it later."

He brightened.

"Maybe I will. I'll call by another day if I do."

It was not until long after he had gone that she realised guiltily that they had both forgotten all about postage. But it had been the same afternoon when he called by again, and he had remembered since then no less than four other books which he must instantly send his mother, and he had taken her to a movie, and she had become his guide about the city, and to-night he was coming to the flat, and how could she, seeing Dad look at Elsa, fail to remember how John B. Grover looked at her?

Was there any reason why Dad shouldn't have a love affair if he wanted to? Mother? It had been quite evident to her for many years now that her parents' marriage, for all its outward decorum, was about as unsuccessful as a marriage could be. She played with the blind cord, thinking unhappily of poor mother, and wondering, reluctantly, if she might not be happier freed from a husband whose every thought and word repelled her. The idea came to her, too, though she shrank a little from it, that there was actually something in her mother which might welcome (without, of course, admitting it) the supreme martyrdom of being a deserted wife. She must always be right—and how right that would make her! Yes, she must always be right. Not all the

burned cakes and iron-hard pastries of her married life, not all
the scones which did not rise, or the jellies which did not "jell"
had convinced her that she was anything but an excellent cook.
Not all the clumsy frocks her daughters had worn as children, or
the shapeless rompers which had clothed Pete's baby chubbiness,
had shaken her faith in herself as a seamstress. She saved three-
pences in triumph, and wasted pounds in muddling, but she still
thought of herself as a "good manager." And yet if you took
away from her that faith in her own rightness what would she
have left? So that even if her life were to be "wrecked" by
Dad's unfaithfulness, would she not save out of the wreckage a
triumphant vindication of herself? His wrongness would make her
more right than she had ever been before . . .

Marty watched her, feeling slightly disturbed. There had been
quite enough in that enquiry about Gilbert's age to set her on the
right track; it was indeed a track down which her thoughts had
already started once or twice. With the difference that she herself, watching the course of her brother's marriage, had for many
years half expected some such development, whereas to his daughter it was evidently a new and alarming idea. She asked:

"Who's going to your party to-night?"

"It isn't a party." Prue returned to the bed and perched herself again on its foot. "Only Gerald and a friend of his from
Melbourne, and Elsa Kay and . . ." the sombreness of her expression broke up suddenly into a smile that was half-mischievous and
half shy: ". . . my American."

Marty's eyebrows rose.

"Have you an American, darling? Don't tell me you beat Virginia to it."

"I didn't. She has two—so she tells me—I haven't seen them.
Mine just drifted into the shop one day to buy—what do you
think?"

"Nothing would surprise me. Omar Khayyam?"

"No. A book on wildflowers—for his mother."

"How charming. What's his name?"

"Grover. John B. Grover. He's going to be an architect—in
fact, he's practically one already—and build houses out of glass
and plastics." She looked round suddenly at the doorway. "Here's
Dad."

Marty thought as Gilbert entered that his daughter looked at
him like an anxious mother, uncertain whether he deserved sympathy or a spanking.

[185]

II

DOORS marked 1 and 2 opened from a small porch in a narrow asphalt lane. Elsa, balancing her parcels on one arm, felt in her bag for her latchkey, and inserted it in the door marked 1. Two seconds of pause before she turned it, expressed her unwillingness to step into the solitary life which this cramped, furnished flat represented. She looked at the little cupboard on the wall where the empty milk-bottles of her own, and the next-door flat waited to be collected to-morrow morning; she thought of the food in her parcels, food for one, the half-loaf of bread, the fragment of cheese, the two apples; she felt the empty silence of the rooms even before she opened the door, and, having opened it, hesitated again on the threshold, repelled less by the solitude and the shabby cheerlessness of the place than by its impersonality. Her depression mounted towards panic because it met her with its customary resistance. She did not belong here—and if not here, which was all the home she had, then where . . . ?

The door of No. 2 Flat opened before she had closed her own behind her. Bulky, exuding geniality, her neighbour cried:

"So it *was* you coming in! Tom said it was someone going down to the end of the lane, but I said: 'You don't tell me!' I said. 'I know her footsteps!' Look, dear, we wondered if you wouldn't come in to-night—we're having a few friends in for cards. How about it?"

Elsa said hurriedly:

"Oh, thank you, Mrs. Slade, but not to-night. I have rather a headache, and I'm going straight to bed."

Mrs. Slade's broad smile contracted sympathetically.

"Well, that's bad luck. My married daughter's coming with her husband. You and she'd get on well—she's just about your age, and I thought it might cheer you up and take you out of yourself . . ." She looked from Elsa to the cupboard with the milk-bottles—her own two large ones, and Elsa's small, half-pint one—and added with motherly solicitude. "You know, dear, you should drink more milk than you do. Put some flesh on you— why, there's nothing *of* you!"

Elsa managed a polite, mechanical smile.

"I don't like milk except in tea," she explained, "and really I don't need it. I'm quite well. It's just a headache."

"Have you got some aspirins, dear, because I could let you have . . . ?"

"Yes, thank you, I have some." Elsa began to close the door. "I'm sorry I can't come to-night."

"Oh, well," Mrs. Slade said cheerfully, "never mind! Another night, eh? You just run in to see me any time you want anything, dear. Don't be shy!"

"No." Elsa's jaws ached with maintaining her smile. She said: "Good-night, Mrs. Slade," and closed the door. She stood inside it with a sense of having escaped, listening, her smile altering, transforming her expression from that touching pathos which had more than once disturbed the kindly soul of Mrs. Slade into one of rather grim contempt. She thought derisively: "Shy!"

She went through the living-room into the tiny kitchenette where she ate her meals, and put her parcels down on the table. There were nights—and this was going to be one of them—when her sense of estrangement from life, unbearable any longer as a torment, became transmuted into a perverse sense of luxury. She felt a dark hostility towards the neighbour who had sought to come between her and the masochistic pleasures of self-torture. Her eyes, as she pulled off her hat, already had the abstracted stare of one who is about to enjoy the dangerous indulgence of looking inward with a fury of concentration. Barred and barricaded in herself, she could already feel the heady power of moving at will in the fourth dimension; the triumph of escaping, not to a next-door flat to be "taken out of herself," but, retreating deeper and deeper into herself, to destroy not only place but time itself; to be back in a little country town, going to school, playing hockey, helping to wash up at night . . .

Coming home from school to hear the inevitable sound of scales from behind the closed door of the sitting-room. To be poor, to know that Mother must give piano lessons which she hated, was the least part of the misery which her memory had kept fiercely alive through the years. To have no real father was not a misery at all. The misery, all tangled up with joy, was in tales of another father called Scott Laughlin, who was not her father. That father had had a daughter who was Mother's daughter, too, and yet was not herself. The confusion of that knowledge, growing with the still less bearable knowledge of her mother's unhappy longing for an old life in which she had no part had driven her to destroy herself. Somewhere within the real world of her home, within the walls of the little weatherboard cottage filled with her mother's presence, and the sound of scales, there was another, unseen world. Somewhere inside her mother's life there was another hidden life. Somewhere behind herself, her mother's daughter, there was another daughter, unknown and invisible, but so deeply loved that she became real—and a rival. Janet—Janet—Janet . . . !

Elsa sat down wearily at the table. She found a packet of cigarettes in her bag, reached behind her to the stove for matches. She watched the first mouthful of bluish smoke fan out and dissolve, and she watched herself, a skinny six-year-old, wriggling impatiently under the hair-brush.

"Janet didn't like having her hair brushed, either."

"Did she have long hair like mine, Mummy?"

"Even longer than yours—down to her waist in a pigtail."

"Mine's growing longer . . ."

But it hadn't ever grown down to her waist. Elsa pushed her hand through her thick, short bob, and flicked the ash from her cigarette on to the floor. Was mother a stupid woman, or only a very unhappy woman, a lonely woman obsessed by the knowledge of an irrevocable mistake? How is a child to know that its mother is poisoning it with a legend? How should it know better than to come back again and again, like a drug addict, for one more, and one more, and still one more dose? How can it differentiate between the tale of Janet and the tales of those other legendary children—the Annes, the Pollyannas, the families of Misrule and Billabong—whose innocent serial adventures carry no doom with them? It can only know with strange stirrings of fear, anger and jealousy that somewhere (but why in a story?) there is an enemy. Mother is here, and here she is mine. But she is also there—and there she is Janet's. Mother lives here in this house —but also she lives there in that other house with a broken front gate, and a deodar in the garden . . .

"Was the garden as big as this, Mummy?"

"Just about."

"Did it have an iron gate like ours?"

"No, it was a wooden one, and it always used to stand half open."

"Why?"

"Well, I don't know, really. I suppose the posts had sagged, or a hinge was broken, or something. It didn't seem to matter, and we never fixed it. Why do you want to know?"

Why? How did I answer that? How could I tell her that love was in her eyes and her voice when she spoke of that home—but in my home she was quiet and cold, so I must follow her to the warmth? In my mind the gate of that world stood ajar on its broken hinge; inviting me. . . .

The room was almost dark. Elsa dropped her cigarette-butt on a saucer and watched the red glow of its end fade and blacken. It had crossed her mind that no adult, save in madness, takes that terrible step across the shadowy line that divides the real from the not-real; she felt a faint shiver, watching the red cigarette-stub intently because it was real, real, and while she watched it she felt safe. When it died she was in darkness, with no anchorage; she was a child crossing the frontier between fact and fantasy without thought, as children do, every day, every moment, and return unscathed—if they have something to return to. But she, crossing it, had made a ghost of herself, and returned to her real world to find it melting and dissolving, her mother half here and half there, nothing stable, nothing that lasted except a story that went on and on . . .

"Did you have fruit trees, like we have?"

"No, but the Masseys, next door, had quite a big orchard. Janet and Marty used to sit up in the trees and eat apples. And we used to go blackberrying in the paddock opposite. That was one of the things they all wrote poems about once."

"Going blackberrying?"

"Yes."

"Whose was the best?"

"I think Gilbert's was that time, though Janet's father used to say that hers were usually the best. Marty wrote a funny one about getting her stockings torn, and having purple teeth from eating the blackberries."

"Was Gilbert's funny too?"

"I don't remember—but I should think not. Gilbert was rather a serious sort of boy."

"Mummy, shall I write a poem about blackberries too?"

There was a passport to that world which invited her; the play-mates who awaited her there were always busy with this mysterious writing. So she must write things, to be admitted. The mere act of scribbling words on paper became a mystic rite, identifying her with them; and yet she was conscious of this compulsion as a burden. She could not know why, nor, at that age, recognise it as an addition to the load which, straw by straw, anecdote by anecdote, was crushing her own life and her own individuality out of existence. She only knew that there were moments of temper and panic and blind revolt, violent fits of hatred for Janet which manifested themselves as hatred of her mother because her mother was accessible, and Janet, remote and inviolate, was not. Moments of terror, too, when, growing up, she looked at what she had written and realised that a page covered with laborious words can be still a blank page.

She lit another cigarette. The brief flare of the match showed her face mirrored in the black window opposite, a white face, two dark eye-sockets, an apparition seen for a second or two, and then swallowed up again by night. It seemed to her a symbol. She had never seen herself more clearly than that, or less briefly. She smoked fast and nervously, invoking conceptions of herself which she had built at different times to furnish emptiness. If Bill hadn't been killed, if he had come back, if we had been married and had children. . . . She saw that Elsa had loved her passionately; and yet she could not subdue her intelligence enough to ignore the knowledge that this Elsa was no more real than any other. She was a myth, seen through the honest, admiring, unanalytical eye of a young man who, having decided to love her, saw her as perfect. But at least she insisted with angry despair, he *did* see me. To him I was there, I was real, more real than anything in the world. That made me real.

So it was less grief than panic which his death had brought, for going out of life he took his conception of her with him, and left her a ghost again. She had no longer any part to play, she was no longer classifiable to herself; the engagement ring on her finger was the last thread between herself and that ideal, beloved Elsa.

To join the Writers' Guild was the shadow of a substitute, and yet it gave her a place, however small, however insecure. Someone had said:

"There's Gilbert Massey. He doesn't often turn up."

The curious shock of excitement she had felt then ran through her again now. Once more the legend had closed round her; and yet, for the first time, fantasy had touched fact with a crackle like the contact of electric wires . . .

"Where?"

"Over there near the wall. Chap with the greyish hair, smoking a pipe."

There he was. She had watched him with a kind of unbelief; with a kind of jealousy because he had once belonged in a life to which she had won only in pretence; with a kind of sardonic amusement because she knew him so well, because she had been eavesdropping on his life for so long, because she could see in the middle-aged man the "serious sort of boy" who had written a serious poem about blackberries. But with a kind of avidity, too, because he was solid, material evidence that the legend was rooted in reality.

She stabbed her half-smoked cigarette out sharply in the saucer, and immediately lit another. The word "parasite" flashed through her mind, and set her hand trembling. What can you do, she thought furiously, if you have no life of your own, but get into someone else's? Isn't he the ideal, heaven-sent host? Get into his real life as you got into his legendary one, find it now, as it was then, the life of a writer, produce the passport which once admitted you to a child's make-believe, and use it now as admittance to a more stable world . . .

Will it deceive him—this spurious document? She stood up, switched on the light, and walked through into the other room where her typewriter stood on the table among a litter of papers. There was a half-typed page in the machine; she read a few lines of it, ripped it out, crumpled it into a ball and threw it on the floor. She went across to the bookshelf, took out her own book and fingered it, turning its pages idly as she had done a hundred times, seeking to convince hgerself that if you have written a book you are a writer. "Ideology" that young brother of Gilbert's had found in it, had he? But Gilbert had spoken of it with a curious reserve. She could feel him watching her, studying her, searching her for something which he must never know was simply not there. She smiled sourly to herself, pushing the book back into its place. She knew the patter of this "ideology," and she had used it, but to herself she could acknowledge with fierce unregeneracy that she cared not a hoot about the world and its problems. Blast the

world. You couldn't say that to Gilbert without antagonising
him. You could perhaps bluff it out in conversation with him,
but he would find it in what you wrote. Or in what you didn't
write. He was securely at home among written words. She
couldn't deceive him there. Yet when she struggled to coerce her
words into patterns which would not betray her, they were empty;
they didn't even deceive herself. Over and over again, sitting at
her table at night with her paper before her, she read what she
had written and heard her brain stating with monotonous persistence that of course it was no good—how could it be any good?
I can't—said her brain—do this work of yours quite alone, you
know. You aren't feeling it. You don't care. If you write with
only half of yourself, you are only half writing . . .

She thought of Gilbert with bitter resentment. He to talk of
productive paralysis! He to be halted by a war! What did he
know of the real paralysis, when you write with your brain, and
your brain refers what you have written back to you—and there
is no you! She thought enviously of him, and Marty, and Gerald
Avery, who could set themselves in the background of their own
thoughts, while she must spend herself all the time appeasing a
ghostly ego that blotted out the whole horizon. Appeasing it—
and concealing it. For if they saw it they would no longer look
at her, but through her, like a pane of glass. They would say
nothing, but a door which must at all costs be kept open would
slam in her face. So she must talk their language, she must joke,
and evade, and use enigmatic silences. She thought of them as
people warm and dry in a strong house, blandly inviting her,
frozen and half-drowned outside, to observe the portents of the
storm. She resented them, but she must get into their house; she
must have a personality again; she must achieve faith in her own
individuality by becoming the centre of someone's world. And
what world better than Gilbert's, in which legend fused with
reality, and an old conflict could be resolved?

She wandered into her bedroom, switched on the light, and
stood at her dressing-table, looking intently at her dark, small-
featured face in the mirror. She was always conscious of the need
to discipline it, to relax the tightness of her mouth, to soften the
nervous watchfulness of her gaze. People didn't like faces which
betrayed an inner tension too clearly. Yet in Gilbert she had
recognised some remnant of repression which was, perhaps, suf-

ficiently akin to her own to make him tolerant. He, too, had known what it was to be imprisoned in himself, and the fact that he had, quite obviously, escaped, lent him an added fascination. He knew how to do it.

She stared at herself steadily. Her body was so small and thin as to be almost childish, her wrists and ankles fragile. She knew that the contrast between her starveling appearance and her dry, assured manner was not without its piquancy—and its pathos. It intrigued people, she had discovered, to see her as appealing, and then, when she chose it, to find her aggressive; and though their failure to see through the falseness of her assurance made her faintly contemptuous of them, she realised that she must capture attention by what means she could. She gave her reflection a faint, involuntary smile, saluting it as an ally in her campaign to capture the attention of Gilbert Massey. Already she had established a relationship which could not, she knew, stand still; it must progress to its logical conclusion, or it must die. She saw in her mirrored eyes the hungry questioning which solitude allowed them to express quite nakedly, and promised herself with wordless passion that it would not die.

III

EVENTS, which had determined his separation from Phyllis, and reorganised the circumstances of his life, now also upset Gilbert's soberly determined and at first conscientiously observed efforts at self-discipline. He found that he could not, without altogether withdrawing himself from those interests and activities which normally claimed him, continue to avoid Elsa. He found her at meetings he attended, at homes he visited. Now that he occupied Nick's flat, they were neighbours; he saw her often in the mornings just ahead of him in the street, making for the station; he met her in the train; he encountered her again in the heart of the homeward-bound five o'clock crowds at Wynyard. She lent him books which, in due course, had to be returned; he passed on to her a paper or a pamphlet he was reading—and what more natural than that she should look out for him next morning to hand it back, and sit with him in the train to discuss it?

Always conscious of Marty's affectionate accusation that he was "soft," he was still unable to subdue the feeling of compassion she aroused in him. There was so much menace in the air in those early months of the year, so steady and oppressive a consciousness of possibly impending disaster, that her solitariness acquired for him an almost painful poignancy. She was too small and thin, there was too much of the child still clinging to her physical appearance, for him to look at her without the stirring of a protective impulse; and he remembered too much of his own fiercely reserved and defensive youth to be quite convinced by the paradoxical assurance of her manner.

He walked down alone to the Domain one Sunday afternoon early in May. This proletarian forum was an endless source of interest to him; he strolled across the wide stretch of parched grass and attached himself to a small crowd which had gathered round a banner exhorting it to Come to God. The middle-aged lady, for whose platform this somewhat peremptory invitation in white and crimson formed the decor, was speaking rapidly in a high, shrill voice, but Gilbert, glancing at the faces about him, found on them the look of observation rather than of listening. They were interested, he conjectured, not in what she said, but in the sight of

one made in their own image, and yet possessed by some impulse
which removed her farther from them than if she were an ape.
They were mostly men, too, and he suspected that there moved in
them some dim conviction that so very plain a female should not
thus obtrude herself; on the heels of his thought came a hoarse
voice from the outskirts of the crowd:

"Lidy! Can I ask a question?"

The speaker bent on him a beaming, spectacled gaze of benevolent encouragement.

"Certainly, brother!"

"Is that yer own face, lidy, or is it a retread?"

The poor woman's meeting was finished, Gilbert thought, compassion struggling with his amusement. It was blown away like a
leaf on a gale of laughter. He drifted with the disintegrating
crowd that turned its back so lightly on the summons to celestial
bliss, and found Elsa at his elbow with a fair, plumpish young man
whom she introduced as Jimmy Baxter.

They sat on a seat in the shade of a Moreton Bay fig, and talked
desultorily, smoking and watching humanity in twos and threes
converge, fuse into groups, groups moving together to fuse into
crowds, platforms being set up, flags draped, banners displayed,
calico signs arranged, and the unofficial Parliament of the people
assembled. Not far from them a Union Jack, flanked by the
Stars and Stripes and the Hammer and Sickle, began to act as a
magnet upon the surrounding groups, sucking people away from
their edges and adding them to the already swollen ranks of its
own audience. Elsa, turning to Gilbert, said in an amused undertone which excluded Mr. Baxter:

"The Comrades are stealing the show!"

Mr. Baxter, smiling with vacant amiability, leaned across her to
offer Gilbert a cigarette.

"Quite a circus, eh?" He looked at the platforms, the flags, the
printed slogans, and the speakers, with the innocent curiosity of a
baby. "Never been to one of these do's before," he confided.
"Happy hunting ground for the cranks, isn't it?"

It was an unusually hot day for May, and in her thin, bright
cotton frock Elsa seemed to Gilbert, for the first time, physically
attractive. She said lightly:

"You should come often, Jimmy; it would be good for your
education."

He laughed appreciatively, and waved his cigarette at the declaiming figure on the platform.

"Get some hints on how to drop my aitches, eh?" His round cheeks reddened with the heartiness of his merriment, and Gilbert, filling his pipe, felt his own face freeze into the foolishly forbidding lines of one who is not amused by another's joke. Mr. Baxter laid his hat carefully on the grass, smoothed his blond hair, and gave the speaker a moment's puzzled attention.

"Second Front, eh?" He leaned forward again to address Gilbert, leaving Elsa out of a conversation which he clearly regarded as being of purely male interest. "Mistake, you know—all this agitation. People in charge know best."

Gilbert answered without looking at him:

"A dangerous theory."

Mr. Baxter's jaw dropped slightly, and he said "Huh?" in a startled voice. He had only been quoting a formula, and never before had he known it to be received with anything but a grave murmur of acquiescence. Gilbert repeated with irritated distinctness:

"I said that the theory that those in power know best and mustn't be criticised is a dangerous one. Unless you *want* a dictatorship. It's Hitler's favourite—in fact, his only theory."

Mr. Baxter's disturbed glance wandered from him to Elsa, questioningly, as if asking her what kind of oddity this was to whom she had introduced him. He looked bewildered and injured, like a child unjustly rebuked. Elsa, smiling vaguely into space, suddenly pointed upward and cried: "Look!" More like a child than ever, Mr. Baxter was instantly diverted from his uneasiness, restored to confidence and simple-minded enthusiasm by the spectacle of 'planes swooping down over the tops of the Macquarie Street buildings. The sea of hats became a sea of white faces as the crowd turned and gaped upward at a dazzling display of aerobatics. The 'planes soared and dipped and looped, but the crowd, only temporarily beguiled, grew impatient as they returned again and again, the roar of their engines drowning the voice of the speaker. It swayed restlessly, like seaweed in a strong tide; futile shouts of protest went up from it; fists were even shaken at the flashing, sunlit wings. The 'planes climbed, plunged, wheeled, sank and turned; and then they were away like dragonflies, darting low over the harbour, vanishing out to sea in a diminuendo of sound.

"By jove!" said Mr. Baxter, following them lovingly with his eyes. The vacant bewilderment of his expression when confronted by an idea had changed to an ardent glow of admiring interest when confronted by a spectacle; he looked as if, at any moment, he would clap his plump hands in an ecstacy of delight. Gilbert stood up abruptly:

"Are you going?" Elsa asked.

He said "Yes" baldly, added a curt good-bye, nodded to Mr. Baxter, and went off across the grass towards the Gardens. Why the devil, he had thought irritably, did she want to go around with a fellow like that? He had felt impatient with her, but it was an impatience that faded with their next meeting when she came to the office to return a book he had lent her, and stayed talking to him for half an hour. She talked well. She had a logical, methodical mind, and a good memory for what she had read. He discovered that his casual invitation to her on that first evening at the Writers' Guild, Marty's subsequent gesture of hospitality, and the link, tenuous as it was, of his boyhood acquaintance with her mother, had established them on a footing of intimacy which he had certainly not anticipated. He accepted a developing situation, finding her company a pleasant novelty in a life whose friendships had been almost exclusively masculine; but he did not ask himself any longer what the end of that development might be.

*   *   *   *

Marty, as was her habit, both asked and answered herself. She said one day to her husband:

"Do you know, Rick, I think that little alley-cat is getting her claws into Gilbert."

He looked up from his paper, politely incredulous.

"Elsa Kay, do you mean?"

"Yes, of course."

"Don't worry," he said with a laugh. "Gilbert's no impressionable youth." She cried impatiently:

"Gilbert's a perfect innocent where women are concerned. He was a shy, inarticulate boy, emotionally repressed, and he married Phyllis when he was twenty-three after being engaged to her since he was nineteen. Any woman not actually cross-eyed or humpbacked who wanted to capture Gil could do it without even exerting herself."

"Why haven't they, then?" he asked reasonably. She shrugged.

"The merest luck, I suppose. For the past fifteen years I've been wondering when it would happen. I believe," she added thoughtfully, "that if it hadn't been for me he might have begun to prowl on his own account long ago."

Richard stared at her in amusement.

"What did you do to save him?"

She sat down beside him and began to explain with slightly exasperated patience:

"Look. Men like to have a woman to talk to. It makes them feel good. Don't ask me why. Maybe because women are trained to listening respectfully . . ."

"I'm good at that, too," he pointed out.

She said severely:

"The point is that Gilbert, having a wife to whom he couldn't possibly talk about all the things that have been harassing him over the last ten years, was fortunate in having a sister to whom he *could* talk . . ."

"And you listened respectfully?"

She scowled.

"Anyhow, I listened. And now, simultaneously, his domestic life has become utterly impossible, and someone has turned up who wants him. And if it had to be someone I wish it weren't that little bag of bones and neurosis."

Richard looked puzzled.

"Is he at all likely to be attracted by her?"

"He's at an age," Marty said shortly, "and in a mood to be attracted by anything wearing the female form and having the desire to attract him."

"She's rather a pathetic little creature, I thought."

Marty nodded.

"She's very pathetic. I don't blame her for being sex-starved. I just wish she wasn't out to make a meal of Gilbert."

"You make her sound like a praying mantis." He picked up his paper again. "Anyhow I don't think you do justice to Gilbert's understanding. He has a good nose for insincerity."

"Insincerity?" Marty tore her hair. "Who said anything about insincerity? Is one insincere in desiring to be rescued from starvation? That girl's emotionally unstable to begin with. Then her fiancé's snatched away from her just at the time when they should have been married,, and now he's dead. She has to make

good that loss. I'm giving you her point of view. She's every
bit as sincere as the praying mantis—and it's not fooling."

He looked at her over his paper and over the rims of his
spectacles.

"The female of the species is undoubtedly more deadly than the
male."

Marty snapped:

"She's had to learn to be deadly." She sighed. "Oh, well, if
it happens Gil can charge it up to experience. And next time he
writes a novel maybe his women will be a bit more convincing."

*   *   *   *

Answering the telephone one day towards the end of May, she
heard his voice.

"I have to drive up to *Glenwood* next Sunday, Marty—they
want to see me about some plumbing repairs. I'll call in on the
way and leave those books for Richard."

"All right, Gil."

"Elsa Kay will be with me."

"Good," said Marty, thinking: "Bad, very bad!"

Gilbert replaced the receiver and leaned back in his chair. He
wondered if the next generation—Pete's generation—would find it
easier to think globally; his own technique, he recognised, was
pitiably inadequate. In this last month his mind had leapt feverishly from continent to continent, from island to island in the wake
of the headlines. From the always oppressive knowledge of near-
northern peril to India, from India to Corregidor, fallen at last;
from Corregidor, in a sharp flare of hope to the battle of the Coral
Sea; from the Coral Sea to China; from China to the faraway
Crimea, following the fortunes of the Red Army to the gates of
Kharkov, and from there, like a skidding movie camera to the
Libyan Desert. Yet there was always a pull like the pull of
gravity which drew his thoughts back to his own threatened homeland. Not only to the major issue, still deadly in its reality, of
whether it was or was not to remain his homeland, but to its
minor difficulties of internal adjustment, to innovations which disordered its once casual but familiar pattern of life; to railway
priorities, to shortages of this and that, to dim streets, and queues,
and the steady pressure of increasing regimentation; to the problem of manpower, calling for some miraculous multiplication like
that of the loaves and fishes; even to the great trek of cattle

moving south to replenish the larders of the Commonwealth against emergency. The centuries-old habit of thinking locally was not easily discarded, and the widening of the mental horizon was as painful as the stretching of the body on a rack. So he hardly knew whether he felt resentful towards Elsa for her in-trusion into a mind already exactingly preoccupied, or grateful because, in thinking of her, he could find an occasional temporary respite from the demanding world.

What she gave him, he decided, was stimulation—and differ-ence. Difference from Phyllis. The sharp contrast between her dark young thinness and his wife's fair, middle-aged lumpishness was the least part of that difference. The greatest was in the fact that she intrigued him, which poor Phyllis, with her stereotyped ideas, her obvious reactions, her transparent manœuvres, and her platitudinous phrases, had never been able to do. She stirred his compassion—and his curiosity. He was more conscious than ever of a slow, inevitable development in their relationship, passing from acquaintance to something more intimate, with a bright, disturbing hint of excitement. She, who had seemed as prickly as a hedgehog, as elusive as a black cat in darkness, began to show him moods of disarming gentleness, and a hesitant willingness to confide. Yet for all that he seemed to learn no more of her, and there were times, indeed, when she lost all reality for him. They were times when his mind, having had its respite, turned again to its restless ranging over world-wide chaos. When he seemed in flashes almost to capture the thinking technique of some future world-citizen, dispassionate but not detached, critical but not aloof, god-like in its scope, but entirely human in its allegiance. In such moments he was able to gather the chaos together, to see it as a whole, to fall with energy, faith and ardour on the problem of reducing it to order. But in such moments, too, he felt her break away from him, and stand back. It was as if she said: Don't ask me to go with you there. And he found himself looking at her and through her as he looked through the empty air. Even Phyllis, true to her own confusions and illusions, had more substance.

Alienated by what seemed to him a wilful, determined unre-sponsiveness, he was still endlessly tempted by her intelligence, and a certain dry, epigrammatic wit and aptness in her comments, to try again. And again. She would let him talk, watching him from under her black brows. She would answer with understanding, with sympathy, even with endorsement, but he was always conscious of a stubborn passivity in her. Her shrug, her faint smile, her significant silences all warned him that no passion lit her acquiescent theory.

She worked all day as secretary to the manager of a large city store, and they had fallen into the habit of lunching together several times a week at a small café in Elizabeth Street. It was of their last meeting that he thought now, remembering the faint, irritated annoyance he had felt when he saw her walking towards him with Jimmy Baxter, and pausing for a moment at the Market Street corner where their ways parted, to wave him a smiling farewell. He asked himself with distaste if jealousy could have inspired that mood, and was relieved to be able to deny it. His momentary exasperation had been born of puzzlement and pique— a cranky inability to understand why she should want to associate with him *and* with Mr. Baxter. He tried to tell himself that he was making a mystery out of nothing. The young man, he knew now, was an assistant manager of the store where she worked; inevitably she would see a good deal of him. Nor should there be anything surprising in the fact that she appeared to like variety in her acquaintences. She was a writer; it was not only a writer's business, but his natural instinct, to make first-hand observations of all kinds of people. Yet he continued to wonder irritably what she *said* to Mr. Baxter. What did they talk about? What could you talk about now except the war and politics, and politics and the war? Then did she sit listening to him, too, with that acquiescent smile? Damn it all—what *were* her beliefs? What *was* her attitude—not only to the world, but to herself?

Stirring the man thus to speculations and emotions, she was also stirring the writer. Curious about her, not only in a personal way, but professionally, because he saw her as the continuation of a story which had been, for him, rudely interrupted at an interesting stage, he had led her on to speak of her childhood. Sometimes she was loquacious, and at such times she seemed to tell him no more than in her moods of taciturnity. But during that last meeting, without her telling him anything at all, he had seemed—well, not to learn, but to come close to learning a great deal.

She had asked suddenly:

"Is the cottage my mother lived in when you knew her still there?"

They had been sitting on a park bench with pigeons and sparrows hopping and pecking round their feet. He had asked her, a few moments earlier, a question which had been on the tip of his tongue many times, and she had answered with a sharp decision: "Yes, of course I loved him. But he's dead; it's over. Don't talk about it, Gilbert." He had been silent, disturbed by the unexpected sharpness of his hurt, and her abrupt question about the cottage took him by surprise. He answered:

"Yes, it's there. Why?"

She had brought a scrap of bread from their lunch table to feed the birds, and she stood up now, causing a scurry among them, and brushing crumbs from her skirt.

"It's cold. Let's walk, shall we?"

They had set off briskly along the path towards the War Memorial. She interrupted his gloomy vision of a world becoming, generation by generation, obscenely cluttered with bigger and better memorials to bigger and better wars.

"I rather want to see it," she said. "I've had an idea lately that I'd like to do a novel with a character based on Scott Laughlin. What do you think?"

Then he had come near to some kind of revelation, for what he had thought, with a violence like a shout, was "You? *No!*" Marty and Nick had often teased him for the deliberate conscientiousness with which he considered questions before he answered them, and he supposed, hearing his own silence like thunder, that Elsa was used to waiting for his replies by now. Why should the suggestion have so shocked him? The wraith of a suspicion that her own convictions were not deeply rooted enough to tackle the portrayal of a man whose convictions had been his life, vanished before the kinder thought that she was not yet sufficiently mature as a writer for so large a subject. He said slowly:

"I think it's a grand idea. But why not—keep it in your mind for a few years? Chew on it. Do something else in the meantime."

"Why?" She had sounded slightly truculent, and he glanced at her apologetically.

"I don't believe you're quite ready for it yet."

She gave a little laugh that sounded hurt and angry.

"You don't think much of my writing, do you?"

He answered that in the only way he could answer it honestly.

"I think a good deal of the possibilities of your writing. Once you get—on better terms with yourself." He filled the heavy silence hurriedly: "Look here, I'm driving up on Sunday to see the tenants in our house. What about coming with me?"

"Thanks, Gilbert, I'd like to."

The meekness of her tone had overwhelmed him with contrition. He found himself saying, almost as if he were pleading with her:

"I do think the idea's fine, Elsa. I hope you'll do it some day. It should be done. But—it would be a big subject—do you realise how big? Laughlin was one of those obscure men who—embody great issues. A story about him—do you realise what it would involve . . . ? What he was up against . . . ?"

She said, still in the same submissive tone:

"I expect you're right, Gilbert. But I can be thinking about it —and I'd like to see the house."

IV

THERE was very little traffic on the road. Gilbert, with Elsa by his side, drove slowly, thinking that petrol rationing had returned to it an old-fashioned flavour of the more leisurely days of his boyhood, when cars were still rare, and bicycles abounded. That was only a momentary impression, born perhaps of the very nature of this expedition, which was a deliberate excursion into the past. For despite its emptiness it was the road of its time, smoothly paved, neatly kerbed and guttered, sprouting groves of bowsers at intervals—though most of them no longer functioned; flanked by the neon signs of shops—though they would not blaze at night. And in this retreat from modern techniques, this enforced abandonment of modern devices, this deserted road which shrieked aloud of immobilised machines, he suddenly felt something horrible—an advertisement of failure, the smell of a dying epoch.

Yet, after all, he asked himself impatiently, why feel so pessimistic? Things had gone not so badly—infinitely better, indeed, than he had dared to hope in the first grim months of the year. Slowly, like a man bracing his muscles, shifting his foothold, and concentrating his attention to take an increasing weight, the country had adjusted itself to the strains and stresses of war. Its people were no strangers to war's bereavements; there were already corners of many a foreign field which were for ever Australia, and beyond that tragedy they felt, now, no hardship comparable to the martyrdom of other lands. Merely an ever-present knowledge of danger, a gradual accumulation of restrictions and inconveniences, adding up in their minds to a consciousness of challenge. Take this weight and hold it—or else . . . !

They shrugged and held it good-humouredly enough, growling only because they had always growled, criticising blunders as they had always done, with vociferous protest and pungent sarcasm, failing here and there, a few at a time, but never all at once. They complained about raceless Saturdays, they complained because there was no beer, they complained because there were no cigarettes, no houses, no matches, no mustard, no blankets, no soft-drinks; they complained individually about everything; and collectively they complained with vigour and bitterness not because the burden was too heavy, but because it was not heavy enough. They learned to carry parcels, to wait in queues, to stand packed like sardines in trams and buses, to be patient at shop counters, to walk instead of driving, to carry identity cards and answer endless questions. By degrees, as successive call-ups skinned the population of its fighting men, the social structure lost what remained of its pre-war equilibrium, its centre of gravity shifted, the armed forces swelled, the civilian population shrank, the unrelenting logic of mathematics began to pose the questions: How many fighting men can a nation of seven million support and supply? When do you reach that point where no more can be taken from industry, from agriculture, from medical services, without overbalancing the whole giddy erection? In a vast, slow, organised General Post, women moved into men's places, men moved into the services, children began to suffer the psychological upheaval of insufficiently tended homes. The whole pattern of life disintegrated, and its particles re-grouped themselves—human particles, each one of which carried to his place in the major problem the multitudinous, demanding problems of his individual life.

Watching it happen, realising the magnitude of the change, and the appalling intricacy of these manœuvres, Gilbert had felt a growing respect for the Government whose advent he had welcomed only because it seemed the lesser of two evils. The administrative machine, he acknowledged, was no streamlined model of efficiency. It creaked badly; almost continually threatened with breakdown, it was forced into hasty improvisations, not always successful. Nevertheless, it kept lumbering along towards a complete mobilisation of national resources with the stolid, dogged persistence of a tank, the sniping of the Opposition rattling against its sides.

It had far more than a war effort to contend with. To that outer pressure, bearing down every month more heavily, was added the internal strain of an old, old conflict, not yet resolved. The once overt war between capital and labour, now subsided into an uneasy truce, still flared out spasmodically in clashes of guerrilla warfare. People who had understood from infancy that the concessions they had won so laboriously over the last century had been won only by the strength of unity, and the weapon of the strike, saw no guarantee that they might safely revise the conditioning of that long and bitter experience. Not all the alarums and excursions of the official war could make them altogether forget the unofficial war they had been waging for generations, or persuade them to lay down, quite out of reach, the traditional weapon of their struggle. They could win the official war and still lose the other; that knowledge kept them wary.

They were going to win the official war. They knew now that life held no future at all for them and their kind unless they did. Years ago, out of the stench and lunacy and brute destruction of another war they had seen "the future" as Galahad saw the Holy Grail. They had lived through that future; now it was the past, and they looked back on it with memories which kept them immune forever from anticipatory worship of a mere succession of days. Gilbert, quoting to one of them the phrase: "I have seen the future—and it works," had been answered by a dour, sidelong glance, and three ominous words: "It'd *better* work!"

That was their mood. Yet more than a mood, he thought restlessly, was needed. The necessity was a re-making not only of policies and laws, but of the whole human outlook, so that the vague emotionalism of a mood became a strong conviction, based on understanding. There was a vast edifice of false values to be demolished. And he was reminded, suddenly, of the naïve, shocked surprise with which officialdom had observed the public reaction to an announcement of imminent clothes-rationing. Do men gather grapes of thorns, he asked himself irritably, or figs of thistles?

He glanced at Elsa.

"How did your store stand the siege last week?"

She shrugged her thin shoulders.

"We were taken by assault, like all the others. It was an unedifying sight."

"What else could you expect?" he asked shortly, swinging the car from the main road into the quiet street where Marty lived. What else, his thought insisted, *could* you expect of people nourished from birth on an immoral doctrine—every man for himself, and the devil take the hindmost? Did our so-called "leaders" protest during the last twenty years while the cult of beauty mounted to a frenzy, wrenching our common-sense askew that the pockets of the clothes and cosmetic manufacturers might be filled?

Did they direct our faith away from the doctrine that Fashion's decrees carry the same authority as Holy Writ? Did they raise their voices to warn us that our minds were being doped and our very souls debauched by the synthetic glamour of fantasies in celluloid? Did they crusade against that misbegotten monstrosity that we call our Education System for turning us loose on the world at fourteen with no more sense of values than a bunch of chimpanzees? They did not. But now, overnight, they call on thorns to give forth grapes, and thistles figs.

He stopped the car at Marty's front gate, gathered the books for Richard under his arm, and got out. But Elsa sat still, smiling at him rather appealingly:

"You know, Gilbert, your sister scares me."

"Marty? Scares you?" He looked at her in astonishment. "Why?"

"Somehow," said Elsa, studying her locked fingers in her lap, unsmiling now, "I don't think she likes me much."

"Nonsense!" Now, as often before, some expression, some inflection in her voice, made him painfully conscious of her solitude. He said emphatically: "Of course she likes you!"

She stared at him with a pathetic, searching anxiety.

"Are you sure?"

He was not sure. Disconcerted by the discovery, at a loss for encouraging words, he fell back on an encouraging gesture. "Come along," he said, as he might have spoken to a nervous child, and held out his hand to her. She put her own in it, and left it there while she slid out of the seat. Until he felt her faint, responsive pressure, he had not realised that he was holding it tighter than was necessary; but her glance at him, half glad and half timid, made his fingers close harder than ever, and when they looked at each other as she stood beside him on the footpath, it was with a mutual question and a mutual answer in their eyes. She drew her hand away, and said with a confused little laugh:

"I suppose I'm imagining. Don't take any notice of me."

She looked back at him over her shoulder. He was still staring at her, but absently. He had never been quick in his emotional adjustments, and now he needed a moment or two for contemplation of his sudden, curious excitement. He had become accustomed to a life in monotint; its abrupt irradiation in rainbow colours

was startling as well as intoxicating. Disturbed by his silent regard, resistant to the intensity of his reaction, she retreated hurriedly, pushing the gate open, running down the steps, leaving
him to follow.

He found Richard turning over the last few feet of a freshly-
dug vegetable plot; Marty, stripping off her earthy gardening
gloves, was already escorting Elsa to the verandah. He said to
his brother-in-law:

"Will the sciatica stand this?"

Richard drove his spade into the earth and straightened his
back carefully.

"Between ourselves," he said, "no. I've had a twinge or two."
His sharp, kindly blue eyes slid from Gilbert to Elsa and back
again. "Are those the books?" he asked. "I'll join you in a
moment when I've washed my hands."

Gilbert went across to the verandah. Elsa, small, still and
silent in her deck-chair, was nevertheless far from inconspicuous.
It was not only because her frock, gaily patterned in orange and
yellow, flamed in the sun like a bed of Iceland poppies. Silence
and stillness were not qualities of tranquillity in her; and as he
handed the books to Marty and sat down on the edge of the
verandah, he was conscious of the turmoil she had aroused in him.

Marty asked:

"Has Prue gone up the mountains this week-end?"

He answered: "Yes." As he said it the thought flashed across
his mind that he need not return to the flat that night. He heard
Elsa saying, politely conversational:

"We were just talking about the rush to buy clothes, Mrs.
Ransom. Gilbert thinks it was only to be expected."

"Why not?" Marty agreed rather curtly, and left it at that.
Richard, emerging from the doorway, filled in what threatened to
become a heavy pause.

"Is it too much to expect some sense of proportion at a time
like this?"

Marty said in a depressed voice:

"That's exactly what we got. A demonstration of the sense of
proportion we've been educated to. A highly and carefully conditioned reflex. Have we ever been taught that there's anything
more important than being smartly dressed?"

"Sometimes," her husband answered mildly. "But not very

consistently or very effectively, I admit. Perhaps," he added after a pause, aware that there was a constraint in the silence of his three companions, "we're a bit bemused by our achievements in the matter of physical speed. Perhaps we assume that if we can move our bodies at four hundred miles an hour, we ought to be able to re-make our minds, and revolutionise our beliefs, and alter our lifelong habits with corresponding rapidity?"

"It isn't only that," Marty said. "Beliefs can be changed quickly enough. They *are* being changed. The problem is to make people relate belief and action—theory and practice." She looked at Gilbert's impassive profile, and then at Elsa. "That was Scott Laughlin's problem, for instance, and the problem of all the others like him. That was what he tried to do once with our father—and failed."

Elsa asked politely:

"Yes?"

Gilbert shot a suspicious glance at his sister. For a moment he wished he had not shown her that old letter about the houses. She was saying emphatically:

"Yes. It isn't the beliefs people quarrel about—it's whether they're to be implemented or not. Our father saw himself as a godly and upright man because he held a certain belief. Scott Laughlin described him as a hypocritical, Pharisaical, cocoanut-stealing, sewer-minded slum landlord because he didn't put it into practice."

Gilbert frowned at her.

"How do you know he said that?"

"I heard him," she said shortly. "I didn't know at the time who he was talking about, but I know now."

Elsa said in her neutral voice:

"He must have been a very—uncompromising person."

"He was." Something in Marty's voice disturbed her brother like a warning. He shifted his position so that he could glance at Elsa, because that tone had seemed to invite his scrutiny of her; yet even as he looked he knew that whatever Marty was drawing his attention to, it would not be visible to his physical eyes. Nor was it. Elsa was sitting quietly with her elbows on her knees, looking out over the garden, and all his glance did was to reinforce the memory of her hand in his, her eyes questioning and answering his own. She was right, he thought with a vague, hurt surprise—Marty didn't like her. His sister had, he thought with an astonished indignation, literally dragged Scott Laughlin's name into the conversation—and why, unless it were to convey, through her own expressed admiration for his qualities, an implicit condemnation of Elsa's mother, who had deserted him? He looked at her with a sudden hostility which vanished in bewilderment. No, it wasn't that. She had been talking at him, not at Elsa. And Elsa was continuing, still in that non-committal tone:

"Rather a one-track mind, perhaps . . . ?"

"Certainly not!" He was surprised by the sharpness of his swift contradiction. "His interests were enormously wide and varied." She agreed quickly:

"Yes, they were, of course. I should have said a tenacious mind."

He looked at her doubtfully.

"Much more than that . . ." he began, and stopped. Why was she going with him this afternoon? To see a house where a man had once lived—a man she wanted to write about. What did she expect to learn from it? She would get her "setting" right. But it was what she put in the setting that mattered, and he was acutely depressed by a conviction that whatever it was it would not be the truth about Scott Laughlin. He picked up a pebble from the path and tossed it idly from hand to hand, moody like a child because something with the promise of ecstacy in it had been interrupted, and because, after a few seconds of nearness, she had receded from him again. Marty said:

"There wasn't any of the narrowness of fanaticism in him. And he didn't dramatise his faiths, or himself for holding them. Do you remember, Gil, how he always jibed at forms and ceremonies?"

"Yes," Gilbert answered, and became unhelpfully silent again.

"I know, Marty," Richard put in, "that you dislike the kink in human nature that makes a plain idea seem intolerable till it's decked out in some kind of ritual. But—let's face it—people like ritual, and adore symbols."

Marty scowled. Flags! she thought sourly. Salutes, clenched fists, and V for Victory! Robes, badges, medals, processions! Songs, signs and oaths! She snapped truculently: "I *loathe* symbols!"

Her husband nodded teasingly at her left hand.

"And yet you wear one."

She shrugged.

"Oh, yes, I wear it. I bow before the tribal ju-ju. If I keep my tongue in my cheek that's my business." Gilbert, glancing idly at her wedding-ring, was moved by the association of ideas to look from it to Elsa's thin, left hand, lying on the arm of her chair. Marty went on: "We won't ever be civilised until we can keep an idea in our heads without a symbol to help us."

Her husband said dryly:

"Then I'm afraid civilisation's a long way off."

"Not that they aren't funny, sometimes," Marty observed reflectively.

Gilbert was listening with the surface of a mind whose depths were grappling with a new, secret, exhilarating conjecture. No sign of it appeared on his face or in his voice, but he flicked the pebble away across the path suddenly with a marble-player's action and a burst of animation.

"Swastikas, for instance," he said cheerfully. "I remember when Mother wore one on her watch-chain to church."

Marty grinned.

"I bet the Lord raised an eyebrow at that, even in those days. Are you going, Gilbert?"

For he had stood up, impatient, under the stress of his discovery, to be alone again with Elsa; he answered, looking at his watch:

"Yes, I said we'd be there before four."

Elsa, rising obediently, met his eyes for the first time since that long, communicative look they had exchanged on the footpath. Her smile seemed to convey both docility and eagerness; it said: "Whither thou goest . . ." and added: "I want to, anyhow." Whatever malaise he had felt before, it was gone now, routed by the possible implications of the startling fact that she was no longer wearing her engagement ring. He asked himself as he followed her up the steps: "Now what does that—symbolise?"

* * * *

He slid the car in to the footpath in the shade of the *Glenwood* pines, and turned to her. It had been a silent drive. Silence had grown on him during the years because so much of his wife's garrulity was of the kind which requires no answer; he found it pleasant to be with the woman who could, on occasion, match his

own taciturnity. Methodical and conscientious, it did not occur
to him to delay his business because her presence marked the day
as significant, and filled it with nebulous promises. He would see
about the plumbing first; and then he would be free to devote
himself to a personal life in which, it now seemed evident, she
was irrevocably involved. He asked:

"Will you wait here or . . . ?"

Her expression stopped him. She was looking past him at the
house, intently, with something of both fear and dislike in her
eyes. Feeling his glance on her she met it with a faint start, and
said, smiling:

"So this is where you've lived all your life."

"Yes."

He turned and looked at the house himself. He remembered
that Prue's American, young Grover, talking on his own particular
subject at their flat one night, had advanced the theory that no
building should be allowed to stand more than a century. "Don't
get me wrong," he had protested to Gilbert's raised eyebrows, "I
don't mean we should build so our houses fall down on us. I
mean we should *take* 'em down before they lay hold of our imaginations—before they set us going all misty-eyed over the glorious
past. The past never was so glorious." He remembered, too, his
own easy reply: "Well, we aren't old enough here to have succumbed very badly to that particular form of sentimentality. A
house a hundred years old is quite a rarity in this country." Now,
looking at his own house, not yet a hundred years old, but getting
towards it, he found fragments of that conversation pricking his
memory persistently. "When a country gets to be a museum of
old buildings, I guess the people are likely to develop a museum
mentality." And: "Haunted houses aren't a superstition, the way
I see it—they're a fact. Every old building's full of the ghosts
of everything that happened in it. One generation lives in a
house—all right. When the second generation lives in it, it
starts being haunted. By the time five or six generations have
lived in it the ghosts have got to be more real than the living
people. It's got round to being more important who slept in it
two hundred years ago than who's going to sleep in it to-night.
That's bad—that's very bad . . ." Gilbert stared hard at the
square, stone building with its shuttered french windows opening
on to its worn, stone-flagged verandah, and admitted that the

atmosphere of even two generations of his forbears clung about it too pervadingly for comfort. He stared at the pine trees. They had grown, he supposed, during his own lifetime, though they still looked to him much the same as they had when he was a child; and had he not himself seen the ghosts of a small boy and girl standing beneath them, hand in hand? The ghost of young Aunt Bee, rustling her frilled petticoats up the path? The ghosts of his father and his mother, the ghosts of little fair-haired Phyllis importunately wooing life, and of little dark-haired Marty implacably defying it? Wasn't the ghost of Scott Laughlin sitting on that old, iron-framed verandah seat? If he, after so comparatively short a time, could feel a garrison of ghosts holding this house like a besieged fortress against the future, what of the inhabitants and the frequenters of much older buildings? He saw John Grover in his khaki uniform waving his cigarette and saying earnestly: "They end by being crazy about their ghosts. They're so taken up with their past that they don't get around to attending to their present—and the future scares them stiff!" He remembered that he had protested: "But why blame the buildings? We needn't sentimentalise them." And the young man had answered darkly: "I guess we always would while they're there. So I say take 'em down in self-defence. Evict the ghosts."

He heard Elsa say dreamily:

"It's a darling old place. You know I could have drawn a picture of it—if I could draw."

He got out of the car. In his present mood it seemed not a darling, but a sinister old place. He said:

"I won't be long. Would you like to walk on? It's down that side street, right at the bottom of the hill."

She answered quietly:

"No, I'd rather wait for you."

When he came out again she was standing at the corner, looking down the street. He stood beside her, finding that it needed no effort of his memory to annihilate the row of brick cottages and replace them with an open paddock; to blot out the neat, suburban picket-fences, and see rotting, lichen-covered posts and rails instead; to ignore the tar-macadam road, and remember how the tracks of cart-wheels had meandered down its uneven, red-earth surface many years ago, and how weeds and clover had smothered the now sedately-kerbed footpath. He thought, "It's too easy, this looking back." He felt, and resisted an insidious nostalgia.

As they began to walk down the hill beside the fence which enclosed his own orchard, he said rather stiffly:

"I'm afraid it's a good deal changed."

"That side of the road," she agreed, "but not this. Your orchard looks just as it should." She gave him a glance and a smile. "I suppose my reactions seem all upside down to you. You'll think how strange that my picture should be so like reality —but I'm pleased with reality for being so like my picture."

But was she pleased? Standing before the cottage at the foot of the hill, he became conscious of her silence and looked down at her curiously. It was not a pleased expression which he surprised on her face, and again he felt uneasiness as he remembered why she had come. Or *was* that why she had come? Whatever her mood or her motive, he thought restlessly—and he could not analyse them—they were neither the motive which should inspire a book about Scott Laughlin, nor the mood in which it should be written. Was she—*afraid* of this place? He seemed to feel fear in her, or to read it in that curious expression, but his mind could make no sense of it. Resentment? Anger? Could she feel that here was the background of a life and family into which she should have been born—and wasn't? Dismissing the idea impatiently, he was still fretted by a suspicion that no idea was too fantastic to take root in a mind that was—overstrained. His thoughts actually halted before supplying the last word, actually avoided with a blind instinct the words "neurotic" and "hysterical." Yet fear and resentment were not all, by any means, what he seemed to read in her face. There was some sort of satisfaction, too. Not triumph, exactly, but perhaps an anticipation of triumph? He felt a sudden conviction that if she wrote of this place, and of the life that had been lived here, she would write cruelly, paying off some old score, getting even with something whose nature he could not even guess. She would never recognise, and therefore could never express, the fragment of social evolution which had worked itself out in that man; she would never give his story the dignity of its broad, human significance. She would reduce it to a novel of personalities, a little domestic drama . . .

She said almost dreamily:

"The deodar's still there."

He looked at it and answered in some bewilderment:

"I suppose it was always there . . . I don't remember, really . . . How do you know . . . ?"

"Oh," she said (and he thought sharply that people in trances must speak like this), "I know all about it. That trellis is new, of course, and the garage, and they've altered the verandah some-how . . . But I expect it's the same inside. A room on either side of the passage, and then another passage at right angles . . . and you go down a step from the kitchen on to a back porch . . . with red and cream tiles . . . Down that side at the back, only you can't see now because of the trellis, there used to be a swing for Janet . . ."

He said blankly:

"Yes, there was. I do remember that. I didn't know the in-side of the house much—except one room . . ."

"A piano," she said, "in the near corner, and a table at the far end with a green serge cloth on it, and one big, leather armchair, and a sofa with a chintz cover . . ."

He was dumbfounded to discover that he himself remembered the pattern on the chintz—so dumbfounded that he hardly heard her continuing recitation until his brain picked up its last words:

". . . and the gate shuts now. Of course it's a new gate. The old one was wooden, painted dark green . . ."

He looked at the gate with a sensation of nightmare. He saw himself struggling in the dusk, with the wooden one it had sup-planted, heard Scott Laughlin's footsteps going up the hall, his voice saying: "Denny, I want to talk to you—let me in, darling." He felt again the confused interrelation of past and future. Had she let him in? Listened to him? Had he failed to move her, or convince her? Were those the moments which had decided whether Elsa Kay was or was not to exist? He could at least remember that they had been, for him, moments of extraordinary psychological stress. He had wrestled with that gate in some-thing approaching a panic, and it seemed now, for a dazed second or two, that he must have known there was some significance for himself in the scene he had just witnessed. Annoyed with his mind for allowing itself to be tricked into even a flash of what he thought of as mysticism, and believed foreign to his whole nature, he said shortly:

"Of course it's a different gate. Shall we walk on a little way—or do you want to look some more?"

She did not want to look any more. Across the bridge the street became rural again. It wound gently up the hill, and before it turned the corner houses had ceased, the tar-macadam had petered out, and they were walking a road which seemed to him almost eerily the same as it had been thirty years ago. He found himself saying abruptly:

"Elsa—you must tell me—do you still—are you still in love with him?"

She said with furious vehemence:

"No, I'm not! Leave me alone, Gilbert—it only torments me to talk of it. He's dead. There's nothing to be in love with any more."

Suddenly she began to cry. Not at all noisily: he only knew she was crying because she lifted a handkerchief now and again beneath the wide brim of her hat to dab at her eyes. He put his hand through her arm, holding it tightly in a distressed attempt to comfort her, and she leaned against him, stumbling a little as they walked.

It was years, he thought wonderingly, since he had been along this road. The routine of life had claimed him, and every morning he had driven out of his gate and turned in the same direction as if he, too, were a machine. It was unexpectedly poignant to him to find how little it had altered, and when they came to the spot where he and Marty had so strangely happened to meet Janet and her father every Thursday afternoon at half-past four, his pace slackened. The big gum-tree was dead; someone, he saw, with anger, had ringbarked it. He remembered that, sitting beneath it, Scott Laughlin had said to him once: "You treat your mind as if it were an unreliable horse, Gilbert. Don't hold it in so tightly—let it bolt a bit now and then." It had been bolting this afternoon—but his habit was too strong. He was still sawing on the reins, still trying to use his reason, still trying to state in words and to analyse the impulses which had made it bolt. He did not trust, and had never trusted, such impulses; indeed, he usually had them subdued almost before he was conscious of them. All his reason told him that this obviously unhappy girl needed compassion; his own need reinforced the assertion with a knowledge that the compassion he felt was akin—or, surely, sufficiently akin—to love. The vague uneasiness and bewilderment she had always roused in him, the instinctive withdrawal, the groping among nebulous uncertainties, were warnings unsupported by reason, and his habit of thought rejected them. But when she turned to him suddenly with a sobbed "Oh, Gilbert . . . !" there came to him, even in the confused moment when his arms went round her, the sharp recollection that, years ago, under the apple-trees, those had been Phyllis' words, too.

*   *   *   *

It was nearly ten o'clock when he stopped the car outside her flat. His mood was unfamiliar to the point of being startling, and yet he contemplated it with recognition. An occasional surge of elation was surely everyone's right, and he felt curiously aggrieved by the discovery that so pleasurable a sensation had remained buried in him all his life. Once released, it brought with it, he was amused to discover, its own techniques of recklessness and irresponsibility, and it interested him to learn that its total effect was not unlike the effect of creative enthusiasm—of what Phyllis called "inspiration." In those rare moments when he had been able to write fast and freely, he had felt something like this to-hell-with-it intoxication. He had thrown literary restraint to the winds and his pen had perpetrated verbal audacities at which, normally, it would have baulked. Recognising this, he was momentarily damped by the recollection that he had usually returned to such passages when his moment of fine careless rapture was over, and smoothed them to soberer rhythms, and more characteristic patterns. Such extravagances, he had felt, were not himself. Was he, then, himself to-night, full of absurd cheerfulness, inconsequentially talkative, detached from all his accustomed allegiances, light as air in a new sense of freedom? It was only the shadow of a doubt; his elated self refused to entertain it—or any other doubts.

It had been a strange nightfall that gathered round the car, standing incongruously on a deserted track, the bush screening it indifferently. Even now he could only remember it as a dream of twilight and emotion deepening together until both reached blackness and silence. Then the moonlight had come, washing like an incoming tide through the treetops, and lying in white pools across the track. As the darkness had borne him down into a mood of almost vacant peacefulness, so the coming of that unreal semivisibility had lifted him again to the elation which still possessed him; he remembered tales of moon-madness, and was almost smugly content to imagine that he had been its victim. Driving home, it had not seemed worth considering which road to take. The car had described an erratic and eccentric course for which his own hands on the wheel blithely disclaimed responsibility. They had been lost; cruising past rows of blacked-out bungalows, their own dimmed headlights hardly competing with the moon, they had drifted bemusedly into blind alleys, and as bemusedly backed out again. Passing down unsuspected lanes and byways, their final emergence on the main road had been an amusing and unimportant accident; they laughed at it lightly and allowed it to lead them home, because it did not matter, really, where they went.

And now it seemed only natural to leave the car where it was against the kerb, and cross the street together, talking about bacon and eggs.

"And coffee, Gilbert? Strong coffee? And buttered toast?"

He objected:

"But then what do we have for breakfast?"

Fitting her key in the lock she looked up at him, and the moon-light flickered across her eyes as it flickered across the black har-bour water, just visible through a gap in the trees.

"Will you be here for breakfast?"

He said almost impatiently that yes, of course he would be here for breakfast; and in the dark hall with the door shut behind them she laughed, and slid away from him, leaving him groping among unfamiliar furniture. Light sprang on in the kitchen; he followed her there, and sat down on a hard chair by the table, and watched her rummaging in a cupboard for a frying-pan. Freed from the moonlight, and transported to a gentle atmosphere of domesticity, he yawned, and subsided again into peacefulness. Only now that he was released from it could he realise the tension at which he had been living; the change from it to his present idle, beatific tenderness seemed to be its own explanation, its own justification. It was so miraculous a mood to have achieved after years of stress that he felt no impulse to do anything but accept it. While they ate and drank and talked and washed up the dishes, the world narrowed to this one room, and narrowed again till it was nothing but his body and hers, and a hunger no longer to be endured, but at last to be satisfied.

*   *   *   *

For the first time in years he fell asleep with his mind blank. Sleep was not a slow-rising tide, submerging a brain exhausted but still helplessly active—it was a tidal wave of obliteration. The war did not go with him into this blessed nothingness, but snatched him from it by way of a split-second dream that was all climax. It rolled into a tight, hard ball; it grew fiery red, and then, at its core, white, as if fire were consuming itself. This central vacuum contracted, sucking flame inward like a whirlpool, spinning and absorbing with such intensity that he knew it must explode. Then he was awake; it had exploded, and he was looking into a darkness that still seemed to shake with sound. He felt Elsa stir beside him.

"What was that?"

"I don't know . . ."

He was listening, his heart thumping from the shock of a dream colliding with reality. There was gunfire now, but it was not gunfire which had burst his dream and set the floor vibrating. His brain, returning slowly from the confusion of sleep, reminded him that he had heard the window rattle in its frame.

"They're practising," Elsa said sleepily.

"Yes."

He heard her sigh, felt her huddle down beneath the blankets, and lay down again himself. She fell asleep quickly; he heard her light breathing. He listened to the distant sound of heavy guns, and then to the sharp clatter of nearer firing. A shaft of vivid light swept across the window blind. He got out of bed, felt his way cautiously into the dark living-room and across to the window; as he reached it the air split with noise again, and the floor shivered under his feet. He pulled the curtains back and lifted the window, feeling a rush of sharp wintry cold on his face. The sky was reeling drunkenly on long stilts of light, the trees were black and silver under the moon, the glimpse of harbour between them was flat and polished like a steel plate; the air was full of the roaring of 'planes.

Elsa, wrapped in a thick dressing-gown, came to stand beside him.

"What is it?"

"There's something up."

"An—air-raid?"

"There wasn't any siren—was there?"

"I didn't hear it. Those guns sound close."

"Yes."

The next explosion seemed to hit them like a blow, but by now his mind had seized on its muffled quality, and he said quickly:

"Depth charges. There must be a sub. about."

"In the harbour?"

"Sounds like it."

She shivered, and he put his arm round her. She said with a faint note of annoyance, pulling away from him:

"I'm cold."

He watched the searchlights sweeping low over the water. Something in her tone and her withdrawal had disturbed him, but he could not think about it now. There was an urgency of sound which anchored all his attention to listening. The crescendo and diminuendo of the 'planes, the agitated noise of patrol vessels and the vicious challenge of the guns were all grotesque against the still serenity of the moonlight; his eyes denied the possibility of what his ears were hearing. Another detonation shook the house; they heard the glass in the window of the next flat crack. He realised that he was cold too. Someone knocked at the door.

"For goodness' sake," Elsa whispered sharply, "go back into the bedroom!"

He felt a sudden irritation at having this small furtiveness imposed on him, but he obeyed, closing the door behind him, and stood in the dark listening with only half his attention to her voice and another woman's, while the other half still concentrated on the noise from the harbour. Elsa came back.

"It's no good standing about and getting cold, Gilbert. It was Mrs. Slade from the next door flat. She's a motherly old dear who's always telling me I should drink more milk because I'm too thin. She was afraid I might be scared and like some company. She thought it must be an air raid. I had quite a job convincing her it wasn't."

He stretched out in the grateful warmth of the bed, felt her hand groping for his, and held it.

She said:

"There's less noise now."

"Yes."

"Do you think they've—got it?"

"If they haven't they will."

"Gilbert."

"Yes?"

"I'm glad you're here."

"There's no danger—to us."

Her hand moved impatiently in his.

"I know. I wasn't thinking of that. I'm just glad you're here."

He supposed that he should have responded to that in some loverlike way, but the most he could do was to tighten his grip on her hand, and refrain from asking "Why?" He could not refrain, however, from wondering rather dejectedly why he should want to ask such a question. The war and the world had crowded back into his life while he slept, and the noises of their devastation had wakened him to a dreary sanity. He knew now that no physical union, no shared emotional tumult between himself and Elsa could bring them together while they stood apart on the issues raised by those searchlights and explosions. Unless you were together there, you were together nowhere. Stretched beside him in the dark she was a thousand miles away; his thought was as solitary as ever, brooding over men—perhaps not half-a-mile from where he lay—dead or dying, trapped under the moon-cold water in a steel prison. There was a sort of imperviousness about Elsa, he thought; barricaded behind her armour of egotism she paid for her inaccessibility to the world by being inaccessible to everyone. She had said that she was not afraid. Is fear only for oneself? He was afraid; not only cold was making his body rigid, and stretching his nerves to a tense wakefulness. Though you are not yourself a military objective at the moment, can you not fear the destructive mechanisms of war merely because they exist? Can you not fear for a world that makes and uses them? And as the room shook suddenly to another explosion his memory brought him a picture of two men whom he had seen die in France in 1917. Though he had not thought of them for many years, their faces were vivid to him now, literally blasted to the surface of his mind by the association of the sound of high explosive. They, he thought, had been military objectives, but they had not looked afraid. They had looked angry—and astonished. And why not? For drill people as you like, discipline their minds, condition their reactions, regiment their thoughts—they still keep an obstinate conviction that there is a certain bit of time—round about threescore years and ten—which is *theirs*. Old people, dying in bed, don't

[221]

look angry or astonished. Why should they? They are not being cheated. Yet in that last second when a man knows that his half-spent life is being snatched from him in an explosion and a red flame—then, surely, there is enough righteous anger in him to have reformed the world single-handed. It's when our bodies are not in danger, he thought, that our minds can leave them unattended, go out and have a look at the world—and be afraid.

Yet from her stillness beside him, and from his own sense of isolation from her, there did come a gleam of illumination. Did not at least some of his own fear have its roots in a deep, but now brutally baffled protective instinct? Her withdrawal from his arm, the impatient tone which had answered his reassurance, became significant, and he asked himself whether there might not lie at the back of every man's fear the knowledge of himself as no longer a protector. Some disembodied voice of composite womanhood said to him dryly: In the past we have been grateful for the shelter of your strong right arm against tigers, spears, swords. But can you shield us from the weapons of your scientific warfare—this precious, ultimate bloom of your masculine inventiveness? Forgive us, gentlemen, if we are no longer greatly impressed by your protective instinct. Forgive us if we feel that our children now need a more reliable guardianship—our own. . . . The thought was his, but the tone was the tone of Marty. The monstrous unnaturalness of modern warfare oppressed him like suffocation. You could not any longer respond with jungle-action to jungle-law. You could not leap up to join a battle outside your windows, for science had removed it from your reach, into the sky and under the sea. You could not strike the attitudes of courage to sustain your cowering woman; she did not cower—she slept. She slept, knowing you as helpless as herself. She slept, stronger than yourself, now, because unburdened by the tradition of belligerence, and therefore free of your unnatural frustrations . . .

He was watching the blind, shining and fading as the searchlights swept across it; listening to noises which, though they meant death to other men, touched him only as a disturbance of his night's sleep. That was a thought so outrageous that it was almost unendurable. That he should so sharply feel his identification with that chaos outside, and yet be forced to lie here with a raging, denunciatory spirit imprisoned in an inactive body, gave him a feeling of forcible banishment from his world, of solitude which amounted to torture. And suddenly he was bored, bored, bored with the whole business. He was sick to death of going about his daily affairs, waking every morning to the grinding labour of thought and the omnipresent burden of anxiety. Suddenly he felt the true danger of war assail him in a flood of longing to stop thinking and act instead. He wanted to go and find a Jap and kill him—not for any logical reason, but merely in an explosion of resentment against a world which denied him peace. He felt an insane desire to be rid of the self which the long years of life had built—to throw his faiths overboard, to abandon his convictions, to repudiate life because it had become an intolerable nuisance. Nothing had ever frightened him so much before. For he knew now, not only intellectually, but from actual experience, what moral collapse meant. He had felt the temptation of self-sabotage. In the roar of another explosion, louder than all the others, instinct turned him to Elsa—not because she was Elsa, but because she was a woman with the power to black-out his temporarily not-to-be-trusted mind. He knew as he took her in his arms that it was better to be, for a little while, an honest animal than a renegade human being.

V

THOUGH he had arrived a full quarter of an hour earlier, Gilbert was still wearing his overcoat and standing in the square of sunlight that came through his window when Prue arrived at the office next morning. To-day seemed a long way from yesterday; the night had not only drawn a sharp dividing line across his own life, but had marked his city with a new experience. Reluctant to leave the warmth of the morning sun, he looked at the distant glimpse of water, blue, sparkling, innocent, and was filled with a sort of indignation. In some way, quite apart from its implication as an act of warfare, he resented the invasion of the harbour very bitterly. Thinking of it as it had been last night, its silver surface broken by the conning-tower of a hostile submarine, swept by rocking searchlights, churned and blasted by falling depth-charges, he felt obscurely that mankind was being made to pay for its violation of the earth, the sea, the air. The payment was not being made, he felt, in death, or physical mutilation, or physical perils, but more subtly and profoundly in a torment of mental and moral confusion. Making an enemy of his home, criminally assaulting his earth, destroying the harmony which should exist between himself and his environment, man was cutting himself adrift from his spiritual anchorage. That communion with nature, celebrated by all artists, handed on by them to unhappy generations as sustenance and unfailing refreshment, could not survive quite unharmed so callous a betrayal. It was not the scarred earth, the blasted sea, or the air shivering with the speed of murderous wings which would suffer; it was man himself, made alien by his own action in his three elements, who would find himself impoverished. And the air seemed, somehow, the worst of all. That, he recognised, remembering Marty with a flicker of amusement, was the result of a deeply-rooted and age-old symbolism. For had not the air been, from the dawn of recorded thought, man's symbol of freedom, and wings his symbol of the spirit? Even primitive man, gnawing his bone over the embers of his fire, must have felt some wonder stir in him as a shadow crossed his foot, and he looked up at the mystery of a bird's flight —must have felt some aching dissatisfaction with his own slow,

[224]

earthbound body, toyed with some dim, fantastic, hopeful dream. Then what was this violation of the air but the betrayal of that immemorial flight-dream? He thought heavily: It was a good dream, and we've made a nightmare of it—flung it back in the face of our ancestors like a jibe, like a sneer . . .

He glanced round as Prue entered, and she was at once aware of some tension in him. He looked tired and unutterably depressed. Living alone together at the flat, they had by degrees lost some of their awkwardness with each other, and she went to stand beside him at the window and slip a hand through his arm. He gave it a squeeze.

"Hullo!"

"Hullo, Dad. Are you all right?"

He looked down at her in surprise.

"Of course I'm all right. Why?"

"Oh, I don't know. I thought you looked sort of—miserable. Was there much disturbance last night? I only heard about the raid when I got to town just now."

"A lot of noise, that's all." He asked mechanically: "How's everything at home?"

"Well, Virginia's in bed. She said she was feeling a bit sick when she came home on leave, and the day before yesterday she had a slight temperature. The doctor says it might be appendicitis, but he can't be sure yet."

He asked quickly:

"Why didn't your mother let me know?"

She moved away from him, taking her hat off, smoothing her hair, looking worried.

"She did try to ·ring you last night, Dad—twice. But she couldn't get any answer."

He had, of course, known that sooner or later he would find himself lying about Elsa, but it had never occurred to him that he would have to lie to Prue. He said, stalling:

"When was that?"

"About eleven o'clock, first. And then again later."

He began to say: "I . . ." She interrupted him with nervous rapidity:

"She rang Aunt Marty, too. She thought you might be there."

He left the window, pulling off his overcoat. He hung it in the cupboard and crossed to his desk, his movements brisk and purposeful, an unconscious camouflage for his confusion and dismay. Good God, was the child *warning* him? Don't try that alibi —it's busted already! Not that he would have tried it, he protested to himself angrily: he wasn't going to drag Marty and Richard into this. The suspicion that somehow—but how?—his daughter was in it already, disturbed him profoundly. But was she? Might he not be imagining—the imagining, he told himself wryly, of a "guilty conscience"? He found to his consternation that when he tried to answer her his mind was perfectly blank. He had come up against the wall of a psychological obstruction, and like a flash he was back in childhood, seeking and finding out its nature. He remembered innumerable occasions when it had seemed to him that to allow his father's tyranny to drive him into lying would be a confession of defeat. To maintain, in the tight corners of family life, a stubborn and stoical honesty had been his way of asserting himself—his declaration of independence. He remembered that he had wondered, quite without disapproval, and sometimes even with envy that Marty's technique should be so different. Her honesty was to herself and her own standards; evasions, lies, blank looks, tears, or any of the histrionic devices at which she was so adept, had seemed to her but legitimate weapons in the war against their father, and she had wielded them quite without scruples. For himself truthfulness had become a habit; as a liar he was inhibited.

Fiddling with something in her bag, not looking at him, Prue said:

"Of course we didn't know anything about the submarine trouble when I left. So when I got down to town and heard about it I rang Mum up and explained that you probably hadn't heard the 'phone because of the noise . . ."

He sat down and pulled some papers towards him blindly. He still had nothing to say. Was he to thank his daughter for "covering up" for him? He tried to think of Elsa, and found her curiously dim. Only one thing seemed clear—that Elsa or no Elsa he must get a divorce from Phyllis. It was intolerable—a sudden gust of anger made the papers he was holding shake slightly—that he should be *accountable* to Phyllis! Good Heavens, he thought furiously, I've never felt free in my life—never!

Prue asked in a carefully casual voice:

"Well, shall we do those accounts now, or some other time? I have them all here."

"Eh?" He looked up sharply. "Oh, yes, we may as well do them now."

It was a relief to escape to the austere, unambiguous certitude of figures, but he had to admit to himself, studying them, that Prue was not a financially successful business woman. That knowledge wakened a small fear in him. Could he go on indefinitely carrying her shop now that almost nothing was coming in from the Burt Street property—now that he was committed in his own business to a policy which had already lost him one or two substantial customers—now that he faced, sooner or later, the prospect of divorce costs and alimony?

When they had finished and Prue was putting on her hat again, she asked:

"You'll be going up to the mountains next week-end, Dad?"

"Yes."

"Driving?"

"No. It'll be the train in future."

"I've asked John Grover up for the week-end. Mother said it would be all right—if Virginia's better, of course."

"Good. We'll all go up together, eh?"

She came over to him suddenly, kissed him hard on the cheek, and was disappearing out the door before he had recovered from his surprise. Left alone, he lit a cigarette and began to wander restlessly about the room. It was not easy, he found, with world chaos and personal chaos making their simultaneous assaults, to keep track of his own motives. Working on those accounts with his daughter he had felt a violent impulse to issue an ultimatum. How would he have phrased it? We got off lightly last night, Prue, but we may not be so lucky another time. The war's right on top of us now. You'll have to give up the shop and go up the mountains for the duration—I don't want you in the city just now.

He hadn't said it because, true as it would have been, he was not sure that there were not two other less acceptable truths hiding slyly beneath it. Was it not true that her shop was beginning to look like a financial burden, and that he, as a writer, feared nothing more than a time when he might find himself forced to write, not by an inner need, but by a monetary necessity? Was it not true, also, that he—and Elsa—would be much freer if Prue no longer shared his flat?

He lifted the telephone receiver, and called the number of his mountain home. Phyllis answered. She cried agitatedly at the sound of his voice:

"Oh, Gilbert, where *have* you been? I was so worried . . ."

He answered abruptly:

"Prue's just told me that Virginia's ill. How is she?"

"She seems better this morning. Her temperature's down. Gilbert, I was trying to get you for *hours* last night. Where were you?"

He answered with an effort:

"I was there."

After a brief silence her voice came with a hint of suspicion:

"But they said you weren't answering . . ."

He had been unable to invent a lie for himself, and now, uttering the one Prue had provided for him, his voice failed to give it, even to his own ears, a convincing inflection. It sounded what it was —an awkward quotation.

"There was a row going on—I suppose I just didn't hear it."

He added hurriedly:

"What does the doctor say about Virginia?"

"He thinks it may be appendicitis, but he says it's impossible to be certain yet. He says the symptoms are too indefinite."

"She isn't going back on duty, is she?"

"Goodness, no! She's still in bed."

"Has she still got a temperature?"

"It's only up a little. The doctor says he wants to keep an eye on her for a week or so." After a pause she asked: "I suppose you'll be coming up *next* week-end?" There was a faint acid emphasis on the "next." He replied flatly:

"Yes, we'll be up on Friday night. Let me know if Virginia seems worse."

"All right." She added sourly: "If I can get you."

He said "Good-bye" shortly, and she hung up without answering. He put the receiver back on its hook, and swore.

*　　　*　　　*　　　*

When her father and sister arrived with their American guest in time for a late dinner on Friday night, Virginia did not look as if she had ever been ill in her life. She opened the front door as they came up the path and stood there with her mother, the light making a halo of her hair. She was wearing a blue frock that matched her eyes, and a housewifely apron gaily printed with bright flowers. There was a pause in the hall for greetings and introductions. Gilbert touched with his lips the cheek that his wife perfunctorily lifted to him. Prue said:

"Mummy, this is John Grover."

Phyllis responded with a characteristic mixture of hospitality and tactlessness.

"So very nice to have you! Your train must have been late—I do hope the dinner isn't spoiled. Gilbert, we're all upset—Dulcie just walked out this morning—said she was going to work in a factory. Can you imagine? John—I'm sure I may call you John? —you must be frozen! Come along to the fire. So inconsiderate, these maids. Virginia and I have had to do everything ourselves. This is Virginia."

"Hullo," said Virginia. Even her father was a little dazzled by her smile. She had spent most of the week in bed, but she had no intention of remaining invisible while there was a young man in the house. She looked him over swiftly, passed him in her mind as presentable, and held out her hand. He shook it with admirable composure. "Virginia," Phyllis was explaining, trotting out her formula absent-mindedly, "is my home-girl."

Gilbert gave his elder daughter a quick glance. She was going to accept that, he thought, and he felt something that was half amusement and half pain. And even while he was trying to defend her with the excuse that she was dressed for the part, and must live up to her apron, he found himself correcting dryly:

"Not now."

"No, not now, Mummy," Virginia agreed brightly. She explained smilingly to John: "I'm a W.A.A.F. nowadays."

"Is that so?" he replied politely. Gilbert saw his eyes turn from the home-girl to Prue; a faint smile passed between them. He had seen that smile before. Sitting opposite them in the train he had studied his daughter and the young American with a certain paternal reserve. He had noticed that they spoke seldom, but beneath the casual decorum of their manner he felt a kind of intimacy which intrigued him. It was not the light, excited, challenging intimacy or flirtation, but rather the quietly confident intimacy of a long-married couple. Their occasional conversational exchanges had ended always with that look, that faint smile. Seeing it again now, he thought that there was a hint of patience in it, as if they were sending a wordless signal of reassurance to each other. As if they were telling each other that tiresome formalities must be endured, and other people suffered sometimes, for a while. He felt a little startled, and looked at Prue more narrowly. Standing beside her sister in the bright light, she faded. Her hair was a shade less golden than Virginia's, her eyes a shade less blue, her lips a dozen shades less brilliant. She looked subdued. No wonder, he thought. They had both been wakened on Wednesday night by the crash of more depth-charges in the harbour. For an hour or so it had been impossible to sleep, so they had sat up together, smoking and talking. She had spoken of human beings sealed in a tiny death-trap under the water from which they knew they would almost certainly never emerge alive; and since then he several times read that recurring thought on her face, like a shadow. He could see happiness there now, but he found it poignant because it was so sternly disciplined. Both in her eyes and in John Grover's, happiness was under strict control; their instinct was already to defeat the intrusion of the world with an exchanged glance, but they were not yet admitting it to each other, or even to themselves. He looked hard at the young man. Something in him was standing to attention. This was a parade. He was going through the necessary motions, but beneath his polite smile there was that look of waiting, that terrible patience. He was buying the joy of being near Prue with the boredom of sharing her with other people . . .

And this," Phyllis was continuing, "is Pete." Pete had arrived with his accustomed boisterousness, and was studying this fabulous being suddenly translated from the movie-screen to his home with ardent interest. The breadth of his smile was in itself a treaty of alliance; he shook hands and continued to stare. His mother betrayed him coyly. "I do believe he's disappointed because you aren't wearing a cowboy hat!"

Pete's smile died suddenly. He blushed and scowled.

"I'm not!" he denied fiercely.

"Small boys imagine," laughed Virginia, "that all Americans are born in Texas!"

"They don't!" stormed Pete. John said quickly:

"I guess they don't either. There's a guy I know, Pete, who *was* born in Texas, and he just can't get the boys here to believe it."

Pete, enraptured by this enlightened championship, pinched Virginia surreptitiously. Gilbert intervened.

[230]

"Pete, you show John where he sleeps, and look after him."
Phyllis began to bustle.

"Dinner will be ready almost at once. I do *hope* it isn't spoiled.
Virginia, you might just have a look at the fire. Gilbert, will you
be ready in ten minutes?"

He put his hat and overcoat down, and went slowly to the
bedroom which for so many years he had shared with Phyllis.
He had been thankful at the time, and was more thankful than
ever now that her re-furnishing of the house had banished the
double bed; and while he listened to the sounds from across the
hall of Pete's voice in affable conversation with their guest, he
wondered if he was going to get through this week-end without
a domestic storm.

If it were to break he knew when to expect it, and late that
night, switching off the bedside light, hearing Phyllis turn heavily
on her mattress, he waited for it.

"Did you go up to *Glenwood* last Sunday, Gilbert?"

"Yes."

"Did you arrange about the plumbing?"

"Yes."

There was a pause then, but he knew that she was only preparing
another question, and reflected that his tense nervousness was
rather like the nervousness he might feel during an oral examination in some subject on which he knew himself to be inadequately
primed.

"Did Marty and Richard go with you?"

"No."

"I thought they might have liked the drive now that they can't
use their own car."

That was not a question, so he did not reply. The pause was
longer this time, and when she spoke again she had moved to
direct attack.

"Where *were* you on Sunday night?"

"I told you," he answered. "I was at the flat."

Her voice shook and heightened.

"I don't believe you!" The silence this time was hostile and
dangerous. "I can't believe you! You *couldn't* have been there—
in that tiny place—and not heard the 'phone!" Suddenly, to his
dismay, he heard her getting out of bed, and then she was sitting
beside him, heavy against his thigh, clutching at him. "Oh,

Gilbert, why should you tell me lies? Haven't I been a good
wife? Where have I failed? What have I done to make you
stop loving me?"

He prayed that she would go on talking—anything to get past
that impossible question which he could answer neither with
truth or untruth. She did. She must tell him something. She
had been waiting so eagerly to tell him. During these months
when she had been so much alone she had had a new spiritual
experience, and it had changed her and brought her so much peace
that she wanted to share it with him. . You're so moody, Gilbert,
you worry so much, but it's only because you use your mind
wrongly. There's a woman here who explained it all to me—
she's been in India, and she says it's all in breathing and relaxation. You have to relax entirely, mind and body, and abandon
yourself to the Life Principle. It takes practice, but anyone can do
it, she says, and when you come out of the relaxation you find
that all the heaviness and the worry have gone and you feel free.
Gilbert, I know there's something on your mind, and I wish you'd
confide in me and let me help you, because I can if you'll only
let me lead you in the beginning. But you have to purge yourself
of untruth first, because you can't relax properly when there's a
lie between you and the Life Principle, so you must tell me where
you were when I rang up—not because I'm curious, but for your
own sake, to free yourself . . .

He repeated, doggedly and wearily, his unconvincing lie:

"I was at the flat. I didn't hear the 'phone."

Her hands fell away from him, and in that moment he came
near enough to her for pity, and a dull remorse that he should
be contributing to the misery which she was trying to defeat by
calling it Peace. She said in a voice that shook between despair
and anger:

"I don't believe it, I tell you!" She cried out suddenly with a
shrill note of accusation: "It was some woman!"

She waited through a few moments of leaden silence for a denial
which did not come. She rose; he heard her bed creak as she got
back into it. Abruptly, with a sharp, contemptuous laugh, she
jeered:

"At your age!"

Then there was silence, and he kept still, almost holding his
breath, as a man might who has been flicked with a whip, and

waits for the pain to pass. But it did not pass. He lay awake, thinking of Elsa, trying to break through the mist of illusion which now obscured his image of her, and failing all the time because his body had been starved for too long, and was now obsessed by the memory of its newly discovered ecstacies. He tried to kill that derisive "at your age" with the sober truth that forty-six was a man's physical prime, but he went on feeling ashamed and dissatisfied, not because of what he had done, but because his motives and impulses in doing it were not clear to himself. It was not until he had heard the clock in the hall strike three that he fell into a restless sleep, and was awakened in the dim light of dawn by the sound of Phyllis weeping.

He thought desperately: "Oh, *God!*" and lay without moving. But it was evident that she meant him to hear. Her sobs grew louder and wilder until he thought they would waken the rest of the household, and he sat up in sudden irritation, saying abruptly:

"For Heaven's sake, Phyllis, keep quiet! What's the matter?"

Before she had said a dozen words he knew that there was only one thing to do, and he got out of bed and began to dress hurriedly, fumbling in the half-light, his fingers growing stiff with cold. He hardly listened to the words of her tirade; his brain was anxiously busy with it only as a symptom of her disintegrating self-control. She had nothing to live for any longer, she had thrown away her life on him and the children, and they thought none the more of her because of it, and I swear to you, Gilbert, that if you bring any more scandal and disgrace on me I'll end my own life, I won't endure it; you don't believe in spiritual experiences because you shut your mind to them, so of course you don't have them, but when you open your mind by prayer you're given guidance, you *are*. I know, because it came to me only the other night; it was like a sort of trance, and I saw that if I failed to save you I must go on a long journey—into death—I saw myself walking into a sort of mist that divides this world from the next and I knew that if I couldn't make you see I would have to . . .

He laced his shoes, shrugged himself into his coat.

"Where are you going, Gilbert? You must listen to me, you must! I'm trying to help you; how can I if you won't even listen, if you run away from the truth I want to make you understand, if you have brought that woman up here I . . ."

He fought down his impulse to answer her. .There was nothing he could say that would not add to her frenzy, because it was frenzy she wanted. He instructed himself with desperate detachment: This is exhibitionism; it will stop when she has no audience —not before. He had not so much as looked at her while he dressed, but crossing the room to the door he had a glimpse of her sitting up in bed in her thick nightdress, rocking backwards and forwards with her hands buried in her greying hair, and he actually baulked for a second, almost overwhelmed by pity, hesitating on the brink of attempting once more to offer her a false comfort and an empty compassion.

The door banged behind him as he went out. He had not meant to bang it; his cold hand had slipped, and the bitter little wind that ran along the passage had done the rest, but he knew very well that to Phyllis it would seem only an expression of his callous hatred of her, his merciless, implacable unregeneracy. He snatched up his overcoat as he went through the hall, and stood for a moment outside the gate buttoning it round him and turning up its collar about his chin. He thrust his hands into his pockets and began to walk down the hill, his footsteps ringing on the frosty ground. In a hundred yards or so the pavement ceased, he passed the last of the row of dark, sleeping houses, the road faded into an earth track, and the bush enclosed it.

While he walked the violence of his agitation subsided. It seemed to leave him in rhythmical, almost measurable jerks, to be jolted out of him with each impact of a foot upon the ground, and as he was freed of it his thought ceased to be a tumult inside his head, and put out feelers to the world. It found and sent back to him from his surroundings a kind of relief. Still hesitant, still incoherent and disconnected, still shaken by that grotesque and horrible scene, it assured him that its disorganisation had been only temporary, that it would make him a rational creature again if he would leave it alone for a while, not force it . . .

All right. Leave it alone, and just keep on walking. Here is something that's real, tramping along a bush road in that grey hour before sunrise when the prickly bright stars are beginning to fade. What gives it this benison of reality? Divorcement from the insanities of human life, bare earth underfoot instead of asphalt . . . ? That's forcing it. Why bother about what it is? Isn't it enough that in feeling it you slowly recover your composure and gather the tatters of your confidence about you? That you can admit, almost calmly, that your own sins of omission and commission have contributed not only to the mess of that single human life you have just left behind, but to the other far greater mess in which the whole world is struggling? You can admit that here, almost with serenity, for here nothing shouts condemnation at you because of it. Neither wireless, nor headlines, nor dimmed lights, nor buckets of sand in the hallway. Here you need not hold back a frenetic outburst of anger and despair, a sort of animal howl for the violated humanity of the human animal. Instead you are again part of something whose survival is quite certain; you feel that if you stood still for a moment your feet would put down roots . . .

Roots. Good, faithful, conscientious brain, bringing the right word as a dog might bring something you have lost and lay it before you. But too tired still, too shocked and played out to do more than bring the word, with its blessed implications—anchorage, nourishment, growth. Keep on walking, and don't try to think yet . . .

The stars were gone now, and the wind had dropped. He came out from the track on to another road, conscious that he was growing warmer, naïvely pleased to discover that he had become normal enough to observe and hate the plane trees. There they stood, shivering nakedly in the steely morning light—two rows of them pruned harshly, mechanically, by men who knew only that they must not grow high enough to foul the telephone wires. There they stood in summer, their flat-topped, mutilated shape hardly disguised by their dense foliage; there they stood in the windy autumn with their fallen leaves swirling about them like brown paper bags. And down in the valleys grew the trees which belonged to the place—the tall gums tapering like the white masts of ships, the cedar wattles with dark, frond-like leaves and clusters of heady, honey-scented blossom, the gnarled angophora, twisting its branches into curly patterns, the tristania, bordering the creeks with gold, the coachwoods and the majestic turpentines . . .

He was ready, now, to think of Phyllis and the thing she had threatened. In the suffocating, antagonistic intimacy of the bedroom nothing could have seemed too grotesque, and he had been filled with a foreboding fury. Literally filled; he had felt in his body and his brain and his eyes and his very finger-tips a suffusion such as victims of the drinking torture might feel, a tightness, a drumming, a confusion of the senses which now, in the sharp solitude out of doors, had left him once more capable of coherent thought.

She was drifting, he recognised, into some sort of neurosis. He tried to tell himself that her threat of suicide was no more than an attempt at blackmail, and that having served its turn, it would be the easiest threat in the world to rationalise out of existence. She would only have to think of the children to tell herself what she would very easily believe—that she was indispensable to them. She would invoke Duty—not the concept, but the word which she saw as a fetish, a totem, a Stern Daughter of the Voice of God—and, bowing down before it, she would renounce her suicide and then wonder why no rewarding flood of peace and light invaded her life in return for such devotion. Just as she had wondered why her prayers for their reconciliation had not instantly smoothed away all those fundamental differences of thought and temperament which were driving them apart. She had prayed; she had begged him with frantic earnestness to join her in her prayers; for she was right and he was wrong, and that settled once and for all, she claimed, any question of her own deviation. How could one step aside from a path one knew to be right? And when he agreed, and pointed out that she must not, therefore, ask him to do so, she only stared and wept. The deviation must be his; the fact that he, also, believed himself to be saving his soul alive as best he knew how, meant simply that he was the victim of a delusion to be vanquished by her own faith and prayer. All their married life, he thought, they had been like two people of different nationality with an imperfect knowledge of each other's tongues. They could stumble along, awkwardly enough, haltingly enough, so long as the matter of their conversation was commonplace and elementary. But once they began to adventure into the mysteries of each other's thoughts, desires, and convictions, it was as though speech failed them utterly; they had no longer any means of communication.

She could not—or would not—acknowledge that. Nothing would ever alter her belief that any two people had only to "try" in order to surmount all differences of taste and temperament. He wondered dejectedly what comfort she was getting out of being a Christian Watcher, and had a sudden vivid memory of her coming in one winter night from a meeting of the "Circle," big and un-gainly, her face red with cold, her glasses dewed with mist, her faded, grey-streaked hair escaping untidily from beneath her hat. He remembered the badge she wore so conspicuously on the lapel of her coat—a gilt cross on a blue ground, with the words "Watch and Pray" wreathed about it. Her eyes, her whole face had been bright then with a benevolent happiness which had, nevertheless, left him unconvinced. It had seemed a happiness that was a little too aware of itself, and the gentleness of her usually querulous voice was a little too gentle. From heights of serenity which, in their blind stubbornness, they would not share, she had seemed to be pitying them—her husband and her children —loving them, forgiving them—and inviting them to watch her doing it. But during the summer, he had noticed, when the walks up to the hall where the meetings were held became pleasant strolls in the cool of the evening, her enthusiasm had waned a little. For of all pleasures, he thought hopelessly, discomfort and self-mortification were the ones she really enjoyed. And he could not subdue a faint, uneasy thought that these were pleasures which, under stress, might be pursued to their logical conclusion.

*   *   *   *

When Phyllis realised that her husband was up and dressed and out in the winter cold before sunrise while she still lay warmly in bed, her first impulse was to get up too. It was her custom, and from years of habit had become her cherished right, to be more uncomfortable than anyone else in the family; but for once her body ruled though it could not altogether subdue the muddled, unhappy chaos of her emotions. For she was really tired; she had been worried about Virginia, and now the violence of her misery, which had driven Gilbert away, had left her so exhausted that her limbs would not obey the goading of her impulse. So, as she lay there—even before she had relaxed into comfort again, while the tears were still drying on her cheeks, and her body was still shaken by an occasional convulsive sob—the impulse began gradu-ally to adjust and modify itself, and that process of rationalisation at which she was so unconsciously adept had already advanced a stage or two. The wind, which would have been raw and bitter if she had been out in it herself, was bracing because it blew on Gilbert. His tormented escape had become another of those in-vigorating walks which he selfishly took while she worked or moped at home.

[237]

With this achieved, she was home again on the familiar ground of martyrdom; here she could recognise herself, and embrace her own odd, perverted comfort. She could lie still now, and let her thoughts roam luxuriously over all the years, all the happenings which had brought them to this pass. She could repeat endlessly her favourite phrases: 'If only he had . . ." and "If only he would . . ." and even "If only he were . . ."

For she could think of Gilbert made over, Gilbert without his emotional restraints, without his demanding intelligence, without his agnosticism, and above all without his convictions, and see him as still Gilbert. She could insist with passion that he must be different, different, *different*—but she would not admit that, being different, he would no longer be Gilbert. Nor could she be content with the slow, inevitable changes of natural development. To possess her soul not only in patience but in interest and amuse-ment, and observe through the twenty odd years of their marriage the metamorphosis of the 1919 Gilbert into the 1942 Gilbert was a feat quite beyond her capacity. Such deliberate and unhurried growth was, indeed, unacceptable to her—a violation of her whole creed—for it had that quality of the inevitable, the evolutionary, which always aroused in her a spirit of bustling defiance. Not life, but she herself, armed with faith and rectitude, should be the force to work such a miracle. It would have seemed to her intolerable and faintly blasphemous to assert that "I will" and "I ought" must wait upon "I am." She saw "I am," in fact, as a sly enemy, and was never without a wary and mistrustful eye upon it. She treated it very much as she treated a housemaid—as something which would achieve excellence only by being never left alone, by being subjected to continual precept and exhortation, to incessant and suspicious vigilance.

So now she thought about Gilbert; and behind the formidable inventory which her memory instantly presented to her, of all his sins and failings over the last twenty years, there still welled up in a painful tide her love for him, her pride in him, her ambition for him, and the grateful astonishment which she had never quite been able to subdue, that he had married her at all. Like a patient and industrious gardener coaxing a creeper over an ugly fence, she had managed to grow a screen of illusion over the hurtful memory of her girlhood. She had never recovered from the blow which had been dealt to her self-esteem by the refusal of the young Masseys to accept her fully as one of themselves. Not all Uncle Walter's commendations had really compensated for Gilbert's polite, schoolboy indifference to her. Nor had she ever forgiven Nick for accepting her dog-like devotion without even realising that she was bargaining with it for his affection. Most of all she had suffered from Marty's antagonism, and Marty's easy superiority. This girl, four years younger than herself, did everything better than she did, and did it without apparent effort. She had friends and secrets, and would share neither; she had some kind of mysterious resource in herself which could not be harmed or even reached; her ruthless, uncompromising contempt had been a continuous torture, and the strong intimacy of her relationship to Gilbert a slow poison of jealousy. Growing up into a lumpish, emotionally disturbed adolescence, Phyllis had been forced to wrestle with her self-mistrust as with the devil. Prudery, ignorance, and the blighting restrictions of Walter Massey's narrow religious dogma had made her attitude to the other sex one which was half a recoil and half an uncontrollable, excited curiosity. Here again she had confronted her own ineptitude, and had fled to fantasy in an effort to restore her self-confidence. One youth who had walked home with her twice from the station had evolved with the passage of time into a serious aspirant for her hand; a tongue-tied young missionary who had come to visit her mother, and had helped her to pick plums for jam-making, lived now in her memory as a suitor who might have cherished and shielded her—as Gilbert had not—from a world which had incomprehensibly departed from the pattern of a good world which she understood.

Yet the astonishment remained. A hard little core of truth in the middle of her fantasies made it inevitable that Gilbert should preserve in her eyes something of the character of a knight-errant. There was an obscure torment in this, for she was not meek and she was not humble, though she accepted those qualities as essential to a Christian. She had the terrible pride of the self-consciously inferior, which is like an itch, and through all the aimless, wretched wandering of her thoughts as she lay there, the process of setting herself right with herself went on.

So that by the time Gilbert came home, timing his arrival for eight o'clock when the family would be assembled for breakfast, she was firmly re-established in a rôle which had acquired even more than its customary merit and poignancy from his transgressions. Her voice was patient, her smile brave, her eyes lit with the faint, faraway exaltation of forgiveness. She produced bacon and eggs kept hot for him, and insisted on making him fresh toast. She chided him gently for not putting on his pullover. She enquired his plans for the day so that she might adjust her own to them. She heaped coals of fire upon his head.

* * * *

That afternoon, rather in the mood in which he might have visited the dentist, Gilbert went into his study and sat down hopelessly at his desk. There was, as Phyllis would have said, nothing to disturb him. The girls and their visitor had betaken themselves with rugs and cushions to the sunny lawn outside; he could hear their voices and their laughter occasionally through his open window. Pete had gone riding on his bicycle. Phyllis, taking two aspirins for a headache, had set out soon after lunch to sell pots of jam and cakes at a Red Cross stall. He had the house to himself. With some desperate idea that by making a bonfire of all the disconnected oddments which he had written in the last four years he might clear the decks of his mind, and prepare it for action, he emptied the drawers of his desk, and sat contemplating the formidable pile of papers with something approaching nausea. He wanted to be rid of them and yet he knew that burning would not really destroy them. They were there because they had been in his mind, and though he reduced the paper on which they were written to ashes, they would still be in his mind, and he would find himself writing them all over again. He began sorting them, reading here and there, at first with a forced and reluctant attention, and then, as the time passed, and the late afternoon sun began to slant across his desk, with a gathering excitement. He began to see that they were, after all, separate parts of a whole, and he began to have, at last—*at last*—a glimpse of that whole, only to find his intoxicating sense of discovery quenched by the bleak realisation that he could not use it. It was not his. It belonged to Elsa. His mind began to work, as he went on reading, with that fever of constructiveness which had been so long denied to it. He saw this bit and that bit falling into place, bound together by the central theme of one man's fidelity to an idea. He saw with a kind of despairing amazement that, unknown to himself, he had already written half a book about Scott Laughlin. A book not about the man himself, but about the issues which would hold the attention and engage the loyalties of such a man. A book into which some such man would fit, growing as it progressed away from his prototype in the details of circumstances, and in the externals of personality, but following the same road, and informed by the same passion. Here were words which would go straight into his mouth, and which, already, called up the ghost of him in the mind of his potential creator; here was an idea which could be his idea, and by which a thin, mysterious line of communication was stretched from his shadowy half-realised character to the pencil in Gilbert's hand. A line like a telegraph wire, faintly thrumming.

The pencil moved with sudden purpose. It crossed a word out, substituted another, hovered, wrote, and was still again. The misty outlines of the ghost stood out a little clearer, the wire thrummed louder, the pencil scribbled confidently, the ghost solidified into flesh and blood, the wire sang and quivered, the pencil raced, the circle of contact was established.

It seemed to Gilbert now, in this blaze of illumination, that he must have been mad or bewitched not to have realised how these apparently irrelevant fragments belonged together. It could be, he saw now, a story with its roots in a time far back beyond the birth of Scott Laughlin, and still growing now, long after he was dead. It could be the old but always new story of the dynamic of humanity pulling against its inertia, condensed in time, narrowed down in place, expressed in terms of one obscure life, and yet still heroic by virtue of its timeless social implications. "Damnation!" he said to himself fiercely, "why didn't I see it before?"

He lit his pipe and stared at the pile of papers in an almost incredulous fury of frustration. He got up and began to walk about the room, restless, nervous and violently rebellious. There it is, he thought. Whether I recognised it or not, it's half *done!* He stopped and gave the stack of manuscript an angry, calculating stare. A hundred thousand words? A hundred and fifty thousand? Have I got to waste it? It was her idea. Even when she spoke of it I didn't realise. . . . And yet, there it is . . .

He stood at the window looking out blindly, thinking of her. He tried to detach himself from his personal relationship with her and consider her coldly—a critic assessing the potentialities of a young writer who was unknown to him. *Could* she do this book?

He was miserably grateful for the recollection that long before he had been seized with the desire to do it himself he had decided that she could not. Then he began to argue tormentedly that perhaps his belief had been influenced even then by a subconscious jealousy; that without being aware of it he had recognised it, the moment she spoke, as *his* subject. Nor could he subdue a certain resentful clamour in himself which insisted that he had earned the right to do it. He had equipped himself, he had read and studied and subjected his mind to an arduous training just so that he might be capable of handling such a theme as this. And I knew him, he argued, I really knew him, and to her he is only a story at second hand . . .

Agitation and rage subsided, leaving him depressed. The hard fact remained. She had got in first, she had pegged out a claim. He left the study and went out into the garden. Phyllis had left a spade standing upright in the patch she was devoting to vege-tables. He grabbed it and began to dig. He told himself that Elsa was young, and she must learn by trial and error like all writers. She would write this book—not as he would have written it, but who was he to say that her way would be inferior? Need it be inferior—even to him? Might she not surprise and confound him? It was a subject, evidently, which did stir some emotional depths in her, even if they were not the same depths which it stirred in him. It might be the subject through which she would find herself as a writer—and was he to grudge her that? He shut his mind altogether, then, against the thought of her as a writer, and consciously evoked closer and more intimate memories. His life had been sexually barren for so long that it was not dif-ficult to summon such images, or to allow himself to be swamped by them; the peril of feeling antagonism towards her was averted by the pleasure of feeling something near enough to love.

He went on digging with determined energy till the sun was gone and the cold air stung the sweat on his forehead, and he heard the voices of the young people in the house, and the sound of the gramophone. Looking up at the verandah, he saw Prue dancing with young Grover.

*   *   *   *

The next day was one of those fragile, perfect days with which the capricious mountain climate occasionally obliterated all memory of its harsher moods. He woke early, and, though the night had left him unrefreshed, he dressed and went outside, leaving Phyllis still asleep. Such small manœuvrings had been part of his life for a long time now; whether she knew it or not, the outward peace of their domestic scene had rested for years on his conscious policy of being alone with her as little as possible.

Standing on the verandah and looking down at the garden, he noticed that it was behaving with some eccentricity. Trees, shrubs and plants which, during four parched years, had fought a grim holding war against extinction, were now bemused by the rain's reprieve, and waking out of turn. For so long there had been no seasons—only drought. They had pursued a scorched-earth policy, retreating and destroying as they went, shedding leaves, dying back along their branches, retiring underground to concentrate what remained of life in their roots, and stand a stubborn siege. The rhythm of life provided that after the long suspension of winter came spring; and now, seeking to re-establish that rhythm, they were returning to the upper world. Saved by the rain, and beguiled by the mildness of the June weather, they were confusedly setting in motion the alchemies which belonged properly to September. There were actually a few flowers out on the azalea bushes; the lilac seemed on the verge of bloom; the furry silver of the pussy-willow was breaking here and there, and the japonica flaunted fat pink buds along its bare branches.

It was cold in the shade, but surprisingly warm in the sun; Gilbert, strolling up the path towards the front gate, saw Prue and her young American walking smartly back towards the house from the direction of the falls, carrying their coats slung over their shoulders. He watched them benevolently. Round the fire last night, mostly silent himself, he had listened to their conversation, feeling at once amused and touched by the careful tact of their visitor. Not once, though the trenchant remarks of his own children provided many an opening, had he been betrayed into even the mildest criticism. Everything, said his attitude—yes, everything—was swell. The people, the scenery, the food, the beaches; even his reply to a frontal attack from Virginia on the subject of the coffee had framed itself adroitly as a graceful compliment to the tea. And Gilbert had noticed, too, with approval and not without relief, that the young man's eyes were more often upon Prue's face than upon the lovely silken legs which Virginia was displaying to advantage.

He pushed the gate open for them. They were laughing as they walked towards him, and arguing about something—food, he supposed, for he heard John say: "Well, I guess it doesn't matter after all; right now I could eat anything!" Prue called out gaily:

"Hullo, Dad!"

He asked as they came up:

"Where did you go?"

"Down under the falls. The valleys are all full of mist, like cottonwool."

She looked so happy that he felt a stab of fear. This morning, he thought, she had forgotten the horrors of war and the dangers of peace, she had forgotten luxury and poverty, and anti-semitism, and the status of women, and the machinations of capital and the counter-machinations of labour—everything, in fact, except that she's twenty-one, and out walking on a crisp, winter morning with a congenial young man. He touched her shoulder in an awkward, unaccustomed caress as she passed through the gate.

"Is everyone up?" she asked. "I must go and help hurry the breakfast along. John's starving—aren't you, John?"

She left them and ran into the house and down the passage to the room she shared with Virginia. Her sister was sitting up in bed with her golden hair falling about her face, and her fingers pushed into it. She yawned and asked:

"Where have you been?"

"Oh, just down by the falls." Prue, running a comb through her hair, began to hum to herself. Exercise had set her blood racing; happiness was making her feel almost light-headed; for a moment she asked herself what she had to feel so happy about, and laughed because she could find no answer, and didn't want one anyhow. It had been fun going down the steps, down, down, through shady tunnels of green into a dark, quiet world where the sky was lost, and the cliffs and tree-trunks ran up towards it out of sight, and the path was so slippery that it seemed sensible to go arm in arm, and you drank water that was liquid ice from your cupped hands, and dried them on handkerchiefs, and went on again, still down and down.

John had asked:

"Don't you have any animals?"

"Only a few wallabies, and an occasional wombat."

"What about those things like Teddy bears?"

"Koalas? Not here; snakes now and then."

"No birds?"

"Oh, yes. Heaps of birds. Why?"

"I haven't heard any, or seen any."

"Didn't you hear the kookaburras this morning?"

"No." He looked at her sharply. "Jesus, were those kooka-burras? I thought it was a bunch of fowls gone haywire." He stood still for a moment, looking round at the greenish, semi-twilight under the towering trees and the giant ferns, and up at the green roof of foliage where a few patches of pale blue sky, infinitely remote, showed through the twinkling leaves. He added: "Gosh, it's quiet here!"

She laughed, and he asked, grinning:

"Did I say something funny?"

"No—only I like the way you say 'Garsh'."

Then he had tried to say it her way; and what with running down the steps and laughing at each other's accents, they had been so breathless by the time they reached the bottom that they stopped on a little bridge near the foot of the falls, and then he kissed her.

For a second her hands on his shoulders had reminded her that he wore a uniform, and she had felt the carefree exuberance of her mood menaced. If you stopped even for an instant to think about khaki, you thought on and on through a nightmare, so she forced her mind away, and used her lips as soon as they were free to say, blinking:

"Garsh!"

That had restored the proper mood. Warm with exercise, they had pottered about among the huge, mossy boulders and the rotting logs; they had used a monkey-vine for a swing; they had watched a flight of gaudy parrots flash out from the shade into the sunlight.

"So now you've seen some birds."

"I can hear one, too."

"That's a lyrebird. You won't see it, though—they're shy."

"I've seen pictures of them. Don't they mimic, or something?"

"They mimic anything. Even your haywire fowlyard."

"They must be good."

"You'd better buy a book about them," she teased lightly, "for your mother."

He said seriously:

"You know, I nearly didn't go into your shop that morning."

She looked at him quickly, and looked away. It was one of those remarks for which Virginia would have known the provocative and inviting answer. She could only say awkwardly: "I'm glad you did," and retreat from a momentary emotion by glancing hurriedly at her watch.

"We'd better go back. It's nearly eight o'clock."

So they had set off up the steps again, running at first, and then subsiding breathless, to a steady trudge, arm-in-arm, their coats slung over their shoulders. Just before they came up into the sunlight he had stopped and said:

"Prue."

"Yes."

"Kiss me again."

She had known, lifting her face to him, just how much and how little it meant. He would have said "Give me food" in exactly the same way, and she would have given it as she gave the kiss, wanting nothing but to see his hunger eased. She felt, now, a curiously defiant sense of triumph because they had stolen an hour or two of life and made it their own; played hookey from a war-maddened world, possessed themselves of something, at least, which they had not needed to share with any living thing but a flight of parrots and an unseen lyrebird.

Virginia, still yawning, climbed out of bed and stretched her lovely body in its bright silk pyjamas.

"What do we do with the boy-friend to-day?"

"I don't know."

Prue, now that her sister was in action, moved automatically away from the mirror. It didn't seem to matter in the least what they did. She asked:

"Are you really all right again?"

"I feel all right." Virginia began to rummage in a drawer. "Lend me some stockings, Prue—mine are all ladders."

Prue threw her a pair. Virginia sat down at the mirror and picked up a brush. She said suddenly:

"Lord, how I loathe men!"

Prue glanced at her sideways. She felt irritated, and said dryly: "Since when?"

"All right, all right!" Virginia snapped. "Don't believe me!"

Prue looked uneasily at the reflection of her sister's face in the mirror, and was startled by its expression of unhappy discontent. Virginia said, brushing angrily:

"Always mauling you about, always pestering you . . . !"

Prue asked:

"What's become of George English?"

"Him?" Virginia tossed her hair back and threw the brush down. "I hardly ever see him now. I've been going out mostly with Tim Webster and a couple of American boys. But I'm sick of the lot of them. You look out, Prue. This one of yours'll be just the same as all the rest. They only want . . ."

Prue interrupted her disgustedly:

"Oh, don't be so *childish?* Of course they do! Why make a hullaballoo about it?"

Virginia put her head down on the dressing-table and began to cry. Prue looked at her frowningly. She had always felt older than her sister, but now, warring with a vague sense of responsibility, came impatience. What could you say to Virginia? How could you influence or argue with anyone so unstable, so wayward and undisciplined, so entirely governed by her appetites and impulses? She realised helplessly that for years they had talked only of trivialities; beyond those trivialities they confronted each other without comprehension. She had seen her sister cry often enough before—because she was disappointed in a new frock, because her hair would not set properly, because she was not able to go to some dance she had set her heart on, because their father refused to increase her allowance. Why she was crying now Prue did not know, but experience had taught her not to take Virginia's tears very seriously. She patted the bent shoulders and said hastily:

"Oh, buck up, darling. It's just that you're still a bit seedy. Hurry up and have your bath, or Mother'll be coming in to see where you are. I must rush and give her a hand with the breakfast . . ."

From the doorway she glanced back, vaguely troubled. But Virginia was already anxiously examining her reddened eyes in the mirror.

*   *   *   *

The happiness of that week-end holiday, Prue found, was too brittle to survive their return to the city. The morning papers met them with news that shells from a submarine standing off the coast had fallen the night before in several of the suburbs; and, saying good-bye to John at Central, she knew that there was no re-capturing of the mood of twenty-four hours ago. Gilbert, watching her as they travelled down in the train, had been hurt by the shadowing of that brilliance he had seen on her face yesterday, and, with a hurried farewell, left them alone together on the crowded platform. John held her hand and said:

"It's been a swell week-end, Prue."

She answered valiantly:

"There'll be more."

"Maybe there will."

"Your train goes in only a few minutes."

"I know. I'll call you up soon."

"Yes. You don't think . . . I mean you'll know if you're going to be moved on . . . somewhere?"

He made a little gesture—the fatalistic gesture of youth captured by the war machine.

"I guess so. We don't really know anything."

"You must go, John, or you'll miss your train."

"I'll make it all right. I've got five minutes yet."

If Gilbert had been there he might have recognised the moment as a counterpart of the one which had swept himself, years ago, into an engagement; he might have reflected that those years had altered the reactions of such young people, giving them at once a maturer clarity of vision, and a deep mistrust, not of life itself, but of the forces in life which could tear up and discard their little personal plans like so much waste paper. The moment held a secret between them which, by unspoken consent, they refused to expose by so much as a word or look to the world's indifferent destructiveness; so they parted with a smile and a backward wave of the hand, and Prue walked soberly off alone to catch her tram.

VI

THE mild winter slid almost imperceptibly into spring. June, momentarily brightened by the American naval success at Midway Island, and the Anglo-Soviet treaty, grew darker again with the unfolding tale of retreat in North Africa. In July the headlines offered encouragement with one hand only to snatch it away with the other. Things were better in Libya, but in Russia the name Stalingrad leapt into the news to remain there for long months, flaring like a sombre beacon. Commentators and newspapermen juggled with those talismanic words "a second front," and the people, hungrily hopeful, irritably impatient, starving for even a crumb of comfort, devoured their conjectures, and added their own stubbornly insistent clamours.

Danger accumulated in the north, but the material for resistance accumulated too. Along the hundreds of miles of road from Alice Springs to Darwin, which three hundred men had toiled to build in eighty-eight days, went the incessant stream of motor convoys carrying war supplies, and troops, and food. By August the enemy was building up a formidable strength in New Guinea, and fighting bitterly for supremacy in the Solomons. Yet the relentless logic of global war dragged even the most parochial minds away from exclusive contemplation of their own territories; the opposing forces of history in the making pulled those minds and stretched them till they sang and thrummed like wires. India thrust itself forward into their consciousness, and issues which had roused no response in them once, were now a painful plucking on their thought, a challenge to sharply-awakened moralities. If you are fighting domination, suppression, overlordship, said the singing in those minds, you are fighting it everywhere; if you believe in freedom, self-determination, democracy, you believe in it for everyone. Global war? Well, then, global peace, global co-operation, global justice . . .

The people learned now—or remembered—that the diagram of man's emotions is not a straight line with grief at one end and joy at the other, but a circle where the extreme of ecstacy blurs into pain. They learned that not only in their bodies and in their mysticisms, but also in their thoughts, the sharpest effort towards achievement must be shot with agony. They began to under-stand—not willingly, but because they must—that if no conflict in themselves hold more torture than mental conflict, no resolving of conflict brings more unassailable serenity. They began to grope towards that serenity, taking the knocks they had shirked before, sloughing off protective layers of prejudice, and wincing with the pain of exposure. They were worried, they were anxious, they were asking; they were on the way to salvation.

This was a background, a semi-conscious reaction to events. With the front of their minds they went on living from day to day, studying their newly-acquired ration-books, writing letters to the papers, taking sides on trivial domestic issues, growing vegetables, practising for air-raids, grumbling, quarrelling, laughing, filling the war loans, going to the movies. By the beginning of Sep-tember their grim and irritable defence-mood had undergone a subtle change. Stalingrad was performing the impossible; Rommel was baulking in the desert; they had had their own taste of vic-tory at Milne Bay. They had been running a Marathon, concen-trating on keeping their place; now they were ready to sprint. The Japanese were pushing up the Kokoda trail, the Prime Minister was talking sternly of austerity, and still more austerity, but—whether because there was the feel of spring and the scent of brown boronia in the air, or whether from some obscure, psychological current of conviction—that mood added exhilaration to its grimness, and gained impetus.

The people expressed it in the streets, showering confetti on marching troops returned from the Middle East, surging forward from footpaths, hanging like clusters of fruit from trees, packing windows and awnings, sending out vitality in waves with their tumultuous cheering. Gilbert, jammed in the crowd with Marty and Prue, felt some of his own despondency lift, and regretted (but only for a moment) his inability to become completely identified with mass emotion. There was power here. Manpower. It occurred to him that that was a dangerous word, linking itself by association with horsepower, and becoming, thus, a word with merely physical implications. He felt it now as a spiritual power, and his own individual fragment of it as something straining almost beyond endurance to pull it in the direction he wanted it to go. Out of this experience as out of every other experience, the same old question emerged to confront him. If you could split this manpower into its component parts, how much of it would pull on his side, and how much on the other? What was going to be the result of the final tug-of-peace? The victorious arms of this nation or that nation were merely factors in the struggle to decide the fate of an epoch. What would be born out of the ultimate encounter? What idea would win in the last, inevitable showdown?

Marty was restless. She liked to observe crowds in the same way that she liked to observe the sea—from a distance. She hated the emotionalism of humanity in the mass, and profoundly distrusted the symbolisms that fed it. She loathed a national flag because it fluttered between her and her own inner conception of the land it represented; she shut her ears obstinately against martial music because it attempted to shape the emotions she felt quite capable of shaping for herself; she detested the hypnotic tramp-tramp of marching feet because it debased the natural contact of man with his mother earth to the rhythmic insensitiveness of a machine; she condemned all uniforms because they masked the final value of the human being—his uniqueness. She looked at the flowing river of cocked hats, which was all she could see of the procession, and said irritably to Prue:

"I'm going to extricate myself—if I can."

"Wait a bit—we'll come with you." Prue yelled above the din: "Do you want to watch any more, Dad?"

He shook his head. They pushed laboriously through the crowd, and emerged at last, dishevelled. Marty adjusted her hat, and said:

"I'll leave you here. I have some shopping to do."

She set off along Pitt Street, walking briskly, and thinking about the book which was beginning to take shape in her mind. She was actually more interested in the way it was taking shape than in the prospect of writing it, for her brain, with a bland, momentous inconsistency, was reversing its usual procedure. Always before she had seen a character, and spun a story out of it. Now she had seen a story, but its central character remained misty She wasted no time on speculating which was the "better" method but she was acutely intrigued to discover the machinery of her mind behaving so little like machinery that it elected, suddenly, serenely, and purposefully, to work backwards. She decided without either approbation or regret that it might be a result of several years during which her attention had been fixed on problems rather than on personalities, and she was, for the moment, simply waiting—an attentive spectator—to discover how, and at what stage, her story would become inhabited. At present it was merely a scene and a few impressions. There was a little cottage, a basket of darning, a stove, pots and pans, pipes, toys, school-books, a pram. The woman who presided over it was, so far, not a person, but an abstraction. Her functions as well as her possessions were clear enough; her busy little days, her routine of chores, her flitting, disconnected little preoccupations. Her domestic annoyances were vivid—the butcher late, the gas-stove out of order, the leaking roof, the washing fallen in the muddy yard; and so were her small relaxations—the movies, the tea-party, the wireless serial. Her anxieties were the baby's lack of appetite, the son's disobedience, the daughter's sullenness, the husband's fits of moroseness, the mounting household bills. And yet, though the spotlight never moved from this little scene, and the courageous, ant-like activity of this little creature, the story itself was not there. Behind her, governing her every action, hampering her every effort, frustrating her every achievement, was the social organisation of her community. She was exhibited in all her pitiable help-lessness, her mind, hemmed in by the four walls of her domestic environment, undergoing a slow atrophy, seeing bills only as her bills, illness only as the illness of her family, the moods of her husband, her children, herself, only as mysterious personal mani-festations. Down to its most trivial detail this woman's little life appeared as dominated by remote political forces in which, irritably and impatiently, she proclaimed herself not a bit interested.

But who was she? No doubt, Marty reflected resignedly, plung-ing down a flight of steps, and pushing her way towards a crowded grocery counter, she would materialise in time. Until she did there was, obviously, nothing to be done about it. Am I Nick, she asked herself, that I should deal in Type Number So-and-so, housewife, lower middle-class? But for all her determined con-fidence she could not avoid a stab of anxiety for her own brain—that curious, un-mechanical machine—clogged by her own domestic inertia, endlessly halted by the demands of her own stove and vacuum-cleaner. I'm getting too old, she thought, with sudden despondency, to cope with this splitting of my energies.

And then, waiting list in hand, she became aware of eyes upon her which looked hastily away as she turned. Something in the sallow face, the blue-green eyes under sandy lashes, the faded red hair of that middle-aged woman was familiar. She looked away, searching her memory; but it was not until she saw the shabby, meagre figure leave the counter, struggling with a suitcase, a string bag, and two small children, that recognition came. Abandoning her place in the queue, she dived in pursuit.

"Sally!" she cried, grabbing at an arm in a cheap tweed coat. "Aren't you Sally Dodd?"

The smaller of the two children burst into loud screams. Sally said hurriedly:

"Yes—I thought I knew you, but I wasn't sure. Be quiet, Joyce! Les, you give 'er back 'er tank this minute!" She looked at Marty again, and asked with awkward formality: "And 'ow 'ave you been keeping?"

"I'm very well," Marty said hastily. "Can't we—wouldn't you and the children have a cup of tea with me, and we can talk? Look, there's a cafeteria just through the archway . . . ?"

She thought as they found a table and set down their laden trays that the years had not changed Sally's habit of fatalistic acceptance. Nor, she admitted wryly, her own habit of bossiness. They had reverted instantly to the old relationship; Marty proposed and disposed—Sally followed acquiescently. Not only the exhaustion of city shopping, not only the effort of buying groceries, stowing them in bags, finding money and accepting change, and trying at the same time to shepherd and control two restless children, gave Sally that battered and dishevelled appearance. Life, Marty thought, has been shoving her around ever since she was born; it's still shoving her. There was that curious suggestion of waiting detachment in her eyes—the expression of poor women who look neither back nor forward, but husband their resources for what each passing moment may bring. A passing moment had brought Marty—so there Sally sat, accepting it, waiting passively for developments. Even observation of her children, even the movements she made to seat them properly, to place plates before them, to steady the brimming glass of milk-shake which Joyce was lifting rapturously to her lips, were automatic; her eyes remained absent. If it had been a bomb through the roof, Marty thought, instead of me, she would have accepted that just the same. Gone through the necessary motions, faced it as part of a life which had always been incomprehensible, and against which there had never been any defence but a patiently and stubbornly continued existence. She asked, pouring tea:

"Where are you living now, Sally?"

"Leichhardt."

Sally had never wasted words, and she did not waste them now. One hand went out to steady the glass again, and the other, machine-like, intercepted a plump, predatory hand hovering above the plate of cakes. "You can't 'ave that one, love; you know the cream makes you bilious."

Les disputed the statement with vigour; Joyce pounced on her opportunity.

"C'n I 'ave it, then? It don't make *me* bilious."

Sally said sharply:

"You can't neither of you 'ave it. Here's two with jam in them. There. Now eat 'em up nicely, or you won't get no more."

She sat back and sighed wearily. Marty asked:

"Have you any others besides these?"

Sally's eyes lost none of their detachment. She said briefly: "Four more. These are the youngest." She looked at Marty and asked, in a tone which made the question a mere civility. "You got any?"

"I had one boy," Marty answered. "He died."

She found herself looking anxiously for some sign of softening or sympathy in Sally's eyes, and found none. It was not for herself that she desired to see it, but as a reassurance that the effort of living had not left her old friend quite emotionally numbed. Sally, putting her cup down, said matter-of-factly: "I lost two when they was little." She made a small sound like a laugh, but without mirth. "Six is enough to provide for."

Marty said: "Yes, indeed." And added: "Are the others old enough to have jobs yet?"

"The eldest—'e's nineteen—went to Malaya. We 'aven't 'eard from 'im in months. Janet's eighteen. She 'as a good job in a factory. Billy's fourteen next month, so 'e'll be leavin' school soon, but Ken's only eleven." She drank some more tea, and added in an absent-minded way: "Kids are an 'andful, all right."

"And your husband?"

" 'E's up North—workin' on some aerodrome."

"Janet . . . ?" Marty asked. "Did you—name her after Janet Laughlin?"

Now there really was a flicker of something in Sally's pale eyes.

"I seen about 'er death in the paper not long before my baby was born. So I called 'er Janet for a sort of remembrance. Mr. Laughlin was real good to us."

Marty felt her old hatred of her father stir. She said slowly:

"Yes, I expect he would have been. You had a hard time in those days, Sally. I've often thought of it since."

"We got along," Sally said unemotionally. She looked at Marty again after a moment's pause, adding, as a bald statement: "And now it's the war."

"Yes," Marty plunged. "What do you think of the war, Sally?"

"I s'pose we got to get it over with."

"And then . . . ?"

"Well," Sally said heavily, "let's 'ope we 'ave more sense than we did last time."

"Do you think we will?"

Sally was silent for a moment, stirring her tea. There was the faintest note of defiance in her voice when she said at last:

"My eldest boy and girl's both Reds. They reckon they under-stand what this New Order ought to be like. I don't know. I never 'ad no time to study these things. But I reckon it couldn't be no worse than what we've 'ad."

"It might. What does your husband think?"

" 'E used to get wild with Ted and Janet. But 'e's comin' round to thinkin' they might be right now. Janet's a bright sort of girl." She drank her tea and twisted the cup automatically to study the tealeaves. "Sometimes seems," she said remotely, "as if namin' 'er Janet made 'er a bit like the other Janet. Sort of serious, wasn't she? Old for 'er age. My Janet's like that too. Says she isn't goin' to bring up no family like I've 'ad to."

"I wanna sambwidge," said Joyce.

Sally gave her one; she waved it away.

"Wanna bermata one."

Les swallowed hastily.

"I wanna bermata one too."

Sally cut the tomato one in two, and gave them each half. She asked Marty:

" 'Ow's Gil . . . your brother?"

Marty winced. She had, more consciously, the same idea which had manifested itself to Gilbert as a vague emotion when he was fifteen. There was a child-world, and if you were a child you belonged in it. But the adult world was split into sections, and from her section Sally found herself instinctively baulking at the Christian name she had used so naturally long ago.

"He's well," she replied wearily. "He married Phyllis, you know. They have three children."

"Writes books, don't 'e?" Sally remarked.

"Yes."

"Seen write-ups about them in the papers. I don't get no time to read. You write things too, don't you?"

"Yes."

"Always did. I remember you and Janet—always writin' things. Where's your other brother—the little one?"

"Nick? He's in the army—somewhere up North." She added: "He's a Red, too."

Sally looked at her with an innocent, transparent curiosity. As clearly as if she had said it, her expression asked: "What's *he* want to be a Red for?" Marty recognised, unhappily, the origin of yet another cleavage in the adult world—the mistrust of the "worker," who knew by experience, for the "intellectual," who knew by observation, by mental effort, by imagination. If your life were a struggle for the bare necessities, she admitted, could you help doubting the good faith of people like herself, and Nick, and Gilbert . . . ?

Sally was wiping the children's mouths and fingers with her handkerchief. They sat still now, happily replete, staring at Marty with round, observant eyes. Looking about her, she noticed the placards hung over the various counters in the huge basement, and felt her mind check in momentary astonished blankness, followed by a sharp, childish delight. "CUTLERY" said one placard. "WOOL" said another. "NECKWEAR" said a third. And a fourth said "VISIONS." Alas, only for a second. From where she sat a thick pillar hid the "PRO" which made melancholy sense of it. She felt an insane desire to point it out to Sally—to ask her what vision she would care to buy. A vision of the New Order? Of her eldest son, wherever he might be? Of some cottage, garden, farm, to which her longing turned in rare, unguarded moments? Of an electric stove, a lounge suite, the brotherhood of man? But Sally was preparing for departure, adjusting Joyce's hat, brushing crumbs from Les' trousers, pulling on her own worn cotton gloves. Marty followed the little party to the doorway with a curious sense of failure and frustration.

"It's been real nice seein' you again," Sally said with formal politeness. "Good-bye."

* * * *

"I'll have to get a stronger bulb for that light," Elsa thought, "*and* a new typewriter ribbon." From the page before her, covered with Gilbert's thick, sloped writing, she peered at her typescript, bending forward. "It's 'inevitably,' and I've got 'invariably.' Damn!" She dropped her hands on the table, looked across the room at him, and said:

"Gilbert?"

"Yes?"

"Will they publish this?"

He laid his book face downward on his knee, and took his pipe out of his mouth.

"I don't know."

She asked dryly:

"What are your chances?"

"As good as the lottery."

"And you think it's worth the bother?"

His brows contracted slightly.

"It isn't a bother." He looked at her sharply. "To me, I mean. Leave it, Elsa—I should have remembered that you're typing all day. I can do it myself to-morrow."

She said impatiently:

"I didn't mean that. Goodness, it's only a letter—five minutes' work. I was just wondering if it accomplished anything."

She thought with exasperation: "If only he'd answer *quickly!* Those long pauses while what you've said sinks in, and what he's going to say comes out! And when it comes out it's always so damned fair, and careful, and considered, and reasonable! Well, here it comes!"

"I suppose it's a drop in an ocean of protest."

"*If* it's published."

"If it's published," he agreed, and then added slowly, "and even if it isn't published."

"What's the good of a protest that nobody sees?"

He struck a match and re-lit his pipe; she saw the reflections of its tiny flame dance in his glasses.

"It's made," he said.

"You mean it's good for yourself?"

"It'd be bad for myself if I didn't make it."

She lit a cigarette and went on typing. A sudden thought struck her, and she burst out laughing.

' Wasn't your mother a missionary, Gilbert?"

"Yes. Why?"

She sat back in her chair and studied him with faintly malicious amusement.

"There's something in heredity, isn't there?"

"You see signs of the missionary spirit in me?"

"And how! Your brother and sister, too. You're all missionaries."

He asked rather wearily:

"What's the alternative?"

She suggested lightly:

"Leave things alone . . . ?"

He looked at her. She fidgeted, puffed at her cigarette, and acknowledged irritably:

"Oh, yes, yes, I know all about *laissez faire!* You're right, of course—you're always right, darn you! So what? So we must all turn into missionaries, one way or another. We take in each other's salvation instead of each other's washing."

"Don't blame me," he said shortly. "I didn't originate the idea. Are we our brothers' keepers, or aren't we? Are we members one of another, or aren't we? It's a choice people have had to make ever since they had brains to think with."

She shrugged.

"It's a great life if you don't weaken."

"An unspeakable life," he retorted with some heat, "if you do weaken." He was looking at her, but the light shone on his spectacles so that she couldn't see his eyes. She knew only from his voice that she had antagonised him. "And we aren't all missionaries," he said, "not by a long shot. Lots of us are apathetic —just plain dumb, and some of us are . . . fence-sitters . . ."

Her dark eyes snapped, and her mouth tightened.

"Meaning me, Gilbert?"

The words were out, a challenge, before she could stop them.

They stared at each other for a startled, silent moment. This was the first time that hidden hostility, of which they had both been conscious from the beginning, had thrust itself into the open. He took his glasses off, laid them on his book, and put the book on the mantelpiece as he rose. He came over to the table and stood opposite her with his pipe in his hand, and that familiar frown of concentration on his forehead.

"I don't know what you are," he said, looking hard at her. "Surely I should, by now? I know my wife's mind, I know my brother's, and Marty's, and Prue's. I know the minds of all my friends, and most of my acquaintances—but I don't know yours."

She was looking down at her left hand, resting on the edge of the table; it was shaking so that the thin coil of smoke from her cigarette broke into tiny whirls and circles. She had wanted reality, hadn't she? She had attached herself to this man so that she could go with him into the reality he so obviously knew, and discover herself there. But it was no good; even to him she was a ghost. She said incoherently:

"I suppose you can't have reality—in sections . . ."

"What?"

She looked up at him in a sort of terror. He pulled up a chair and sat down, resting his folded arms on the table. She went on with nervous rapidity:

"I wanted—companionship, Gilbert. That's all. I wanted another human being to be with me—can't you understand that?"

"Of course. Well?"

"Just that. Not anything else."

"I don't understand what you mean."

"I won't be dragged into things."

"You mean you want a relationship that's purely personal?"

"I suppose so . . ."

"There isn't any such thing, Elsa."

She said confusedly:

"Perhaps there isn't. That's what I meant when I said you can't have reality in sections."

"What are you afraid of?"

"Afraid . . . ?"

"Yes!" he said with sudden rough emphasis. "Afraid!" And while she groped for an answer he remembered her denial of fear during their first night together, and his own acknowledgment of it. He knew the answer and spoke it for her.

"You're not afraid of outside things—only of yourself—some-how. Aren't you?"

She muttered sulkily:

"I suppose so. I don't know. Yes, I think I am . . ."

"Why?"

Suddenly she found words.

"Why? You said you didn't know me. How could you? I don't know myself. There isn't any me—isn't that something to be afraid of?"

He looked at her in bewilderment.

"It would be if it were true. What do you mean? What do you want—care about?"

She asked with painful eagerness:

"What *should* I want or care about? What do *you* want or care about? You're real enough!"

"If I am," he said, "you should know what I care about by now."

"People," she said slowly, as if remembering and repeating a lesson. "People—and writing. Isn't that it?"

"Yes, that's it. Don't you care about those too?"

Something was hypnotising her into an alarming honesty. She shook her head.

"No."

"Not at all?"

"Not a bit. Not really."

"Not even writing?" He was almost pleading with her.

"No. Not your way, Gilbert. Only as—something for myself. I don't want to be a writer—I just want to write things . . ."

For the first time he smiled.

"It's a subtle distinction, but I see what you mean. And people?"

She avoided his eyes; her own, losing their dazed honesty, were becoming wary and secretive again.

"I . . . like people . . . all right."

He had nothing to say to that, and his silence angered her into words that resisted him. "*People*, I said! Not 'the people'! Not your blasted proletariat, and your everlasting toiling masses! I want a personal life, Gilbert. I've never had one—I don't seem to be a real person at all . . ."

"How can you be," he asked impatiently, "if you persist in shutting the world out? You make a ghost of yourself."

That word on his lips, actually spoken aloud, which had been so often in her own thoughts, gave her an almost superstitious chill. She said angrily, but so low that he could not hear:

"My mother made a ghost of me."

"What did you say?"

"It was my mother!" she said loudly and fiercely. "She never let me forget her first marriage, and her first home. She never let me forget Janet. She adored Scott Laughlin, and all my life I heard about him, and about Janet, about that house you took me to see, about her life there, even about you and your family. My own life wasn't ever real to me—it always played second fiddle to the life mother told me about. I heard so much about Janet, Janet, Janet, that when I was little I played at *being* Janet. So that my mother would love me as much as she loved Janet. Can't you see, Gilbert, I've got to escape from that—I've got to have a life that's mine, and people who are mine . . ."

She was crying. He began to understand it all now, and he looked at her with the horrified pity he would have felt for a human being incurably maimed or deformed. He pushed his chair back hurriedly and went round the table to her. She flung her arms round his waist and held him desperately, and while his hands stroked her hair his mind was hunting for words of comfort. You have me. But had she? You *are* a writer. But was she? Failing comfort, there was warning. Don't try to escape, Elsa; there's no escape. . . . That was only telling her what she was so bitterly discovering—only turning the knife in her wound. He said nothing. What was there to say?

*　　　*　　　*　　　*

Yes, Marty was right, he supposed, when she said that he was "soft." Ruthlessness was not in his nature. He fell back on his compassion for Elsa and the bond of their physical intimacy. For the next month or so he made a deliberate effort to provide her with the "purely personal" relationship which he knew to be an illusion. He stopped discussing the news with her, he gave up the interchange of books and pamphlets, he took her to movies instead of meetings; and all the time he knew that she was too intelligent not to feel the growing artificiality of their companionship. He admitted to himself that his "missionary spirit" found obstinate cause for hope in this. She would learn from experience, perhaps, what he had told her—that no human relationship can exist in a vacuum. She would find that every road which promised escape, no matter how alluringly it might seem at first to lead away from all she wanted to avoid, sooner or later took a sly turn, and led her back to confront her world. She would feel the impossible, tedious emptiness of conversations which may go just so far, and then must stop, cut short, left in the air, because danger lay ahead. She would acknowledge at last the grim simplicity of the issue: not "Will you go?" but "Will you choose your path or be pushed?"

Her attitude to himself during this time was one of casual affection, flaring out sometimes into a defiant hostility. He knew that she was going out more and more with Jimmy Baxter, and wondered sometimes if she were trying to make him jealous. He felt sorry for her when this thought crossed his mind, for absence from her now was a relief—an opportunity to return to himself and his own thoughts. He found them less oppressive than they had been before; they were still hard, but at least they had substance, and thinking them released him from his self-imposed task of becoming a ghost to console her ghostliness. They lifted and lightened to the news of the Japanese retreat over the Owen Stanley Range, of greater air strength in Egypt. They checked in painful suspension, awaiting the outcome of the naval battle in the Solomons. Some part of them was always alert, an unsleeping eye, a listening ear, conscious of Stalingrad.

He was able to take the buffetings of thought more calmly now, and was aware of indebtedness to Elsa. He had not fully realised the strain of a life grown almost celibate until he escaped from it with her; and his worried knowledge that he had given her less than she had given him was not altogether quieted by the knowledge that she had no use for what he could offer. She was right about him, he admitted. No missionary had ever more ardently desired to wrestle with the devil for a soul's salvation, but during this month he began to appreciate the stress of such spiritual wrestlings. It was a month of torrential rains and wild weather. Prue succumbed to influenza, and retired for a week to the mountains, and Gilbert, thus released from the necessity for sleeping at his own flat, spent most of the nights with Elsa. She met his patience with flippancy, his sometimes clumsy sympathy with ridicule, his conversation with indifference, and his passion with passion. He went to and fro between the office and her flat, and the boisterous weather was only an extension of his own struggle with her. The harbour woke from its placidity in a fury of white-capped waves, breakers dashed high over cliffs and quiet beaches, the Manly ferry stopped running, small craft were damaged at their moorings, and with the further easing of water restrictions came warnings against floods. Fresh from Elsa's unrestful presence, he plunged out into the rain and wind-swept streets with a feeling that he had left the worst of the storm indoors.

The night before Prue was to return he tried what he felt must be the last line of attack.

"Have you begun on your book yet?"

"I thought you said I wasn't ready for it."

"I may have been wrong. Why don't you try?"

"You wouldn't like my way of doing it."

"Does that matter?"

She shrugged.

"Not a bit, I suppose. Why do you want me to do it, anyhow?"

He spent longer than usual thinking out the best reply to that, and she forestalled him with her bitter comprehension.

"I know, of course. You want me to come up against the 'realities' of the story, and find myself unable to cope with them. You want me to make a mirror for myself to look into. Supposing I don't choose to treat it that way?"

"Supposing you don't? How would you treat it?"

"I might make fun of it."

Suddenly he laughed outright. She had said that, he knew, with a vicious perversity intended to hurt him, but after the first second of shock he had seen how safe Scott Laughlin would be from any such portrayal. He said:

"You could do that, of course, but it would be nothing but a little invented tale. You can ignore truth if you want to—but if you do you have nothing left but falseness. Obviously."

The look she gave him was almost one of hatred.

VII

HE found himself thankful, now, for Prue's return, but disturbed by a suggestion of constraint in her manner. He asked about Virginia:

"Have you seen her since she went back?"

"No—I've only spoken to her on the 'phone."

"How is she?"

"She says she feels quite well."

He enquired after a pause.

"That chap English—is he still about?"

"I don't think she sees much of him now."

"Has she," he enquired dryly, "found a substitute yet?"

Prue shrugged.

"Several, I should think."

"I suppose she's enjoying life, then." She gave him a faintly worried glance.

"I don't know that she's enjoying it—exactly . . ."

He frowned. Her tone and the word "exactly" seemed to have left him an opening—a mere crack—for further enquiries. He did not make them. During these early days of November his first waking thoughts were always of the morning headlines, his breakfast a tasteless something which he swallowed mechanically while his mind fastened on El Alamein and Stalingrad. Yet though this overwhelming world-worry claimed priority over all lesser worries, the lesser worries were there. The problem of his marriage was an incessant, nagging unrest, and lately there had been added to it anxiety about Prue. And at this shadow of a hint that Virginia, also, might confront him with a problem, his mind jibbed and retreated. He felt an irritable impatience with his elder daughter and her flirtations. He could not invest them with reality. Try as he would, Virginia remained as remote from him as one of the seductive screen beauties whom she so resembled. He could not readjust his conception of her life as a series of shallow romances in which she played lead with glamorous efficiency, but which were of no more real interest or significance than a dozen streamlined celluloid love-stories which he had seen and forgotten in the past couple of years. He turned from the thought of her as he turned from the screen when the velvet curtain swung across it. He could not so easily dismiss Prue from his thoughts, and sometimes, catching a glimpse of her face over his morning newspaper, he gave her a second sharp glance, wondering uneasily if she had really recovered from her attack of 'flu.

Sometimes she wondered herself, and found a kind of reassurance in the thought that she was physically run down. It was a neat and simple and plausible way of accounting for the unfamiliar mixture of nervy excitement and weary depression which she felt; one hot day when she came near to fainting in the shop, she was almost pleased. But she said nothing about it to her father, fearing that he might urge a return to the cooler air of the mountains. She didn't want that—not only because while she was in town she could still see John Grover occasionally, but because she dreaded the company of her mother. Her feeling—which she found some comfort in believing was the result of illness—was that she did not want to be bothered with her family's troubles. It was a resentful and defensive feeling. She was suffering from the effect of falling in love; she was egotistical, she was isolationist, her instinct was to shut the rest of the world out—to withdraw into her own life, and commune with a new experience. That communion was being threatened by the knowledge of dangerous undercurrents in the family relationships. Mother and Virginia were both on edge, both restless with secret preoccupations, and bitter with unexpressed grievances. Waking on one night which Virginia had spent at home, Prue had heard muffled sobbing from her sister's bed; her questions had been met with an irritable "Oh, leave me alone!" Her mother had kept on inventing reasons for ringing her father up at night—reasons so obviously phoney that Prue blushed for her. Each time she had waited until well after midnight to do it, and twice she had come away from the telephone looking tight-lipped and saying: "He isn't there." She had looked at Prue with suspicious intentness, and asked: "Where *can* he be?" Questions had seemed to burst from her, beyond her control: "You said that meeting he was going to was on *Tuesday* night, didn't you?" "Who comes to see him at the flat?" "What time does he usually get home at night?" "I suppose you know all your father's extraordinary friends?"

She had answered shortly; but often, impatient to escape with all her mind and heart into her own jealously enclosed world, those questions had intruded, goading her into unwilling speculation. She had kept Elsa's name out of her answers, but she found herself remembering that quiet, dark, watchful face with almost passionate hostility. Her youth could not but assert that her father was behaving rather absurdly. The thought hurt her, not because it made him seem culpable in her eyes, but because it made him seem foolish. That was intolerable. She had cherished her respect for him the more because respect was something that her mother had never been able to inspire, and she wrestled now with a feeling that he had let her down. He had let her down not only by deviating from her conception of him as calm, self-possessed, and stable, but far more unbearably by introducing doubt and hesitation into her own attitude to John. Understand as she might that the demands of sex were not only upon the young, the fact remained that in the first excitements of love they had come to seem peculiarly the prerogative of her own romance. They were bound up with emotions which were new, fragile, delicate, scarcely to be breathed upon, and it was not easy, during hurried meetings always burdened with the menace of an incalculable world, to keep faith in those emotions—tenderness, pride, solicitude, anxiety. Nevertheless, these were her secret riches, her exclusive and jealously - guarded discovery; it offended her to find others pretending to her treasure. It frightened her to have that treasure exposed in such a way that she was forced to question its worth. Was this marriage—this unbeautiful relationship between her father and her mother? Was this love—this snatched, furtive relationship between her father and Elsa? Was it any part of love that made Virginia cry at night, that made her eyes brooding and discontented, that edged her voice with sharp cynicism when she spoke of men? Prue refused to be altogether overwhelmed by such doubts, but the sole source of resistance which she had was her own unfolding experience, and that was, as yet, too young, too uncertain and sensitive to escape quite unbruised.

She made only desultory attempts to see the situation as one involving a conventional right and wrong. The sympathy she felt for her mother was less sympathy for an individual than a vague sex-solidarity. She still liked her father strongly, if unhappily; for her mother she could find nothing but a faintly exasperated pity, and the strong, painful, inescapable affection of the maternal bond. Almost reluctantly, she made, towards the middle of the month, one effort to intervene:

"Couldn't you come up the mountains with me this week-end, Dad?"

"Not this time. I have the V.D.C. on Sunday."

"Do you have to go?" She added with an effort: "I think Mother gets a bit hurt when she doesn't see anything of you for a long time."

He had a note from Elsa in his pocket. *"You haven't been near me for almost a fortnight—I want to talk about the book . . ."* He answered curtly:

"I can't go this time. I'll try to manage it next week-end."

She said no more. He returned to his paper, trying to distract his mind from a hint of dissatisfaction with himself. He read: JAP REMNANTS FACE ANNIHILATION. He passed on to official commendation of the previous night's blackout. He skimmed impatiently a paragraph on the banning of iced cakes. He could not escape from contempt for Elsa's disingenuousness. *"I want to talk about the book!"* He could not escape from contempt for himself because, disingenuous as the summons was, he would answer it.

*   *   *   *

He found her friendlier, more cheerful and unshadowed than she had been for a long time. Pleasantly tired after a long, out-door day of military exercises, he was glad enough to relax in an armchair, drink the iced beer she produced for him, allow himself to be soothed and made welcome. It was not till he had been there for an hour that he felt something surprising in her halcyon mood, and was stung into alertness, startled by the conviction that he was not the source of that mood, but merely basking in its reflected glow. He became silent on this discovery.

She was saying:

"You didn't ring me last night, did you?"

"I did, as a matter of fact. About half-past eight."

"Oh, I'm sorry!" Passing his chair, she bent and kissed his forehead lightly. "Jimmy took me to a party an aunt of his was giving. To celebrate her daughter's engagement to an apoplectic-looking middle-aged colonel." She dropped into the chair opposite him, laughing. "You never *saw* such a place, Gilbert! Statues in the garden, a Hollywood staircase, mirrors, lights—everything one glittering bedazzlement . . ."

She talked and he listened; the malicious wit of her descriptions made him smile even at a time when he was not feeling particularly cheerful. She had, he acknowledged, looking at her thoughtfully, a fine flair for light, satirical and sophisticated comedy.

". . . the only thing that didn't glitter," she was continuing, "was the conversation. The moment I got in I felt that I was plugged into the conversational wave-length. I agreed fifteen times that the flowers were lovely, seventeen times that Tuesday had been dreadfully hot, and at least twenty-three times that it was socialistic tyranny to deprive the children of their Father Christmas. One pearl-encrusted dowager told me . . ."

He did not hear the rest. He could see her standing there, small and demure in the glitter she described, smiling and agreeing, keeping the brighter glitter of her own superior intelligence carefully invisible, using it only for sharp observation and subsequent derision. Accepting the flowers, the weather, and the issue of a banned Father Christmas as topics of conversation all on the same plane, all to be met with the same bright acquiescence. He understood more clearly than ever why she was retreating from him. She could enjoy her own intelligence only if she sabotaged it by refusing the demands of life made upon it. She must keep it locked up inside her, using it as a toy to make existence acidly amusing, referring experience to it only for ridicule, dipping her pen into it to write with edged irony, and cruel wit, and sour humour. What she could not endure, and would not tolerate, was to have it dragged out of her and set to forced labour on problems not to be resolved by wit and satire. She had been happy and stimulated last night because her intelligence had been titillated instead of challenged. Nothing in that glittering evening had disturbed her private consciousness and enjoyment of her own alert mentality, and nothing had interfered with her chosen method of exercising it. That was left, inevitably to her association with himself and his kind, when every conversation implied that to possess an intellect was not enough; when every silence thundered with unspoken criticism of mental activity wedded to spiritual inertia; when the implicit challenge of every topic that was raised forced her back into herself, warily defensive.

Already, in the oppression of his helpless silence, she was fading. The animation was dying out of her face; her hands, expressive in gesture, were stilled; her dark eyes lost their lively snap and sparkle. She was suddenly subdued, watchful, and again curiously pathetic. Her forlorn expression seemed to beg some overture from him, and his hand made a brief, instinctive gesture of invitation. She came to sit on the arm of his chair, and pulled his head into the crook of her arm, stroking his forehead.

She whispered:

"I've missed you, Gilbert. I really have missed you dreadfully."

*　　　　　*　　　　　*　　　　　*

Opening the door of his flat at eight o'clock next morning to collect some papers on his way to the office, he found Prue and Phyllis there. Prue, avoiding his eyes, said: "Hullo, Dad," and went past him hurriedly into her bedroom. Phyllis confronted him, and he knew that he was no better at facial dissimulation than he was at verbal lying; she had accused and he had admitted before they spoke a word. She demanded fiercely, without preamble:

"Where have you been?"

Prue, with her bag under her arm, came out of her room, pulling on her hat. She said nervously:

"I'm going now, Mummy. I'll meet you at the hospital this afternoon. See you to-night, Dad."

He stared after her till the front door of the flat closed. He said sharply to Phyllis:

"Hospital? What did she mean?"

"I asked where you were last night?"

Jealousy, hostility, even hatred, he had been prepared to see in her face, but the impression he had now of cruelty—of information deliberately withheld from him as a sort of punishment—made him furious.

"Who's in hospital? Is it Virginia? Pete? What's happened? What brought you down here?"

Her face was flushed and her hands trembling; she spoke fast and excitedly:

"Evidently it's very inconvenient for you, though I should have thought that a wife could turn up unexpectedly at her husband's flat if she liked. I want to know where you were last night."

He knew that she had been trying for weeks to find fuel for the small flame of suspicion that had been lit months ago. Now she had it. All right. His obstinacy and antagonism rose to meet hers.

[269]

"Is Virginia ill, Phyllis?"

She asked, trembling:

"Why should you be so anxious? Do you care about your wife and children?"

He shouted at her furiously:

"*Answer me*—is Virginia ill?"

She made a vague, clumsy gesture with her hand and turned away from him suddenly, but he had seen her eyes fill, and her face twist with misery. She sat down at the table and said sullenly:

"It's her appendix again. She came home on leave and simply collapsed. She'd had pains in her side all the week and wouldn't report sick because of some dance she wanted to go to. We brought her down in the ambulance and got her into hospital straight away—I wanted Dr. Hale to do the operation . . ."

She began to cry. He said as gently as he could:

"Don't worry—she'll be all right. When is it to be done?"

"To-morrow morning."

"Why didn't you let me know?"

She looked up at him, her eyes drying in a blaze of anger.

"How can I let you know anything? I rang up before we left, but you weren't here. Where *were* you? That's what I'd like . . ."

He was angry and impatient again.

"Actually you didn't *want* to get me on the 'phone. You *wanted* to come here and find me away. Well—you did."

He turned his back on her abruptly, walked into the bedroom, stood staring at the disordered bed, and as abruptly returned to her.

"Need we quarrel," he asked, trying—and failing—to drive the formal stiffness from his tone, "when Virginia's ill? I don't think I've ever given you any reason to think I don't care about the children."

She replied to that only by asking again, doggedly:

"Where were you last night?"

He exploded: "I won't be spied on, Phyllis!"

"Spied on?" She stared at him with such a genuine expression of outraged indignation that he could not meet her eyes. "Can't a wife want to know where her husband spends his nights without being accused of spying?"

He sat down exhaustedly on the edge of the table, oppressed by a sense of hopelessness which left his mind blank. She was crying again. He felt incapable of thought, but he listened instead with a curious intentness to her weeping, and the other sounds which intruded upon it. A ferry hooting. A window being opened in the flat above. A wireless playing, and children's voices. He glanced down at her sideways—a glance which was pure observation, which collected her like a specimen. His ears and eyes worked involuntarily; his very skin worked, registering the lazy, gathering heat of the summer morning; his own identity forsook him so that he became nothing but a group of senses absorbing impressions.

He heard her say unsteadily:

"Can you tell me that you haven't . . ."

In the slight pause that followed, her words remained in his mind as an unfinished sentence less spoken than written. Other words must go on the end of that sentence—what would they be? His interest was purely professional. His mind tried over the possible alternatives as if he were writing a bit of dialogue. "That you haven't got a mistress?" "That you haven't committed adultery?" "That you haven't been unfaithful to me?"

But what she said was: ". . . that you haven't betrayed our marriage vows?"

He felt a sharp annoyance. He thought: "I wouldn't have got that. And yet it's right. She doesn't only dramatise—she melodramatises. And of course she has to link it up with religion, with the marriage ceremony, because that's the only way she can bear to think of sex at all." She was not his wife, but a "character" he must understand . . .

"Well? Can you?"

He came back to himself with a start. He was abashed to find himself concerned with such things at such a time, and yet it intrigued him to learn that no matter what his own mental stress, his writing consciousness stood apart from it, taking notes. Incorrigibly, it noted now that his mounting rebelliousness against the tiresome, stupid, humiliating business of lying and concealment had reached a climax. He answered shortly:

"No, I can't."

He was wondering now at what point she would become hysterical. He did not look at her, but her voice warned him that it would be soon.

"Who is it?"

"I won't tell you that."

"Are you—in love with her?"

His attention detached itself from her to search himself for the answer, and he recognised a faint impulse to lie struggling against the stronger revulsion against lying; he, too, was not quite inno-cent of rationalising. He would, perhaps, stand better with him-self if he could say "Yes" and believe it. But he could not believe it, so he replied with unemotional flatness.

"No."

It left him with a feeling of emptiness and freedom. He stood up and went across to Nick's desk, and began rummaging in the top drawer for the papers he wanted. He heard her say: "I think you're the most immoral . . . *evil* man I've ever known!" The words made no impression on him. He found his papers and crossed the room to the bedroom door without looking at her. He felt her clutch his arm.

"Gilbert—look at me . . . !"

He looked briefly, and looked away. This was the starting-point of hysteria, and he knew a moment of panic, fearing nothing she could say or do, but only the awakening of his own impotent, intolerable pity for her. She began to sob, rail, plead and accuse, all in the same breath. How dare you do this to your children, don't you love me any more, what have I done, where have I failed, all through our married life you've never given me any sympathy or loyalty, I've put up with twenty years of neglect, you never had any reason to complain of your home, no man could have had a better wife than I've been, I've worked my fingers to the bone for you and the children, and what thanks do I get? I'm pushed aside for some other woman, you should be ashamed of yourself at your age with grown-up daughters, not that it isn't what anyone would expect of a man with your ideas, but I warn you I won't stand it, and I have tried always, and I love you still, I could even forgive, oh, Gilbert . . .

He freed his arm and went into the bedroom, saying nothing, trying to shut his ears to the crescendo of her voice. A rhythmic thudding made him turn sharply, and he saw, feeling sick, that she was beating her head against the frame of the door. He pulled her away and shook her roughly by the shoulders.

"Stop that at once!" She made a queer sound between a sob and a groan; from an angry crimson her face faded with alarming suddenness to a greyish pallor, and she slumped against him. He lowered her into a chair and stood staring at her for a moment while the title of a book he had read began to beat in his mind like a drum. Beware of pity. Beware of pity. Beware . . .

He said in a neutral, matter-of-fact voice:

"Sit still and I'll make you a cup of tea."

She moaned: "I don't want it. I couldn't . . ."

"Don't think I'm not sorry about this, Phyllis. We must . . ."

"But Gilbert . . . *why?* What have I done? Where have I failed . . . ?"

He said desperately:

"Don't talk about it now. You're tired."

"Of course I'm tired!" she cried shrilly. "What with worrying about Virginia, and breaking my heart over you, I haven't had a decent night for weeks. I lay awake all last night listening for you, and hoping you'd come in . . ."

"We'll talk about it when Virginia's better."

She snorted contemptuously: "A lot you care . . . !"

It was no use. He left her and went into the kitchen. She called after him fiercely: "Never expect me to live under the same roof with you again!" With a lighted match half-way to the gas-stove, he paused, almost smiled, wondering if she meant that, or whether she had said it only because it seemed a suitable utterance for a wronged wife. He decided that he would take her at her word, anyhow. The match singed his fingers; he lit the gas, and waited, listening for the sound of her weeping. By the time the kettle boiled she was silent, and when he returned to her with a cup of tea she was lying back in the chair, her face still blotched with tears, breathing heavily and fast asleep.

＊   ＊   ＊   ＊

Less than a week later, coming home late from his office to Marty's house, he found his sister typing on the balcony, and looked at the stack of manuscript beside her with an experienced eye.

"What are you up to? That's no broadcast script."

She said triumphantly:

"It's twenty thousand words, no less, of a brand new novel. About a Sally Dodd."

"What on earth put her into your head?"

"I met her in town one day, and she fitted into an idea I had.

The villain of the piece is the little cross she puts on her ballot paper—she and all the other Sally Dodds both in and above her financial class."

"I see. X marks the spot where the tragedy occurs."

"Exactly. How's Virginia?"

"The doctor says she's doing very well. He told me to-day that they had some anxious moments during the operation—she had the anaesthetist worried, apparently. Anyhow, she was looking cheerful enough when I saw her this afternoon. Sitting up in bed putting stuff on her fingernails."

"An excellent sign."

"I thought so."

She lit a cigarette and passed him the packet.

"And Prue?"

"She's a bit subdued, poor kid. Her young American has vanished somewhere up North." After a pause he added, frowning: "She's been having a bad time with Phyllis. And with me, I suppose."

Marty waited. She was accustomed to his uncommunicativeness. He had turned up with his bag, saying no more than: "Can you put me up for a while?" She had answered: "Yes, of course." By degrees he had told her a few bare facts. Virginia was ill and about to be operated on; Phyllis had come down and was staying at the flat; he thought it better not to be there himself just at present. She had understood their significance because of a lifelong knowledge of him which made her able to interpret his tones and expressions, his long silences. He sat down now on the end of a cane seat, put his newspaper and a couple of books beside him, and said at last:

"It's my fault, of course . . ."

"Don't be absurd!" Marty left the table and sat in a deckchair opposite him. "You might as well get it off your chest, Gilbert. So far as I'm concerned we start with the axiom that Phyllis is an impossible woman."

"I know you never liked her."

"I always loathed her. Presumably you went through a stage of caring for her—you always had far more of the milk of human kindness than I had—but that was all over long ago. It was quite inevitable, and you must know it. Why talk about 'faults'?"

"There are certain—obligations, I suppose."

"Ah!" She looked at him with exasperated compassion. "So Elsa captured you at last?"

He gave her a quick, half-annoyed glance.

"Your perspicacity never fails you, does it?"

She shrugged and flicked the ash from her cigarette over the balcony rail.

"If you had to—break your marriage vows, as Phyllis would describe it—what's the matter? What are you grinning at?"

"Nothing."

"Well, I wish it had been a love-affair instead of just—an affair."

"How do you know it wasn't?"

"I know you very well, and I know Elsa—well enough. What's the position now? Phyllis knows?"

"Yes."

"And she's raising hell?"

"Yes. It's Prue I'm worried about really. She bears the brunt of it."

"What are you going to do?"

He stood up and began walking restlessly about the balcony.

"I suppose I'll ask Phyllis to divorce me."

"You aren't thinking, by any chance, of marrying Elsa?"

"Elsa," he replied dryly, "has other ideas, I think."

Her eyebrows shot up.

"Already?"

He stopped walking, and felt for his pipe and tobacco pouch. Not even his clear knowledge that there had really been nothing of importance between himself and Elsa made him quite proof against the hurt of his last visit to her. He had gone to tell her of Virginia's illness, and his wife's presence at the flat, but even while he was speaking he had noticed her curious air of abstraction. She had said at last: "Perhaps it's just as well, Gilbert. It was fun while it lasted, but I suppose you'll want to go back to being a respectable family man again now .And I . . ." He had looked at her closely then, noticing the absent look in her eyes, as if, already, she had seen another mirage, and set her face towards it. He realised that he was nothing but something she had "tried." She would go on all her life trying new people, new situations, new relationships—rather as she would try on hats, discarding them because what did not suit her was non-existent, and there was always hope that the next might end her search.

She was the perfect egoist; he had been a hopeless failure, he told himself with self-derision—atrociously unbecoming to her ego. So he had asked:

"Yes? What about you?"

"I . . . well, Gil, I think I may be getting married."

He had asked with polite, ridiculous formality:

"Mr. Baxter?"

"Yes, Jimmy."

So that ended it. He wondered if her intelligence would find Mr. Baxter's lack of demand on it (or, even worse, his lack of appreciation of it) any more tolerable than his own importunity. It had been a calm, unemotional, and on her part, at least, a rather pre-occupied parting. The absurd humiliation he felt he had not betrayed to her, but alone he was forced to confront it. He was a middle-aged man who had made a fool of himself; who had allowed himself to become emotionally involved in what was no more than a physical incident. His suspicion—now finally confirmed by Marty's "so Elsa captured you at last"—that the situation had been of her making, filled him with a self-contempt which was not less painful because he knew it to be salutary. He even told himself by way of sour consolation that though he had never really known what love was, he did, now, know more than ever what it was not. He pressed the tobacco carefully into the bowl of his pipe, and answered Marty's question with composure.

"She has—naturally—found someone nearer to her own age."

He glanced at his sister, read her expression of angry contempt, and laughed.

"You're an incorrigible partisan, Marty. Forget my domestic problems for a moment, and bend your attention to a literary one."

"With pleasure," she snapped. "I prefer them."

"It's queer," he observed, "that you should have begun a Sally Dodd novel—because I want to do a Scott Laughlin one."

She stared at him with an almost open-mouthed astonishment that merged into delight as the idea took root."

"Why, of course!" she cried. "Why on earth didn't you ever think of that before? When will you start?"

"Actually," he answered, "I've started already. There was a question of—what shall I call it?—professional ethics holding me up. I wrote all this stuff—bits and pieces—over the last four years, and—incredible as it seems—didn't realise what I was doing.

I mean I didn't identify it with Laughlin. Then I got the idea—from Elsa."

"From Elsa?"

"She told me she wanted to do a book with a character that would be Laughlin's prototype."

"Ridiculous," said Marty, with such calm decision that it was not even an exclamation.

"Yes," he agreed. "I think that too, now."

"Do you mean to tell me," she demanded, "that you were going to abandon the idea yourself because she wanted to do it too?"

"It wasn't my idea—it was hers."

Marty glared at him.

"Gilbert, you're a fool. She could no more write a book about that man than I could write one on relativity."

"All the same, she did think of it first."

"Didn't you say you had been writing it over the last four years?"

"Yes, but I hadn't related it to Scott Laughlin. It's practically all usable. Inevitably, because the things I was thinking about and trying to get down on paper were essentially the same things that he was thinking about thirty years ago."

"If you allow absurd scruples . . ."

"Scruples aren't absurd. But I don't think I have any scruples now. Elsa talked about it enough for me to know that if she does tackle it no one on earth would recognise the same story or the same character in her book and mine. So now I see them as different books. I'm going ahead."

Marty relaxed with a sigh of relief.

"I should hope so. Was that the telephone? No, I'll go. Look, Gil, there's a letter from Nick on the table. It came this morning . . ."

When she had gone he picked it up and began to read. It was a characteristic document, he thought. Nick dealt concisely with the preliminaries on the agenda. He was well. Thanks for the socks. Gilbert's letter had not yet arrived. He wanted some razor-blades. And then to the real business of the meeting. Some comment of Marty's—unwary, Gilbert wondered, or impishly deliberate?—had evidently seemed to him to call for firm rebuke. *"My dear girl, your thinking is all crooked, as usual . . ."* His handwriting, clear and decisive as his voice, expounded the principles by which alone she could be delivered from error. Coming to the end of the first page, Gilbert felt his lips twitch as he realised that he could complete the sentence quite accurately without looking at the next one. The words, by now, flowed from Nick's tongue or pen as glibly as traditional legal phrases from a lawyer drawing up a declaration, or religious ones from a clergyman intoning I Believe in God, the Father Almighty, Maker of Heaven and Earth. . . . The gramophone, Gilbert thought, remembering Marty's metaphor, was still functioning with unimpaired efficiency. The record was still good, uncracked by shot or shell, unwarped by the jungle climate. His amusement faded to soberness with the thought that his brother would go on thus reciting his faith till he died, and die still reciting it. *"The political unawareness of the masses is fostered and used by reactionary elements, and this can be countered only by intensive education in the Marxist teaching of dialectical materialism. This insists on CHANGE, and is therefore, as Marx pointed out, entirely different from your bourgeois philosophies. Engels called dialectics 'the laws of movement,' as you very well know, so to accuse a Marxist thinker of 'rigidity' is nonsense. It simply demonstrates that you have not yet mastered . . ."*

Behind him, Marty said in a worried voice:

"Gilbert, that was Prue . . ."

He looked up from the letter. "Yes?"

"She was speaking from the hospital. It seems that Virginia's suddenly worse again. She says you had better go at once."

He looked bewildered.

"Worse? But they said yesterday she was doing splendidly." He picked up his hat from the chair where he had thrown it. "Is Phyllis there?"

"Yes, she's there."

Marty followed him down the stairs and out the front door to the gate. Through the nervous, defensive years of their childhood, the confused and inhibited years of their adolescence, and the increasingly anxious years of their maturity, she had never felt her affection for him as strong or as painful as now. He, so tolerant of others, had an infinite capacity for self-condemnation; she stared after him anxiously as he walked down the road.

VIII

PRUE met him at the hospital entrance. It was nearly dark, and she was walking up and down the gravel drive, smoking. She said:

"I've been waiting for you." She threw her cigarette away and walked beside him. "They had to operate again—it was urgent."

He peered down at her in consternation.

"What was wrong?"

"They said something about an internal haemorrhage. I don't know. She may be out by now. I've been down here for about a quarter of an hour."

"Where's your mother?"

"She's waiting—up there. Dad . . ."—for the first time her voice lost a tone whose brisk, detached unemotionalism had disturbed him—"Mother's—well, I just couldn't cope with her a little while ago. When she knew they were operating again. She—made quite a scene, she seemed not to know what she was doing. I . . ."

He stopped her with a sharp, repudiating gesture. Alarmed by this new development of his daughter's illness, he refused irritably even to think of his wife. He said impatiently:

"Don't worry, Prue; of course she's upset. It'll be all right . . ."

Preposterous words, inept and feeble! What was this "it" that would be all right? But he found every other thought being crowded out of his mind by painful memories of his intense pride in Virginia's beauty and her lively charm during childhood; of the slow waning of that pride—its metamorphosis into secret disappointment and growing uneasiness; of his gradual detachment from her, then—his defeated acquiescence. He looked at Prue as they went up in the lift. Standing tensely in the corner, looking plain and pale and tired, she infected him suddenly and horribly with her own obvious fear; so that when he stood a few moments later by the bed and moved his shocked gaze slowly to the face of the nurse standing opposite, he was not surprised by what he read there. Virginia was unconscious, and slid from unconsciousness to death almost imperceptibly. With her dying the small, still room lost its unreality. The living, grouped round the bed, eluded, deserted by something upon which all their thought had been tormentedly concentrated, were aware of themselves not as alive, but as left behind. They looked at each other vaguely, with the unquiet mistrust of strangers; stirred uncertainly, almost guiltily conscious of their own breathing, and the beat of their own hearts. And he, looking across the bed, felt that beat check, and then hammer fast and violently under his wife's bitter stare. Still tranced, still for a few more moments immobilised by shock, she crouched and stared at him with such hatred that he flinched from her gaze as from a lethal weapon. It was almost a relief when realisation broke down her paralysed stillness and silence like flood-waters breaking a dam; they were out in the mid-stream of her hysteria, he and Prue, swept along by it, helpless and horrified.

The efficient hospital routine intervened; she was quietened with sharp, authoritative words; a sedative appeared and was swal-lowed. The tumult was, if not over, at least subdued. But she still watched him. In her mind, he knew, condemnation and judgment did not wait even upon accusation; her distracted brain was at work upon an indictment, but he was already convicted. Here was calamity. Calamity was punishment. Who was being punished? Not herself—never herself who lived righteously! Who but Gilbert—renegade, rebel, trouble-maker, atheist, adul-terer, and Heaven knew what else besides? He felt his helpless-ness like a wound; no words which came to him, search as he would, seemed worth speaking, so he was dumb, making—only once—an attempt to comfort her with an arm about her shoulders; and finding that between them even so casual a caress was now an outrage.

By degrees he began to wonder, and to feel a tired, sluggish anger. It moved only as an undercurrent to his awareness that Virginia was dead, and death was final; but when the doctor beckoned him outside he felt it swell and break through the surface of his grief. He heard himself saying sharply:

"You told me the first operation was perfectly successful . . ."

The doctor took off his glasses and polished them on a large white handkerchief. Without them his eyes looked small, naked, and worried.

"It *was* perfectly successful." He replaced the glasses. "Mr. Massey, I take it that . . ." He stopped, seemed to consider, began again: "Your daughter did have an inflamed appendix, and

it was successfully removed. Ordinarily, during an appendicec-
tomy, a routine examination of the pelvis would be made, but you
may remember that I told you we had some trouble with the
anaesthetic. Dr. Holmes was worried—and I, of course, had to
finish the operation as quickly as possible . . ."

He paused. Gilbert said impatiently:

"Yes?"

"This afternoon she suffered a severe internal haemorrhage, and
collapsed. So far as I knew there was nothing to account for this,
but the only possible course was to operate again immediately."
He paused again, cleared his throat, and finished abruptly: "Your
daughter died of a ruptured ectopic pregnancy."

Even in the first moments the inner meaning of those words was
as clear as if had been shouted aloud. They meant parental
failure. With no recollection of having left the doctor, he found
himself standing at the other end of the long corridor, staring down
at the pattern on the rubber floor-covering, and thinking that it
looked like curdled milk. Contemplating himself, too, with a
faintly scandalised curiosity because once more it was clear that
everything which touched him—no matter how it overturned his
life and the lives of those near to him—was automatically referred
by some dictatorial inner sentry to his writing consciousness.
Parental failure had been instantly ranged in his mind beside
marital failure, and failure in his one belated attempt at a love-
affair; yet he found himself confronting these failures less as
failures in living than as the ingredients of failure as a writer. Can
you fail in all your closest personal relationships, and still succeed
in what is essentially an interpretation of such things? There was
a hint of panic in the question. He made a brief struggle against
a line of thought whose surface egotism revolted him, and then
gave up, acknowledging that in moments of crisis truth broke loose
and must be accepted. Even faced with his own imminent death,
he thought, feeling a sharp resentment against such tyranny, he
would be less conscious of it as the death of his body than as the
sealing off of a tap that dripped words, words, words . . .

At the other end of the corridor, as if through a small, brightly-
lit tunnel, he saw Phyllis come out of the room where Virginia
lay, walking blindly, with Prue on one side and a nurse on the
other. He saw them joined by the doctor; he heard their voices—
a quick, low interchange of words, broken by the sudden high

note of Phyllis' question. He heard the doctor answer something, saw a gesture which referred her to himself, saw her turn and stare at him with the length of the corridor between them like a life or a world. He knew another moment of panic when they began to walk towards him—Prue and her mother and the nurse. Yet when they reached him he saw that for the moment he need not find the necessary, impossible words. Phyllis' eyes were dull and her feet dragging. The nurse left them at the lift, and they went down silently. By the time he had found a taxi his wife was comatose; they got her into the back seat and she slumped there against Prue's shoulder during the drive home, murmuring incoherently.

His dread of the question which she must ask and he must answer tempted him to wonder momentarily if he could keep the truth from her altogether. His own instant reaction of furious, blazing denial shocked him. Why should she escape? This is her failure as well as mine! He told himself that she was suspicious and persistent—she would find out the truth anyhow. It was a sound argument. It was the final argument. Nevertheless his anger remained; his knowledge that she must hear his answer was less strong than his implacable determination that she should hear it.

* * * *

That night he slept restlessly for a few hours on the couch in the living-room. In the early morning he was wakened by the sound of Phyllis sobbing wildly in the next room, and the murmur of Prue's voice. He got up and went out into the kitchen. When Prue joined him, looking haggard after a sleepless night, he had coffee made, and handed her a cup silently. She sipped it, saying nothing, avoiding his eyes. In the last week or so she had been exiled from her own life, forced to thrust it into the background; now, in the sudden weakness of fatigue she slid back into it helplessly, too fast to save herself. She was back in the last day of her own life; since then she had been merely struggling through an existence in which she was a stranger. All this had nothing to do with her. On the last morning which had reality a man with a barrow of flowers had taken up his stand outside her shop. The scent of pink boronia was strong in her nostrils as she went to the door from time to time, looked out into the street, felt a quick, warm nervousness when an American uniform appeared, and a dull disappointment when it passed. He was late. Five

minutes late. She said to her assistant: "Joyce, you needn't wait
—I'll shut up. I have some things to do still." She was alone,
and she went into the little cubby-hole behind the shop where the
mirror was, and looked earnestly at her reflection. She powdered
her face, put on some more lipstick, and wiped it off. She re-
arranged her hair, wished she had bought the blue frock instead
of this silly, multi-coloured thing, and craned backwards to see
if the seams of her stockings were straight. She went out into the
shop again and stood still in the middle of the floor, attentive,
wondering at her own disquiet. She looked at her watch. He
was ten minutes late. The desk was tidy, but she tidied it again.
She opened a book, turned its pages without seeing them, shut it,
replaced it carefully on the shelf. She went back to the mirror
and confronted her own questioning face in it. The question was
written so clearly there that in the first unwary second she stared,
nonplussed, and even shook her head faintly, as if saying to those
arched eyebrows and uncertain eyes: "*I* don't know!" She took
out her lipstick and emphasised the curve of her mouth vividly.
She looked at her watch. She thought: He won't come now; he
must have had his leave stopped. I may as well go. There's that
letter I should have written; I could do it now . . .

Someone had come in. She thought, defying the sudden leap
of her heart: I should have shut the door. Some idiot woman
wanting some idiotic romance she doesn't know the name of. . . .
And all the time, staring into the mirror, she was wiping off the
extra lipstick she had put on, and listening. She went out into
the shop with a rush and found him standing there, staring anxiously about and breathing fast as if he had been running.

"Oh!" she said, "you *did* get here! I was just leaving. I
thought . . ."

They both laughed, conscious of betraying their relief to each
other, and happy because they did not mind the betrayal. He
said:

"I only just made it, didn't I? The train was late, and then I
missed out on a stree—on a tram. But I figured you'd wait if you
could . . ." He held out a package. "I brought you some
candy . . ." But the parcel, when her hand touched it, made a
kind of contact between them which he seemed unwilling to re-
linquish. He continued to hold it, looking hard at her. He said
suddenly: "We're being moved on. I won't see you any more . . ."

That was the last bit of life that she had to think about. Standing there—in his arms by some movement which neither of them remembered making. From then on she had quite realised that there was to be nothing more but waiting, but that moment was something she had been hoarding until a quiet time should come when she would be alone, selfishly and jealously alone, to think of it. Now, because she was too tired to keep that taste of living away from this dreary existence any longer, its past beauty clashed unendurably with present ugliness, and her eyes began to ache with tears. She heard her father say:

"I must talk to your mother, Prue. Is she awake?"

"Yes," Prue answered. "She's been awake for hours. I'll tell her."

When she had disappeared into the bedroom he heard through the open door the rising clamour of his wife's voice. He heard her cry out fiercely: "I won't! Don't let that man in here! I can't bear the sight of him! Keep him away from me!" Prue came back, white-faced, sat down at the table, swallowed some more coffee, and told him sharply:

"It's no use, Dad. You'd better leave her alone. Do you want me to tell her anything?"

He said violently:

"*No!* I'm going to tell her myself. Whether she likes it or not." He looked at his daughter and added unwillingly: "I suppose you must know too. Virginia died of a—complication of pregnancy."

He felt a bitter anger which lent him unaccustomed ruthlessness. Phyllis tried to shut the door against him, and for the first time in his life he used his superior physical strength without compunction. When she attacked him with venomous words he found words himself, loud enough and brutal enough to silence her. She stopped her ears, and he wondered as he dragged her hands away and made her listen whether she were already subconsciously afraid of what he had to say. When it was said, and heard, and understood, he found himself back in the living-room, his anger gone, energy drained out of him, wearily aware that when it came to scenes she could outlast him, and that the situation was now beyond his control—and hers.

That heavy interval of silence was thunderous with her mental manœuvrings. He could hear them in his own brain as clearly as if she were talking aloud. The very air which she had so filled with emotional stress accused him of selfishness, egotism, dissoluteness, subversiveness, apostasy. He knew that her mind was working with a concentrated passion, an inevitable instinct of self-preservation, to bring against him any and every charge which could not, by any stretch of the imagination, be brought against herself, and which thus helped her to preserve intact the conception of her own blamelessness. Somehow she must shift from her shoulders that intolerable share of responsibility which he had so mercilessly placed there—and how, save by transferring it to his? How, save by arguing that where one failing, or one vice, or one sin can be proved, others may lavishly be added? How, save by rummaging in the past for every long-hoarded grievance, by patching them together into one lurid, all-enveloping fabric of callous guilt, and clothing him in it?

He realised uneasily that there was a power in the atmosphere engendered by such frenzied minds. His own admission of culpability—up to a point—made it more difficult for him to resist accusations which went beyond it. He, too, in that brief, silent interval was engaged in self-preservation. It required no inconsiderable effort of will to recognise a clear line beyond which remorse became masochistic, and to hold the scales steady between self-reproach and self-respect. When the door opened behind him and he saw her there, still buoyed up by that dreadful energy of supercharged emotion which had died so quickly in himself, he shut his mind deliberately against her denunciations. He would be his own accuser.

Prue appeared in the kitchen doorway, apprehensive. She said pleadingly:

"Oh, *mother* . . . !"

But Phyllis was conscious of nothing but the unbearable load of hatred she had generated and must now expel. Through the first moments of her tirade Gilbert saw nothing but Prue's face, twisted with distress, alternately burning red and sallow with fatigue. For all the miseries and frustrations of Phyllis' life were exhibited now, and even to himself the revelation was shocking. There was nothing of which she did not accuse him, up to deliberate perversion of his daughters' sexual morals; and at that he felt his hands make a murderous movement, checked them, stared at them, and said to Prue:

[285]

"Go away. Leave us alone, Prue . . ."

She walked between them to the door. He followed her, and it was the expression of bitter indignation on her face which calmed him. He said: "Go up to Marty and stay there." He shut the door behind her and went back to Phyllis. He found that he was now quite immune from the contagion of her hysteria. It was merely a matter of waiting for her to exhaust herself. Detached, even bored, he stood between her and the high window, snatched knives out of her hand, took boxes of matches away from her, turned off the taps of the gas-stove, and watched almost with indifference when she dropped at last across the bed in a stupor, moaning and whimpering until she slept.

*   *   *   *

Prue, returning in the evening, found her mother not only shut, but absurdly barricaded in her room. Edging through a crack in the door to find furniture piled against it, she felt her exasperation well up towards an explosion which was checked by her first glimpse of Phyllis' face. It was absent, ruminative, the face of one living in some secret, inner world. She was already well advanced in the task of building a high and dangerous wall between herself and an unendurable reality. She was silent, absorbed, enclosed, implacably hostile. At the funeral, dressed heavily in black, she ignored her husband. Later, listening to Prue's anxious argument and pleading, she said only, with bitter finality:

"I'm finished with him. For ever."

Prue, packing their bags, told her father:

"I'll take her up the mountains. You'd better keep away for a while. It only makes her worse to have you around. She'll get over it . . ."

To please her mother she had found a long-sleeved black dinner-frock and shortened it. Her father thought that it made her seem frail, and slenderer than ever; he looked at her pallor, and the unyouthful lines of strain round her mouth with helpless anger and rebellion.

"I'd rather go with her myself. You stay here with Marty." She shook her head impatiently.

"You know that's silly, Dad. The minute you come near her she begins to—to get excitable again. For goodness' sake keep right away from her for a time, and I'll try to make her see things differently."

"She won't ever do that," he said. He asked unwillingly, when she made no reply: "Has she spoken of divorce to you?"

Prue sighed.

"Oh, yes, she has. She says that's what you want—so she won't."

"I see."

"*Is* it what you want?"

"Yes. Yes, it is—but not for the reason she thinks."

"You don't want to marry—anyone else?"

"No." He added quickly: "You know, Prue, marriage isn't— I mean it *can* be quite different from this . . ."

"Of course it can." She spoke kindly, indulgently, and almost absent-mindedly, as if reassuring a child, but watching the cold, settled unhappiness of her face, he was not reassured.

*   *   *   *

They left him to a strange solitary life whose routine was interrupted towards the end of November by a telegram from Nick. At the military hospital he found his brother looking thin and curiously aged. One hand was swollen with some tropical infection and monstrously bandaged; he had had malaria, and the treatment had left him yellow. Nevertheless, he was still undefeatedly Nick, alert, confident and critical, his impressions of a campaign already neatly arranged and analysed, his interpretation made, his conclusions drawn.

Listening to him, and giving at last, in answer to inevitable questions, his own account of a very different ordeal, Gilbert found himself clambering back to some kind of normality. Nick, having exhausted the analysis of his own experiences, brought to his brother's the same dry, theoretical approach. His brief, matter-of-fact comments anchored personal torments once more to the world-torment of social maladjustment, and under his calm observant eye Gilbert recovered his emotional equilibrium. He began to feel the confusion of his own life, Phyllis' corrosive hatred, and Elsa's futile escapism as small things, having importance only as manifestations of a greater malaise. There was relief in the detachment of Nick's condemnations. In his company Gilbert felt his own mind emerging for the first time in weeks from a fog of emotionalism, his thoughts clarifying, his psychological balance

[287]

and even his sense of humour reasserting themselves. The last, indeed, was a quality which Nick always stimulated—not intentionally, but because, he suspected, there must always be to the creative mind something faintly comic in the spectacle of sternly detached intellect. He did not even begin to accept Nick's viewpoint, but standing back to examine his own life from it, he became a spectator as well as a participant, and the effect was salutary. He found himself hungrily ready to discuss again things which had been imprisoned in the back of his mind—the disquieting implications of Allied negotiations with Darlan—the Beveridge Plan—the North African campaign—the miracle of Stalingrad's resistance, now developing into a terrific offensive like a crescendo of triumphant music.

Yet there were times still when a letter from Prue made him slide again into abstracted brooding. He sat by his open window one evening early in December, his thoughts swinging helplessly between the printed columns of his newspaper and her small, round handwriting.

"Mother has seemed a bit better the last few days," she wrote, *"and this afternoon she came out in the garden and pottered about with me for an hour or so. Pete had an invitation to stay with the Johnsons for a fortnight, and I persuaded her to let him go, because he gets quite upset when she has crying fits, or suddenly starts praying out loud, which she still does at all sorts of odd moments. I found her in your study one day reading some of your MS. I didn't say anything, but I've packed it up and am sending it down to you with this, because the way she looked at it made me think she might take it into her head to burn it, as she did all your other books that were in the house. I'm glad my copies are safe at the flat. It's just the shock about Virginia, of course, and I do think she's getting better. No, I think it would only make her worse again if you came up. And I don't think it would be any use Aunt Marty coming either—Mother gets nearly as angry about her as about you . . ."*

He threw the letter down and looked at the large, brown-paper parcel of manuscript lying on the table. Soon he would have to tackle it again. He contemplated it with distaste and yet with craving, wondering if drunkards felt the same way about their tipple. Wondering, also, whether this latest addition to his life's experience were something which might bring his conception of Scott Laughlin into clearer light and sharper perspective when he began to write again. For had not he, too, known at one time the stress of domestic catastrophe, and had he not been forced to relate it to other less personal preoccupations? And had he not also had a well-loved daughter?

But distaste was still stronger than craving. The mere thought of undertaking once more the long labour of expression revolted him. He recoiled from the necessity for thinking in words, knowing how the very process of finding words revealed flaws, fallacies and inaccuracies; how his mind had to struggle to keep the thought whole and find the right words at the same time; how sometimes, belabouring his brain for the word, the thought eluded him. Confronted by the threat of this sustained effort, this drawn-out discipline, he was seized by an immense, despairing boredom and disgust with the whole human race. Why write about it? Generation after generation, he thought angrily, century after century, we reproduce endlessly the same old drama and the same old leading actors. It's as if the plot had been worked out at the beginning of time, and performed with minor variations ever since; as if the same old programme that announced the cast of characters B.C., still serves, two thousand years later. Human History, a comedy-drama in five hundred million acts! Characters in the order of their appearance—the Inert Onlooker, the Reactionary, the Revolutionary Idealist. He saw it—this tiresome performance—with jaded, jaundiced eyes. He saw the Inert Onlooker being hauled and pushed and bustled this way and that by the other two principal characters, but he told himself sourly that there had never been, nor would there be now, any climax, any denouement. He knew that the curtain would fall upon the Onlooker, still gaping in glassy-eyed equanimity, while the others, behind his back and far, far beyond his consciousness, would remain locked in an endless, unresolved struggle. It might be a struggle which rocked the stage beneath his feet; the clamour of their argument might drown thunder; but while he had some tinkling toy of an idea to play with, some trivial topical issue to engage his wayward attention, he would neither heed the volcanic tremors, nor hear the sound and fury of his disintegrating world . . .

He never failed to feel a surprised relief when the moods which

[289]

induced such depression and despair were promptly routed by a faith which, though it might be caught napping occasionally, always awakened belligerently to their challenge. He reached out resignedly for the parcel, untied it, and with the manuscript on his knee, began to read.

*   *   *   *

The insistent double-ring of the telephone roused him, an hour later, from a page like a battlefield. Scribbled words had filled the gaps in ranks where other words had fallen; whole sentences had been mown down by a ruthless pencil-stroke; a routed paragraph stood imprisoned behind an entanglement of criss-cross lines. Tired but victorious, he threw it down and went to answer the summons—and because Prue had been so much in his thoughts, her voice, ghostly with distance, seemed something which his own forebodings had conjured up.

"Is that you, Dad? Oh, thank goodness—I was afraid you might be out . . ."

"Is anything wrong?"

There was a brief, hesitating pause.

"Well, it might be. . . . I thought I'd better let you know. Mother went out very early this morning, and she isn't back yet."

"Went out? Where?"

"I don't know. She was in bed about two o'clock, because I . . . could hear her. And when I went in with her tea about seven she was gone. I've been out looking for her all day. And coming home again to see if she was back . . ."

He heard a faint break in her voice and said quickly:

"I'll come up. Yes—to-night. Straight away."

"There isn't a train till after ten, Dad."

"Then I'll get the car out and drive up. Prue . . . ?"

"Yes?"

"Have you told anyone?"

"Not—not yet. I kept thinking she'd come in. But when it got dark and she still wasn't home I began to get worried. Shall I call the police and ask them to look for her?"

"Yes. Yes, you'd better do that, Prue. Tell them I'm on my way up. And you stay at home in case she comes in."

"All right, Dad. Good-bye."

He replaced the receiver and stood for a moment staring blankly across the room. He felt himself being haled back into the over-charged atmosphere of Phyllis' emotional un-control. He was not Nick, and to him his wife was still a person; he could not reduce her to an abstract problem, or the subject for a thesis—Sex Ignorance and Female Parasitism as Factors in Maintaining the Capitalistic Status Quo. She was Phyllis, bewildered by life into a frenzy, her attempted method of escape no more rational than Elsa's, no more rational than that of a panic-stricken animal butting its head blindly against a wall. He lifted the receiver again and called Marty. She listened in a silence which, enduring for a moment after he had finished speaking, made him see her standing there in her hall frowning with an expression of nauseated consternation. He said:

"I'm going to send Prue down to you as soon as possible."

"All right, Gil."

"Tell Nick, will you? He expected me out at the hospital to-morrow."

"I'll tell him."

He rang off, and went out to get the car.

IX

PRUE woke uneasily from an uneasy sleep. She had been dreaming, but her dreams vanished as she opened her eyes, leaving nothing behind but an impression of frightening chaos and effort. She sat up, listening. The house was absolutely silent. It was nearly dark; she must have slept for several hours. She could see the foot of Virginia's empty bed, and she thought miserably how strange it was that her wish for a room of her own should have been granted at last in so tragic a way.

It had always been Mother, of course, who discouraged the idea. Virginia hadn't cared, so long as she could have three-quarters of the wardrobe space, and all the mirror whenever she wanted it; and this thought came to her sister now without even a shadow of bitterness, appearing merely as the understandable foible of a beautiful young woman—a foible not serious enough to be paid for with death. Yet that, really, was how it had been paid for . . .

It had been one of Mother's pretty little articles of faith that her daughters could not bear to be separated, and she had found her own pleasure in coming when they were both in bed to "tuck them up." The memory scalded Prue's eyes with sudden tears— tears not for the sentiments which this ritual was supposed to honour, but for their falsity, which made them pitiable. For though she had felt an affection for Virginia, she had never really known her; even as children they had had different friends, and different interests. It seemed to Prue, now, almost sinister that they had never quarrelled. They had never been deeply enough concerned with each other's lives to argue over anything but trifles; never intimate enough for anything but minor disagreements. Ever since the funeral Prue had been reproaching herself for having known Virginia so little; for assuming that her brilliant self-confidence meant invulnerability; for having been so absorbed, lately, in her own affairs that her sister's evident unhappiness had seemed only more of her wilful tantrums. She found that she could not now forget that curious outburst: "Gosh, how I loathe men!" But, accusing herself, Prue defended herself too. She remembered that week-end as a time when it had been necessary to believe. Necessary, she thought vaguely, to be—*ready*. She had to resist the cynicism of Virginia's disillusionment. I couldn't, she argued desperately, I didn't *dare* to take her seriously—just then! And yet — just then — Virginia must have been floundering in the confusions of excitement and revulsion, invitation and withholding, desire and recoil, which had trapped her at last. Blaming herself, Prue could not avoid, any more than her father could, the conviction that her mother was to blame too. On Phyllis' inhibited tongue enlightenment had merely become deeper mystification; her embarrassed sidestepping, her panicky avoidances, had long ago made a chasm between her daughters and herself. Such thoughts made ugly and painful the memory of those tender tuckings-up.

Prue switched on the bedside lamp and looked at her watch. Twenty-five to eight. She swung her feet to the floor and sat still, with her elbows on her knees and her head between her hands, thinking of Phyllis.

Poor Mother, driven and defeated by herself! Always prodding herself on from one foredoomed effort to another. Poor Mother, whose life was one long succession of blunders and ineptitudes. Who couldn't even name her daughters without being proved grotesquely wrong! Prudence, who chose to follow in the dangerous footsteps of her imprudent father—and Virginia . . . !

Prue's hands clasped her temples tighter. Where were they now—her father and her mother? How long had they been gone? She seemed to have lost track of time lately. There had been nothing but waiting. Waiting at the hospital during Virginia's two operations; waiting through an endless day for her mother to return; waiting for her father to arrive from town; and now this further waiting, not yet ended. And all of it enclosed in the one vast waiting which had begun with John's departure . . .

She looked at her watch again, and began a laborious calculation. Mother disappeared on Tuesday morning—and this was Wednesday night. Only Wednesday? Dad had arrived at about eleven last night, and by midnight he was gone again with a police sergeant and three volunteer searchers. She had waited up till it was nearly daylight, and then, still dressed, she had lain on her bed for a few hours, wide awake, listening, hoping against hope for the sounds of their return. But she knew the mountains. She had tramped them with her father and Nick, and in groups of young hikers; she set the minuteness of one human being against their vastness of tangled valleys and tortuous ridges, and her hope became fear. All day she had waited, walked restlessly to the gate to watch, returned to the house again, tried to read, tried to sew, tried to write to John, and found herself at the gate once more, staring anxiously down the road. Hours had expanded in that endless waiting; only by fixing her eyes and her mind sternly on her watch, to whose busy ticking an hour was sixty minutes—neither more nor less—could she get time disentangled again. A milkman, rattling along in his cart yesterday, just after sunrise, had met a woman walking towards the Falls. Thirty-six—thirty-seven—nearly thirty-nine hours ago. . . . "Thought she looked a bit queer," he had told the sergeant. "Seemed to be talkin' to 'erself. Stopped and asked her was she all right. Said she was just out for a walk. Didn't bother no more—'ad me round to finish . . ."

That was some sort of a clue. At least they needn't search on the north side. Talking to herself. Of course. Prue's ears were still full of the sound of that talking—a fretful, complaining, accusing, self-justifying monologue addressed to God. Mother had been talking to herself—or God—for weeks. Prue clutched her head again, and pressed the palms of her hands hard against her burning eyes. Should they have—done something about it before it came to this? What *could* they have done? Was mother really . . . was her mind . . . ? Of course not. Absurd. Surely, Prue insisted to herself, there had been enough to account for what she had been fiercely telling herself was only a temporary psychological breakdown.

Quite, quite enough. If you accepted her as she was—and what else could you do?—you had to admit that she had been under an intolerable strain for years. Father, iconoclastic, overthrowing her cherished idols one by one, disturbing her peace of mind, making the firm ground of her social respectability tremble beneath her feet. . . . Accepting her as she was, it was inevitable, too, that she should attempt repeatedly to "forgive" him—and Mother being forgiving was enough to drive anyone into veritable orgies of wickedness . . .

That Elsa Kay affair . . .

There still warred in Prue's heart a nagging disappointment in her father because he had been "silly" about Elsa, and a defensive, almost maternal condoning of his silliness because she understood better, now, something of the barrenness of his married life. So Elsa had been inevitable, too.

And, finally, Virginia. Coming on the heels of the revelation of Dad's unfaithfulness, what *could* Mother—plunging madly about in her mind for her own alibi—think of her daughter's transgression save that it was an inheritance of dissoluteness from her husband? And a fruit of his shameless example? As a result of his freethinking, his lack of paternal exhortation, his stubborn refusal to exert paternal discipline? Feeling her last remnant of respectability tottering, what could she do but manufacture an interpretation which absolved her by pinning the whole obloquy on him? Here, she could feel, was the ultimate and irrevocable wrong that he had done to her and their marriage.

Prue lifted her head from her hands, frowning painfully. If Mother had really convinced herself by this interpretation, why was she not recovering, and climbing back to the only kind of normality she had ever known? Surely she must believe it? She had an impetuousness of belief which matched her impetuousness of action. She had only to make a plan to act on it, and she had only to frame a thought to believe in it; that her plans all turned out badly, and her beliefs all let her down, seemed to her only the undeserved buffettings of a malevolent fortune. Heaven knows, Prue thought despairingly, we wouldn't have grudged her her conviction of rightness! Then why this disappearance? Was there some inner judge, some arbiter of awful and implacable honesty, whom she could never quite convince? Was that the "God" she was talking to—haranguing—arguing with . . . ?

Prue jumped up and began to walk about the room. Suddenly she could think of nothing but her mother's clumsy body, her vague expression, her anxious, harassed activity, her busy, blundering hands, her faded-blue, spectacled eyes. She saw the thin, chill light of the young moon filtering through treetops, breaking up the ground into confusing patterns of black and silver; and she imagined that familiar figure clambering, slipping, stumbling, but obstinately refusing to be still because her whole philosophy was that you must *never* be still, never wait, never admit that any situation can arise which may not be mastered by physical bustling. And then, when the moonlight faded, crouching alone somewhere in that unendurable darkness, silence and solemnity until dawn came, and with dawn a new urge to bustle—a panic-stricken hurrying that fell at last into aimless, dazed trudging while the bush met her with deceitfully yielding walls of scrub, and fern, and trees, and her calls were answered only by echoes . . .

Prue flung herself face downward on the bed again. For the first time in these long, unreal weeks, she wept frantically until she fell asleep, exhausted.

*   *   *   *

Still sleeping heavily, she did not hear the front door open some two hours later. Gilbert switched on the light and stood in the hall, squirming his shoulders out of his pack, lowering it to the floor, pursuing through his mind an elusive problem: whether to ring Marty now, or wait till the morning? He was so tired that he could not deal with more than one simple thought at a time, and uppermost in his mind was Prue's closed door, and the silence from her room. He called her softly, and got no answer. He pushed the door open and saw her in the pool of light from her reading-lamp, lying fully dressed and sound asleep on her bed. Turning away, he tried to think what it was that he had been considering. Something he had thought of doing. . . . It was gone. Whatever it was, it must wait.

He went into his bedroom and stood looking stupidly at the two beds. The light from the hall fell dimly across them, and his heart gave a sudden shocked leap because for one second he thought that he saw Phyllis lying on hers. But it was only her old coat that Prue had been wearing, and had thrown down there. He took his hand from the frame of the door, and felt himself stumble on the first step he made. He found the rail of his own bed, gripped it, and sat down, staring at his long, mud-stained boots. He was thinking that he should get them off before he slept, but he could not relate his exhaustion to the irritable disinclination for stooping which he felt; he just sat looking at them, conscious of another problem.

His body solved it for him; he stretched out on the bed and slept immediately. The first hint of dawn was making a pale square of the window-blind when he woke with a start, listening. The room was still feebly illuminated by the light from the hall, the house still quiet. He was so stiff that he could hardly move, but the mental vagueness of fatigue was gone. He sat up slowly and bent to unlace his boots.

He began to wonder why it had taken him so long to realise where Phyllis would be found. Then he was annoyed by his wonder, for only now, after his respite of sleep, the certainty of his sudden conviction began to seem strange. He hovered uncomfortably between seeing his revelation as mysterious, and seeing it as natural. Was it possible that mental tension and physical tiredness could actually release some sort of inspired, irrational perception which was normally inhibited by rational thinking? He did not like the idea; it made him uneasy. Opposing it, he told himself that he had simply been deceived by the sight, from the cliff-tops, of a far-away fire in the valley. Naturally it had been necessary to investigate that first; she *might* have had matches with her, though it seemed unlikely. . . . So they had made their laborious way round to where a descent was possible; in the shadow of a towering cliff the darkness was inky, but they had scrambled down, sliding and stumbling, by the light of their torches, and made their way along the talus—only to find a camping party of four men asleep round the dying embers of their fire.

By that time the dawn was breaking. The campers, roused from their sleeping bags, had heard their tale, made a billy of tea, and prepared to join in the search. That brief halt remained in Gilbert's memory with a curious vividness. The fire had been a fixed point in his mind, and a fixed point in the dark immensity of the night. When it failed he felt his purpose begin to swing and waver. What now? Where now?

Drinking his mug of scalding tea, he had looked about him. This was the hour of all hours when the bush could be terrifying. Its silence and loneliness could be friendly by daylight to one who accepted silence, and welcomed occasional solitude, and by night, about a roaring fire, its darkness was only the encircling wall of a brightly-lit room. But in this suspended hour between night and day, when the grey light made ghosts of the trees, and all colour was washed out to greyness, and grey ashes stirred like feathers over a few live embers, and the silence itself was grey and heavy, like lead, it was no longer a place at all. It was the essence of quiet, and the ultimate experience of loneliness. You could not draw it into yourself, make it your own; instead it sucked you out of your body, absorbed your thought, and struck your sense of time and being away from you. In this stillness and this waiting quiet he had seemed to feel madness and sanity merging in him so that his thoughts functioned with a terrible detachment. Where was Phyllis? There was no longer any fixed point where one could look for her. Anywhere. Anywhere at all in these thousands of acres of bush. Miles and miles of it surrounded them. She might be above them on the high tableland whose perpendicular cliffs rose out of the valley like fabulous castle-walls; or below them in some hidden gorge where a creek trickled secretly between its rocks and ferns. She might be wandering and calling. She might be lying in pain or delirium, injured by a fall. She might be dead. Had it been sane or insane, the actual relief with which he had contemplated that possibility? Contemplating it, recognising the relief, he had felt no shock and no recoil. The sky should have split and the landscape shivered under the impact of that monstrous relief; but it had remained undisturbed. This vast, impersonal, impassive quiet could assimilate any frenzy of human emotion, and make it negligible. He had been able to think the truth with perfect calm. Was that to be mad—or sane?

But the memory of it shook him now with a sudden rigor. Not even the other shocking moment later in the day seemed so shocking as that period of cool, mad acceptance. He could think of the later moment without feeling goose-flesh prickle his skin. Daylight had banished, by then, whatever mood it was that had captured him before; he was thinking again, functioning by himself, conscious of familiar standards. They had made plans, brisk and business-like. They had split up into two parties, and separated. They had detached themselves from the unreality of that dawn hour, and offered the bush a challenge. And, discarding its mysteries, admitting sunshine to replace its dim, other-worldly light, it had taken up the challenge with a kind of remote, careless indifference. I will give you every advantage. Use any means you like. Find her if you can.

They had tramped all the morning, they had shouted and coo-eed. The undergrowth impeded and wearied them, the day grew fiercely hot, the cliffs tossed back at them the echoes of their voices. But at midday, stopping to drink from a little creek, the sergeant had uttered the word "mist." "She might have taken any direction," he said gloomily, "the mist was that thick yesterday morning . . ."

It had meant nothing to Gilbert at first. The word dropped like a stone into the deep water of his memory, sinking deeper than his consciousness, disturbing some black depth of association, setting up vibrations of conviction that rose slowly like bubbles to the surface of his mind. They had been walking again for nearly an hour before he became aware of them. He went on tramping mechanically, all his startled attention concentrated on his mind, threshing about for a memory, for words, for something about mist . . .

Phyllis, storming and sobbing on her bed. . . . *"You're given guidance . . ."* Himself, lacing up his shoes, snatching his coat. . . . *"If I failed to save you I must go on a long journey. . . . I saw myself walking into a sort of mist . . ."*

That was it—and the second bad moment was upon him. Remembering it now as he straightened up slowly, because stiffness made stooping painful, he pulled his boot off, dropped it on the floor, and sat with his hands hanging limply between his knees, looking back with vague astonishment at himself performing a bizarre mental feat. He had done a curious thing. A curious, interesting thing. He had become Phyllis. But it was not, after all, an entirely new experience. There had been, he remembered, writing hours from which he had emerged with a feeling that there were adjustments to be made in himself before he could rise from his desk completely free. There was something to be cast loose—some power-current between himself and a character of whom he had been writing—to be disconnected. Some wraith which he had created—or perhaps merely recognised—must hear the throwing down of his pen as a signal, and sink back into its paper tomb like the ghost of Hamlet's father returning to its grave at cockcrow. That had often happened.

Yet he was still disturbed. He told himself that he had merely applied a writing-technique to life—and it had worked. Why shouldn't it? Probably it was really a primitive living-technique, grown rusty with disuse, and now only occasionally applied, clumsily and ineptly, by groping artists. He had found Phyllis by being Phyllis; what could be simpler or more rational? Plodding along in the heat of the day, wrestling with those half-remembered words, he had known that they were a clue, and that he could use them to find Phyllis. It was the sudden temptation he felt to repudiate them which gave him the shock he had failed to feel earlier in the day. It was reassuring to be able to feel horrified with himself for the impulse to turn his back on this clue. It was a relief to shout down his cold, idiotically sane reason which told him contemptuously that all this was just mystical nonsense. Forget it, take no notice of it, it means nothing . . .

He had refused furiously to forget it. He had fastened his mind on to it with an always intenser concentration. Somewhere in him was Phyllis—the only person who knew where Phyllis had gone. He began to hunt for her in himself as he hunted for people in his books; his mind began to worm its way into her mind as it wormed its way into the minds of his fictional characters. Inevitably, imperceptibly, the current was established, the conception merged into experience . . .

Now, outside that experience again, he felt impelled to explain it all to himself because, though he did not mistrust and suppress emotion as Nick did, he liked to ride it on a tight rein of intellectual comprehension. He understood that, looking out from Phyllis' mind, he had seen a track, a trodden track just wide enough for one, always visible far ahead, winding among stunted, wind-blown scrub, skirting cliffs and rocky outcrops, climbing hills, swerving round contours, vanishing, reappearing—a stubborn, toilsome, persistent track.

Stubborn, toilsome, persistent Phyllis. People like Phyllis, nourished on symbolism, turn to the symbolic action and the symbolic place like a compass to the North. People like Phyllis, treading the beaten paths of faith and custom, can never leave a track unfollowed. So the mist into which she stepped must have become the mist of her crazed vision; the track must have become the stony path of her life, and she a small, shapeless figure, obstinate and driven, toiling along it up and down the hills, up and down the years, threading her way between undergrowth and bewilderments, tired with ascents and failures, sticking to the track with that dogged, stupid courage of hers, sustained by the conviction of an ultimate goal, a haven . . .

He bent down again and began to struggle with the other boot. He felt a peevish annoyance because he could not stop trying to explain to himself something which still seemed too simple to require an explanation. He had *been* there. He had shared her physical effort, and felt it with her as sublimation; he had seen the crest of the next hill through her bemused eyes as some spiritual summit; he had known her misery and solitude and mortification of the flesh as ransom for the sins of a loved and hated stranger whom he now recognised as himself.

So that when his mind had reached with her the point where the track faded out, he was able to feel the shocked baulking of her thought, the hesitation of her tired, trudging feet, the vacant, bewildered wandering of her gaze. For she was up against an old frustration now; her symbol had let her down, it had beguiled her on and then vanished, leaving her at a loss, floundering for a new direction.

She was no pioneer, poor Phyllis. Many and many a time, adventuring too deep into the mysteries of her various esoteric faiths, and finding himself unwilling or unable to proceed farther, she had backed out, disengaged herself, turned in her hunger for peace to examine enviously his own deep-rooted calm. He had seen it happen over and over again, sometimes with amusement, sometimes with irritation, sometimes with compassion. She could not understand or even imagine what held him steady in the treacherous currents which betrayed her own footholds—but steady he was, and she clutched at him. Hate him, despise him, resent and oppose him as she might, she had depended on him— and, in her own way, loved him too. Her mind had its lifelong techniques, and even in this twilight of confusion where, mentally and physically lost, she stood helpless, it must have performed its inevitable adjustments with the precision of habit. Trackless, it would turn to Gilbert. That was certain. Memories of times when there had no longer been a track for her faith would link themselves to this moment when there was no longer a track for her feet; and she would see him, and herself with him, walking all through one long morning till they came to this spot. From here, as from other dead-ends and blind-alleys where she had halted, he had gone forward confidently. She had a track again; she had something to follow, if it were only a memory, and it would lead her on along a high ridge, and down a long hill to a creek where they had picnicked once. Because the image of him inhabited that place, she would go to it.

You only had to become a little mad, he thought, to recognise the tortuous, involved logic of insanity. For she must, undoubtedly, have been insane for a little while, though she had seemed calm enough and—allowing for weakness and exposure—rational enough when they found her. Arriving at the creek, searching in vain among the long, spiky grass and the dark foliage of the callistemons, he had felt the wrench of a sleep-walker, rudely awakened. He saw his companions looking at him silently, with commiseration, and had to bite back an angry protest: "But she *is* here!" His own conviction began to waver. His everyday common-sense reasserted itself, meeting with contempt the persistent voice which said, diminuendo: "I know she's here—I came *with* her. . . ." He turned his back on that tactful, sympathetic silence, and went on beating about in the underbrush, and calling. The others, exchanging glances and shrugs, began to search again too, desultorily, but it was the sergeant, nearest to the lip of the falls where the thin ribbon of water leapt over into the valley fifteen hundred feet below, who first heard her answer. He shouted excitedly:

"She's here! Mr. Massey! I heard her voice—somewhere. . . . Listen . . . !"

Gilbert had realised then that his freakish temporary tenancy of her mind had been inadequate after all. He knew at once, hurrying down the creek to join the others, what had happened; and the most appalling aspect of her attempt at suicide seemed to him to be that it had failed. She had bungled it. There had been nothing in that thought from which he needed to shrink now, no thought of himself at all. It had been pure pity and despair because everything she did, from making jam to jumping over cliffs, "went wrong." He remembered the little ledge not ten feet from the top, invisible to her in the mist; when he joined his companions, already staring dumbfoundedly over the cliff edge, he could see that she was—physically at least—not even injured.

It had been easy enough with the rope which the sergeant was hastily uncoiling to get her up. Already the other members of the search party were half-way up the hill to send an agreed signal to the ambulance which awaited it at the end of the road. Phyllis had smiled wanly at him when he climbed down to her; standing on his bent shoulders with the rope about her waist, she had been pushed and pulled up the few feet of perpendicular wall. She was weak, her hands and knees were grazed, and she had wrenched one ankle badly when she fell. The rocks above the ledge were wet with soakage and blown spray from the falls, so she had scooped a hollow to drink from, and she said, when they offered her food, that she was not hungry. She said to her husband with faint triumph:

"You see . . . ? I wasn't *meant* to die. . . . When I prayed down there I knew someone would come, because I wasn't *meant* to . . ."

He answered:

"Yes. Lie down now. Don't try to talk . . ."

She lay in the late afternoon sunlight with a rolled-up coat under her head, looking peacefully and contentedly exhausted. She slept for a couple of hours. The sergeant, withdrawing himself tactfully to the other side of the creek, sprawled face downward on the grass and dozed. Gilbert sat beside his wife, and watched the setting sun send long fingers of shadow across the valley, smearing it with twilight.

He wondered how long the effects of this super-gesture she had made would last. For the moment, he knew by that expression of peace, she was purged of her torments, haloed, safely ensconced in her little shrine. You couldn't do more by way of martyrdom than attempt to surrender your life. She lived like a child, he thought, from one moment to the next. At this moment she was in the centre of the stage, and satisfied. She was the focus of attention, care, compassion, even awe. How would she support the return to a world in which this limelight would remain on her for a few days at most? What would happen when she realised that she had solved nothing? What new avenue of escape would she try when she found herself confronting the same life which she had found intolerable before?

It was dark when four men arrived with the stretcher, and it had taken over three hours to get her back to the ambulance. Limp and pale in the hospital bed, she had smiled at him with the old forgiveness when he bent over her. She had even murmured: "Dear Gilbert . . ."

He dragged his other boot off and dropped it on the floor. He didn't know by what mental processes he had been transformed from "that man" to "dear Gilbert," but he was wearily content to remain ignorant. He had handed her back her life, but he couldn't live it for her. He lowered himself stiffly on the bed again; his arms ached from carrying the stretcher, and his body cried out for rest.

X

A FAINT evening breeze made the twinkling leaves of a gum-tree at the foot of Marty's garden rustle, and set its tracery of shadow tossing on the grass. The sun was just setting, and the heat of the day fading to a drowsy warmth. Nick, discharged from hospital, and summarily borne off by Marty to finish his leave and his convalescence at her home, was reading in a deck-chair on the verandah, and Richard, talking to Gilbert, was hosing lettuces where once flowers had grown. The smell of wet earth came strongly to Nick's nostrils; he put his book down and yawned.

He was still near enough to a life filled with physical effort, endurance and danger to feel this interval of peace as miraculous— still sufficiently obsessed by images of sweating, straining, dirty men struggling with mud and jungle, to look at a quiet garden scene with something of incredulity, as he might have looked at a mirage. He found himself understanding the reaction of many of his comrades-in-arms who, fresh from the battlefront, were amazed and angered to find life at home going on "as usual." Nevertheless, his conscientiously disciplined brain endorsed reactions only after they had been submitted to Marxian analysis, and this one, he recognised at once, was superficial. His creed taught him that life, like peace, was indivisible; that a woman knitting, or a man sunbaking on a beach were involved in the s?- e ultimate issues as a soldier on active duty; that the physical a\ des of peaceful relaxation were not necessarily symbols of co. 'acent and care-free minds. It was less the conclusion that he valued than the means by which he arrived at it. When Richard or Marty, or even Aunt Bee, displayed a flash of the same perspicacity, he felt the faint annoyance of a brilliant bridge-player whose untutored opponent flukes a grand slam. He could suffer this illusion of peace only after he had referred it to an intelligence which told him, in sound, dialectical terms, that war or no war, the sun would shine, the shadows fall, the doves coo, and the evening spread its benison; that, idyllic as Nature insisted upon remaining, life was not going on "as usual" at all.

Richard turned off the hose and came towards him along the path with Gilbert. His words, as he lowered himself stiffly into a chair opposite and felt for his pipe and tobacco pouch, were, with curious appropriateness: "On an evening like this the war seems very far away!"

Nick felt the indulgent, friendly impatience which his brother-in-law's utterances usually aroused in him. There was no sense in *saying* such things. You felt them, you analysed them, you dealt with their fallacies, and then they were, very properly, dead. Gilbert, seating himself on the verandah step, asked:

"Is that the morning paper beside you, Nick?"

Nick passed it over. Aunt Bee, appearing from the doorway of the drawing-room with a basket of darning in her hand, sat down in a chair beside him and, innocently apt, sighed:

"Such a lovely evening! You can hardly imagine there's a war going on!"

Nick moved restlessly; his own unwary reaction sounded bad enough on the lips of an indecisive liberal, but even worse from a frankly ignorant old woman. He said firmly:

"It's going on all right!"

Gilbert threw the paper down on the step beside him. Half his mind was thinking that the light was not good enough to read— or perhaps his glasses needed changing; the other half was reflecting that it was precisely in such halcyon moments. when every prospect pleased the eye, that war seemed to him most omnipresent, and man most vile.

Nick's return had stirred in him anew the rebellion he had felt on that strange night with Elsa, when the war outside her very windows had seemed not blessedly, but enragingly far away. He had his own memories of war, and lately he had been forced to admit that they were almost nostalgic. No hesitations in that life, no uncertainties, no will. A life of obedience and action; a life of unbelievable simplicity. Was this the paradox of stillness at the heart of the whirlwind—peace only in the centre of the war? He had found himself looking at his brother with actual envy, coveting his uniform and his rifle, forcing himself only with an effort not to rationalise his emotion by seeing it as martial ardour and selfless patriotism; forcing himself to recognise it as an impulse to escape. To live in a scene set for battle was, he knew from experience, to feel war press upon you from without as well as from within. They cancelled each other out, those pressures; between them you could live and breathe in a sort of careless, fatalistic calm.   But to inhabit an environment which cheated your eyes every moment with the illusion of peace was to carry the whole war inside you, to haunt the empty shell of civilisation like a ghost, to feel the one-way pressure of the world's madness swelling inside your head till your skull cracked. . . .

Richard was saying:

"Well, Nick, I may have—as you're always telling me—a middle-class mind.   But when you use that term as if it were a synonym for blindness, I protest."

Gilbert got up and strolled away again down the path.   Aunt Bee, darning placidly, glanced at him from time to time with anxious, auntly fondness, listening with only half an ear to the lively argument which was developing between Nick and Richard. She felt happy that dear Nick should be so lavishly provided with the potent medicine of controversial discussion, and she knew that Richard was deliberatly continuing a treatment which Marty normally supplied without conscious intention.   For to them—to Nick and Marty—a conversation was a battle, or it was nothing; they sniffed it from afar, and in the space of two sentences were locked in a stimulating encounter.   But Richard, not chronically a controversialist, was now, in the sheer goodness of his heart, measuring out provocation in methodical spoonfuls, and smiling gently to himself as Nick gulped them down.

"You're beginning," he was saying wickedly, "to be dated already, you know.   And why?   Not because you embalmed Lenin in a tomb, but because you embalmed his ideas in your heads.   And," he added, trailing his coat assiduously, "if you hadn't embalmed Lenin he'd be turning in his grave by now."

"You talk," objected Nick, "as if the Party wouldn't accept new ideas.   That's not true.   No contribution is turned away.   No criticism is resented."

"I don't doubt that that's your policy.   All the same, I maintain that there are too many of you who accept the Word of Marx as uncritically as the most ignorant peasant ever accepted the Word —not of God, but of the village priest.   For some of them this Marxian theory is—thanks to a deplorable standard of education— the only intellectual possession they've ever had.   And they guard it from any breath of criticism as a dog guards a bone . . ."

"Rubbish!   They guard it from deliberate reactionary slander and misinterpretation—never from honest criticism."

[307]

" 'Never' is too big a claim," Richard insisted. "Watchdogs, my dear Nick—loyal and fierce, I grant you—but just watchdogs."

Nick thumped the arm of his chair.

"You have an absolutely cock-eyed view! Criticise all you like, but for God's sake have some alternative to offer! What *do* you offer? A sort of mystical *laissez-faire!* Leave it all to the individual! Holy smoke, you know very well . . ."

Aunt Bee looked up from the darning of his khaki sock to beam upon him. Satisfied that he was being suitably entertained, she peered out again into the gathering dusk at Gilbert. She was not so happy about him. She had been unable to detect any outward signs of stress in him; he was no thinner, no paler, there were no telltale lines on his face, and no new grey hairs. Indeed, she thought, all of them—including Prue and Pete—seemed to be by common consent smoothing out the family life which Phyllis had so rudely disordered, mending and re-building it with a thousand everyday actions and ordinary remarks, rather as a colony of ants might rebuild a nest shattered by some clumsy footfall.

At first she had been, in the simplicity of her soul, a little shocked by their calm. A good cry, some exclamations and laments, a busy family conclave in which the whole position could be dissected, discussed, and deplored, would have reassured her. They, who rebelled so violently against things she had always accepted as inevitable, seemed now to regard as inevitable something which was, to her, a bolt from the blue. If they wondered, as she did, how long poor Phyllis would remain in the nursing-home to which she and her nervous breakdown had been transferred, they never spoke of it. If they looked uneasily towards a future in which, restored to her family, she would always be an incalculable factor, they gave no sign. Prue, indeed, looked peaky still—but how much of that was due to anxiety about her mother, and how much to the quite right and proper pining of a young girl in love, her aunt could not determine.

Nick was still explaining to Richard the limitations of the middle-class mind which, so Aunt Bee gathered in a few moments of bewildered attention, rendered him not only blind, but deaf and practically half-witted as well. She sighed, gave it up, and continued to think about the method which the family had adopted to tide it over a domestic crisis. Having been content all her life to admit unsophistication, and rely on goodwill to illuminate her path, she judged their method by its results, and conceded its virtue without attempting to understand it. She could feel peace when it was all about her, even if it manifested itself in the guise of heated argument. She could feel family affection even when its expression was silence, and family unity even when it was demonstrated by six people going their six separate ways. For the time being they had put Phyllis out of their conversation, if not out of their thoughts. They went outside their own lives for matter to speak of, saying by implication that they refused to remain prisoners of personal tragedy. And Aunt Bee discovered her own first shocked agitation over the affair subsiding. Against the terrific backcloth of human chaos and endeavour which their interminable discussions conjured up, she saw not only Phyllis, but herself and all the rest of them shrink till they became not negligible but undoubtedly very small. She was even abashed by lit by a spotlight of egotism, magnified out of its proper proportion, and charged with a febrile excitement, had had something avid in it. Yes, something that Phyllis herself would have enjoyed! She glanced at Nick, thinking how much better he looked now that that dreadful yellow colour was fading from his face, and how reassuring was the belligerent note in his voice.

Gilbert, strolling up and down the path, came near enough to hear fragments of the conversation, and then retreated again till the voices were only a murmur.

"No party," he heard Nick say, "can entirely guard against the intrusion of bad elements. There are always . . ."

The sound of gravel crunching under his feet made the rest inaudible, but his mind held the words and began to consider them. He asked himself if one besetting sin of Nick's "bad elements" were not, perhaps, over-emphasis? Did not their zeal often lead them into a labouring of the obvious? In their determination to get their points across, he thought, they were sometimes like bad amateur actors, mouthing and over-playing, insulting the mother-wit of their audience, hissing "asides" to explain some self-evident fact, striking attitudes until, like the too virtuous hero of melodrama, they made virtue tiresome, and the audience began to fidget . . .

His brother's voice came to meet him as he approached the verandah again:

". . . and in that case, of course, he must either conform or get out."

"Ah, yes," Richard answered, "but that's such an old, old ultimatum. Is the New Order to go into action under that worn-out banner?"

"But how else . . . ," Nick's tone was impatient, and, turning on his heel towards the shadowy garden, Gilbert found himself echoing: "How else?" It *was* an old, old ultimatum. All through the world's history, he thought, one could hear those four words beating like a tom-tom at the back of every great idea, and every noble creed. In primitive tribal rites, in organised religions, in political theories and in social conventions, the same words offered the same old choice. Even in science and the arts adventurous spirits had been forced to confront it. Conform or get out. And searching for progress in those past centuries, one found it always in points of departure; in the minds and actions of the people who —got out. . . .

He turned again; gradually the murmur of Richard's voice sorted itself into words:

"Well, when it comes to deciding what one is to be loyal to, I prefer the Shakespearean *'to thine own self be true, and it shall follow as the night the day . . .'*"

"The trouble with you," Nick told him with grim finality, "is that you're an anarchist."

Pausing for a moment to tread out the stub of his cigarette, Gilbert grinned to himself. Richard had been labelled—or re-labelled. Was the metamorphosis from liberal to anarchist promotion, or still blacker damnation? As he walked down the path again he bore with him the echo of Aunt Bee's voice saying pensively: "You know, Nick dear, I think I must be an anarchist too."

     *   *   *   *

The kitchen was steamy, and smelled pleasantly of soap. Pete, scraping plates, was arguing with Prue about which movie they were going to see that night, and Marty, wearing the faintly revolted frown of concentration with which she always approached household tasks, was staring into the Frigidaire, planning the next day's meals.

"There's some dopey love-picture on with the Tarzan," Pete complained, piling forks and spoons into the washing-up basin. "Can I eat this bit of pudding, Aunt Marty? It's only a little bit."

"Eh? Yes, eat it for Heaven's sake. Prue, does Nick still hate corned beef?"

"Yes, I think so." Prue rolled up her sleeves and tied an apron over her frock. Pete volunteered:

"I don't hate it. But then I won't be here to-morrow."

"No?" Marty cocked an eye at him. "Where are you dining to-morrow?"

"With Dad and Prue. Aren't I, Prue?" He sat down at the table with the pudding dish on his knee and ate happily, thinking how pleasant it was to run footloose between two homes, dropping in for a meal here or a meal there, choosing between the little room upstairs and a stretcher in Dad's room at the flat, enjoying in each the privileges of an inhabitant and the courtesies of a guest. On the whole he liked to be here, because Nick was here, full of tales about New Guinea; and when Nick was disinclined for talk there was Uncle Richard, who would converse endlessly in a grave, adult manner, definitely enlarging to one's self-esteem. It had been necessary for him to have that self-esteem restored, for his confidence in the stability of life had been rudely shaken. Up there in the mountains it had been like a bad dream to hear one's mother talking to herself, or raging against Dad, or praying out loud, or doing one of a dozen things which made one's skin crawl with embarrassment. Even at the Johnsons there had been something in their kindness which was disturbing. When Prue had told him about Virginia he had realised for the first time that death meant—disappearance. It shook his sense of security that a human being so near to him could suddenly vanish, never to be seen again. He had barely recovered from that uneasiness when Mother vanished too—not permanently, like Virginia, but even more strangely; and in silences, glances from his school-mates, tones of commiseration from his teachers, he had felt himself involved in some adult drama which his sensitive adolescent mind angrily repudiated. The holidays had rescued him, and restored him to a family-circle of grown-ups who seemed, sensibly, to be repudiating it too. Life had begun again in a new routine which was orderly enough to make him feel secure, and flexible enough to allow for the impulses of the moment. Scraping the dish with loving care, he announced:

"I think we'll go to the other one, Prue."

"All right," she said. "I don't mind which. Have you finished with that dish?"

He examined it narrowly. "You'd hardly need to wash it," he

sighed, adding it to the pile on the sink. "What'll I do now, Aunt Marty?"

"You can put the milk-jug out, and dispose of those scraps. And then you can go upstairs and wash, and put on a clean shirt."

He squinted down at his chest aggrievedly.

"A clean shirt? But, gee, I only put this one on clean this morning."

"Nevertheless," Marty said inexorably, "it is now dirty."

He suggested tentatively. "I could button up my coat . . . ?" He caught his aunt's eye. "Okay, okay, I'll change it. Gee, I'm hungry! Could I have a banana?"

Marty turned and contemplated him with wonder.

"After two helpings of meat and vegetables, and three helpings of pudding—you're hungry? Take a banana, child. Take two bananas. Heaven knows I wouldn't want you to starve."

When he had gone she picked up a tea-towel and joined Prue at the sink.

"You're tired, aren't you?" Prue asked. "I'll finish this."

Marty answered mechanically: "I'm not tired." She thought: "Of course that's a lie." But it was not the tiredness of aching bone and muscle, which one can admit. It was the tiredness of depression and frustration, the tiredness of feeling behind her one more barren day. A day of dusting, preparing vegetables, carry-ing groceries from the shops, cooking, sewing on buttons for Pete, washing dishes. A day of dragging her mind away from Sally Dodd, who clamoured incessantly for its attention, and bullying it into concentration upon the clock and the routine of domestic duty. Sentences, whole paragraphs, had formed themselves in that rebellious mind, only to slide away unrecorded, and now forgotten; the tiredness born of conflict between what she wanted to do and what she must do, made her feel old. A pang of apprehension shot through her, reminding her that she was, indeed, no longer young enough to afford many such "idle" days . . .

Where had it gone—this oppressive, menacing year, now almost ended? She, for one, had nothing to show for it. She had addressed a few meetings, she had done a few talks over the air, she had knitted more than a few socks, she had a tin hat and a whistle to vouch for her co-operation in N.E.S. She had grown vegetables where once flowers grew. She had invested in war loans, and dipped deep into her purse for "worthy" causes. Yet these things, set against the inactivity of her pen, could not begin to save her from a guilty sense of failure, and the conviction of a wasted year.

At least, she told herself impatiently, she had been spared the domestic stress which had complicated Gilbert's struggle with the same problem. She looked at her niece thoughtfully, realising that Prue, apart from the upheaval in her parents' life, had also had her experience of emotional entanglement to deal with; and remembering the poignancy of her own first, abortive love-affair, she felt a wave of compassion. How much, really, did the child care about this shadowy young American whom war had flung into her path for a few months, and snatched away again? She asked:

"Have you heard from John lately?"

"Yes." Prue peered attentively into a vegetable dish. "He writes as regularly as he can." Marty asked with anxious bluntness:

"You aren't engaged, are you?"

"Engaged?" echoed Prue vaguely. "Oh, no." She added another plate to the pile on the sink, and asked suddenly:

"Dad and Mother got engaged in wartime, didn't they?"

"They did," Marty replied rather sharply. "What of it?"

"Do you think they ever would have got engaged if it hadn't been for the war?"

"Oh!" Marty, impatient, sorted out the dried silver. "How can one know? Quite probably not. Why?"

"I was wondering," Prue said, very intent on the plates, "whether you *can* really get to know people in war-time? Well enough for marriage, I mean. I don't see how you can. For instance, I don't know what I really feel about John—whether I love him, or whether I just loved having patches of happiness in the middle of all this . . ." She stopped, and warned: "That plate's cracked."

"I know," said Marty.

"It might be," Prue went on, "that I was just predisposed to like him because liking Americans is sort of in the air: It might have been that he was just—that he just wanted a girl—any girl . . ."

The cracked plate broke in Marty's hand. She said with an angry sigh:

"It might. No one can know but yourselves. And apparently not even yourselves. How would you like living in America?"

"There you are," said Prue, as if clinching an old argument. "I'd be terribly homesick. And you have to be pretty certain that there's something strong enough to—set against that. Where's some stuff for the saucepans?"

"Under the sink. Well, you have to find the answer for yourself, Prue. Presumably you've had other affairs."

"The usual flirtations," Prue said, scouring busily. "Kisses, and so on. Nothing that ever lasted long enough to get complicated."

"You didn't feel the same about any of those?"

"Goodness, no! I never felt anything about them at all."

"Perhaps it's not a bad thing," Marty suggested lamely, "this separation for a while. He'll come back, and then . . ."

Prue glanced at her. Under that fleeting look with its cold knowledge Marty went dumb. You can't, she thought, camouflage the hideous insecurity of life from the young with encouraging words. They know too much. In a heavy silence Prue scrubbed the sink, washed and dried her hands, and asked: "Shall I sweep the floor?"

"Damn the floor!" said Marty. "Here's Pete all washed and brushed and resplendent in his clean shirt. You look devastating, Pete. Are you ready to go?"

"It's twenty to eight!" Pete discovered with alarm. "Come on, Prue, or we'll miss the newsreel. Can I get a hamburger in the interval?"

"Why not?" asked Marty. "You'll be needing a little something by then. Are you coming back here to sleep, or are you going home with Prue?"

"I think I'll go back with Prue." He added delicately: "If you don't mind, Aunt Marty?"

"Please yourself," Marty reassured him. "So long as I know where you are."

She saw them off at the back door, and went out on to the verandah to join the others. Aunt Bee had lit a cigarette to keep the mosquitoes away, Gilbert was sitting silently on the step, and Richard, still indomitably argumentative, was saying:

"But you must admit that the system of patronage produced some great artists, Nick. After all, there were . . ."

"Why do you say it produced them?" Nick interrupted. "They happened. And there was no other system for them to work under. Artists will never be regarded as effectives under a capitalist system. They'll always be hangers-on, entertainers, protégés of wealthy people who want to satisfy their own vanity by acquiring a reputation for 'culture' as they'd acquire a motor-car . . ."

Marty entered the fray with ardour, for the sake of entering it.

"Are you suggesting that artists haven't achieved anything of value in the last century and a half, with capitalism at full blast?"

"Of course not. But they've achieved it in the teeth of capitalism. For one-tenth of the world's creative energy that has been effective, there's probably been nine-tenths that was frustrated and lost."

"That may be broadly true," Marty conceded, "though I don't know how you arrive at your figures. But what's going to be the fate of artists under a socialist system?"

"You know very well," Nick said calmly. "They'll be accepted and honoured."

Marty retorted nastily: "Honoured, eh? Reverenced and looked up to? Heaven preserve them!"

"From what?" Nick demanded belligerently.

"From a generation just breaking away from old gods, and on the lookout for new ones. You can't simply ignore the human instinct to worship. If you take away people's religious saints they set up political ones. If you take away their glamour-girls, and society debs, and hereditary monarchs, they look round for substitutes. And find—artists! Sanctioned by the party line. And then what?"

"Well," snapped Nick, "what?"

"Then you have a class of artists with a vested interest in the status quo. Which is monstrous. An artist must have a chip on his shoulder or he's nothing. He must be dissatisfied or he's dead."

"Can't he be dissatisfied," Gilbert said mildly from the darkness, "with the minor internal workings of his socialist system? It certainly wouldn't be streamlined perfection. I should think he'd still find plenty to inveigh against."

"But *would* he inveigh? He, with the State as his patron, and everything to lose? Some might—and most wouldn't."

Richard suggested:

"Aren't you underrating the—the essential urge of the artist, Marty? His obsession to produce—whatever it is—books, paintings, music. Isn't that something independent of systems?" Nick said firmly:

"No human activity is independent of the social system."

Richard bent down to knock his pipe out on the edge of the verandah, and decided, not without relief, to retire from the discussion. Gilbert said over his shoulder:

"Yes, that's true, Nick. The system determines the conditions under which the artist must work. But what Richard meant, I think, was that to most artists material rewards over and above what's necessary for a reasonable standard of living aren't very important. And if the artist found his material rewards hampering his work, he'd just—discard them."

"That," said Marty, "might be the reaction of the one-tenth. And as a result it's work might promptly suffer an eclipse. And the nine-tenths, who continued to draw their fat emoluments in return for service rendered, would have the whole weight of official propaganda and approval behind them. Just as those who glorify the capitalist system at present have its endorsement . . ."

"You're presupposing a corrupt Government, aren't you?" Nick enquired patiently.

"Not at all. I'm presupposing a Government composed of fallible human beings, sincere and earnest, and believing in their system. Are they going to cherish an artist who uses it as an Aunt Sally for his verbal missiles? Not on your life!"

Gilbert laughed.

"Just what are you trying to prove, Marty?"

"Simply that a policy of glorifying the artist, and rewarding him with material comforts far in excess of other workers', is not —in the public interest."

"If that's all," Gilbert said, after a moment's careful reflection, "I think I'm with you."

"The whole business of assessing the value of work in terms of money," Marty asserted, "is entirely arbitary. But with most trades you can preserve some sort of consistency. When it comes to artists your system is dealing with intangibles. It can allot such and such a wage to the bricklayer, and at the end of the day it can count up how many bricks he's laid, and estimate if he's worth it. But if you go to a writer and ask how many words he's written for his daily bread, he can stump you with a variety of answers. He can say: 'I wrote five thousand—and tore them up.'

Or he can say: 'I've been walking the streets getting copy.' Or he can say: 'I've been lying out in the sun absorbing beauty.' Or he can just put on an air of superiority and say his Muse has taken the day off. Can you coerce a Muse?"

Nick snorted:

"If you're going to introduce mysticism . . ."

"There's nothing mystical about art. The artist's material is life—just as it's everyone else's material. But it has to be broken down and wrought upon by himself in his own way, and in his own good time before he can produce anything out of it. He can't be driven by any outside agency. He propels himself along like a rocket-ship by a series of explosions . . ."

Gilbert stood up suddenly.

"I'm going," he said. "Good-night."

He walked round the house and up the steps to where he had stood once with Elsa, but she was far from his thoughts. He would remember this year as a good one and a bad one. Bad for its oppression, and the inexorable tension of its dangers; for his own curious emotional abberration, for Virginia's death, for the collapse of Phyllis' defence in her long, losing fight with life. Good for . . . ? For those same things, which had been goads, stimuli, sparks to his tinder. It had all helped to make him ready, he realised—with the usual acknowledgment to Marty's metaphor—for an explosion. Opening the back gate and walking down the road towards the station, he was conscious of the year, good and bad, safely stored in him, ready for manufacture by his own particular craft. In the black mirror of the train window he could see it all like a movie. While it was still sharp he must begin to get it down. Danger, when imagination—not in panic, but soberly—had seen invasion and occupation of his land as something that might actually happen. When it had seen organised resistance shattered, recoiling, regrouping in hasty improvisations, dwindling to desperate guerrilla warfare in remote places. When it had even adjusted itself to the thought of life become primitive and nomadic, a hunted life of constant effort, danger, and hunger.

While it was still a living part of his thought, he must record that to feel that shadow lifting had its painfulness as well as its relief. For there was now no recognisable present to return to, and the "normality" of a few years ago was a no-man's-land, offer-

ing even less foothold than that fantastic, imagined existence. Released from the Stone Age conception of life as a mere need to
survive, you found yourself not restored to a saner present, but
confronting an obscure future. Nothing that happened in this
world-storm could convert the mad succession of nights and days
into a "present." They were suspended in history, born of the
past, a threat or a promise to the future, mere whirling events at
which human beings, whirling with them, clutched in the hope
that they would fall into place some day, somehow, and form a
pattern for rational existence. Yet to see them as utterly chaotic,
he thought, would be to feel oneself annihilated. For man, being
a thinking animal, is a planning animal; he must feel his life
dominated by his thought and purpose, or he is lost. And they
were not chaotic. There was logic behind every event, and
direction in every development, so that it became a spectacle which
one watched, but in which, too, one's own comprehension was a
factor. There was, indeed, nothing left of life but this straining,
unceasing effort towards comprehension. Living was only in one's
mind, for the routine of bodily life had been reduced to a mere
somnambulism, a series of mechanical actions dictated by necessity or governed by habit, a marking time between the past and
the future.

Yes, he had gone through this year like a sleepwalker, awake only
in his mind, watching the headlines, and, even more narrowly, the
obscure little paragraphs; reading not only along the lines of print,
but between them; sorting facts and relating them, sifting evidence,
accumulating and discarding, toiling laboriously like an ant to add
his grain of comprehension to the world's sum. His life was in
that, and in the expression he must give it. Even now, as he
alighted from the train at his own station, he was poring with
miserly concentration over remembered scraps of news. ADMIRAL
DARLAN MURDERED. CABINET LIFTS BAN ON COM-
MUNIST PARTY. ROMMEL NOW IN TRIPOLI AREA.
RUSSIA OPENS FOURTH MAJOR OFFENSIVE. INDUS-
TRIAL INSURANCE COMPANIES LAUNCH CAMPAIGN
AGAINST BEVERIDGE PLAN. MORE TAXES, FEWER
LUXURIES IN 1943 . . .

He felt an urgent, hungry desire to get on with his task of
recording and interpreting even a trivial fragment of this enormous
world-story, and he walked fast along the road towards the flat, like

a man with a tryst to keep. All the evening he had felt restless. He had been impatient of the long, inconclusive verbal sparring between Nick and Richard—exasperated because their talk intruded upon some preparation for activity which his brain was trying to make. He brought all the substance of their contentions with him as one brings dreams out of sleep; he brought all the problems of his somnambulistic living—Phyllis, Prue, Elsa, the Burt Street property, his own long, creative paralysis—into the daylight clarity of thought, and felt them move into position, link up, fuse with the headlines, and become part of one story, clamouring for a pen. He had fled from Nick's argument with Marty, seeing the intricate web of theory which they were weaving about the practice of the arts as a wilful and ridiculous waste of time which should be spent on production. He felt past all that, just now; he was obsessed by a feverish longing for the physical act of writing down words. You can theorise, he thought, as he unlocked the door of the flat and switched on the light, about the sex-relationship—but when desire overtakes you, you stop theorising, and go to bed. He went to his desk, pulled drawers open, gathered papers together, cleared a space, sat down. It felt like health after illness, safety after danger, eleventh-hour triumph. And you can use art as a subject for debate, his mind was telling him irritably, you can make it an excuse for metaphysical hair-splitting; but when the time comes you sweep all that aside, and set up your easel; or sit down at your piano, or reach for your pen. . . .

THE END.